An ___ **O'Neil** spent most of her childhood with her leg ___ ped over the family rocking chair and a book in ___ hand. Novels, baking, and writing too much teen ___ ge angst poetry ate up most of her youth. Now Anni ___ splits her time between corralling her husband into ___ elping her with their cows, baking, reading, barr ___ racing (not really!) and spending some very happ ___ hours at her computer, writing.

Cur ___ with a poor sense of direction and a propensity to r ___ , **Annie Claydon** spent much of her childhood los ___ books. A degree in English Literature followed by a c ___ eer in computing didn't lead directly to her perfect jot ___ —writing romance for Mills & Boon—but she has no ___ egrets in taking the scenic route. She lives in ___ don: a city where getting lost can be a joy.

THE VET'S SECRET SON

ANNIE O'NEIL

HEALING THE VET'S HEART

ANNIE CLAYDON

MILLS & BOON

First Published in Great Britain 2020
by Mills & Boon, an imprint of HarperCollins*Publishers*
1 London Bridge Street, London, SE1 9GF

The Vet's Secret Son © 2020 Annie O'Neil

Healing the Vet's Heart © 2020 Annie Claydon

ISBN: 978-0-263-27980-1

MIX
Paper from
responsible sources
FSC® C007454

This book is produced from independently certified FSC™ paper
to ensure responsible forest management.
For more information visit www.harpercollins.co.uk/green.

Printed and bound in Spain
by CPI, Barcelona

THE VET'S
SECRET SON

ANNIE O'NEIL

MILLS & BOON

This one goes out to every veterinarian I have called out of hours and who has come running.
I thank you. My beasties thank you.
Annie O x

CHAPTER ONE

ELLIE LIFTED THE small ball of fluff up in front of her face and gave it a nuzzle. Puppy time after a difficult surgery was always curative. 'Who's the best little-bitty puppy?'

The pitch-black Labrador put its paw on her nose then gave her a tiny pink-tongued lick on the cheek. Even though she'd had a million puppy moments like it, Ellie's heart strained at the seams.

'You're definitely the cutest.'

As if in protest, the other puppies—a mad mix of golden, red, black and a solitary chocolate one—began tumbling up and over her legs, vying for cuddles.

Four weeks old and full of life. A perfect litter of ten, spanning every colour of the Labrador spectrum. It was the last litter Esmerelda, Ellie's beloved Lab, would have, and even though she knew she wasn't entirely objective, she was certain it was the best.

She picked up another one and breathed in the sweet, scrummy puppy scent. Mmm… Perfect. She couldn't wait for Mav to get back from surf school. Her son's giggles of delight combined with puppy cuddles…sheer heaven.

'Having a bit of puppy therapy, are we?'

Ellie looked up and saw her long-term mentor smiling down at her. 'Ha! You caught me, Henry.'

'Tough surgery?'

'Very.' She told him about the golden retriever who'd been injured when he'd tripped whilst carrying a big stick.

'And the oropharynx?'

'There was a truckload of splinters in his tongue and his mouth. A huge one was lodged in his throat, the poor lad. He's in Recovery now. I don't know who's feeling worse. Him or his owner.'

Henry gave a sympathetic shrug. 'It's a tough call sometimes. I just had a woman sob the entire time I clipped her cat's nails!'

Ellie made an empathetic noise. 'Mrs Coutts?'

Henry grinned. 'You clearly know your patients' owners well.'

'One of the keys to our success here in Dolphin Cove.' She patted the newspaper-covered play area where she was stretched out, puppies using her like a climbing frame. 'Join me?'

Henry, who'd valiantly stepped in to be her emergency locum vet over the last few months, grinned and sat down opposite her. 'How could I resist?'

The puppies climbed and tumbled over him, vying for cuddles. For someone with a puppy tucked in the crook of each arm, her mentor didn't look all that chirpy.

'You're looking serious. Got a new surgery you need to brainstorm?'

Henry shook his head, his white hair flopping across his forehead as he did so. He looked every bit the mad professor. Semi-retired and as smart as a whip, he was also her hero. Who else in the whole of the UK would've given up their summer holidays to come down to Cornwall and take over the roster of complicated surgeries her business partner had lined up?

She shoved aside the niggle of discomfort the question elicited and smiled at him. Just about no one, that's who. No one she cared to lay eyes on, anyway.

'It's not that,' he said, easing yet another puppy into his arms.

Ah. So there *was* something.

Ellie gently extracted her insanely curly ponytail from one of the puppy's mouths. One day she'd get her hair under control. She snorted. And one day pigs would fly. 'Not a pull toy, little one,' she cooed, easing a final golden coil out of its gummy mouth.

She inspected Henry as the pup he was holding scampered away and he pulled one of her favourite pups, the only chocolate Lab in the litter, into his lap. He was looking awfully serious.

The chocolate pup put both of its paws on Henry's beard then slid back down into the nook of his arm and instantly fell asleep.

Ellie laughed. 'I guess that was enough playtime for him.'

'Guess so.' Henry cupped the little pup's head in one of his big old hands. His tone was much more reflective than a vet with over forty years of experience might be. He must have seen thousands of puppies curl up into sleepy little balls of fur and puppy snorts over the years.

'C'mon, Henry. Out with it. There's something playing on your mind. You rescued me in my hour of need. If I can do anything to help you in yours, just say the word.'

She wasn't kidding. When Drew, her business partner and her bestie, was in a horrific car accident, Henry came right down. Drew's long stint in hospital was coming to an end, but there was still ample rehab and healing to keep him away from the surgery for at least the next eight to ten weeks. More if there were any setbacks.

Uh-oh. Drew hadn't had a setback had he?

Henry readjusted the puppy and something about the look in his eyes made her scoop one up into her own arms. She gave it a nuzzle as Henry began to speak. When he'd finished, she could hardly hear for the buzzing in her ears.

It wasn't Drew. It was a favour. And not just any old favour. He was asking her to do the one thing she'd promised she would never do. Let Lucas Williams work at Dolphin Cove.

But she owed Henry. She owed him big time.

Four months ago she'd barely held it together when Drew's life hung in the balance. Henry had come to her rescue. Not only did he tackle Drew's incredibly complicated surgeries, he also brought along students from the Royal Veterinary College down for internships to help ease the load. Much to her embarrassment, he used Ellie as an example of what you could achieve if you stuck to your guns: build one of Britain's most innovative veterinary surgeries in one of its most old-fashioned villages even when your heart had just been smashed to absolute smithereens.

Okay.

He didn't say that end bit.

He focussed on the good. Which was how she'd survived her heartache and the epic life change that came in its wake. The Dolphin Cove Veterinary Clinic was literally her dream come true. And now it could all disappear in the blink of an eye. If she let herself be prone to dramatics. Which she was, because…oh, damn!

This felt almost as bad as— No. Nothing felt worse than having the love of her life take back his proposal and throw all of their hopes and dreams to the wayside to become television's favourite celebrity veterinarian.

The Uber-Vet.

Bleurgh.

Uber-Louse more like.

The man on television—which, obviously, she'd only ever watched season after season by total accident—was so far removed from the geeky, funny, hilariously wonderful man she'd fallen in love with she could barely stand to look at him.

So much for *I've got to save my dad's clinic, Ells. I just want to keep everything low-key to keep the stress down. I'm all they've got now. I don't want to ruin your dream.*

It scared her to realise how raw the old wounds still were. Wounds she had done everything in her power to heal as she'd embarked on the new life she'd built for her and her son.

'He really said you have to go *now*?' Ellie knew she was repeating exactly what Henry had just said, but she didn't seem able to get the facts to sink in.

Lucas Williams, ex-love of her life, wanted Henry to take over his stupid television show. Immediately. And to make that happen? He was going to come to Dolphin Cove and replace Henry.

The skin prickled at the back of her neck.

This was the moment she had hoped against hope would never happen.

Henry scrubbed a hand through his hair. He of all people knew what a bit ask it was, but there was a lot at stake for him as well. 'The students depend on these scholarships, and with money so hard to come by these days—'

She waved her hand to get him to stop talking. She, more than anyone, knew how important the scholarships were. There was no chance she could've attended the Royal Veterinary College without a bursary. Denying other students the chance because of pride? It would be an unspeakably selfish thing to do.

She forced herself to repeat the facts to Henry to make absolutely sure she'd got them right. 'So, what you're saying is, Lucas Williams is giving up his job as the Uber-Vet and he wants you to be the new one?'

'That's right.' Henry nodded. 'We'd film at the veterinary college, raising its profile, and all of the proceeds would go towards scholarships for less well-off students.'

Just like she'd been.

'And you have to go tomorrow?'

'Day after. Lucas is going to drive down tomorrow. The television producers seem to be mad about the idea and they want to start filming...'

'ASAP,' they said in tandem.

She looked out beyond the low wall of the puppy pen to the big old floor-to-ceiling glass windows that faced the private cove beyond the clinic. Still sunny. Still gorgeous. At least something was the same. Another perfect summer's day in Cornwall.

She squinted at the sun. It'd be hours yet before it dipped into the sea, but those hours were quickly evaporating and before she knew it, it would be tomorrow morning, Henry would leave and the man who had changed her life for ever would be arriving. And all of this exactly when she had one of the most important surgeries in Dolphin Cove Veterinary Clinic's entire history on the books.

Prosthetics for a beautiful Bernese mountain dog. A gorgeous beast of a dog called Moose who'd struggled to recover from a car accident a few weeks back. Ellie, a specialist in emergency surgery and internal medicine, had done her best, but had ultimately held up her hands and said, 'It's not enough. This dog needs more.' The type of 'more' only an orthopaedic surgeon could envision. An orthopaedic surgeon exactly like Lucas Williams.

The father of her child. The son he didn't know he had.

She swallowed back an uncomfortable lump of guilt. 'And there's no one else in the entire world who can come down apart from *him*?'

'You want and deserve the best, Ellie. Lucas is the best there is.' She scuffed her foot against the floor exactly the way Maverick would've if she'd told him it was time for bed.

'Of course, I could always turn down the offer and stay here.'

'Don't be ridiculous.' Of course Henry must go. It was a once in a lifetime offer. Putting the finest veterinary college in the UK in the limelight as well as giving its poorer students a critical financial lifeline? There was no way she could insist Henry stay. Even so. 'Just…give me a minute to process this, all right?'

Henry opened his mouth, presumably to say she'd be fine, but…urgh! She didn't want *fine*. She wanted everything to stay exactly as it was. Well. Not *exactly*. She'd rather Drew wasn't in recovery from his accident and that he'd never been through the emotional and physical wringers the past couple of years had thrown at him, but what was the point in working your fingers to the bone and aiming for the moon and the stars beyond it only for life to throw her biggest fear into her path?

A clammy skittering of goosebumps ran across her skin.

She could've done what her parents and Drew had suggested when she'd found out she was pregnant. Told Lucas she was having his son. But to do so precisely when the papers had started crowing about a rumoured engagement between the Uber-Vet and his producer? No chance. Instead, she'd poured all her hurt and anger into building the clinic even Lucas would admire.

She gave her arms a rub as a chill swept through her.

What good was venom or comeuppance when the secret she held would change his life?

Lucas would be angry. He had every right to be. Over five years of not knowing he had a son… She'd be raging if she were in his shoes. But she'd done what she'd done for a reason. Lots of reasons. One of which was ensuring she had full custody of Maverick.

All that might change now.

Who was she kidding? Everything would change once Lucas found out Maverick was his son. Anyone who cared for animals the way he did couldn't be all evil.

Henry slipped the sleeping puppy in his arm onto a bed. 'I'd better get up to the flat and start packing.'

'Don't leave.' Ellie gestured for him to stay then twisted her coils of strawberry blonde curls into a messy topknot. 'Not just yet.'

'How many more weeks until Drew's out of hospital?' Henry asked as he sat back down, even though he knew the answer as well as she did.

'He's home in the next couple of weeks, but he's got a good two months of rehab before he can come back here to the clinic and even then...' She glowered, the frown quickly softening as a pair of puppies began to climb a small set of steps onto a short slide and...whoosh. So adorable! Maybe she'd give Drew a puppy as part of his rehab. He hadn't seemed so keen on doing all the exercises they'd given him last time she'd visited him in hospital, but once he was home and had a puppy to entice him out on a walk...

'And his recovery is going well?' Henry asked.

What was going on here? Henry had visited Drew practically as much as Ellie had. Saying that... Ellie knew Drew better than just about anyone in the village. Not only was he her best friend from Dolphin Cove, he had been a student alongside Lucas and Ellie at the Royal Veterinary College. He'd watched her fall in love. He'd been part of the plotting and planning for each and every component of their dream clinic. He'd been there to mop up the tears when Lucas had ripped her heart out of her chest and walked away from each and every one of their plans. He'd also been sitting beside her as she'd watched the smiley face appear on that fateful pregnancy test nine weeks after they'd returned to Dolphin Cove to set up the clinic without Lucas. She'd clocked one missed period up to stress and heartache. Two?

Well.

She had her boy and she loved him to bits, so...not *everything* about her time with Lucas had turned out badly.

She forced herself back onto topic. 'I think it's fair to say being a patient doesn't really suit him.' Poor Drew had already suffered so much loss. If he was permanently disabled because of his leg injuries? Nightmare. She couldn't imagine him living a sedentary life. Not happily anyway. The man was made of motion. Except for these past few months. Suffice it to say her bestie was going to have to pull some hardcore determination out of the bag if he wanted to stand at an operating table for eight-plus hours ever again.

Henry tapped Ellie on the knee, presumably having seen her drift off into A World Without Drew. 'Ellie, love. I know you've been through a lot lately, but I wouldn't be doing this if it wasn't the right thing to do. Think of all of those amazing vets I can send down here for internships.'

Ellie heaved a melodramatic sigh, hoping Henry knew she wasn't actually angry, just…digesting things. 'I know. I should be cracking open the champagne for you. I just… It's one of those crossroads moments.'

'One you, of all people, have the strength to get through.'

'You think?' The last thing she felt right now was strong. Terrified, shaky, anxious and defensive? Definitely. Able to hold her own against the man she'd once loved with every fibre of her being? Not so much.

'You're made of stronger stuff than you ever give yourself credit for,' Henry said, scooching over to her side of the puppy pen and giving her a half-hug. 'Who knows? Maybe it'll be the best thing that ever happened.'

'Ha!' She crinkled her nose up. 'Having the Uber-Vet here is *not* going to be the best thing that ever happened to me.'

'No.' Henry gave his beard a thoughtful stroke. 'But having Lucas Williams here might be.' Henry smiled as if he knew something she didn't then left the room, Ellie's jaw still hanging open in disbelief.

Lucas pulled off the main road, such as it was, and onto the long, wooded drive leading down to the clinic. Seeing the clinic sign and then glimpses of the cove peek through the woodland felt as familiar to him as if he'd done it a thousand times. In a way he had.

They'd talked about every detail of their 'fantasy clinic' a thousand times. More.

Back when this site had been private land, they couldn't have dreamt of affording let alone building a state-of-the-art clinic on it. Dreaming the impossible was easy with Ellie. She was a woman who could look at anything and spot nothing but possibility. Nothing but hope. Which went a long way towards explaining why he'd fallen in love with her the instant she'd walked into that first day of veterinary college wearing a studious expression and a tiger onesie.

It surprised him how raw he felt, seeing their shared dream as a reality he wasn't a part of.

Sure, he was proud of turning his father's failing clinic into something extraordinary, too. It had saved his family from unimaginable problems, but…looking at Ellie's clinic on the website before he'd come down here had stirred something in him he hadn't been sure still existed. *Hope.* Hope that the two of them might be able to find a peace with their complicated past.

Most of the staff photos were action shots, unlike his well-lit posed one taken by the production photographer. There were loads of Drew, of course, but the pictures of Ellie were the ones that had punched him in the solar plexus. Ellie deep in concentration in surgery. Ellie playing with the pups she bred as service dogs from Esmerelda, the puppy he'd given to her with a diamond ring on her collar and a question on his lips.

Will you marry me?

If only—

He loosened his white-knuckled grip on the steering wheel and continued to drive. If only a lot of things.

As he drove through the woodland, a broad expanse of lawn opened out before him and then the drive split— one lane signposted for the main clinic and community petting zoo and the other for the surgical ward. He let out a low whistle.

Ellie and Drew had clearly worked their socks off. He felt a burst of pride on their behalf and then, in its wake, an all too familiar stab of guilt.

He steered the car towards the main clinic. The car park was still relatively full, even though it was near the end of the day. The building was a glass, beam and wood-shingled number that oozed confidence and comfort. Exactly the type of place you'd want to bring your pet if they were hurt. Exactly the type of place he and Ellie had envisioned opening all those years ago. He huffed out a laugh. She'd really gone and done it. With her trusty childhood friend Drew, who she had no doubt fallen in love with by now. Had kids with. Pets of their own.

At least she'd kept Esmerelda.

A dog isn't just for a proposal...

He imagined Drew slipping a ring on Ellie's finger, felt a surge of something fiery and hot fill his chest, then checked himself. He had no rights in that area. And certainly no right to be jealous. Who Ellie loved or didn't love was no longer his business. Helping her was.

He parked the car, clapped his hands together and gave them a rub. He'd waited a long time to make amends. Maybe too long. Tunnel vision had been the only thing that had kept him going as he'd dealt with the massive debt his father's London-based veterinary clinic had accrued as Parkinson's had begun to take its toll on his father's health, then dementia and then, six months ago, his passing.

There were countless other threads to his family's complicated story, and making sure Ellie wasn't mired down with them had made breaking things off seem like the only option. Now, with Henry taking over the reins of the show he'd created to save his family from financial ruin, he felt as if he was breathing freely for the first time in years.

A bell tinkled above his head as he entered the bright, welcoming atrium-style reception area. At its heart stood a small oak tree. The tree, a couple of metres in height, was planted in the centre of a wraparound bench seat where patients and their owners sat waiting for their appointments.

The sight threw him back in time, feeling his hand close over Ellie's smaller, more delicate hand as he'd passed the acorn from his to her palm when they'd decided this was the perfect spot to build their clinic.

From the tiny acorn...

He gave his head a shake. It was probably a fake. Who planted an oak tree in their atrium lobby?

Ellie Stone, that's who.

He scrubbed a hand through his hair and made himself examine the place with a more practised eye. This was, after all, to be his workplace for the next few weeks. If Ellie didn't chuck him out on his ear.

Pushing her reaction to the side, he scanned the atrium. The interior, whilst modern and clearly designed for animals, was as warm and welcoming as a classic country hotel. A huge stone and wood reception desk stood a few metres back from the door. In lieu of the near obligatory plastic chairs or benches most vet surgeries had, the

Dolphin Cove Veterinary Clinic had inviting sofas and window seats built into the multi-angled reception area in addition to the bench seat round the tree. There was a floor-to-ceiling cat scratch and even a little cave off in a corner with a sign on it reading 'For pooches who prefer a quiet space.'

Behind the reception desk, a young woman who would've looked more at home on the back of a horse at an elite show jumping event was tapping something into the computer. She looked up when he approached. 'Hello, may I—? Oh, my gawd! Are you…?' She waved at the other two people sitting in the reception area. An elderly woman with a cat in a soft carrying case and a stylish young man with a tiny Pekingese on his lap. 'It's the Uber-Vet!'

Lucas shook his head. Fame and recognition were his least favourite aspects of his job. That and the non-stop rumours about his imaginary engagements. He'd barely had time for dating let alone having enough head space to think about falling in love. And that was the thing, wasn't it? You didn't think about falling in love. You just did it. Precisely as he'd done with Ellie.

'Don't move!' The girl scuttled round the desk with her phone pinched between her immaculately manicured nails, 'Can we do a selfie?'

Check that. Selfies were his least favourite part of being the Uber-Vet.

'I'm getting a selfie with the Uber-Vet!' The girl sing-songed at the two pet owners as Lucas resisted a sigh and put on an obliging smile.

The flash on her phone went off, and then, as she took a couple more, she launched into a monologue. 'I'm Tegan. I work here. Obvs. This is Mrs Cartwright and her very well-loved Siamese cat, Tabatha.' She stage-whispered, 'Bit of a hypochondriac but we love her.' She raised her voice. 'Mrs Cartwright? Would you and Tabatha like your photo taken with the Uber-Vet?'

'Who?' Mrs Cartwright, an immaculately turned-out, birdlike woman, peered at him with bright blue eyes. 'Oh, no,' she said, after she'd given him a quick once over. 'No, thank you. I'll wait for Ellie. As you know, I'd far rather Tabatha saw Drew as he is very familiar with her ailments, but...' She heaved a weary sigh. 'My poor, poor Tabatha.'

Tegan dropped to her knees in front of Tabatha and began making *meow* noises.

'I'd like a photo,' the young man holding the Pekingese said. The dog's immaculately groomed coat flowed over his arms as he swept her up and alongside Lucas. 'Here...' He handed him his phone. 'Can you take it? Your arms are longer. And stronger. My boyfriend would be so totally jel if he knew I was cuddling up to you. Teegs! Come over and get in the photo with us.'

Tegan obliged, happily squishing Lucas into the centre of a Tegan and Pekingese sandwich.

Lucas grinned and bore it. Nearly six years on Britain's television screens had kept his father's clinic from closing and miring his family in debt, so...he held up the phone, 'Ready? Smile!'

When the flash went off, he saw stars for a moment. When they cleared his heart smashed against his chest. There she was.

Ellie Stone. Even more beautiful than he'd remembered her. Wild golden red curls. Her lean, athletic body wearing scrubs as if they'd been handmade for her every curve. A pair of trendy trainers on her feet. No surprise there. Shoes had always been her weakness. Green eyes, as pure and welcoming as the sea beyond the clinic. They flashed brightly then narrowed.

Maybe not so welcoming.

'You're late.'

'Ellie!' Tegan swotted at her arm. 'Don't be rude. It's the Uber-Vet!'

'I know exactly who he is,' she bit out.

'Cool.' Tegan grinned. 'Then you won't mind if I run out and get Torky, yeah?' She turned to Lucas and gave his arm a squeeze. 'He's my twin and, like, totally wants to be a vet, just like you.'

Lucas sucked in a breath. Not the right thing to say in front of your boss who was an excellent vet herself.

Tegan continued, oblivious to the icy stare Ellie was giving her. 'Ells? Would you take our picture when we get back? Me and Torks. What? Why are you so frowny?'

Lucas's eyes zapped to Ellie's. He'd stupidly held onto a sliver of hope that enough time had passed that she might be the tiniest bit happy to see him. She arched an eyebrow as if to say, *This is a veterinary clinic, not a red carpet.*

No smile. No glimmer of delight. No, *Oh, my goodness, my Prince Charming has just walked through the door.*

Not quite the happy reunion he'd been hoping for.

Ellie sniffed and gave Tegan what he used to teasingly call her 'Mum look'. Teasing because he'd imagined her giving that look to their own children one day. He'd loved that look. Hell. Who was he kidding? He'd loved all her looks. Happy, triumphant, giddy, loving...

'I do mind, Tegan. Torquil is busy in the surgical ward and you should be busy answering the phone.' She tipped her head towards the reception desk, where the phone was, indeed, ringing.

Tegan, full of attitude, swept back behind the reception desk and very pointedly answered the phone, 'Hello, Dolphin Cove Veterinary Clinic, Tegan speaking. How may I help you?'

'Sorry about that—' Lucas began, but Ellie cut him off with an eye-roll.

'She's young. She'll get over it.'

'It's good to see you, Ellie,' Lucas said, meaning it. 'How are you?'

She crossed her arms over the dark blue scrubs dotted with…were those toy poodles?…and glowered at him. Funny how toy poodles took the edge off a glare.

'Hmm. Good question.' She tapped her chin with her index finger. 'Do you mean…how *are you*, Ellie, after six years of not ever speaking to you? Or, how are you, Ellie, seeing me swan into your clinic as if I owned the place. Or…wait a minute.' She put her finger up in the air as if a lightbulb had just gone off, her green eyes blazing with emotion. 'Best yet…how *are you*, Ellie, after I dumped you and made it very clear there was no place in my life for you despite the fact *you* were the one to always say there is no I in team?'

'*What?*' screeched Tegan from the reception desk, hand over the phone receiver. 'You used to date the Uber-Vet? Ells. You are a dark horse, girlfriend! Ellie and the Uber-Vet. Who knew?'

'His name's Lucas!' Ellie ground out.

At the same time Lucas said, 'Lucas is just fine.'

'Ah! Lucas!' Henry appeared from one of the long corridors stretching out beyond the reception desk. 'There you are. I see you've caught up with Ellie.'

'Henry.' Ellie wheeled on him. 'This was a terrible idea. I'm going to find someone else.'

'Someone else to who can do the Bernese surgery?' Lucas said, knowing he was on solid ground. 'I don't think so. The only one on the British Isles who can do that surgery is standing right here.'

Ellie opened her mouth, presumably to protest, but nothing came out.

'Oh, dear. Well, I…' Henry's eyes bounced between the pair of them as his brows dived towards his nose in consternation.

'Actually, Henry,' Lucas continued with a smile, 'Ellie and I were just discussing where I should put my things. Weren't we, Ellie?'

'We were doing no such thing,' she growled.

'Oh, well.' Henry gave his beard a thoughtful stroke. 'You're more than welcome to stay in the guest flat with me. I believe there's a sofa bed for the night or I can move out of the bedroom tonight and sleep on the—'

'No!' Ellie snapped. 'My house? My rules. My veterinary clinic? My decision whether or not you even touch one solitary hair on an animal's head.'

The young man with the Pekingese piped up, 'It's a bit late for that. He's already held my Audrey here.'

Ellie's eyebrows shot up to her hairline. 'And you are?'

'Caspian Smythe-Bingham.'

She opened her mouth, presumably to say 'Who?' when a look of recognition flared then softened her features into a welcoming glow of recognition. 'Caspian, yes, of course. I'm ever so sorry. I'm not normally so… um…' She gave Lucas a dismissive flick of her eyes then looked at Henry. 'Henry, if you don't mind showing our *temporary* guest into the coffee room, I'll meet

with you both after we take a look at… Audrey, right?'
She reached out her hands for the Pekingese who curled
up against his owner's chest.

'Oh, no.' Caspian stroked his dog's long hair. 'Audrey
doesn't seem to like you.'

Ellie gave a nervous laugh. 'Not to worry. Sometimes
it takes a minute or two to get to know one another. Why
don't you bring her into the examination room, and we'll
take a look there?'

Caspian arched an imperious eyebrow. 'If you don't
mind, I'd really rather the Uber-Vet took a look at her.
They have a bond already, you see?'

The expression on Ellie's face was so cross it took all
of Lucas's power not to laugh. Not that he wanted to irri-
tate her more than he had, but…this was actually a little
bit funny. Maybe the funnier later variety of funny, but…

'Why are you laughing?' Ellie's glare bored into him.

'I'm not laughing.'

'Course you are,' Ellie snipped. Her eyes darted to
the door as a young boy and an older woman who looked
very familiar came in. Ellie's entire demeanour changed.
'Exam room three,' she crisply instructed Lucas. 'You
take Audrey. We'll all have a look.'

'Only if you're sure.' Stepping on her toes was the last
thing he wanted to do.

'Of course I'm sure.' She pointed him down the corridor towards the exam room then gave a little hip-height
wave to the two who'd just come in.

'Did you want to see them?'

'No,' she snapped. When her eyes met his, the sparks
flew hard and fast. Like a fresh log had been thrown on
a bed of hot coals that had been lying in wait…smoulder-

ing…waiting for the perfect moment to flare and burn as brightly as they once had.

'Right you are, then.' Lucas stepped to the side so that Caspian could follow Ellie. 'After you.'

With a rather pointed swish, Ellie whirled around and headed down the corridor as briskly as her trademark trendy trainers would take her. Henry mouthed a silent *'Good luck'* to Lucas as he followed in her wake.

It was going to be an interesting few weeks. Truth be told, he hadn't been convinced she'd let him in. But now that she had he was going to keep his foot firmly in the door, no matter how many times she tried to slam it. The fire in her eyes had told him everything he'd needed to know. There was something to salvage between them. And he wasn't leaving until he found out exactly what it was.

CHAPTER TWO

ELLIE DIDN'T THINK her heart had ever hammered so hard.

She pictured the village defibrillator in the old-fashioned phone box outside her parents' pub just in case her heart decided to fly straight out of her chest and directly into Lucas's very lovely surgeon's hands.

Err...no! Her heart would stay precisely where it was, thank you very much.

Then why was her hand shaking as she reached out to close the exam-room door?

She'd known Lucas was coming. For an entire twenty-four hours.

Time in which she'd steeled herself to see him. Made plans even.

She had decided to be cool, calm, collected, introduce him to his son, make it clear he'd never ever have custody and then send him on his merry way.

So what had she done instead?

Not prepped her son at all. Made a panicked phone call to her parents then hung up before she could take any of their advice, paced and paced and paced in between trying to sleep, which had worked for about...oh, sixty seconds.

Only to go berserk and all but bare her soul in front of the entire village.

Well.

A bit of her soul in front of two villagers and one visitor who wanted his pet to be seen by Lucas and not her. Still. Talk about heaping one humiliation on another.

As the exam-room door clicked shut, she turned round, only to find herself face to chest with the chest she had once been so familiar with that it was pure instinct to reach out and touch it. As she stood, hand raised between them, Lucas asked, 'Where do you want me?'

Their eyes caught and locked. Electricity buzzed between them, just as it had the night of their very first kiss all those years ago. His clear blue eyes bored into her, asking about a hundred questions all at once.

Am I forgiven? Do you mind that I'm not leaving even if I'm not? What have you been up to for the past six years?

Uh...having and raising the son I still have to tell you about.

'I'll just put Audrey here, shall I?' Caspian's plaintive tone mercifully pulled Lucas's attention away from her. Her nerve endings crackled with discomfort as he settled in front of the exam table as naturally as if he'd worked in this room for years. He'd always had that knack. Putting people instantly at ease. The Lucas Effect, she'd called it. No one was immune. Even a young Cornish girl who'd never been to London or had sushi or a million other things life in Dolphin Cove hadn't prepared her for.

One glimpse of that warm smile of his and...swoon!

And look at him now. Taking over her patients as easily as he'd stepped in front of the cameras and won Britain's heart over as the Uber-Vet.

Uber-Jerk, more like.

She gave him a sidelong glance as she washed her hands and popped on a pair of gloves. Where was the goofy, nerdy funster she'd fallen in love with?

The glasses had been replaced by contacts. Laser surgery?

The short haircut complete with cowlick was gone.

Even the usual glob of jam or spaghetti on his shirt was nowhere to be seen. Just an immaculately kitted out 'smart casual' ensemble, which he filled to perfection.

Nope. The twenty-something veterinary science geek was gone and in his place was the suave, sophisticated and properly grown-up Uber-Vet.

Lucas gave the Pekingese a scratch on the head and an admiring look. Owners loved that and Caspian was no exception.

If Caspian looked at him any more adoringly, sugar cubes would start popping out of his eyes.

In fairness, it was difficult not to be sucked into the Lucas Williams vortex of lust. His dark blond hair was combed back in a wavy invitation to run your fingers through it. His sea-blue eyes spoke volumes, darkening when he saw an injured or abused animal, flashing with a jewel-bright brilliance when he did things like, oh, propose to a woman with a puppy only to take it back the next day. A few freckles. A crooked front tooth that made his dazzling smile just a tiny bit mortal.

Water under the bridge, love. You've put it off long enough. Find a way to have him in your life for Maverick. Your boy deserves to know the truth. So does Lucas.

Ellie could hear her mother's earlier counsel as clearly as if she was in the room. Even so, she hoped her mother had seen that Lucas had arrived and had steered Mav straight to the 'puppy wing', as her son had taken to calling the purpose-built whelping and puppy-rearing pens at the far end of the clinic when she'd dropped him off. He loved it there. Seeing the puppies born and raised before being given to the various families who fostered them until they were old enough for training at specialised centres around the country.

As they all shifted into place around the exam table, a waft of Lucas's man scent enveloped her. How a Londoner managed to smell of warm summer air, freshly chopped wood and oranges was beyond her. She began to mouth-breathe, asking herself on a loop why she hadn't given him his marching papers the instant she'd laid eyes on him.

She'd known this moment was coming ever since she'd seen that smiley face on the pregnancy test. You'd have thought six years would've given her enough time to prepare herself and her son, but...nope! No such luck.

'Ellie?'

'Hmm?'

Lucas gave her a look. The kind that meant she'd been staring at him but not actually speaking words.

'Mind if I get started?'

'Not at all.' Why would she? Just because the father of her child had re-entered her life seemingly out of nowhere was absolutely no reason to get all tetchy about when he started a canine exam.

Smile and nod.

She should call Drew. Drew would know what to do. He'd been the one to tape her together all of those years ago when her life had fallen apart and come back together in a totally different shape. Drew, who was still in hospital healing from all sorts of injuries—emotional and physical—himself. No. She should not call Drew. She was a grown woman perfectly capable of handling herself in this entirely unnatural situation.

Work!

That was something she knew how to do.

She grabbed her tablet and began tapping in Audrey's details. She pulled up her chart from a previous visit and placed it on the exam table so Lucas could see it.

'About three years, is she?' Lucas asked.

Caspian all but swooned. 'Oh, my goodness, me. *Yes!* How did you know? Are you, like, an animal whisperer as well?'

'Erm, no… Ellie's just pulled up her chart.'

'Oh, right, well, I'm sure it doesn't have all of the details because we've only been here once before, when poor little Aud had a sliver. We live in London, where you are based if I'm not mistaken?' Caspian didn't pause for breath, launching into a long story about how he was down for the weekend, visiting his Aunt Viola.

Ellie tuned in. Her hunch in the reception area had been right. Caspian was one of Viola Smythe-Bingham's great-nephews. Viola had five cats, a pair of wolfhounds, a herd of alpacas and a nineteen-year-old pony called Arthur, all of which were under Ellie's care.

Caspian must be down on one of his annual 'make sure I'm listed in the will trips' Viola frequently complained about. Viola was very rich, very single and had no children of her own. And her family never let her forget it. What they didn't know was that Viola had made an incredibly generous donation towards the construction of their new clinic after they had saved her favourite alpaca, Starburst, from certain death. She had also promised a substantial donation to the Dolphin Cove

Veterinary Clinic when she passed away. At ninety-two Viola showed few signs of slowing down. Ellie hoped she never died. Viola was far more fun than any stack of money would be. So were her alpacas.

As Caspian wittered on about Audrey's pedigree, her agility classes, her specialised diet and grooming routine, Ellie's gaze drifted back to Lucas, who was nodding along whilst deftly examining the dog who, although looking a bit wan and listless, was also gazing up at him as if he were a Greek god.

Traitors. The lot of them.

She wondered when Drew came back if he would go all googly-eyed, too. Ask his advice on everything. Treat him like the superstar he was and always would be.

Audrey yelped when Lucas palpated her tummy, then tried to climb into his arms. For comforting, no doubt. Arms that had failed to comfort her when he'd explained he wasn't breaking up with her because he didn't love her but because he didn't want to 'drag her down'. Drag her into the limelight more like. She wasn't nearly as camera ready as the women she saw on his arm at all those star-studded charity events he attended. The swine. He made it very, very difficult to hate him seeing as he had single-handedly quadrupled the amount of donations Britons gave to animal charities.

Wasn't life just great?

Her heart softened as she pictured her gorgeous boy. She wouldn't have him without Lucas. So for that alone she owed him a thank you.

'Her gums are a bit pale and her tummy does seem sore. Ellie, sorry, where do you keep your stethoscopes?'

'My what?'

Caspian and Lucas were both looking at her expectantly.

'Stethoscope?' Lucas took one of his lovely, beautiful surgeon's hands—hands she'd traced again and again with her own fingertips—and put it to his broad expanse of chest as if explaining it to a five-year-old.

She did a weird *ha-ha-ha* laugh. 'I know what a stethoscope is.'

'I know,' He gave her a funny look and put his hand on the small of her back just as he used to whenever her nerves had got the better of her.

She lurched backwards, then gave him a wide-eyed look, pretending his touch hadn't just swept through her body in a honeyed spray of heated sparkles. 'I would've thought the Uber-Vet would have his own, super-special stethoscope.'

Everything at the Uber-Vet's was 'super special'.

Not that she'd watched the show.

Much.

The comment hung in the air like a discordant note.

It had been a low blow. And not really her style. She wasn't a sniper.

'As you know, I'm not the Uber-Vet any more.'

Caspian gasped and asked for details. Ellie pulled out the stethoscope she always kept stuffed in her front scrubs pocket and handed it to him with what she hoped was an apologetic look.

Lucas popped the ear tips in and pressed the chest piece to Audrey's tiny frame.

Caspian lowered his head in a reverent silence as Lucas's features shifted into a deeply attractive expression of studied concentration.

No, she chided herself. It was not attractive. And he probably wasn't even listening.

The Lucas Williams she'd once believed he was didn't

exist. That Lucas Williams had been the kindest, most generous, gentle, intelligent, capable, loving man she had ever had the privilege to meet.

This one?

This one was a stranger to her.

We'll start our own practice, we'll get married, we'll have a family of our own.

Urgh. Why did it still hurt so much?

Because all of his reasons had felt like lies in the end.

It had been a Grand Canyon-sized break-up and just like the river that ran through it, she could already feel the self-loathing, disbelief and hurt wash back into her system.

The air in the exam room suddenly felt stifling. She had to get out.

'May I...?' She scooched round the examination table, trying not to brush up against him. All six feet two of his gorgeously fit body. The body she'd once thought would be the one that, at the end of a long day at the clinic, would curl round her in bed, tugging her into his perfect arms. Kiss her with his perfect lips.

Tingles began blossoming in a most inconvenient area at the memory of their kisses.

Anyway.

Lucas looked up, unhooking the stethoscope from his ears. 'You're not leaving, are you?'

Ha-ha-ha. 'No. I was just...erm...finding the scale.' She slipped a small scale onto the exam table and lowered her voice an octave, trying to sound soft and demure and, more to the point, like the owner of the veterinarian surgery they were standing in as she addressed Caspian. 'So, Audrey here has been under the weather?'

Caspian gave her a quick glance then poured all his

attention on Lucas, explaining how Audrey had gone off her food and he was ever so worried.

As he rattled through Audrey's diet, Ellie noticed the dog constantly trying to nuzzle into Caspian. More specifically, into Caspian's pocket.

'What have you got in there? Cheese?'

Caspian went deadly serious. 'No. It's her treat food.'

'Which is…?'

'*Foie gras*. It's not normally *foie gras*, but Audrey does hate car travel so I fed her a bowlful last night and then again this morning…but since we've arrived…' He threw up his hands in despair. 'She's been vomiting and exhausted and plodding around as if the weight of the world is around her neck. I've tried and tried to give her more to cheer her up. She likes the scent but won't eat it!'

Ellie tried to keep the judgement out of her voice when she said, 'Perhaps that's because *foie gras* is effectively poisonous to dogs.' Grapes, onions, garlic and almost pure fat? A classic recipe for a good old-fashioned case of pancreatitis.

Lucas took a step back from the exam table. He knew the rule and, astonishingly, was adhering to it. One vet gave the news, the other vet nodded along unless vet number one was floundering and even then…you had to wait for the signal. Theirs had been a tug on an earlobe.

The blood had drained from Caspian's face. 'You mean I've poisoned my precious Audrey?' He clutched the dog to him, her mournful eyes meeting his as if to say, yes, you have.

Lucas and Ellie flew into action. If it was indeed pancreatitis and poor Audrey's distended belly meant a severe, potentially lethal infection was underway, they needed to act and fast.

Ellie swiftly put a drip into her little leg after Lucas had shaved a small spot, despite Caspian's cries of despair. 'It's critical that if she's lost any fluids they be replaced.'

They spent the next few minutes with Ellie doing a more studied examination of Audrey and, after escorting Caspian to the kennel area of the clinic and assuring him he could visit Audrey as often as he liked, they finally convinced him that what she really needed was a good rest and monitoring by their team of vet nurses.

'And you'll call me if anything goes…you know…' Caspian's voice caught in his throat, unable to voice his worst fear. She got it. She felt the same way about her pets.

'I promise we'll ring. Well done for noticing she needed care.' She gave his shoulder a squeeze then added, 'Do give my best to your Aunt Viola, won't you?'

'Course, darling.' Caspian leant in for a kiss on first one cheek and then the other. 'And sorry about, you know, earlier.'

She smirked a 'yeah right' after he'd left, only to have her expression freeze when she saw her son running towards the front door. 'Maverick?' Her heart leapt into her throat as she rushed out to meet him. 'What are you doing there?'

He held out a notebook and pen in his hands. 'I wanted to get the Uber-Vet's autograph. Torky told me he was in here. Can I, Mum?'

His little forehead, high like his father's, was crinkled all the way up his brow. She swept a hand through his dark blond hair, his bright blue eyes looking up at her with such hope. Such expectation.

How could she say no to that face? How could she explain that what he was asking was so much more complicated than asking for a celebrity's autograph? Lucas Williams wasn't just the man who'd broken her heart. He was also Maverick's father. The fear that had haunted her ever since she discovered that she was carrying this little boy swept through her afresh. The fear that Lucas would take him away from her.

'Ah! There you are, Ellie. I thought maybe we should sit down and—' Lucas stopped. Ellie was kneeling in front of a little boy who was holding a notebook and pen. His little forehead was screwed up as if he was trying to digest some very complicated information. When he saw Lucas, his eyes brightened and his big ear-to-ear smile instantly made Lucas smile, too.

'Mum, look! It's him! He's still here!'

Ellie stood up so fast she wobbled.

Lucas reached out a hand to steady her, but she pulled back as if his touch burnt her.

'I'm Maverick.' The little boy stepped forward, his hands holding out his notebook. 'I wanted to get your autograph, but my mum said you'd gone back to London.'

'Lucas is very busy, love. He's got a patient.' She nodded towards the elderly woman sitting patiently with her cat.

Lucas threw Ellie a confused look and caught a flare of guilt lance through her green eyes. She looked pale, her hands shaking as she feebly tried to wave away her white lie. He looked back at the little boy, registered his hair colour, his eye colour, the way they sloped a bit, like his mother's…and his. Almond shaped, he called them. Sleepy sexy, Ellie had called them. He had the strangest feeling of déjà vu. As if he was looking at a photo of himself from when he had been a little boy.

He tried to estimate the little boy's age and then, with the power of a lightning strike, he got it.

Maverick was his son.

His heart crashed against his ribcage with a ferocity he wouldn't have believed possible.

One look at Ellie, eyes bright with a sheen of tears, and he knew he was right.

Trying his best not to frighten the boy, who quite clearly did not know Lucas was his father, he knelt down in front of him, took the paper and signed it, drawing in his signature pawprint at the end of the 's' in Williams.

This was not the way he'd expected to meet his son. Not even close.

He felt Ellie's eye boring into him throughout the short interlude.

When he looked up at her, she was shaking her head, *No, no, no—don't you dare tell him.*

So what was he meant to do? Leave?

Not a chance.

Emotions assaulted him like knife wounds. Elation. Pride. Loss at having missed so many precious moments. His birth. His first word. His first tooth. Disbelief that Ellie had kept Maverick a secret all these years.

He knew things hadn't ended with any sort of grace between them but hiding a *child*? *His* child? What the hell had she been thinking? This little boy…this gorgeous little boy was his flesh and blood. More than any of their shared hopes and dreams, Ellie knew he'd wanted a family of his own. With her! But life had ripped that possibility away from him.

And now, thanks to her, he'd missed the first five years of his son's life.

He forced his raging thoughts into a cage as he reminded himself, thanks to Ellie, he had a son. A beautiful, healthy, happy little boy. But at this moment? The gratitude ended there. She should have told him.

He rose and looked her straight in the eye. 'You and I need to talk.'

Fifteen minutes later, after a delighted Maverick had been assured he would be able to introduce Lucas to the puppies he and Torky were currently playing with and Mrs Cartwright was assured, once again, that her beautiful Siamese, Tabatha, was in fine fettle, Ellie shakily handed Lucas a mug of hot tea in the small kitchen that stood at the heart of the immaculate surgical ward.

'Two sugars with milk,' she said before he could ask and then, 'So…'

'Yeah.' He scrubbed a hand through his hair, noticing Ellie's pupils were dilated and her eyes had gone that green-grey colour they'd used to turn when her emotions had been running riot. 'So…'

'Mav's…' she began, her voice catching in her throat. 'Maverick's yours. In case you were wondering.'

'Oh, I figured that out.' Maverick, now that he'd spent a few more minutes with him, was a little carbon copy of him. 'I just— Ells—'

'Don't call me that,' she interrupted. Her eyes were darting everywhere but at him.

'What? Do you want me to call you Miss Stone?' He glanced at her hands. 'Or is it Mrs now?'

'No,' she snapped. 'I'm a single mum.'

A complex fury that she'd gone through this all of this on her own swept through him. 'You didn't have to be.'

She rolled her eyes at him. 'Oh, really? Because I thought when you told me the engagement was off, that meant you didn't want to marry me.'

She opened her mouth to continue then clamped it shut. There was clearly a lot more on her mind, but she wasn't going to make this easy on him. In some ways? Deservedly so. But keeping the fact he had a son from him? It was an unforgivable omission.

'So... I'm guessing you decided not to tell me because of the split?' Not the best of conversation starters, but... he wasn't going to let her clam up.

Her eyes widened. 'Seriously? Lucas, there were a thousand reasons why I didn't tell you.'

His anger was simmering so close to the surface he forced himself to take a drink of the sweet tea rather than lash out and make it incredibly clear that nothing in the world was more important than family. And this little boy... Maverick...was his son.

The few seconds of silence afforded him a vital reminder that he'd been in a desperate place and, he supposed, she must've been, too. Even so... He levelled his voice. 'How about giving me one of them?'

She scrunched her eyes tight and pressed her thumbs to the bridge of her nose. When she opened her eyes again, instead of seeing the guilt and fear he'd seen before he saw strength. The fierce love of a mother determined to protect her son. 'I didn't think you were in a place to handle a son as well as your other "more relevant" responsibilities.'

He flinched at the turn of phrase. His own. Back then he'd been less experienced at juggling his family problems with his romantic life. He'd grown up a lot since then and had definitely learned to choose his words more carefully, but this…this was whiplashing him straight back to a time and place he'd hoped to never revisit.

'It was a complicated time.'

'Complicated?' Ellie's laugh was utterly bereft of humour. 'It seemed pretty straightforward to me. You dumped me to "help your family", then swanned off to become a media darling without me.'

'That wasn't how it happened, Ellie.' He'd been crushed between a rock and damn tight hard place. His options had been limited and by limited he meant he'd had one choice.

Ellie put on a posh voice. 'Swanning into the limelight and dazzling the UK's female fans with your many talents.' Her tone turned dark. 'No wonder you sent me back to my poky village to get on with "a country girl's hopes and dreams".' She crossed her arms defensively. 'You told me I'd be better off without you. Admit it, Lucas. It wasn't that you didn't want to drag me down. It was that you wanted to push your own star higher.'

The tang of bile rose in his throat.

His father had been barely able to work because his Parkinson's had become so bad. His mother had been exhausted from worry and being his full-time carer. His older brother, also a vet, had up and vanished. A string of debts Lucas had uncovered had explained the disappearance. So he'd been the only one left to try and keep the debt-ridden clinic afloat. There was no way he had wanted to subject Ellie to that. Crush her dreams. Sideline her while his focus had to be on his family.

The show had come about through a completely chance encounter. One day, a couple of weeks into his gruelling schedule, a woman had come in with a dog she'd found that had been hit by a car. She'd stayed throughout the exam and had insisted he talk her through the operation when they'd discovered he had a broken pelvis. Lucas had organised for her to watch him operate on the poor little chap on a monitor they had in one of the private waiting rooms.

When he'd come out of the operating theatre, she'd told him she was a TV producer and that watching him at work had given her an idea. The Uber-Vet. The money they had offered him had gone a long way to keeping the clinic open, getting his father proper medical care and his mother some much-needed rest. So Lucas had lunged at the offer and done what he could to make the show a success. A slick haircut and slightly whiter teeth hadn't changed who he was inside!

He'd wanted to tell Ellie when the offer had come in, but the producers had been very clear. They'd wanted him and only him. The idea of ringing her with yet another rejection had simply been out of the question. So he'd signed on the dotted line and got to work.

He gave his jaw a scrub. Yeah. He'd made mistakes. But his choices about how to save his family from crippling debt weren't up for discussion now. Why she had kept his son a secret was. 'Pushing you away was not what I wanted. You know that, Ellie. I needed to help my family and, as I said, things were complicated.'

Ellie's green eyes met his in a blaze of indignation. 'You're right. What would a simple country girl like me know about all those big complicated city things?'

'Ellie—stop it. Don't put yourself down.'

'It's hard not to, sitting face to face with the one person who I stupidly thought would always put me first.'

Her words landed in his gut like a boulder.

Rock. Hard place.

He was feeling the squeeze all over again. Only this time…this time the only person he had to look out for was himself. Complications with his father's Parkinson's had taken his life a couple of years back. He'd built up enough of a rainy-day fund to keep his mother busy with her charity lunches, and as for Jonty? He'd finally resurfaced. Was getting the help he needed for a gambling problem he'd hidden from them for far too long.

Ellie clapped her hands to her face, took in a couple of slow breaths then dropped them to the table with a slapping sound. They had to sting but maybe, like him, her body was buzzing with the type of adrenaline no one should experience. Fear of loss.

She wove her fingers together then finally met his gaze. 'I was going to call you when I found out I was pregnant.'

'When was that?' He was hungry for details.

'About nine weeks after you chose fame and fortune over a humble life in the country.' She took a pointed sip of her tea, her eyes glued to his. 'And a new girlfriend.'

Lucas felt as though a searing hot knife had been slipped between his ribs. 'What? I didn't have a new girlfriend!'

'Katrina Shandwick would probably beg to differ,' Ellie parried, then pushed herself up and away from the wooden table and began muttering something he couldn't make out apart from the 'Don't let him see you cry' part.

Katrina Shandwick had been his producer. They'd gone to countless red-carpet events and she'd always insisted she be his plus one, but it had never been anything more than that—mostly because he'd had no idea how to talk to the press. Especially in the beginning.

As Ellie noisily washed her mug at the sink, every

part of him ached to go to her, hold her in his arms, but instinct told him to stay away. Especially if he wanted to be involved in his son's life.

'Ells—Ellie,' he corrected himself. 'Did you really think I would've started dating someone so soon after we split? I'm not like that. And I would never suggest that you or your work were anything less than exemplary. C'mon. That's not me. You knew me better than anyone.'

'Precisely.' Ellie whirled around. 'I *used* to know you. This guy here?' She circled her hand in the air between them. 'I have no clue who he is. You changed overnight. And there was no way I was going to let you into my son's life.'

Our son, he said silently, and then, because he knew he had to fix this if he wanted any sort of relationship with Maverick, 'Ellie, there have been some seriously crossed wires here. I don't think you understand what—'

Ellie cut him off quick smart. 'You're right! I don't understand a thing! I don't understand how, after six years of blanking me, you could just swan in—'

'I hardly swanned in.'

'Selfies in the exam room? Stealing my patients?' She arched an imperious eyebrow. 'Taking forever to diagnose Audrey?' A shadow flickered across her features as an idea struck. 'Oh, my God. You waited, didn't you? You *let me* figure out what was wrong with her to cut me a break? In front of my *own* patient? Are you trying to do me favours? What the actual freaking heck, Lucas? I don't need favours. Especially not from you.'

Lucas looked over his shoulder as if an invisible crowd was giving Ellie hints—the role of the producers in his previous life. If three days ago could count as previous. 'I did no such thing,' he protested, nanoseconds too late. He had. It was her clinic. Her diagnosis to make. He'd done enough guest visits to know it rankled other vets that pet owners would hang on his every word rather than their loyal, committed, local vet. One of many downsides of being part of the fame game.

Ellie dropped her head into her hands again, groaning with the injustice of it all.

'Can't you just go? Go and pretend none of this ever happened?'

'Now that I know I have a son?' He wasn't going to broach the other part—the part about how his heart had stood still when he'd first laid eyes on her. 'Not a chance.'

'Fine,' she eventually said. 'But you're not staying here.'

'But Henry said you needed help—'

Ellie cut him off. 'Thanks to your offer to Henry, I have no choice but to accept your help in the clinic. But, believe me, if we didn't have so many important surgeries coming up, you'd be in your car heading back to the bright lights of London right now.' She huffed out a sigh. 'What I meant was you're not staying *here* here.' She flashed him a look that spoke volumes. She still had feelings for him. Hurt ones definitely. But pain was a bedfellow of love and…damn, this was complicated. Did he still love her?

'Not until I work out how we're going to tell my son you're his…' She gave a little shudder, unable to actually say the words. She pointed up to the ceiling. 'Mav and I live upstairs in a two-bedroomed flat, all the beds are taken. Henry's in the guest flat next door. Ditto. You'll stay…' A slow satisfied smile crept onto her lips. A smile that unleashed another hammering of heartbeats against his bruised ribcage. 'You'll stay at the Hungry Pelican.'

'What? With your parents?'

Ellie's expression went all doe-eyed. 'You're not frightened of seeing my parents, are you? After breaking their little girl's heart, leaving her to raise your son on her own and crushing all her hopes and dreams about love?'

A flicker of something he couldn't quite identify darkened her eyes, though her smile remained bright. Guilt maybe? Had her parents encouraged her to tell him? If they had…excellent. Far be it from him to disagree.

'Great.' He clapped his hands together and gave them a rub. 'If I remember correctly, they're about a two-minute drive away?'

'Or a ten-minute walk,' she answered, and then, a bit superciliously, 'The Dolphin Cove residents are trying to keep city slickers and their big fancy cars out of the town centre. You know, preserve that country feeling.'

Lucas covered his mouth to mask a smile. Here was the Ellie he knew. The mischievous one who drew the best out of people whether they liked it or not. 'Great. Say the word and I'm ready to go.'

CHAPTER THREE

ELLIE FLUNG THE pub door open and stomped inside.

'Hello, darling!' her mother trilled from her usual post in the kitchen pass, where she slid gorgeously delicious plates of food through to the serving staff. 'I wasn't expecting you tonight.'

'I've brought you a guest,' Ellie said tightly. 'A *paying* guest.'

'Actually,' Lucas firmly corrected in a low voice, 'I think you'll find I'm family.' He raised his voice again. 'But I'm more than happy to pay.' A steely determination added a timbre to his voice Ellie hadn't remembered hearing before and that six-year-old thread of guilt cinched just the tiniest bit tighter round her heart. Tighter still when her mother appeared in front of them.

Lucas stepped out from behind her and towards her mum. 'Hello, Mrs Stone. It's been a long time…'

Her mum held up a hand, her expression impossible to read. 'Stop right there.' Wyn disappeared from sight and reappeared moments later with Ellie's father Gordon—Gordo to friends. He normally looked like a cross between Santa Claus and your typical jolly old sailor type. Right now, he looked like a very protective father.

'Lucas,' he said tightly.

'Lucas,' Ellie's mum said, with a bit more warmth than Ellie was comfortable with. 'What can I get you to drink?'

Ellie glared at her. Weren't they all meant to be being mean to Lucas? Her mother glared back. One of those multi-faceted glares that said, *This is the father of your child, child.* And, *This is long overdue, young woman. Humph.*

She was thirty-five years old, not a stroppy teen!

Well. Perhaps she felt a little bit stroppy. Okay, very stroppy, but this was one of the moments she'd been avoiding for five years. The bigger one—the one where she explained to her son that he did have a father…

Sudden rushes of hot and cold swept through her. Five precious years she'd cared for and protected her boy, ensuring that, above all, he knew he was loved. Valued. Her parents adored him. Surprise, surprise. He was and would remain their only grandchild. His 'cool Uncle Drew' had been an awesome dad stand-in. Not on the romantic front because—*ew!*—she'd grown up with Drew and the idea of even— *Ew!* Not because he was icky looking. Quite the opposite, in fact, but…no. Her heart had always belonged to one man and one man only. Anyway, the point was that she had never wanted, for one solitary second, Maverick to think he was unwanted—like *some* people had made her feel. And now, with Lucas here, her son could very well turn the same accusatory look on her that Lucas had given her when he'd found he'd been denied five years of loving the world's most perfect little boy.

'A soft drink will be fine,' Lucas finally said.

Gordon gave a tight nod and went back behind the bar. 'I'll take it you'll have a wine, Ellie?'

She nodded and mouthed, 'Large, please.' She didn't

normally drink on a 'school night' but…extenuating circumstances.

'Where's—?' Wyn began to ask, and then clapped her hands over her mouth.

'Don't worry, Mum. He knows.' Ellie flicked a look at Lucas who, to his credit, didn't launch into a high and mighty speech about Ellie's failure to tell him about Maverick.

Neither did he start telling her mum how she'd made him hide in the operating clinic while she'd extracted Maverick from the kennels without the promised show-and-tell session with the Uber-Vet. Or how he hadn't insisted on coming along when she'd escorted a very grumpy Maverick up to Henry's flat for an evening of spaghetti Bolognese and yet another showing of his favourite animated movie about pets.

He hadn't even brought up the topic of how she was going to run the clinic single-handedly when Henry left in the morning for London and she would, inevitably, try to make him leave again. Even the walk to the pub had been low maintenance. He'd pointed out a few things he thought had changed since he'd been down last—seven Christmases ago. He'd complimented her on the clinic—as well he should—and asked how they'd managed to create such an impressive facility on ten acres of prime real estate—with a lot of blue-sky thinking, some lottery funding, some private donations and the inclusion of a community petting zoo.

In all honesty, he'd been exactly like the Lucas she'd known six years ago minus the part about how they used to know everything about one another. Everything and then some. Her insides had been tingling from the moment she'd laid eyes on him. Still were.

'And here we are.' Gordon carried their drinks over to a quiet table at the back of the pub. It was a gorgeous evening so most of the customers were sitting on the picnic benches outside or in the small but pretty garden area behind the pub.

'So! Lucas,' her mother began. 'What brings you to town?'

Ellie was tempted to jump in but thought she'd leave this one to Lucas.

'The official reason is to replace Henry.'

'Oh?' Her mother threw her a questioning look.

Ellie parried the look to Lucas.

Lucas explained, 'My contract was up for renewal with the Uber-Vet, but I felt it was the right time to pass on the baton.'

Wyn spluttered her wine out. 'I thought that's what you wanted. The show.'

Lucas shot Ellie a look. One that asked why on earth she hadn't explained the situation with his family to them.

Because her brain had pretty much exploded and been unable to receive more information when he'd told her he couldn't marry her any more, that's why. By the time she'd even begun to process what Lucas had been going through, she'd found out she was pregnant, and he had been appearing on the red carpet with another woman and…well…that was pretty much the story from then on.

'The show was a means to an end,' Lucas finally explained. 'My father's illness had put the clinic in a difficult financial position and my brother—'

'He's a vet, too, right?' Ellie's father asked.

'Yes. He…' A dark look shadowed Lucas's bright eyes. 'Jonty had his own problems to deal with, so…' He leant back in the booth and swept his fingers through his hair.

'Suffice it to say there were a lot of factors that led up to my decision to do the show and just as many to step away from it.'

One of the bar staff called out to her parents for some assistance. Ellie barely noticed them leave as a wave of understanding crashed through her.

Had Lucas been genuinely torn? She hadn't been able to believe him. Proposing one day. Taking it back the next. Who *did* that?

But...maybe it hadn't been his decision at all. She desperately tried to remember exactly what Lucas had said to her that day.

There's been a change of plan. My priorities have changed. I don't want to drag you down with me.

She'd stopped listening then. The roar of blood blocking out everything else other than the fact that the love of her life had just dumped her.

But...had he?

There's been a change of plan.

She replayed the lines again.

I don't want to drag you down with me.

Had Lucas done the show because he'd *had* to?

The softening of her heart hardened. No. They'd been a couple. Deeply in love. When he'd proposed he had been prepared to announce to everyone they knew that he would be with her in sickness and in health, for richer, for poorer, all the terrible things—because weathering terrible things together made anything seem endurable. By pushing her to the side, he'd made it clear he hadn't trusted her to stick with him. That...that was the pain she'd born through the years.

Lucas scraped his crooked front tooth over his bottom lip, the blood draining from it as it dragged over the full, kissable mouth she'd never thought she'd lay eyes on again. Not in person anyway. The look he gave her said, *Please. Please give me a chance to explain.*

She gestured for him to continue.

'Since Dad died—'

'Wait! Your father passed away?'

'Didn't you know?' Lucas looked genuinely surprised.

'No. How would I—?' She stopped herself. It would've been in the papers. Or the veterinary magazines she subscribed to. 'I'm sorry. That must've been very difficult.'

Lucas nodded silently, his shoulders slumping as if reliving the weight of losing his father all over again.

'Is your mother all right?'

'She's better now.' His eyes shot to hers and in them she saw a wealth of pain.

Instinct kicked in and she pulled him into a quick tight hug and just as quickly pulled away. His scent, the familiarity of how they fitted together, his touch…it was all too much. She took a gulp of her wine then said hoarsely, 'How're you going to tell her about Maverick?' She dropped her head into her heads and moaned. 'Don't answer that. I don't have the slightest clue how to tell Mav that his TV hero is his father.'

'I'm his hero?' Lucas's expression lightened. The tension and pain dropped away from his features, leaving nothing but pure joy.

'Well,' she snipped. 'On television anyway.'

And then, completely unexpectedly, they shared a smile that reached into the very centre of her heart.

Dangerous? Absolutely.

Worth exploring?

Her brain threw that one back and forth for a second. Maybe for Maverick's sake. But only if Lucas were to meet about a hundred thousand criteria, including assuring her, beyond any reasonable doubt, that he would never, ever let her boy down.

Ellie's parents arrived back at the table just as Lucas took her hand in his and said, 'We need to talk.'

Wyn did an about face and turned her husband round with a cheeky smile. 'Darling? I think we might be needed in the kitchen.'

'Oh, right. Course.' Gordon gave the thick-slabbed table a knock. 'We'll leave you two lovebirds…erm… um…we'll leave you two to it. We'll be right behind the bar if you need anything.'

'What they need is to be alone, Gordo.' Wyn tugged him away from the table, lowering her voice as her gentle chiding continued.

Despite themselves, Ellie and Lucas both sniggered as Ellie's parents very indiscreetly tiptoed back to the kitchen and parked themselves at the pass, pretending not to stare at them.

'Excuse me.' A pair of tween-aged girls approached the table with white paper napkins in their hands, their parents sending them encouraging smiles from the far end of the pub. 'Would you mind signing our napkins? We just love your show.'

Lucas smiled and signed their napkins. The girls giggled and told him the names of all their pets and how Uber-Vet was, like, *totally* their favourite show. He tried to introduce them to Ellie, but it was clear they didn't really care who she was. They just wanted to talk to him, and it was easy to see why. He was warm, personable, and—*ha!*—he drew a little dog paw at the end of his signature. Adorable. Of course it was. Everything about him was perfect, except for the fact that when it had mattered most, he hadn't wanted her.

And just like that all the warm and fuzzy feelings

percolating inside her evaporated. This wasn't a fairy-tale ending. It was the beginning of what would be a long, complicated emotional mess she'd be unravelling for years to come.

When they'd gone, Lucas leant in close to her. Goose-pimple close.

'Ells, do you think we could go somewhere a bit more private?'

Ellie arched an eyebrow. 'What? And deny your adoring fans a chance to meet the one and only Uber-Vet?'

Something hot fired in him and she knew she'd taken a step too far. Mocking him wasn't like her and while she might think of Lucas as many things, vain was definitely not one of them.

'I'd never begrudge the fans anything. The viewership kept my family from… I owe them a lot.' His eyes darkened with something she couldn't put a finger on and then that familiar smile softened them again as he rose from the bench seat. 'C'mon. We need to talk about this without an audience.'

She quickly told her parents they were going for a walk but that Lucas would need a room for the night. Her mum threw her one of those looks. *You'd better not mess this up, young lady. Your son deserves his father.*

Her stomach churned as they left the pub. Her mother's look was a blunt reminder that Ellie wasn't entirely free to raise a flag on the moral high ground.

When they'd reached the beach path at the edge of the village, she turned to him. 'Why are you here, Lucas? Really?'

'Don't beat round the bush, Ells.' He laughed, then quickly corrected himself. 'Sorry. Ellie. Eleanor? Shall I call you Eleanor from now on?'

'No.' She gave him a play punch on the arm because after all the water under their particular bridge, using a formal name seemed ridiculous. 'But c'mon. Answer the question. Why are you really here? I doubt it's because you need the work.'

'No,' he said, much more seriously than she would've anticipated as their footsteps fell into a natural, matching stride. 'I want the work.'

She pursed her lips. 'Oh, c'mon, you're famous! You could work anywhere in the world. And you want to do a locum post in Dolphin Cove?'

He stopped and turned her to him, the heat in his hands easily filtering through her light linen top. 'I want to work with *you*. I never liked how we left things and a stupid part of me believed that if I came down…' He lifted his hands away and held them between them before she could interrupt him, her shoulders already feeling the loss of his touch. 'The plan wasn't exactly fully formed, but when Henry told me he was working here when I rang him a month back—'

'A month?'

Lucas nodded, looking as confused as she felt. 'Yeah. I rang him weeks ago to ask him to take over on the show. These things don't happen overnight.'

Ellie felt her jaw twitch. So it wasn't just her parents who'd wanted her to tell Lucas the truth. It was Henry. She knew Drew thought the same, though he'd never dared say as much. Was this the universe telling her she'd been wrong all of these years?'

'Ellie,' Lucas focused on her with an intensity that roared through her bloodstream, 'I am staying.'

She glared at him. It wasn't his call. It was hers! Wasn't it?

The memory of *that day* surged back to the fore.

I don't want you being dragged down with me.

Had Lucas genuinely been trying to protect her from something? Ensuring she'd be free to follow her dreams? Why hadn't he seen that her dreams had included him?

He stood, silently, waiting. The man looked immovable. Gorgeously immovable. That. And he was the only vet in the country with enough skill to tackle the list of surgeries Henry had been scheduled to do.

'Oh, hell.' Her resistance faltered. 'It would be very useful if you could stay and work, but we need to figure out a plan with Maverick.'

'We?' He said, hope lighting up his eyes.

'Me,' she corrected. 'And your job will be to prove to me you respect my wishes. And my son's.'

Lucas nearly corrected her. Nearly said 'our son', then thought better of it. He would have his son in his life, and he'd take every step to ensure nothing got in the way of it. Even Mav's mama bear of a mum. She might be igniting all sorts of fires in him he'd long thought extinguished, but the one that burnt brightest… That flame burnt for his son.

At a split in the path, Ellie pointed him towards a sandy path edged with tall grasses. 'If we head off here, we can go to the beach in front of the clinic.'

'Beachfront property. That's quite a coup, Ellie.' He was impressed. 'I thought you and Drew were going to set up in the village. Renovate an old shop.'

Ellie's eyebrows shot up in exactly the way Mav's had when he'd first spotted Lucas. 'No. The plan was that you, Drew and I were going to set up in the village.

Drew and I decided to aim higher. Go for more of a community outreach angle.'

They rounded the corner into the idyllic cove where the veterinary clinic's windows shone in the ever-darkening hues of the remaining sunlight.

Ellie huffed out a sigh. 'Sorry. I'm being a pedant. You did your thing, we did ours. There's no need to stick the knife in.'

'It's me who owes you the apology, Ellie. Seriously. I know saying I left you in the lurch is a pretty massive understatement, but… I genuinely didn't feel as though I had a choice.'

'I got by,' she said in a voice that didn't sound entirely convinced.

He had too. Just. The bright lights and constant need to be 'in character' had never sat well with him. He loved being a vet. Plain and simple. He'd also loved Ellie every bit as much, but…he'd made what he had thought was the best choice. The only choice. Leaving his parents to battle debt and his father's debilitating disease on their own? He'd simply unable to do it. Not without dragging Ellie away from her dreams and her beloved Cornwall. The fact things had turned around so quickly with the Uber-Vet had seemed little short of divine intervention.

He opened his mouth to explain but clamped it shut, knowing anything he said on that front would only be digging himself a deeper hole.

What's done was done. The only thing he could do now was to look forward and the one thing he knew he'd have in his future was his son. No matter what Ellie thought.

Taking a step back from the heated emotions, Lucas opened his arms wide and turned away from the beach towards the clinic. 'You've done more than get by, Ells. Look at what you've accomplished. You've set up this incredible clinic, a surgical unit—'

'A petting zoo and a teaching centre,' Ellie said, a flush colouring her lightly tanned cheeks. A sense of accomplishment she clearly hadn't let herself feel added a couple more inches to her athletic five-foot-eight frame.

Without thinking, he reached out and gave her shoulder a rub, feeling her pride by proxy. For a nanosecond he felt her lean into his touch and then, as if it had never happened, the only thing he felt was the distance between them. 'You should be proud. You two have accomplished so much.'

The dark laugh that was so unlike her surfaced again. 'We probably would be in a crummy old shop if you hadn't dumped me.'

'What?' He made a noise indicating he doubted it. Not the Ellie he'd known anyway.

'We found a place in the village and it would've been perfectly fine, but when I found out about Mav there was no chance I was going to have him think he had a second-rate parent. If he ever found out about you, that is.'

Wow. There was a lot to unload in there. The last thing he would've ever said to his son was that he'd got a second-rate parent. Ellie was in her own class. An exemplary one.

Lucas felt as if she had reached inside his chest and crushed his own heart. He knew he'd hurt her. If he'd had any idea the pain had run this deep...

They stared at one another, their eyes searching each other's for answers to myriad questions until the atmosphere between them thickened. Lucas took a step forward. A bone-deep urge to pull her into his arms and promise her she'd never have to feel that harrowing pain again took hold of him, right up until a flat palm on the centre of his chest put a quick stop to that.

'We are going to discuss Mav and what to do about the fact you're his dad. And that's it.'

She was right. He had overstepped the mark but… hell's teeth. He would've done everything in his power to be with Ellie and Maverick if he'd known. Which did beg the follow-up question…why hadn't he wanted Ellie to be a part of his life as he'd untangled his family's almighty mess?

He'd thought he'd been protecting her. Plain and simple.

From the tiny acorn…grows the mighty oak.

After he'd proposed they'd gone on a walk. Soon enough they'd been laughing about all their hopes and dreams. Insane, considering they'd had no money, no clinic and zero clients. *Oh, well*, they'd said… *From the tiny acorn…* They'd stopped and kissed under an oak that must've been a good four hundred years old, vowing to leave a legacy of kindness and love in their wake that lasted as long as the tree.

That evening his father had rung and asked him to come home. Things, he'd said, weren't quite tickety-boo.

It had been the biggest understatement in the universe.

When he'd got there and learnt of the debt, the struggling clinic, his father's ever-increasing battle with Parkinson's and his AWOL older brother, it had been too much. He'd needed to focus. He'd not wanted to test the limits of their relationship—not when Ellie had had all the opportunities in the world.

As if reading his mind, she asked, 'Why wasn't I enough?'

'It wasn't you, honestly.'

Her eyes widened. 'You told me you loved me. You asked me to marry you. How could I have not taken it personally?' Before he could answer, she pointed at a log further down the beach. 'This isn't about you and me anymore. C'mon. Let's hash this out before I change my mind. Maverick is the priority here.'

'Absolutely,' Lucas said, swallowing down yet another lump of remorse into a gut already churning with discord. So much for a few weeks down in Cornwall making his peace then moving on with their lives. Ellie would be in his life for ever. It was up to the pair of them what form that relationship took. For his son's sake, he prayed it would be amicable.

'So!' She sat down on the log and tugged a hand through her curls, the sun lighting them in shades of fire and gold as if she were a Hollywood starlet. 'As you know from Henry, my *loyal* friend and colleague, Drew was in an awful car accident.'

Lucas nodded. He'd be stopping by to see him when time allowed. But his priority was to be here for Ellie and, as soon as possible, Maverick. 'I am happy to work all the hours you need.'

Ellie smirked. 'They're a lot longer than your fancy telly vet hours.'

He let that one slide. There was a lot more to it than swanning into an exam room, making a diagnosis then heading into surgery with a gaggle of nurses and vets in his wake. There had been planning meetings, research, actual vet work to ensure he was at the absolute top of his game, networking, scouting out difficult cases, media appearances with Katrina, and the list went on.

His father had helped with what he could but, in the end, his Parkinson's had got the better of him and soon even going through case files had been too exhausting. His death, whilst gut-wrenching, had meant he had no longer been in pain. His brother had resurfaced periodically, but after his father's death, a stint in rehab had been the only solution for his addiction. An expensive rehab clinic that had meant renewing the Uber-Vet contract again and chaining himself to a lifestyle in which he'd never felt entirely at home.

It had been worth it, though. His brother had found a small horse-centric clinic out in the countryside to practise in, joining Lucas and his mum for Sunday lunches to hash over difficult cases. Those meals had brought his family some much-needed peace. Enough for Lucas to finally say it was enough. It was time for him to live his own life now. So when his contract had come up for renewal? That was precisely what he'd done.

'Ellie.' Lucas shifted round on the log so that he was facing her. 'I know you think I'm different now, but for the most part I'm still the Lucas you met in vet school.' He held up a hand. 'I know you don't believe it and there are things I wish I could explain better than I did at the time.' He looked at Ellie, only to receive an eye-roll and a flick of the hand. She didn't want to hear it. Fine. It was painful terrain to hash over again and, just as he'd done all those years ago, he put the blinkers on again. But this time for his son. 'Are you happy for Maverick to know I'm his father?'

Ellie peered at him though her fingers. 'God, that's weird.'

'What?'

'Hearing you say Maverick's name. Seeing you take ownership of him as his father.'

Another well-aimed kick in the gut. She didn't trust him. Fair enough. He'd have to earn that too. And he would.

'I want to be his father, Ellie. I know there is no way I can make up for the years I've lost—but I can swear to you right now that I am going to do my damnedest trying.'

She gave him a look that echoed the mix of emotions he was experiencing. A mix of hope and fear. But mostly, *How can I believe you after you left me when it mattered most?*

He'd known the boy a matter of minutes, but primal instinct had lit a white-hot coil of connection in him. He'd sacrifice for Maverick. Protect. Honour. Cherish. Love. He was a father. He was Maverick's father and he'd do everything he could to ensure his little boy knew he was loved by both of his parents.

His own father had been a complicated man. Scientific. Dedicated to the animals he'd cared for. Close to his sons when he'd needed something. Like sacrifice. Distant when he hadn't. It had been the pain most likely. And pride. He had been a highly respected vet until Parkinson's had robbed him of his ability to perform surgery. Hobbled by his own body's frailty. It must've been a devastating blow to his pride.

Ellie stretched her legs out, her foot tracing an infinity pattern in the sand. It was the same pattern he'd had designed in diamonds for her engagement ring. The one she'd thrown at him when he'd told her he'd made a terrible mistake. 'I don't want him to hear a single lie.'

'No. Absolutely not,' he agreed.

'I don't want you making promises you can't keep.'

'I would never do that.'

She pursed her lips at him. He could almost feel the

diamond ring bouncing off his chest as she whirled on one trendy trainered foot and out of his life. 'We'll see about that.'

Oh, she would. She'd see his commitment in spades.

They spoke about the logistics. Mav had surf school and science camp and also helped out at the vet's petting zoo, showing the other children that goats were fun to pet, and cows had scratchy tongues and no upper teeth. He liked to spend time with Torky, Tegan's twin, in the whelping unit during the socialisation hours and—she softened at this bit—nap time. School began again in September. He loved books so there would be lots of story-reading duties.

The list went on. Completely unlike the lists of duties that went with being the Uber-Vet, Lucas was loving each and every detail. His respect for Ellie also went up a significant notch. 'How do you do all of it? Motherhood and running the clinic.'

She shrugged. 'It's hard, but Mum and Dad are amazing. Drew's a brilliant uncle and, well, pretty much the whole village has helped because they all want their animals looked after and the only way that happened in the early years was if Mav came along.'

'You took him with you?'

'I didn't have much choice, did I?' Their eyes clashed and held.

Choice.

What a loaded word.

She'd not given him a choice. Not even a chance to offer help. Then again, he'd not given her a choice either. Not much of a leg to stand on in the self-righteous department. So he stayed quiet, his frustration humming through him in sharp bursts filled with static.

'Here's how I see it playing out,' Ellie continued officiously. 'If, and only if, Maverick takes the news well, you can stay the eight weeks the clinic needs you. After that?' She gave her head a little shake. 'We'll see.' She flicked her thumb over her shoulder towards the flat she and Mav shared. 'Tonight you're staying at the Pelican. I'm sure my mother has a million more questions for you. After that, whilst I'm not entirely thrilled about this, it makes more sense for you to move into the staff flat. I've been doing most of the night duty calls.'

He looked at her through fresh, professional eyes. She looked tired. The strain, no doubt, of taking up the slack whilst her partner recovered from his accident. Something tugged at his heart that he'd tamped down in order to get through his own trials. Compassion. Empathy.

'That's a lot of work for one person, Ellie.'

She scrubbed a hand over her face. 'Yup. Well. We're a young business trying to make a big mark. I normally take Mav to my mum, but it'd be nicer for him not to be woken up, so I'll wake you up instead. Welcome to parenthood!' She briskly began to rattle off more details—Mav's favourite pyjamas, how he liked his pillows, which were his favourite cuddly toys. 'He doesn't like marshmallows in his hot chocolate and is scared of the dark, so don't ever, ever turn off the small lamp on top of his chest of drawers.' She rubbed the heel of her hand against her bare knee, the edges of her A-line skirt fluttering in the light sea breeze. 'And he likes your show.' She threw him a soft smile.

'Why, Ellie Stone. Is that a compliment?'

'No.' She pushed herself up to stand to avoid his gaze. 'Just a fact.'

Speaking of facts… 'What did you tell him about his father? About me?'

She shrugged. 'Nothing much. Just that I loved him and not everyone had a daddy on the scene—a bit like the animal kingdom. You know, daddy lions don't hang around to teach baby lions how the world works because they have prey to stalk. Territory to protect.'

He snorted. Trust Ellie to use lions to explain why mummies hung around and daddies didn't. Then again, it was a fairly apt analogy. Ellie had created an amazing 'den' here. A place to care, protect and feed her son. And all the while Lucas had been protecting her. Not that she saw it that way, but…one day. Maybe one day. Miracles did happen. Like this one. He had a son. A beautiful boy by an equally beautiful mother who, one day, might forgive him for having turned his back on her when he'd thought he'd had no other choice.

She clapped her hands together. 'So! Let's go and rip the plaster off, shall we? Then you can hoof it back to Mum and Dad. Mav'll have a lot of questions and we both have a long day tomorrow.'

Walking behind her as she briskly made her way up to the clinic, Lucas realised he was smiling. An entirely new life was about to begin for him and, unlike the time he'd shut himself off from his own ambitions, this time he couldn't wait to start. Bring it on. Bring it all on.

CHAPTER FOUR

MAVERICK STARED AT Ellie then Lucas then back at Ellie. 'For real?'

Ellie nodded, still a bit shell-shocked herself. She'd just told her son who his father was.

Maverick crossed his legs underneath his endangered animals duvet cover, briefly making the tiger's head look as if it were surging forward to take a bite out of someone. Lucas, preferably. Her son turned his blue-eyed gaze on her. 'I thought you said my daddy was a pirate.'

Ellie's cheeks burnt at the memory. She'd said it on a whim once, never for a second thinking he'd believe her, but…it was how she thought of Lucas sometimes. A swashbuckling love thief. *Stick with the facts, Ellie!* 'Nope. 'Fraid not, love. He's a vet.'

'The Uber-Vet,' Maverick said in a reverent tone, his gaze swinging back to Lucas. 'It's like…it's like… I am *made* of vets!'

Lucas grinned from the foot of the bed where Ellie had made him sit amongst the jumble of cuddly toys. As annoying as it was to have her son all googly-eyed over the fact his father was the Uber-Vet, it was nice to see Mav take the news on board as easily as he accepted being pulled out of bed and slipped into her mother's spare room while she went off to check on a colicky horse or attend a late-night calving. Would that she had taken the news her engagement would only last twenty-four hours with such ease.

Mav popped his elbow onto his knee and his chin into his hand as he stared at Lucas for a moment. 'I suppose we do have the same earlobes.'

Ellie couldn't help herself. She cracked up. Earlobes! They had a lot more than that in common. Eyes. Hair. Dry wit—yes, even at five. And a brain that never stopped whirring with curiosity.

'Are you going to move in with us?' Mav asked Lucas.

Gulp. Case in point.

'Oh, now… I think your daddy…' Crikey, that had felt strange. Saying 'daddy' with Maverick's actual daddy sitting there. Did he even want to be called Daddy? 'Lucas will staying at the Hungry Pelican tonight.'

'But I'll be moving in next door tomorrow,' Lucas said reassuringly to Mav, and then, conciliatory to Ellie, 'To make things easier for Mummy when she's on night calls.'

Mummy.

Oh, jeepers. Who knew hearing that out of Lucas's mouth would give her butterflies? To ignore them she countered with a cheery, 'Unless, of course, Mummy decides to send Daddy on the night call.'

Ellie and Lucas shared a little tug-of-war smile. It reminded her of when they'd gone out on an internship at a huge clinic up north together when, in the dead of winter, they'd used to play rock, paper scissors to decide who went out to do a midnight calving or a pre-dawn set of lamb triplets where the farmer would, inevitably, surprise the vet with a series of 'While I have you here…'

cases in their huge, unheated barns. The butterflies took flight again.

'So…' Maverick gave his curly mop a scratch. 'Will I stay in my bed?'

'Absolutely.' Ellie sent a pointed look in Lucas's direction but refused to meet his eyes. How did a man who'd crushed her heart to bits manage to warm the cockles of that very same heart with one cheeky grin? She took Maverick's hands in hers and began to play pat-a-cake with them. 'I will be in my bed. And your daddy will stay in his bed. Next door.'

'But…don't daddies live with mummies?' Maverick asked.

Ellie could feel Lucas's eyes on her. The butterflies hummed with excitement. Would she like Daddy to live with Mummy? Her body obviously would, but her brain was shouting out the reminder that daddies didn't get to just pop up after six years of absence and pretend they hadn't kicked Mummy to the kerb right after they'd proposed to her. She blew out a little breath before she answered. 'Daddies and mummies who haven't seen each other in a while sometimes have different ways of living.'

'You mean like Rockford and Esmerelda?'

'Who're they?' Lucas asked.

'The stud dog and Mum's golden retriever.'

'Ah,' said Lucas, glints of humour sparking in his eyes and then quickly going out as he put two and two together.

Ellie bit the inside of her lip. Lucas had given her Esmerelda along with a promise to love her until the day she died.

Lucas gave his stubbly chin a rub then said to Mav, 'Yes. I suppose you could compare our situation to that.'

'But Rockford has lots of lady friends.' Maverick began listing them off. It was one of his hobbies. Keeping track of all of the 'lady friends' Rockford had. Perhaps this hadn't been the best of analogies.

Ellie turned to Lucas, interested to see how he handled this one. Definitely a daddy question.

He spluttered for a moment then said, 'True, true. But he also has all sorts of puppies he never gets to spend time with. Or read stories to. I'd like to be able to do that, so I guess I am a bit different from Rockford...' He looked up and met Ellie's eyes. 'I'm a one-woman kind of stud dog.'

Oh, boy. There was so much to unpack from that. So she looked at the clock and announced, 'Bedtime! Unless you have any more questions?'

'No,' Maverick said, snuggling down under his light summer duvet. 'Since I have eight weeks to ask questions, I can put them in my book. Next to your autograph. That way I will always have a record that you were real.'

Tears instantly sprang to Ellie's eyes. He'd already prepared for Lucas to leave. When she heard Lucas clear his throat, she knew her son's statement had hit him right in the solar plexus as well.

Lucas scooched round on the bed until he was sitting right behind Ellie—as if they were a happily married couple who always sat without as much as a hair's breadth between them.

'You'll never have to worry about that, son. I'll always be here for you. Whenever you need me.'

Ellie looked away, trying to make it look like the tears she was wiping away were actually some unfortunate specks of dust in her eyes.

'You just keep the questions coming. Okay?'

Maverick squinted at Lucas for a moment and then asked, 'Do you think our earlobes are the same?'

Lucas gave his hand a squeeze and tucked a stuffed polar bear, Maverick's favourite, into the crook of his little boy's arm. 'Identical,' he said, then leant down and gave his son a kiss on the forehead before getting up to leave. 'I'll let you and your mum have a bit of alone time, yeah?

'Okay, Dad,' Maverick said, as easily as if he'd been calling Lucas 'Dad' from the day he could speak. 'And in the morning I'll introduce you to Esmerelda. She's got ten perfect pups! Mummy says it's because she was a perfect match to Rockford.'

Lucas winked at Maverick then at Ellie. 'Your mother always did have good taste in men.' And just like that Ellie fell a little bit back in love with Lucas Williams who, despite everything she'd done to forget him, was still very, very real.

Lucas was a complicated mix of fidgety and delighted. He'd slept poorly, had gone for a run along the beach but had been expressly forbidden from turning up at the clinic until it opened so he'd filled in some more time by taking up Wyn's offer of a hot breakfast.

At least he knew now that Ellie's parents didn't view him as the enemy. Quite the opposite, in fact. After being hammered with twenty questions about the show—it was rewarding to raise the profile of animal welfare—his future work plans—to stay here in Dolphin Cove until something new surfaced—his late father—missed, but at peace—his mother—reinventing herself as a charity event doyenne—and his brother—living a quiet life in the Cotswolds—Lucas pushed back his plate and gave Wyn a smile.

'That was an incredible English breakfast.'

'Cornish,' she briskly corrected him. 'You won't be getting hog's pudding or Cornish potato cakes up in London, I expect.'

'No. Good point.' He'd be drinking ginger and turmeric smoothies and whatever other ghastly things the craft services truck had supplied to keep him 'camera-ready'. This, he realised, was one of the first proper meals he'd eaten sitting at a table that wasn't a business meeting.

'Neither do you get women the quality of my Ellie, I would think,' Wyn said, eyes trained on him like a hawk's. 'Up there in London.'

Lucas smiled. Okay. So it was sort of a business meeting. 'Very true. She is one of a kind.'

Wyn sat back in her chair, eyes still glued to him as she took a long draught of her tea. 'Six long years,' she said when she had finished. 'I suppose you could've gone and got married yourself in that time.'

His jaw tightened. Nope. There'd just been the one proposal. He'd had a couple of girlfriends over the years, but after the debacle with Ellie he'd vowed never to propose to anyone again. Life threw too many curveballs to make that mistake twice. As such, girlfriends hadn't lasted long. That and the sixteen-hour workdays.

'Oh, no, Mrs. Stone. It's been all work and no play for me, I'm afraid.'

'Wyn,' she corrected him, more gently, he supposed now that she knew he hadn't run off and married someone else. She gave him a pat on the knee and picked up his plate, preparing to head back to the kitchen. He might not have retained number one almost-son-in-law status, but he'd always remembered her saying how important it was never to hold a grudge.

Too many to carry around, she said, *by the time you hit fifty. Who needs extra weight when gravity is already against you?*

'Wyn,' he repeated, grateful for the olive branch.

She narrowed her gaze at him. Here it was. The sting after the sweetening. 'Tell me, Lucas. Why are you here?'

He trotted out his line, knowing it would never be enough. 'Henry said Ellie needed help and I—'

Wyn cut him off. 'Ellie and Drew have needed help ever since they started the clinic. It was meant to be a three-person surgery…' She tapped the side of her nose. 'If memory serves.'

'Yes. Yes, it was.'

She waved in a couple who were peering into the pub, asking after coffees. 'Grab a table and I'll bring the menus over in a second.' Then to Lucas, 'I don't want you telling me anything you haven't told my Ellie yet, but know this—you broke that girl's heart clean through. Don't let her convince you otherwise. The boy of hers, my grandson, is the most precious thing in the world to her. I'm not a woman who issues threats because there's enough hate in the world, but if you hurt one single hair on either my baby girl or my grandson's head…'

'I know, Mrs Stone. I wish I could explain everything, but…'

I wanted to keep Ellie safe. Out of my family's black hole of debt.

Wyn tutted. 'Actions speak louder than words, sonny boy. Actions.'

She was right. Actions did. He'd pushed Ellie aside exactly when the marriage vows he'd never taken had told him he should've pulled her close. Because of that he'd missed the first five years of his son's life.

Like it or not, it was time to re-examine his view on life. He kissed Wyn's cheek and followed it with a solemn smile. 'Guess I'd better start making up for lost time.'

Wyn returned his sober smile. 'I'd guess you'd better.' She tapped her watch face. 'Time's a tickin'.'

Through the small crowd of pet owners arriving for their early appointments, Lucas saw the familiar red gold hair up at Reception and then, as if she sensed him approaching, Ellie lifted her green eyes to meet his.

A zap of connection instantly lit up his nervous system. It felt like being alive again. Properly, completely alive for the first time in…years really. As if part of his heart had died the day he'd told her he had to walk away. Not that he was being all *Boo-hoo, poor me* about this. He'd made the decision and he'd stuck to it. His family was back on track, he'd paid forward the benefits of the show to the veterinary college and now it was time to make amends to the one woman who lit him up from the inside out.

He'd hurt her. He had to own that.

Did the fact she'd kept Maverick a secret burn? No doubt about it. He'd lain awake half the night wishing Ellie had told him. Used the anger she felt for him to present herself on set with what had no doubt been a gorgeous big old pregnant belly and said, *This is yours, pal. Own it.*

Bah. He wouldn't have wanted to raise his son in that household during those first three years and he hardly could've left his parents. It had been one of those times when life had slung everything at a man just to see what he was made of. Stronger stuff than he'd thought, but…

damn…had he been strong enough to have also raised a child amidst all that chaos?

Clipboard in hand, glasses perched on her nose, Ellie gave him a quick smile that didn't exactly exude warmth, but she wasn't telling him to leg it back to London either. Part of the deal, he supposed, when she'd promised her son eight weeks with the father he'd never known.

'So!' He strode up to the counter intent on putting his best foot forward. 'What's on the roster today?'

'Hi, Lucas.' Tegan was beaming at him, half-sprawled across the high reception counter as she threw him a long-limbed wave. Ellie ignored her.

'Morning,' he said to Tegan, then to Ellie, 'Want to run me through the day's list?'

'What? Like one of your producers?' She put on a fancy London voice. 'Well, Mr Uber-Vet…today we have a variety of delights for you to ease yourself in here at Dolphin Cove Clinic.' She held her clipboard at arm's length and ran her finger dramatically down it. 'Let's see. Your first patient is Rufus.' She looked up at him with a bright smile. 'His anal glands need cleaning.'

Ha! That was normally a job for the vet nurses. And usually pretty stinky. Fair enough. She was testing him. He gave her a 'bring it on' smile. Another zap of connection flashed between them. A reminder of the fun they'd had when they'd interned together. Daring each other to do more and more difficult diagnoses whilst mastering the basics. They had brought out the best in each other. Maybe one day they could do it again.

'Ells! Anal glands?' Tegan was looking at her in horror. 'That's no way to treat our guest. Get Mum to do it.'

'Mum?' Lucas asked.

'My mum's the senior vet nurse here,' Tegan explained

officiously, as if she and not Ellie was in charge of the clinic. 'She does all that kind of stuff. Plus laser treatment, dressing changes. She's amazeballs. Ellie! Give him something pukka. The man doesn't want boring.'

Ellie gave her a bright smile. 'Nope. He's an employee. We're all created equal here.'

'Okay...' Tegan rolled her eyes melodramatically. 'Looks like *someone* woke up on the wrong side of the bed.' Before Ellie could protest, Tegan smiled and waved at a harried-looking woman being pulled into the clinic by an enthusiastic Rottweiler. 'I'll just check Mrs Collins in, shall I?'

Ellie handed Lucas the clipboard that held a list of the day's patients and their complaints. He gave it a quick scan.

There were a surprising number of anal glands to be seen to today.

He tried to hide his smirk with a serious look but failed.

'Sounds good.' Snigger.

'You think blocked anal glands are funny?' Ellie asked.

'Not in the slightest.'

Their eyes clashed and held. What was really going on here? Was this Ellie's way of fighting an attraction that obviously hadn't died or was she trying to bore him into leaving?.

He put himself int her shoes. Realistically? This must be an epic nightmare. Well. Too bad. He had a son to think about now. He held her gaze with a look he hoped said, *I'm staying, darlin'. Anal glands or no anal glands.*

Tegan finished with the woman she was checking in

then looked between the pair of them. 'What was that? Did you two just share a look?'

Ellie gave her a scarcely veiled side eye. 'No. I don't even know what that means. *A look.* Pfft.'

Tegan's face lit up with a naughty smile. 'I just remembered. Lucas…you and Ellie used to date at uni, didn't you?'

That was one way to put it. He was just about to leave it to Ellie to put her spin on things when Maverick ran in, boogie board under his arm and a beagle running behind him.

'Mum! I'm off to surf school.' He stopped when he clocked Lucas. 'Hi, Dad!'

'Dad?' Tegan's jaw almost dropped to the counter.

Ellie gave her a tight little smile. 'Yes, well…'

'Ooh.' Tegan was relishing this. Big time. 'You are a dark horse, Ellie. A very dark horse indeed.'

'Maybe I'd better start seeing patients.' Lucas said, easing himself away from the reception desk, ruffling his hand through Lucas's hair as he did so.

Maverick beamed up at him then said, 'Don't forget. You said you'd come with me to the whelping unit before lunch.'

Lucas gave him a nod and a salute. 'Wild horses wouldn't keep me away.'

'Actually,' Ellie began, 'there are some wild ponies out on the moor about twenty miles away. Someone rang in this morning to say she thought one had a bad cut on its forehead. Catching them could be tricky. Might take hours.'

'Oh?' Lucas quirked an eyebrow. He'd not had to round up an animal in ages. Years really. Could be interesting. More interesting than anal glands, anyway.

'Ellie!' cried Tegan, who clearly didn't want Lucas to leave Reception let alone the clinic.

'Mum!' cried Maverick, who had obviously been banking on puppy time.

She threw up her hands.

'Fine! We'll do the ponies together once we've finished with morning surgery, but you...' she pointed at Lucas '...had better get cracking. We'll leave after you've spent time with Mav and the puppies.'

Lucas gave his jaw a scrub and nodded. Actions spoke louder than words and he wasn't above eating a bit of humble pie. He rubbed his hands together and grinned. 'Right. Point me to an exam room and I'll get started. Rufus? Is Rufus Collins here?'

The woman with the Rottweiler lurched forward as the dog bounded towards Lucas. 'Oh, my days,' cried the woman. 'It's the Uber-Vet! Rufus, look! You're going to have a celebrity see to your stinky bot-bot.'

With a huff of irritation, Ellie called her first patient and headed towards her exam room with a pair of chihuahuas in tow.

With a slight bow Lucas led the way into his exam room across the corridor. It was going to be a long day but a fun one.

'Ring me *any time* if you're worried, all right?' Ellie put her patient, a tiny budgie with a cyst under its wing, back into its cage. She ushered the owner out with a gentle suggestion to ease back on the 'free-range flying' sessions in the conservatory. Flying into crystal-clear windows had caused the ruptured air sac and, whilst it would heal, more incidents wouldn't be in the bird's favour. With a smile and wave, she went back into the exam room, aware of the low murmurs and laughter coming from the exam room Lucas was using.

Irritation crackled through her. Everyone seemed to be having a gay old time across the hall, whereas on her side grumpiness had definitely been the order of the day.

She gave her shoulders a bit of a jiggle. This was happening whether she liked it or not. There was no turning back time or changing the facts. Her son knew his father and his father wanted to stay.

For the next eight weeks, she briskly reminded herself as another gale of laughter erupted from his exam room.

She resisted the urge to press her ear to the door to try and figure out what they were talking about. The pet? His show? Her?

Bleurgh. What did it matter? They were all under the spell of the gorgeously perfect Uber-Vet.

Funny how no one remembered the lanky, goofier-looking version of Lucas who had come down to Dolphin Cove a handful of times over the course of their training. The nerdy animal geek who had yet to grow into his six-foot-two frame, figure out a haircut that worked for him and… *Hee-hee*. She started to giggle. The glasses! How could she forget the glasses he used to wear? Thick, tortoiseshell frames he'd thought had made him look studious and French.

She leaned against the wall, the memory of him pretending to speak in French whilst waving his glasses around in an erudite fashion tipping her smile ever upwards.

The door opened and Lucas was there, tall and gorgeous. No glasses. Those bright blue eyes of his hit hers with a heat so direct she could almost feel it. 'You all right?'

'Mmm…' she said, a bit too aware of the warm vibrations the sound produced.

Oh, Lucas, she thought. *Why have you come back? What do you* really *want?*

It terrified her to think the answer might be her. Equally scary was the possibility it wasn't.

Mrs Cartwright and Tabatha appeared from behind his exam-room door.

Ellie's smile dropped away.

'Mrs Cartwright? Lucas saw Tabatha yesterday and she was fine. Has something happened?'

Mrs Cartwright threw her a guilty look then leant a little more heavily on the arm Lucas has proffered her. 'It's ever so nice having a proper gentleman in the surgery, dear, isn't it?'

Humph!

She didn't think Henry or Drew would be very pleased with that pronouncement. It did suggest Tabatha was still in fine fettle but… Mrs Cartwright was looking a bit frailer. Ellie worried that her only human contact was with the vets here at the clinic, so…if she wanted to add Lucas to her list, fair enough. She'd have to brace herself for heartbreak in, oh, about seven weeks and four days. Not that she was making big fat Xs on her mental calendar or anything.

'Why don't we get you a packet of those special treats for Tabatha I was telling you about?' Lucas said as he slowly escorted her down the corridor. 'They'll definitely help with her digestion.'

Smoothie, Ellie thought, primly marching herself back to her exam room to finish up her notes. Her phone began to buzz on the countertop. Drew.

Interesting. She'd been the one ringing him over the

past few weeks. Not that she blamed him for withdrawing from the world for a bit. The poor guy had been hit by several emotional hammer blows over the past couple of years, not to mention the physical ones. First his fiancée died in a tragic accident and now he'd bashed his leg into smithereens after a catastrophic brake failure in his car. Maybe this call was a sign he'd begun to turn the corner. Or it could just be that he was happy to be in his own house again. Several months of hospital food didn't sound that fabulous.

'Hey, there, friend,' she said, lodging the phone against her shoulder whilst typing in the final instructions for Biddy the Budgie's dressing. 'How's the leg?'

'A little birdie tells me Henry has left for the dazzling lure of Hollywood.'

Ellie heaved out a sigh. So much for casual chitchat. 'Yup. Well. London-wood. I should've rung, but things have been a bit crazy.'

'Crazy in what way?' Drew asked in a way that made it very clear that the birdie had also told him Lucas was there.

'Lucas came in to replace him.'

'Huh,' said Drew in his characteristically dry way.

'Exactly.'

'And has he—?'

'Yes. He's met Maverick. He figured it out. And we told him. About Maverick, I mean.'

'Strewth, woman. You don't mess around.'

'Well, it's pretty difficult to disguise the fact that they're related. And, yes, I did try to hide Maverick, but Torky told him the Uber-Vet was in Reception and—'

'Mav came running,' Drew finished for her.

'Yup.'

'Need a shoulder to cry on? I've got some double chocolate salted caramel ice cream.'

'I'd love both of those things,' Ellie said, 'but sadly I have a clinic to run, a son to raise and…' She sniggered.

'What?'

'I told Lucas the ponies out on the moor were wild.'

'What?' He guffawed. 'You're naughty. They'd do everything friendly apart from brush your hair for you.'

'I know, I just…' She tugged her hair out of its ponytail. 'I just wanted…' What *did* she want?

'Him to feel as much of an idiot as you did?'

'Don't mince your words or anything, Drew,' she said, and then wailed, 'It's just not fair! It'd be easier if I wanted revenge or thought he was revolting or—'

'Wait. You still have the hots for him?'

'No!' she shouted. Too fast. Too hotly. *Oh, hell.* She still had the hots for him. Not very useful in the whole build a cage around her heart plan.

'Let's back up a minute here.' Drew took a couple of loud, yoga-style breaths. 'Now. Let's start over. What is it you want while Lucas is here for the remainder of my purgatory?'

'You could start doing more of your exercises.'

'Uh-uh,' Drew tutted. 'We're talking about your problems, not mine.'

Ellie harrumphed. 'Well…revenge is out because it's not like I'm going to propose to him and then take it back.' Or that he would even accept. She couldn't read him as well as she used to be able to. Maybe he genuinely was here to help out at the clinic and that was it. Except… now that he knew he had a son, everything was different.

'I don't know,' she sighed. 'It's complicated. If there

hadn't been a Lucas there wouldn't be a Maverick and as we know...'

Drew joined in with her, 'Maverick is the best little boy in the West.' And he was. She wouldn't trade one ounce of the heartache she'd endured if it meant losing her son, but...this whole father appearing out of the blue thing would be a lot easier to deal with if she felt nothing when she looked at Lucas.

Drew broke into her silent reflection. 'What do the clients think of having the Uber-Vet at their beck and call?'

Ellie had to laugh. 'They love it. Mrs Cartwright's been in.'

'Surprise, surprise.'

'Twice in two days,' she clarified.

'Ah,' there was a note of concern in Drew's voice. 'Are we to worry about Tabatha?'

'No. I think we need to put the kettle on a bit more frequently for Mrs Cartwright, though.'

'Smart. And how's Esmerelda's litter coming along?

'Brilliant. They're all genius puppies.'

Drew laughed. 'Of course they are. I'd expect nothing less.'

'Want one?'

'No.'

'Sure?'

'Yes.'

'How's physio going?'

'Can we change the topic, please, Ells?'

There was a sharp note to Drew's voice Ellie didn't like. 'I'm going to pop one of Mum's lasagnes by tonight.' Even though he was home, she doubted he was hobbling round the house enough to cook.

'I'm fine.'

'You love her lasagne.'

'And you have enough on your plate without fussing about me. Go see the patients. I can hear them howling in the background.'

He couldn't, but he did have a point. The clinic had a gazillion bookings. 'Right you are, my friend. I'll leave you to it, but call me if you need anything, all right? Otherwise I'll sic Mav on you.'

'Ooh. My worst nightmare!'

Ellie signed off with a smile. Cool Uncle Drew was a lifesaver when it came to Mav. More than that, he was family, minus the DNA. He'd been the one to get her boy on a surfboard at the ripe old age of three. The one who'd been with her when he'd taken his first steps. Got his first tooth. Announced he was going to be a vet, just like them...*and* the Uber-Vet. The look they'd shared over Maverick's head when he'd come out with that one...it had been a doozy.

Ellie went out to the central reception desk and grinned. Everyone was talking, petting animals that weren't theirs, discussing summer plans and whether or not they'd change because of Fluffy's cone of shame or Patch's paw in plaster. Every day was different, but she was pretty sure that having Lucas around brought this extra level of wattage to the clinic's waiting room.

Whilst it was mildly irritating that everyone who came to see her asked, for the first time ever, if she was really sure about her diagnosis and maybe they should get Lucas in for a second opinion, she also knew everyone who did see him was in good hands.

One thing she knew for sure about Lucas Williams was that he was a good vet.

Just as well given that everything else was up in the air.

* * *

After a busy morning of seeing numerous cats, dogs and a ferret, Ellie headed out to the van to make sure it was all kitted out for the on-site calls they had lined up next, including the wild pony. Once she'd done her check she headed off to find her son who would no doubt be starving after surf school.

She quietly eased opened the door to the puppy unit and instantly felt the air leave her lungs.

There, sitting amongst the pile of snoozing pups was her son, curled up on a lamb's wool rug, asleep, with two puppies snuggled up close. Sitting next to them, eyes also closed, puppy in one hand, the other gently resting on Mav's leg, was Lucas.

If she could erase the past six years and rewrite them, this was one of many moments she would've written in. Absolute perfection. Despite herself, she tugged her phone out of her pocket and took a photo. For Maverick, obviously.

Lucas's eyes opened at the shutter sound. When they lit on Ellie he smiled exactly the type of smile she should be resisting if she didn't want her heart broken all over again.

He eased himself out of the tangle of puppies and little-boy limbs and joined her at the edge of the pen. 'He's a credit to you.'

The both looked at Maverick, pride swelling in both of their chests. Ellie was struck by what a 'proud parents' moment it was. Something she definitely should not get used to. Lucas might be all about staying now but he hadn't been through a tired little boy tantrum. Or an 'eat your vegetables' standoff. He'd tire of it soon enough. Wish himself back into his old life.

'We should get going.' She went to get Maverick but Lucas beat her to it. More deftly than she would've imagined, he scooped their little boy up into his arms, his head nestling into Lucas's shoulder, exactly where she'd used to snuggle when they had been watching a film or a bit of telly in between study sessions.

'Where do we take him?'

Ellie pointed to the flat. 'Tegan's mum, Cardy, is up there. She'll be there for him when he wakes up and get him some lunch. After that he'll go to my parents'. They're having a board games afternoon at the pub and Maverick has got a jigsaw puzzle on the go.'

Something passed across Lucas's eyes she couldn't quite put her finger on. Remorse? Respect? A mix of both? It was hard to say.

Once he'd tucked Mav into his bed, they tiptoed out of the flat.

'Right,' Ellie said with as bright a smile as she could muster. 'Ready for some cowboy action?'

CHAPTER FIVE

LUCAS PULLED OFF his long glove, wiped his brow and smiled. 'I've never done that before.'

'Seriously? No breech alpaca births in London?' Ellie held out a bag for him to put the gloves in, popped it to the side then took a deep drink from her water bottle, a trendy reusable number with the clinic's logo on it. It was a hot summer's day with only a hint of a sea breeze as they were a few acres inland at Viola's farm, the very aptly named Seaview Farm.

'Nope. Not on my watch anyway.' Lucas leaned against the fence, in awe as the newly born alpaca tried, then succeeded in standing up on his reedy little legs. 'I would say this entire week has been filled with quite a few firsts.'

Ellie threw him a look.

Seeing each other for one.

Learning he had a son for another.

Then finding a weird but strangely workable routine over the past week where, between the two of them, they looked after Mav. More accurately, Ellie showed him how parenting worked whilst keeping her own feelings about things hidden.

Despite the little flashes and flares of frustration that

crackled between them, he liked to think he was settling into the groove of things. He willingly dived into getting Mav sorted for surf class or science camp or supper or bedtime. Making sure he had enough puppy time, nap time and brushed his teeth. Genuine, honest to goodness, quality time.

It didn't mean it was all footloose and fancy free. He hadn't missed Ellie's odd aside about Maverick still being in awe of the fact that his father was the Uber-Vet so was on his best behaviour. She couldn't wait to see how he handled things when Mav had a tantrum in the middle of the supermarket or refused to brush his teeth or, God forbid, came down with anything, because Maverick was many things, but a good patient was not one of them.

'Chickenpox,' she'd whispered. 'You were lucky you missed it.'

'No,' he'd retorted. 'I regret having missed it. That and so much more.'

Not that he'd had much time to wallow in a sea of regrets. The clinic was a constant hive of activity. Very different from the specialised work he'd been focussing on to keep the show's ratings up. The Dolphin Cove Veterinary Clinic was half animal hospital, half community centre. It made sense seeing the place had largely been built from local crowd funding. And, of course, it made sense when you knew Ellie. She loved people every bit as much as she loved animals. And she loved animals a lot.

They'd caught the wild pony in the end. Turned out all you had to do was walk up to it with a carrot. Ellie had let him think otherwise for just a little bit too long on that front. Never mind. There were worse hurdles she could throw in his path. Like refusing to let him have access to Maverick. One week in and his heart had shown an elasticity he'd not believed it capable of. He loved his little boy more than he had ever imagined loving anyone… anyone apart from Ellie. Not that he was free to 'go there' any more. That chapter was well and truly finished. A niggle surfaced. Was it? Could he change his own rules?

Ellie took another drink of water and handed him her bottle. 'Here. Hydrate.' She inspected him for a minute. 'I would've thought you'd have seen every animal under the sun by now.'

'You didn't ever really watch the show, did you?' He handed back the bottle, catching Ellie's eyes observing him as he eased out the kinks from the awkward way he'd had to stand during the birth of the cria. He pretended he didn't see the flush hit her cheeks. 'Cats and dogs were our bread and butter cases. They're more relatable.' She nodded for him to continue. 'We had a python who'd swallowed a football, but wisely brought in a specialist herpetologist.' He ticked off some more animals. 'Ferrets, tortoises, mice and hamsters have made the odd showing. Goats, cows, horses, pigs, but nope. No alpacas.'

Ellie gave him a grin, her golden curls swishing across her shoulders. 'Well. Now you can tick that off your list.'

He folded into a courtly bow. 'Much obliged to you, m'lady. Got any tigers hidden away anywhere?' His eyes flicked up to meet hers. The heat in her cheeks doubled.

'Not unless you count the beast of Bodmin Moor,' she answered loftily.

'Ah…the fabled Beast of Bodmin. Whatever happened to it, I wonder.'

'Probably waiting for the Uber-Vet to show up so it could make a splash on telly.'

Ouch. The jibes weren't frequent, but when Ellie made one, he felt it.

'Ha-ha.' He nudged her with his elbow then turned serious. Finding out he had a son mustn't detract from the fact he had originally come down here to make amends. 'I'm not all about the bright lights big city you know.'

Ellie looked at him. Hard. She swallowed as if she was choking back something not very nice to say then gave a nonchalant shrug. 'I guess.'

Lucas took another swig of water from Ellie's bottle. 'Mmm... Good. Better than the water in London.' It was the closest he could come to saying that he wished things had turned out differently.

'Everything in Cornwall is better than London,' Ellie said with a cheeky grin.

'Ha! That's quite a statement.'

'She's not wrong,' a firm, posh voice cut in. 'Air's better. Sea's cleaner. Sun's warmer. Not a finer place on earth than Cornwall.'

'Viola!' Ellie took two long strides forward and took the small bale of straw out of the elderly woman's hands. 'You should've called. I would've brought the hay. Look. The little lad's up on all fours already. Have you decided what you going to call him?'

'Well,' the white-haired woman said, squinting against the midday sun. 'We're on an X year, so... Xavier? Xander?'

'X?' Lucas echoed. 'You've been raising alpacas for twenty-four years?'

Viola gave Lucas an appraising look. 'Not just a pretty face, are you?'

Lucas laughed. 'I spent some time at a clinic up north where we used to go to quite a few dairy farms.' He glanced at Ellie. They'd done the internship together. It had been the first time they'd lived together. A preview, he'd thought, of the life they would share together. From the pained look on her face she must've thought the same. He rubbed his hands together. 'Anyway, several of the farmers used the alphabet to track the birthing years.'

'X,' said Ellie, turning her attention to the cria, wobbling its way to its mum for a first drink. 'Um…how about Xanthus?'

Viola pressed her wrinkled hands to her heart. 'Xanthus?'

'What on earth made you think of that name?'

Ellie pointed up at the sky and playfully said, 'Divine inspiration?'

Viola's features softened. 'I was once courted by a young man called Xanthus.'

'Oh?' Ellie gave Lucas a *this-should-be-interesting* look.

'Yes.' Viola's gaze drifted out to the sea. 'He was a sailor. Naturally,' she added. 'With a name like that what else would he be?'

'A Greek god?' Lucas suggested.

'He was a touch of that, too,' Viola said, her look growing even more distant as the memories crowded in. 'He had blond hair. A bit like yours… Lucas, was it?'

Lucas smiled and nodded. Viola clearly didn't watch Uber-Vet either.

'Yes. We met when the motor on his fishing vessel gave out a few miles off the coast. One of the other boats saw his emergency signal and towed him and his crew in. He stayed at The Hungry Pelican.'

'Oh?' Ellie said, more interested.

'Long before your parents ran it, of course, Ellie, dear. It was a bit more…rustic, but, as pubs often are, it was the heart of the village, especially on a Saturday night.'

'And did you meet on a Saturday?'

'Friday,' she said wistfully, as if she'd never had a Friday since. 'Yes, we met on a Friday night and by Saturday night we were firmly in love. That's how it was done back in the day. None of these long courtships you young people seem to have.' She arched an eyebrow at Lucas as if she knew all about him.

Lucas shifted uncomfortably. He'd fallen in love with Ellie the moment he'd laid eyes on her. So why had he taken so damn long to propose? It wasn't as if he'd expected his love to run dry once vet school had finished. Putting family first had always seemed the right thing to do, but…he'd wanted a family with Ellie, too. Why had he made them two separate things?

'Three, four, ten years! I don't know what you young folk are waiting for,' Viola continued. 'Of course, with the war and rationing and heaven knows what else, none of us expected to live quite so long back then…'

Her eyes took on a faraway look as she reached out to an alpaca who had spotted the hay and come up to the fence line to have a munch.

As if she couldn't stop the story from being told, Viola continued. 'He asked me to go back with him. Xanthus. Leave Cornwall behind for Greece. Start our own family. I told him not to be ridiculous, we would stay here.'

Her lips pressed into a thin, pink line.

'And…?' prompted Ellie, throwing a *See, it isn't only me* look in Lucas's direction.

'And then his motor got fixed and I never heard from him again.' Viola gave Ellie a tight smile then lavished the alpaca mum with praise about how beautiful she was. How her love was pure. Unconditional.

That one stuck in Lucas's throat. He'd made his love

for Ellie conditional. But what was he meant to have done? Left his family to flounder? Dragged Ellie into unknown levels of debt? The show had been a fluke. He'd thought he'd been protecting everyone. But…to what end?

'I'm so sorry,' Ellie said, her voice scratchy with emotion. Lucas looked over at her. She gave a shake of her head and looked away quickly, but he could've sworn he'd seen a film of tears in her eyes.

'Don't be, dear.' Viola gave her arm a squeeze, the sharp, savvy glint returning to her eyes. 'If I wasn't worth fighting for, then I'm sure it would've all turned out horribly anyway.'

Ellie suddenly became very busy packing up the rest of their equipment.

'I'm sure you were worth fighting for,' Lucas said, his eyes catching Ellie's as Viola batted his comment away. A flash of pain shot across her features so vividly it felt as though it had slashed through his own heart. He ached to say, *I fought for you*. In his own way he had. By setting her free. Would she have really wanted to weather the storm with him? Put her dreams on hold to fulfil a family responsibility?

The thought sank deep into his gut. If she had…he would've been by her side as she'd carried their child. Their son.

Viola gave a wistful sigh. 'Look at you two. So young. So much life left to live Everything exciting that's happened to me happened before either of you were even born.'

Ellie squeaked in dismay. 'Oh, Viola. That's not true. Look at the difference you've made to the clinic. Without you, we wouldn't have the surgical wing.'

Viola waved the statement away.

Ellie persisted. 'You've got such a lovely farm and so many friends. Your family *adore* you.'

Viola gave them a look, dismayed at Ellie's naivety. 'They adore my money, love. Not me. I'd give it all away right now if I didn't have all of these lovely beasts to take care of.'

'I'm sure it's not the money.' Ellie's protest was weakening.

'No, dear. Much like me, my family like animals more than humans. The truth is, the likes of Caspian could do with rolling his sleeves up the way you do. Learn how to earn his keep.' She gave the alpaca another appraising look then spoke as if she were a High Court judge. 'I would strongly advise the two of you to seize the day. You never know what's round the corner. Or who you might lose when you turn it.' She brightened and gave each of them a quick head-to-toe inspection. 'You're both so tall the two of you. You'd make a fine couple. Ellie? What about keeping this one?'

Ellie flushed a deep red and muttered something about having another call to get to. Then, as if she'd been having a tug-of-war with her conscience about what the right thing to do was, she pulled Viola into a quick, fierce hug and said, 'You come down to the clinic anytime. You know we have the kettle on round the clock and there is always someone there to talk with.'

Viola gave her a smile and said she would definitely take her up on the offer.

After Ellie had headed back to the van and was safely out of earshot, Viola gave Lucas a schoolmarmish look and said, 'She won't wait for ever, you know.'

'Sorry?'

'Don't play the fool with me, my dear. I remember you.'

Lucas tried to remember when he might have crossed paths with Viola during one of his visits with Ellie back in the day. Truth was, he'd only had eyes for her, so apart from her parents and Drew he didn't really remember anyone else.

'*Carpe diem*, love,' Viola whispered. '*Carpe diem.*'

He knew what she was saying. This was his chance and he was already risking losing it.

'I'll see what I can do.'

'Yes,' said Viola pointedly. 'Do.'

Ellie slammed the van door shut, barely waiting for Lucas to close his door before reversing the vehicle out of the barnyard and onto the country lane.

She felt his eyes on her, but refused to look at him, finally exhaling when he sat back in a thoughtful silence.

She flicked on the radio and punched up an alternative music show. The singer was howling away about a following his dreams. It was the type of music her mother would've called shouting with instruments.

The perfect atmosphere for letting her own thoughts run wild.

What on earth had possessed Viola? *Keep this one.* She would've if she could've, but if there was one thing she'd learnt when Lucas Williams had handed her her walking papers? It was that no one had the power to make anyone stay.

Yup. That's right. She'd begged. The most humiliating thing she'd ever done. Begged and cried and asked over and over why he was doing this. He'd been immovable. Like a man whose heart had turned to stone.

When she'd gone home, Drew had been the one to tell her parents. She hadn't had the strength. The strength to say it without bawling her eyes out anyway and the last thing she wanted to do was shed a solitary tear for Lucas ever again. She'd vowed to never, ever let herself feel so low. So unworthy.

And, then, of course, she'd felt even lower when a couple of months later he'd popped up on telly with an utterly gorgeous woman on his arm. This, just about when she'd found out she was carrying their child.

'Can you be honest with me, Lucas?' The question was out before she could stop it. 'I need to know why you really came back. I know Henry rang you, but with your contacts you could've surely found someone else to fill in for us here these couple of months.'

Lucas turned in his seat and looked at her. 'I think we both know I'm six years late, Ellie.'

'For what?' she pressed. 'Winning my love? Winning Maverick's? That took about five seconds. What is it you're really after, Lucas? Absolution? A clear conscience? It sure as hell isn't me.'

She saw Lucas give his knees a scrub then balled his hands into fists. Good. He was as frustrated as she was.

'Can we maybe have this talk somewhere stationary?'

'What?' She glared at him. 'Now my driving's not good enough for you either?' She swerved to miss a pothole, silently acquiescing that perhaps he had a point.

'Do we have any more calls to make?'

She threw him a guilty look. 'No. I just…' She stopped herself when her voice cracked then began again. 'I found Viola's story upsetting.'

'Not inspiring?'

She pulled the car off into a little recess in the hedge, twisted her leg round so she was facing him and said, 'Seriously? You think I would find a story about meeting the love of your life only to have him dump you at the first hurdle inspiring?'

'No.' Lucas reached out and swept some of her hair away from her face. 'I suppose not.'

'Lucas,' Ellie said, swiping his hand away. 'Why. Are. You. Here?'

He opened his mouth and closed it for a minute. Annoyingly, he looked completely adorable. All lost for words and clearly wanting to say the right thing but not knowing how. If this were seven years ago, she would've reached out, held his face in her hands, pulled him to her and kissed him.

But it wasn't then. It was now. Six years after he'd taken back his proposal. She had a child to look after. Her own heart to protect. And a veterinary clinic to run.

'Speak, man, or I am quite happy to find however many locums it takes to replace you and hand you your walking papers.'

'No.' Lucas shook his head solidly, the passion in his voice matching hers. 'Not now that I've met Mav.'

A chill ran down Ellie's spine. 'You are not taking him from me.'

'No.' Lucas said. 'But I— Can we walk and talk?'

She nodded. 'There's a footpath down here.'

He gave the thick hedge she'd parked the van alongside a dubious look.

'There's a way through to a lovely little river. I bring Esmerelda down here sometimes with Mav.'

'It's not where you bring people to disappear them?'

'It's where I go for picnics,' she said dryly as she got out of the car and grabbed her backpack from behind her seat. 'C'mon. I've got sandwiches. You want to walk and talk? Follow me.'

They set off at a brisk pace under the cool canopy of trees, Ellie doing her best to stay a step ahead of Lucas. Every emotion under the sun was zipping through her bloodstream right now, but the number one thing she didn't want to do was cry. Neither did she want to shout about her son's future. He was hers. Yes, Lucas had a right to have access to him. It was only fair to Mav, but... she'd go down fighting if Lucas suddenly slapped a custody agreement in front of her.

All of which threw her hackles and her suspicions straight back up into the stratosphere. She wheeled on him. 'Are you sure you didn't know about Maverick before you came down?'

'Absolutely. Henry didn't say a word. He just said you were in a pickle because of Drew's accident.'

'A pickle?' Ellie laughed. 'He called nearly losing my best friend and business partner to a car accident a pickle?'

'Henry was always the master of understatement.'

She threw up her hands. 'Looks like there's yet another person I didn't know as well as I thought I did.' She tipped her head up to the sky and squeezed her eyes shut tight. No. She was not this person. She was not an embittered, angry person. She'd worked so hard to put the past in the past. This was a hiccough. An emotionally charged, life-changing hiccough. She looked at Lucas determined not to let her emotions get the better of her. Stomping away in a huff did not pay dividends. 'What else did he say?' Ellie pointed Lucas towards the path that led to the river, a little too aware of their arms brushing each time the higgledy-piggledy path brought them closer together.

'He said you had an amazing facility. That I should take inspiration from you.'

'What? You've got all of the bells and whistles at your disposal in London.'

'Not any more.'

'What?'

Lucas wiped his hands together. 'That chapter in my life is done and dusted.'

'Right. At the ripe age of thirty-five you've finished with Uber-Vet for ever. What happens when you realise that you miss the celeb lifestyle and change your mind, beg them to take you back?'

'Seriously, Ells—Ellie.' He corrected with one of those goofy *oops* smiles of his. 'Henry's taken over the show permanently.'

It still wasn't an answer.

'Lucas!' She stomped her foot. 'Will you please tell me why, of all the veterinary clinics in the world, you had to come help out at mine?'

'Because I needed you to know how awful I felt about what had happened. Make peace with you. Can we do that? Try to make things right between us?'

Ellie stared at him solidly, her expression still, then after what felt like ages she said, 'You should know by now not to say things you don't mean.'

Lucas meant it. That had always been his intention in coming down here. What had shocked him were the words he hadn't said. *I still love you.*

They reverberated around his heart as if the words had been inscribed there.

He looked deep into Ellie's eyes, wondering if she was feeling the same thing. A long-lost feeling that could be revitalised. Renewed.

I still love you.

The words gained traction as his heart pounded the words out in a syncopated cadence.

I still love you.

He couldn't say them. Not yet anyway.

Viola's words rang in his head. *Carpe diem.* Fine. He'd do something about it. But step by step. No way was he going to scare her away. Not with a relationship with his son on the line. 'I mean it, Ells.' Lucas pressed his fists to his heart. 'Just because things turned out the way they did, it never meant I stopped caring about you. Splitting up hurt me every bit as much—'

'Oh, hold on a minute, Lucas. Splitting up with me served you and you only, so let's ratchet back the sanctimonious *I was doing this for both of us* attitude, shall we?' Ellie distractedly pulled her hair up into a top knot, then tugged it down, then tangled it up again until finally leaving it to its own devices as she sat down on a tree stump by the edge of the river.

Okay. Fair enough. But she was still here. Still listening.

Lucas sat next to her, channelling his energies into digging deep into his soul to find the best solution. He loved her. Now he needed to find out what the hell to do with it. Stuff it back in the box where he'd put it all those years ago? Or rebuild the trust he'd so obviously broken by taking matters into his own hands.

Tension buzzed between them like high-tensile electricity.

'I— There were many things I wish I'd done better.'

She shot him a sharp wounded look.

'I know, I know. It's a cheap way of explaining myself, but...' He tried to lay out the facts so she could understand. 'After I proposed, I called my family to tell them the good news.'

A wary look shadowed her eyes.

'It turned out things at home were very complicated. Nothing to do with you. They all love you and think you're brilliant, but...they'd been waiting until I finished vet school to tell me just how bad things were.'

Her shoulders dropped a notch. 'What happened?'

'Jonty went AWOL, for one.'

'What? He just disappeared?'

'Pretty much.'

'But I thought he was meant to take over your father's practice so you could come to Cornwall?'

Lucas gave her a wry smile. Families. They were complicated. And Lucas's was no different.

'Turns out, as the deadline approached, Jonty's drinking increased. So had his time at the races.'

Ellie raised her eyebrows. She knew too much champagne and access to horseracing wasn't a good combo for Jonty. It was one of the reasons it had been agreed Jonty would work with his father. So he could be reined in, so to speak.

'Long story short,' Lucas continued, 'a lifetime of trying to become the man our father wanted Jonty to be landed him in rehab. The clinic hadn't been doing well the more Dad's Parkinson's progressed, but he'd been too damn proud to tell anyone until Jonty upped and left and I called to tell him I was moving to Cornwall.'

'But didn't he know? We'd talked about it for ages.'

'Course he did. I guess he'd just been hoping Jonty's wild phase would come to an end, but it was one of those awful convergences of bad timing, bad debt and poor health. It was going to take an epic amount of energy to turn things round at my dad's clinic. Years. I didn't know what else to do. There was no way I was going to drag you down with me. Believe me, I genuinely thought I was doing the right thing.'

A wash of compassion softened Ellie's features as she inspected the new landscape of her memories. For the first time since he'd come down he felt a glimmer of hope that they could be like they had once been. Best friends, confidants, lovers. They'd known everything about each other. He'd thought they always would. And then life had intervened.

'Lucas...' Ellie's voice was cautious, as if she wasn't sure she wanted to go down this road but was going to make herself, if only to find peace. 'One of the things I always admired about you was your sense of honour. It was why it shook me to the core when you split up with me.'

'I did what I did because I believed it was honourable. If there had been any other way...' He brushed a bit of her hair behind her ear then ran his finger down her sweet face again. 'It was such an incredibly complicated, unhappy time for my family.'

'So...' Her eyes connected with his with a primeval intensity. As if she could actually see directly into his heart. 'In your weird, backwards way you were protecting me by breaking things off?'

He nodded. That had been exactly it.

The softness in her features hardened again. 'You should've trusted me to stand by you.'

He snorted. 'What? Burden you with debt and put years between you and the dream of opening the Dolphin Cove Clinic? No way. I would never have done that. Not to you or Drew.'

'Drew would've understood.'

He gave his jaw a scrub. Yeah. Drew probably would have. He'd not even bothered asking. It had just seemed too much to ask of a friend.

Ellie poked his thigh. 'And I'd just promised to marry you. To stick with you. Through everything.'

Lucas felt his ribcage expand and contract. The emotional weight of all he'd put her through hit him like a wrecking ball. Little wonder she'd kept Maverick a secret. He didn't know if he would've trusted him to come through for her either. Not after what he'd put her through.

'Do you think there's a chance we could start over? As friends...for Mav?'

She blew out a slow breath. 'I don't know, Lucas. I'm not sure I can go back to the way things were.'

'I disagree.' He softened his tone. 'I know it'll take work. I know it'll take time. But I believe we can fix this, Ellie. What we had was...it was out of this world. And something's telling me you feel it, too.'

She lifted her hands up. 'Whoa, there, sonny boy. Having you here is a reminder of the one time in my entire life when I felt small, insignificant. You made me feel worthless and I promised myself I would never, ever feel that way again.'

'I don't want you to feel that way again.' He meant it with every fibre of his being.

'I know,' she said. 'Maybe. There are six years of resenting you for not believing in me that I need to sort out.' She lifted up a hand so she could explain herself. 'Look. I don't want to be angry at you. I don't want to hate you. I don't want to resent you. I want Maverick to have a dad.' Her serious expression lit up with a gentle smile. 'And even though you're pretty new at it, you seem to be catching onto this whole dad thing pretty well.'

Lucas knew now was not the time to accept kudos. He nodded for her to continue.

'Now that I understand why you did what you did a bit more, I can let a lot of that pent-up *grr* out.' She made another *grr* and feigned watching it disappear down the lane.

'It's a big ask.' Obviously. 'Asking you to forgive me.'

'I want to forgive you. I… I do.' She gave him a look he couldn't read. 'You know what my mum says about things like this.'

He nodded, smiling as she threw some air quotes up and said, 'There's no point carrying around anger or defensiveness when gravity is already against you.' She picked up a stick and began to trace a swirl into the earth. 'Rotten things happen. Quite a few epically rotten things happened to you. But you should've believed that as your fiancée, as your *wife*, I would've wanted nothing more than to be there, by your side, supporting you, loving you. For that alone I… I'm going to struggle, Lucas. I will try to be friends. Honestly, I will, but…sorry. Forgiveness isn't going to come easily to me.' When she met his eyes, he saw all he needed to know. She still loved him. And that's why the hurt ran so deep.

He wanted to push it. Press her to admit she felt that same heated frisson whenever their hands brushed. Notice how charged the atmosphere between them was when their eyes met and the space between them took on a magnetic quality. They were meant for one another. Always had been. He knew it in his marrow. She did too. But she was protecting herself. She was being cautious.

'Friends?' he said, extending a hand.

Friends,' she repeated sadly.

The moment her hand touched his… With work and commitment, one day, somehow, everything would be all right again, and they could finally be a family.

CHAPTER SIX

'LUC!' ELLIE KNOCKED on the guest flat door. 'You in there?'

No answer.

She glanced out at the bay beyond the flat's balcony. The summer sun was just dipping below the horizon, the sea sparkling like diamonds. A perfect night for a romantic stroll...

Er... No, it wasn't. It was a perfect night to perform surgery on a Labrador retriever who could very likely die if someone didn't answer his blinking door soon!

'Lucas?' She tried again, tapping her foot impatiently. Maybe he was out. *Urgh*. Not tonight! She needed him. She glanced at her watch then out at the clinic car park. They'd be arriving any minute now.

She blinked back some frustrated tears. She wasn't sad. Or mad. She was tired, mostly. The last few months of trying to run everything with Drew in hospital had been wearing. Just having him back in Dolphin Cove eased her stress. Saying that, with the amount of rehab he was still facing? The truth of the matter was Drew was still several weeks away from consulting let alone operating. A hard-hitting reminder that the clinic ran much better with two vets and even more smoothly with three.

She knocked again. *C'mon, c'mon, c'mon! Answer the bloody door!*

Maybe he'd gone into the village to visit Drew. When he could prise him out of the house, that was. Drew had definitely become a bit of a hermit. She reeled back through the evening. Nope. Not likely. She'd been down at the Pelican an hour ago to give Mav a goodnight kiss before he went upstairs for Grandma and Grandpa night, a summertime special. She'd not seen Lucas or Drew and Drew would have definitely pulled her aside for an update on the 'Lucas situation'.

Meaning had she decided to fall in love with him again? Drew thought she would. Ellie insisted she wouldn't. Out loud anyway. They'd achieved a perfectly civilised working relationship and she made sure not to be too protective when it came to the time he wanted to spend with Mav. Ignoring the way her heart pounded when she saw the two of them together or the way her body responded whenever his hands brushed against hers was rather tricky but…she was made of stern stuff. She had to stay strong. Resistant to the Lucas Effect.

She banged on the door again. 'Lucas!' She was going to have to do this on her own if he didn't answer in thirty seconds.

She racked her mind. Where could he be? Apart from the pub and a couple of small restaurants, there wasn't really anywhere else to go in Dolphin Cove. Not at this hour anyway. He'd said something about running some errands for Drew a couple of days back. But errands at nine o'clock at night?

Her heart lurched up into her throat.

He wouldn't…no, he wouldn't be out on a date, would he? Not that she cared. He could do what he liked with his life as long as he didn't hurt Mav.

She pictured him laughing with another woman and reaching out to hold her hand.

A swirl of nausea rose in her throat.

She did care.

Well, not tonight she didn't. Tonight she was a vet and vets didn't have time to be all jealous over imaginary dates their ex-fiancé may or may not be on. She knocked one final time. 'Lucas!'

The door swung open and all the silly thoughts that had been swirling round her head disappeared when there, lit by the remaining glow of the evening's sun, was Lucas Williams with nothing but a towel round his waist.

Oh, *my*. She didn't know how, but she'd forgotten how completely and totally gorgeous he was when he wasn't wearing clothes. In fact, he was even more scrumptious if that was at all possible. The golden remains of the day lit him to perfection. Damp hair tumbling in soft waves on his forehead. Little droplets of water shifting their way slowly across his musculature. And then, to her horror, she licked her lips.

She must've looked like the cat who'd got the cream.

He gave her a funny look, then gestured for her to look up from his six-pack to his eyes.

She put on a cranky managerial face and barked, 'Where've you been?'

Why are you speaking like a possessive girlfriend?

'Out for a run. Everything okay?' He looked over her shoulder towards her flat, presumably to check for Mav.

His question snapped her back to the reason why she'd knocked.

'We've got an emergency gastro surgery I need help with.'

Everything about him snapped from relaxed to action man. 'Absolutely. Let me get some clothes on.'

She was about to say *No, don't* because it was exactly the kind of thing she would've said back in the day, but that would've been flirting and maybe sexist and completely because she wanted to keep staring at his utterly luscious torso. It was broad and tanned and screaming to be traced by the tips of her fingers. To her horror, she actually physically ached to be one of the drops of water casually working its way down his pecs all the way to his six-pack. A light strip of blond hair naughtily beckoned to her…wending its way from just below his belly button to the edges of his loosely wrapped towel. The sun flared inside each of the glistening droplets of water dappled along his shoulders, his chest, his mouth. Droplets of water she would envy until the end of time because of that stupid, stupid vow she'd made him take that they would only be friends.

No. Not stupid. Practical.

And she'd done extremely well in compartmentalising everything to get work done, address the fact her son now knew his father and that, more to the point, she absolutely, positively did not and would not ever fall for Lucas Williams ever again.

The pickle was…now that it was mid-August and Lucas only had a few weeks left…it suddenly didn't seem enough. He filled a hole in her life she'd not wanted to admit needed filling. Drew was brilliant and her bestie, but Lucas? Lucas knew what she was going to say before she said it. Could tell which puppy she loved most without her having to say. Knew when she needed a hug and some quiet time after putting down a family's cherished pet. Predicted when she could do with a completely silly three-legged race with her son along the beach with the promise of ice-cream cones at the end. She hated to admit it, but the last three weeks of 'friendship' had been fun.

Oh, who was she kidding? It had been more than that.

It had been a glimpse into the family they might have been if life had been different. The more she'd hashed over the talk she'd had with Lucas, the more she could see why he'd made the decisions he had. Did she agree with them? No. He'd left her with a broken heart and a son to raise on her own, but if her parents' pub had been put in peril and there was no chance she could've done the clinic with Lucas…

How did you choose?

You didn't.

You went with your gut and on that occasion? Family had won. She got it. Her family had been her bedrock throughout her life. Even more so when she'd found herself alone, pregnant, and with nothing more than a dream of opening a veterinary clinic.

Her parents had been pretty awesome this summer, too. Taking Lucas's arrival in their stride. Never mind the fact her mum had been gently prodding at her for years to tell him. But she didn't rub it in. Say, *See? Look how happy your son is with his father.* They simply made Lucas welcome at the occasional 'family' meal down at the pub and never raised a questioning eyebrow when, on the very rare occasion Ellie loosened her mama bear reins, Lucas came to pick up Mav instead of her. Her parents were, in short, the completely reliable, loving, amazing people they'd always been and, perhaps like her, were waiting to see if Lucas really was here to make amends.

'Ells? Is this surgery happening now?'

'Yes,' she said, distractedly flicking her fingers at

his torso. 'Go put some clothes on and I'll see you in the clinic.'

'What's it for?'

'Chocolate Lab who ate an entire bucket of lead fishing weights.'

Lucas let out a low whistle. 'Hell's teeth. Shown any signs of poisoning?'

'Nope. Just clanking.'

His eyes widened. 'Clanking?'

'He ate that many.' She mimed being a Lab with a low hanging stomach that clanked.

Lucas rolled his eyes in disbelief. 'What sort of Dolphin Cove family would let their dog eat a bucket of lead fishing weights?'

Ellie smiled. She'd never admit it, but she loved how he'd taken to speaking about Dolphin Cove as if he were a local. He knew as well as she did that even if he lived here fifty years, they'd still think of him as a Londoner.

'They aren't local.' Ellie gestured towards the main road. 'It's a family visiting from London. They were playing down on the beach, building a sandcastle or something with their little ones, and lost track of the dog who they found wolfing down the last one. There were bits of crab in there, apparently.'

'Ah. Lab, you say?'

'Yup.'

'Chocolate?'

'Mmm-hmm.'

'They're the hungriest, by my estimation.'

'Pretty much.'

Lucas looked over her shoulder. 'Where's Mav? What's our plan for him?'

Ellie's heart unexpectedly bashed against her chest.

Lucas's question had come so organically it felt as if they were a proper family. Sometimes she brought a sleep monitor down with her. Other times she called Drew. Today timing was on their side. 'He's at my parents' tonight. It's board games night at the pub, remember? He usually stays over, so...lucky for the Lab owners you and I have a completely free twelve hours ahead of us. It's you and me, baby.'

She made a face.

You and me, baby? What the hell was that? She readjusted her features to make it look as if she'd said nothing more interesting than *I'll prepare the surgical tray.*

When she met Lucas's blue eyes, something passed through them she couldn't quite put a finger on. A tangle of emotions. Relief that Maverick was being looked after? Something...naughty? Or maybe he was just looking forward to a good juicy surgery. That had to be it. He wouldn't be thinking sexy thoughts at a time like this. With a dog's life in peril.

'See you down there in two minutes,' Lucas said, turning around, door still open, and with a dramatic flourish...he whipped off his towel.

The cheeky bastard.

She stared at his bum and couldn't help but smile. Toned, saucy—if that was any way to describe sexy bum cheeks—and just begging to be squeezed.

He turned back to make sure she was looking.

Oh, she was looking all right.

With a wink and a grin, he was gone.

It was going to be a *long* night.

'Could I have those surgical scissors again, please?'

Lucas was a picture of concentration.

Ellie handed him the specialist scissors. 'Gastronomic incision not big enough?'

'Not…just…yet…' Lucas's brow crinkled. '*Boom*. Now it is. I'll just pop a suture in at either end to bring it closer to the abdominal incision…'

His voice tapered off as he meticulously went through the steps of preparing the chocolate Lab for surgery.

'Antibiotics all right?' Ellie was in full surgical mode now. The poor dog had literally clanked on his weighted walk into the clinic and the longer that lead was inside him, the more likely a case of internal lead poisoning could threaten his life.

'Twenty milligrams for every sixty minutes.' Lucas glanced at the operating theatre's digital clock. 'We've been at it for twenty minutes. Another forty and we'll give him a second injection, unless we've got it wrapped up by then.'

'Right. Let's get going.'

Ellie and Lucas went about the surgery as if no time at all had passed since they'd last been in a surgery together. Surprisingly, this was the first they'd done together since he'd arrived. She suggested he take the lead—not because she wasn't up to it. Adrenaline always kicked her skill levels to the fore whenever an emergency case landed at the clinic. It was more…she really liked watching him work. He had an incredibly exacting but relaxed way of preparing an animal for surgery. Not clinical like some of the locums she'd worked with. It was almost like watching a conductor at work. He always made sure the dog knew he was there, keeping him safe with soft strokes and the odd little massage on his head as he drifted off to sleep when the anaesthetic kicked in.

They worked together in studied silence for a while,

only breaking the atmosphere with a request for a pair of clamps or laparotomy sponges to keep the intestinal loop isolated from the rest of the abdominal cavity.

'Strewth,' said Lucas as he pulled out another lead weight. 'Looks like there are four more to go. There must be almost a kilo's worth of them. Poor pooch.'

'I know, right?' Ellie took the weight and put it in a bag marked for post-operative disposal. 'Lord Fluffingstein may never eat crabs again.'

'I doubt that.' Lucas sniggered. 'A Lab's a Lab no matter what they've been through.' He asked Ellie to secure a clamp to help elevate the stomach. As she worked, he laughed. 'I've come across some cracking dog names before, but his takes the cake. Lord Fluffingstein. What do you think they call him when he's running around at the park?'

'Your Lordship?' Ellie ventured.

Lucas gave a snort, his twinkling eyes and jiggling eyebrows the only things visible above his surgical mask. He put on a fancy voice and intoned, 'Your Lordship would like to offer his utmost gratitude to Her Ladyship Ellie van Stonington for having the very best of clinics to hand at his time of need.'

Mercifully, Lucas couldn't see the flush of red creeping up her neck. Thank goodness for surgical gowns!

'Would Her Ladyship be so kind as to give the saline bag a bit of squeeze, please?' He looked across the operating table, hands poised to retrieve the next weight, and winked.

Gah!

How was it a gastro-intestinal surgery on a greedy chocolate Labrador had turned into a flirtation zone?

No veterinarian brain surgeons necessary to answer that one.

The Lucas Williams Effect had permeated her very finely crafted no-flirtation shield. Naked bums did that to a girl. His anyway.

The long night was turning into a dangerous one. For her erogenous zones anyway. She cleared her thoughts and put on her grown-up voice to veer him off course. 'It could've been a fatal night for him. I know the Penzance clinic has had at least two dogs die this summer from lead poisoning.'

'Sounds like there's a need for some signs to be posted down at the harbour or a bit more diligence by the fishermen.'

'I think the dog owners should be the responsible parties, really. It's not like you'd let your children wander off and stick their heads into a bucket of mystery food.'

'Good point.' Lucas said. 'Although… I seem to remember seeing a picture of Maverick with a face full of spaghetti Bolognese sauce down at the pub.'

Ellie barked a laugh. 'My mum's spaghetti Bolognese is worth a face-dive. And I was obviously there to observe the occasion, as every good parent is.' She eased another laparotomy sponge into place then looked up to catch the tail end of Lucas's wince.

'Sorry. That wasn't meant to be a jibe.'

'No offence taken.' He didn't sound angry. Wistful maybe. Definitely more pensive than he'd just been.

She couldn't even imagine having missed so much of Maverick's life. It had taken all her strength to stop herself from nipping over to the school in her breaks when he'd first started last year. This year would most likely be no different. Even on his nights at her parents' she demanded a full retelling of the evening. Lucas had missed five entire years of his son's life.

For the first time she felt a huge rush of empathy for all the years he'd lost because she'd decided her son would be better off without him. Oh, crumbs. Had her decision-making been as messed up as Lucas's had been? Had she kept Maverick out of his life out of spite? Hurt, definitely. She had to admit to that. She'd told herself over and over that someone who broke such huge promises wouldn't be reliable. She glanced across at him, his attention back on the extraction of yet another lead weight. She'd wanted him to trust her in his darkest moment and then she'd gone and done the exact same thing to him. She'd shut him out. Shut him out when she'd needed him most.

Oh, Lucas. I'm so sorry.

As tangled up as her emotions were about having Lucas here, she knew one thing for certain. They would have to make this work for Maverick's sake. He already adored Lucas and it was easy to see Lucas felt exactly the same way. Not that she blamed him. Her kid was one in a billion.

She adopted a chirpier tone. 'My parents are on the village council. I'll see if they can mention it. Even if the signs are posted in the summer when all of the tourists are here.'

'Nice one. Oh, and can you remind me to send Lord Fluffingstein home with a list of things to watch out for just in case some of the lead did get into his system? And about peritonitis.'

'I already did it. The lead part.'

'They didn't stick around?' His eyebrows rose in surprise.

'I told them I'd ring when we were done. Their children looked knackered and teary. Their holiday cottage is only a five-minute walk away, so I thought a few text updates would be better than them fretting it out in Reception.

Lucas eased another weight out of the dog's intestinal tract and considered it for a moment. 'What's this?'

Ellie leant in, a hint of Lucas's citrusy shower gel hitting her along with another mental image of his cheeky *derrière* sashaying out of the lounge and into his bedroom.

'Someone's initials most likely,' she squeaked.

'The fisherman's?'

'Probably. If they're hand cast like these ones obviously were, they sometimes stamp their IDs into the mould. Must be an old-timer.'

'Smart.'

'Not if you don't want someone taking your crab it isn't. Cornish common sense. The traps will be marked, the buoys, everything. My dad told me the medieval fisherman would use little symbols if they were illiterate. It's a shame really because in theory it should be done on the honour system. Everyone knowing where everyone's patch is and steering clear. Respect and consideration and honesty. That's all the world needs to work properly, isn't it?'

'Is that a variation on love making the world go round?'

Her eyes shot to his. 'I suppose. But love *is* respect and honesty. In an ideal world,' she tacked on, not wanting this to sound like a lecture.

'A village that fishes together stays together?' He suggested.

'Yes! Exactly.'

Crinkles fanned out at Lucas's blue eyes as he handed her yet another weight. He was smiling. A ridiculously large flock of butterflies took flight in her tummy. Mercy. The Lucas Williams Effect. Right here in her OR. She forced herself to become more officious.

'Still an idealist, then, I see,' he said.

'Still a dreamer,' she parried.

'Exactly what I always loved about you,' he said. 'Aiming high and refusing to settle for second best.'

What he'd loved *about her?*

The minute the words came out of Lucas's mouth he knew he'd stepped onto emotional quicksand.

Ellie's eyes flared brightly and then grew distant.

If kicking himself had been an option, he'd be covering himself in bruises.

How the hell had he let that nugget of truth slip out?

Because it *was* the truth. He loved her. Plain and simple. Seeing her again had had exactly the same lightning-strike effect it had had the first time he'd seen her. He loved her and he didn't want to hold the feelings captive any more. But he had to. His feelings on marriage...they were complicated. So much more tangled than being here in Dolphin Cove, with Ellie, with Maverick...

It felt like living again. Living his own life away from the camera, away from his family's intense reliance on him to get them out of a very deep hole. *Breathing* felt more real. He'd quite happily never go back to London again if she would have him here, but another part of him was worried it was all just a bubble. A bubble that would burst just as it had all those years ago when he'd proposed and thought absolutely nothing could break through the intense joy he'd felt.

Despite the dark thoughts, he smiled beneath his surgical mask. The *look* on Ellie's face when he'd whipped off his towel. The attraction they'd once had was there all right. She still fancied him. He definitely fancied her. Could she love him again? Love *and* trust him the way she once had? Could he trust her? She had, after all, kept his son a secret. If he hadn't come down here, would he have ever known he had a son?

They worked in silence for a bit, teasing away the foreign bodies, ensuring the beloved pet was as well cared for as if he were one of their own. It had been their shared motto back in the day. 'Treat them as you'd treat your own.'

He silently cursed himself. He'd treated Ellie incredibly poorly. Turned his back on her precisely when he should've held his arms out wide open and said, *I need you.* Somewhere deep inside him he knew she still had feelings for him. He saw it in her eyes. Not all the time, but…it was there. A core-deep need to earn that trust back gripped him. He wanted his son in his life—no question. But he also wanted Ellie in it. How that relationship took form? He didn't know. But he knew shared trust would be of paramount importance. If it took him the rest of his life to earn back her trust, so be it.

'Here's the last weight,' he said, his voice rough with emotion.

'You all right, Luc?'

Ellie's eyes met his, her forehead crinkled with concern.

She cared. More than she was willing to admit, but she cared.

That flame in his heart burnt a little bit brighter.

He nodded. 'We need to lavage the peritoneal cavity with some warm saline to remove any spillage or blood clots.'

She nodded, the furrows in her brow deepening. He was stating the obvious to avoid saying the words he wanted to say most.

I love you, Ellie.

He used a good two and a half litres of the sterile liquid to clean the area then checked the dog's vitals whilst Ellie used a surgical suction tube to remove the fluid and dry the cavity as much as possible. Hygiene was critical. An iota of infection and the poor pooch risked another visit to the clinic. One he might not return home from. When she'd finished and stepped back from the table, they both changed their gloves and then the instruments. When they'd finished Lucas asked. 'Want to close, or shall I?'

Ellie gave her forehead a swipe with the sleeve of her surgical gown. She looked tired. Really tired.

He couldn't believe he hadn't seen it before, but it was obvious wasn't it? The poor woman had been working herself to the bone since Drew's accident. He made a mental note to up his game on clinic hours. Call in some favours. Get her the time off she needed. Be here for her when she needed him. Properly.

Ellie placed fresh surgical towels around the edges of the laparotomy. 'I'm happy to close. I'm going to use a straightforward continuous suture pattern, so…if you need to get to bed or anything…' Her voice sounded smaller than it had. Less confident.

'No chance. I'm going to see this through with you.'

Her eyes flicked up to meet his. 'Okay. Can you text the family to let them know he'll be out of surgery in half an hour or so? He won't be up to much of a family cuddle, but I'm sure he'd love to hear their voices before we get him snugged down in the kennel overnight.'

'Will you send him home with them tomorrow?'

'Yup. Normally, I'd do it tonight, but it's so late and I'd like to triple-check there aren't any signs of lead poisoning tomorrow.'

Lucas sent the text then fielded the inevitable phone call, assuring the family that Lord Fluffingstein had come through surgery well. Lucas said he'd meet them in the front of the clinic in half an hour, but not before as he was helping Ellie with the final stages of surgery. He watched as Ellie began to weave the synthetic absorbable monofilament sutures into Lord Fluffingstein's stomach. 'Nice,' he said. 'Perfect apposition of the gastrointestinal tract. I always remember you being a dab hand with a needle.'

Her eyes narrowed a bit. Whether she was smiling or shooting him a look, was difficult to tell. Lucas's stomach screwed up into a tight knot. Back in the day he would've been certain it was a smile.

'I've got some socks you could do for me in the morning,' he teased.

He grinned at the inevitable arched eyebrow she was sending him and began to hum.

'What's that?' she asked, tying off the final knot and pronouncing the surgery over. 'Sounds familiar.'

'"Hound Dog",' he said.

Ellie laughed. 'Of course it is! I can't believe I didn't recognise it straight away.'

He began to sing some of the lyrics, enjoying the sound of her laugh, the way her eyes lit up when they met his as she joined in on the chorus.

'Do you remember when you first sang it?' she asked, her voice suddenly thick with nostalgia.

'Course.' He triple-checked that all of the tubes and needles were clear of Lord Fluffingstein before he and Ellie carefully transferred the pooch to a gurney so they could take him to the recovery kennels. 'Karaoke night the first week we met.'

'First night we kissed,' she added, her eyes meeting his as they wheeled the gurney down the short corridor to the recovery kennels, where a chihuahua with a torn cruciate ligament, a tom cat who'd met the wrong end of a barbed-wire fence and a geriatric cocker spaniel who'd had two hip replacements were already sleeping.

Together they slipped him into the kennel, his sleeping form heavy in their arms. There was something so vulnerable about a post-operative animal. 'It makes you feel so responsible, doesn't it? For their welfare.' His voice sounded loud in the quiet room. He lowered it. 'Seeing them so defenceless.'

'I feel that way when Mav's asleep, too.' Ellie shifted her body so that her arm brushed against his.

'I'm not surprised. I've only been with him a couple of times when he's been asleep, but...' He gave his chest a light thump. 'It gets you right here.' He remembered the weight of his sleeping son in his arms when he'd carried him to bed a few evenings back after a particularly long story-reading session at his place. He'd never felt anything more perfect. Never felt a stronger need to care for someone. It was unlike anything he'd ever experienced.

He put his hand on Lord Fluffingstein's soft ear and gave it a gentle caress. 'You just want to make sure they never hurt again. That they're always safe. Don't we, Lord Fluffingstein? We never ever want you to have to go through anything like this again.'

Ellie smiled at him, leaning against his shoulder for a split second. 'I knew you were still in there.'

'What? Who?'

'The big old softie I met all those years ago.'

'He was always in there. He just got a little lost along the way.' Their eyes met and clashed. He hoped his were telling her he was trying to change. Trying to be the man she'd once thought he was.

Her eyes stayed glued to his, a wash of understanding softening her features. 'Life can do that sometimes. Send you down a path you never expected to be on.'

It wasn't an outright 'I forgive you'…but it was close.

A huge warmth filled his chest as the space between them grew smaller, and smaller yet, until the next thing Lucas knew he was holding Ellie's face in his hands, tipping her chin up to his, their lips millimetres apart, then brushing, sparks of heat flaring between them until he couldn't bear the distance between them any longer.

He slid one hand into the small of her back and the other onto the nape of her neck, moulded her soft, curvaceous body to his until they were kissing as their lives depended upon it. Not urgently. More…as if every microsecond of contact mattered. Touching and teasing and parting and tasting. It felt familiar and completely new, as if time had granted them a reprieve from their past and given them this fresh start to see if maybe, just maybe, they could find a way to be together again.

And then the buzzer for the front door went.

Ellie pushed back, her hands on his chest, her eyes glued to his. 'We'd better get that.'

'When they're gone, I want to do this again.'

Ellie said nothing, but her body language told him all he needed to know. She did, too.

'You'd better go get the door.'

'No,' he said solidly. 'I think you should.'

'What? Have you gone all shy?'

He pointed at his scrubs.

Ellie's eyes dipped below his waistline and began to blink rapidly.

'Ah. Oh. Um… I'll just get the door, then, and give you a chance to…' She turned to go.

'Ellie?' He reached out and took her hand. She didn't try to pull it away.

'What?'

'I'm here for you, you know. Whatever you need.'

The flush of her cheeks told him she knew he was offering more than a helping hand in the OR. She gave his hand a quick, tight squeeze. 'Thank you. Now let's let give this family the good news, yeah?'

'Course.' He went to the sink and began to throw cold water on his face and the back of his neck. Once things had subsided down there…he looked in the mirror. Was he the same guy she'd once known? Yes. Was he different as well? Yes.

Older, wiser, hopefully better equipped to handle life's slings and arrows with a bit more perspective than he'd had back then, a twenty-nine-year-old man fresh out of ten years of training to be a vet. As he stared into the mirror, willing it to tell him what he was capable of, he felt a shift in his heart. He could do this. He could stay. Learn to trust himself enough to take another risk. Take his time earning Ellie's trust…and love. And no amount of cold water on his face would put out that fire. Not by a long shot.

CHAPTER SEVEN

ELLIE WAS NODDING and smiling and really wishing Lord Fluffingstein's family would go home and go to sleep because one too many carnal thoughts were getting in the way of her thinking sensibly.

She wanted Lucas.

Badly.

She wanted to run her fingers through his hair. She wanted to trace her fingers along that gorgeous chest and abdomen of his. She wanted to explore what had been happening in his scrubs before that ruddy buzzer had gone off, reminding her she was living in the here and now and not ten years ago when she and Lucas used to sneak off and take a post-operative shower together.

Her attention swung to the corridor where Lucas was taking long-legged strides to join them. And here was the reason why her mind couldn't stay focussed.

He slipped into place beside her, one of his big lovely warm hands on the small of her back as he extended the other. 'Hello, there. I'm Lucas Williams.'

The family went wide-eyed. 'You're the Uber-Vet,' whispered one of the children.

'Not any more,' Lucas said, his smile not faltering for a second. In fact, if Ellie wasn't mistaken, it had just grown brighter. He stood back up and put his hand back on Ellie's back, as if giving her a physical cue that he had really meant it when he'd said he was here for her.

Here for ever?

No.

She batted the thought away.

That would be ridiculous.

She looked up at him.

His eyes met hers and he dropped her a slow, astonishingly cheeky wink.

Oh, my God. He wanted to take a shower with her, too.

'The best thing you all can do for Lord Fluffingstein is to get yourselves a good night's sleep. He'll be needing lots of TLC in the morning.'

If Ellie wasn't mistaken, the pressure on her back had turned into a soft, circular rub at the mention of TLC.

Sprays of glittery anticipation made standing still incredibly awkward.

She was going to have sex. With her gorgeous ex. The father of her child no less. The first time she'd had sex in just about for ever. She'd had a couple of relationships over the years, but...*meh*. None of them had been Lucas and she had a business to run and a child to raise. His child.

'So we'll see you in the morning, then?' Lucas was shaking hands with the owners, then he knelt down to give the children a hug. No wonder he was famous and everyone who'd ever watched television was in love with him.

She was in— Wait, *was* she still in love him?

She watched the family go in a stunned silence.

No. She couldn't be...could she?

Lucas held out a hand, guiding her towards the back

exit that led to their flat—her flat. Her flat at her clinic in her county—

'Shower, Ells?'

'Yes,' she answered way too quickly and hilariously primly for someone filled to the brim with lust that surely could be sated on this one occasion. Once they'd had tonight she could get on with her life and be quite content. 'That would be lovely.'

'Mmm…' Lucas rolled over in bed, feeling the sun on his face. He patted his hand out alongside him. No Ellie. The door creaked. There she was…the woman who'd made him feel whole again. No wonder none of his other relationships had worked out. She toed the door open. 'Ah! You made coffee! You're an angel.'

'A crazy-haired angel.' Ellie grinned, handing him a steaming mug, adding, 'White and two.'

He pushed himself up to sitting, loving the way her light cotton dressing gown fluttered across her curves as she crossed the room to toe open the French doors. 'I just want to keep an eye out for Mav,' she explained.

'Will he be back before he heads off to surf school?'

'Not always. Mum usually sends a text if she's bringing him round, but there's been nothing so far today.'

He took a draught of the coffee. 'Delicious.' He caught her hand in his as she settled in the space next to him on the bed then gave the back of it a kiss. 'Just like you.'

When he looked up at her, he saw she was frowning.

'What's wrong? Don't like being called delicious?'

'No, it's not that.' She gave his arm a rub, her frown softening into something a bit less worried looking. 'I just… Do you think Mav should know about…you know…' she pointed at the two of them '…us?'

'I suppose that depends on where you see this going.' He was going to give her the lead on this. He had to.

'Step by step. Super slowly,' she said with a decisive nod.

'Sounds good.' It did. As he'd learnt, the very best of things were worth waiting for. He scooched over beneath the duvet so they were side by side. 'Does that include more Mummy and Daddy time?'

She giggled and swotted at the air. 'It's so weird to hear you say that.'

'What? Mummy and Daddy?'

'Yeah.' Her nose crinkled up, but she was still smiling. 'It's what we are.'

'It's what we are *now*,' she reminded him as she put her coffee down on the bedside table. 'Ish.'

He put his mug down on the other side table and climbed out from under the light down covers so that he was sitting astride her legs. He took both of her hands and placed them on his chest. 'Feel that?'

She waited a moment, then nodded after the thump-thump of his heartbeat registered. 'Yup.'

'That's all yours. Yours and Mav's.' He leant in and gave her a deep, hungry kiss, her hands still pressed to his heart. 'Feel that?'

Her grin widened. 'I hope that's not for Mav.'

'Nope! That's just for you.' He sat back on his heels. 'It's always been there, Ells. That heartbeat. And I think you feel the same way.'

'What? All tachycardic?' She grinned. 'I'm far too cool for that nonsense.'

'Oh, yeah?' He began to tickle her. Tickle and kiss and nuzzle and play until before he knew it, the two of them were naked again—laughing, touching, kissing, caressing—until once again their lovemaking culminated in a climax that shot the pair of them into the stratosphere.

Lucas fell back on to the bed after their breathing had steadied. 'Well, that was fun.'

'You make it fun.' She poked him with a toe, then picked up her coffee mug.

'Fun like last night fun or fun like carnival fun?'

She pushed her lips out and gave him a studied look over the rim of her lukewarm coffee. 'Mmm…last night wasn't really fun, it was more…' she lowered her voice to a sexy growl '…luxurious. Slow and yummy. Like the way you'd want to enjoy a very, very special box of Christmas truffles.'

He could get on board with this line of thinking. 'Could you get used to having something that decadent on a more regular basis?'

She hesitated before answering. 'Was this what you imagined happening when you came down here? Slipping into my bed after a long day of saving pets' lives?'

It was a fair question. One that deserved an honest answer. But just then the door was bashed open and standing in the bedroom doorway, looking completely bewildered, was Maverick.

Ellie yelped and pulled the duvet up more snugly around her. 'Mav! Hey, there, love.'

'Morning, Mummy.' He looked at Lucas next. 'Hello, Lucas.'

Hmm… Sometimes he was Daddy. Sometimes he was Lucas. Lucas mostly when he wasn't sure about something.

'Morning, Mav. Your mum and I were just—'

'Talking about the day's surgical rota,' Ellie cut in with a cheery grin.

'In bed?' Maverick clearly thought that was a ridiculous place to talk about work.

Ellie threw Lucas a *fix this now* look.

'Absolutely. Did you know that the brain is most creative in the morning?'

'Is that why you always get up before me, Mummy?' Lucas seemed to be buying the explanation.

'It's one of the reasons, love. Um… Do you mind throwing me that T-shirt over there? And the skirt?'

Lucas bit back a laugh as Maverick handed her the items with a bemused expression.

She wriggled into them with rather amusing efficiency, flipped back the covers then threw Lucas the fresh pair of scrubs they'd brought up from the surgery unit last night that had never quite made it onto his body.

'Pancakes?' she asked.

'Love 'em.' He grinned his thanks.

This, he thought with a smile, could well be the perfect start to a proper family life.

A few stacks of pancakes, lashings of maple syrup and several glasses of orange juice later, Ellie breathed a sigh of relief. Lucas had stayed for breakfast but excused himself to make some phone calls for the clinic whilst Ellie and Mav sorted out the day pack he took to camp. Throughout it all? No one mentioned anything about Mummy and Daddy under the covers.

After clearing the table, Ellie ran a comb through her son's unruly mop and then gave him a kiss on the forehead.

He looked up at her, his eyes wide and hopeful. 'Is Lucas going to stay here now?'

Lucas, not Daddy.

Ellie's face froze in a cheery Mummy face as she tried to figure out the best way to answer that.

Maybe?

Probably not?

Not until they had a proper talk about things anyway. And ensured she'd got over the fact he'd proposed, taken it back then at least seemed to have swanned off to live a highly glamorous life without her. He'd explained that part pretty well, but…it didn't mean what had happened still didn't sting. And there was also her guilt about not telling Lucas about Maverick and the fact she'd have to explain that to her son one day.

Not really the simplest of answers for a five-year-old.

'Come here, bub.' She pulled her son into a little half-hug and touched her finger to the tip of his nose. 'Mummy and Daddy are figuring out how things are going to work around here. It's been a while since they've seen each other and I'm pretty used to how things worked with Uncle Drew.'

'Uncle Drew never spends the night with you.'

'Very true.' She gave a serious nod instead of giggling. As if! She'd made sandcastles with Uncle Drew. And mud pies. He was like a brother to her. And an awesome business partner. Not to mention a pretty great vet. But kissing him? Bleurgh. 'But Uncle Drew and I never dated.'

'You and Daddy did?'

'We did. During vet school. And then he had to go and be the Uber-Vet for a few years.'

It was sort of a white lie. More a lie of omission than an actual lie, so…

'Like superheroes have to go and save the world?'

She smiled, wishing Lucas was here to hear this. 'Yeah. A bit like that. So…now that he's not fixing all the animals on telly, he's thinking about what he'd like to do next.'

'Why doesn't he work here?'

'Well…'

'There are all sorts of animals he could fix here,' Maverick said, the idea clearly growing on him. 'All the puppies and Mrs Cartwright's cat and the animals in the petting zoo and…um… Moose! He could fix Moose.'

'Moose could definitely do with some Uber-Vet magic.' Moose was also one of the reasons Ellie hadn't sent Lucas packing. The Bernese mountain dog had suffered some fairly awful injuries in a car accident and Ellie had been hoping Henry might be able to work his magic. Since he'd left, Lucas had had a couple of appointments with him, certain he could help. He'd said prosthetics were possible for the large canine, but that he had something even more ground-breaking in mind.

'If he wants to fix the animals in Dolphin Cove,' Maverick began slowly, avoiding eye contact, 'would he live here like other daddies?'

'Well…' It was a valid question. Particularly from a five-year-old who had been pretty awesome about accepting a previously entirely absent father into his life.

'Not all mummies and daddies sleep in the same bed every night.'

'You mean like I change my cuddly toys around sometimes?'

'Sort of.' Ellie crossed to the sink and pretended to be really busy washing dishes for a minute.

She was on the brink of asking Mav how he would feel if Lucas were to stay around longer term when her son pulled on his snorkel and mask then patted his round tummy. 'I'm ready to hit the waves.'

Ah! The magical mindset of a five-year-old.

'I hope they're good ones today.'

Maverick made a sad face. 'Only one more week before school starts.'

'I know, bub.' She gave his curly head another scrub. 'But you love it there. Learning all sorts of cool things is one of the perks of growing up.' Ellie knelt in front of him and gave each of his pudgy cheeks a kiss then waved him off as he ran down the steps just as Lucas reappeared from the clinic.

Maverick launched himself off the stairs towards Lucas before he'd reached the bottom of the steps. Ellie was about to scream when, as if he'd been doing it all his life, Lucas swept his son up in his arms and whirled him round and round to Maverick's complete and utter delight.

The pair of them looked up at her and grinned. In that moment Ellie knew she wanted Lucas to stay. She was ready to love him again. Really love him the way she once had. Maverick deserved it. She deserved it. And, from the sound of what Lucas had gone through with his family, he deserved some happiness, too.

An hour later the pair of them had barely laid eyes on one another the clinic was so busy. When she ran into him in the surgical unit her heart softened rather than raced. A sign, she realised, that her fear about him leaving was dissipating.

'Ooh.' She gave the supine feline in his arms a stroke. 'This isn't Mrs Cartwright's, is it?'

'No.' Lucas held up the chart. 'This is Shadow.'

'Oh, right.' She scanned the chart. 'The Thomases' cat. Everything okay?'

'She'll be fine. A bit of periodontal disease. I'm thinking too much tinned tuna might be the culprit.'

'SCC?'

He tapped the side of his nose.

'Ouch. How many teeth did you have to extract?'

'Just one. The family noticed her eating habits had changed and of course…'

'Halitosis,' they said together.

'Luckily, they caught it before things got too bad. And they've promised to change her feeding so, fingers crossed, all will be well.'

'Speaking of too much seafood.' Ellie pointed at Lord Fluffingstein, who was giving the pair of them lots of doleful brown-eyed looks. 'Any chance you could help me escort the crab-lover here into the waiting room?'

'Ah! Are his family here?'

'Yup. From the second the clinic opened, bless 'em.'

'Excellent.' He rubbed his hands together. 'I love a good reunion, me.'

Ellie smiled. 'Course you do, you big ol' soppy thing.'

'Who're you calling soppy?' Lucas play-protested, already clearing his throat at the thought of the family being reunited with their cherished dog. It was one of the reasons she'd fallen for him so fast. His genuine affection for the animals they treated was infectious.

After ensuring his post-surgical shirt was snapped into place, Lucas and Ellie slowly escorted Lord Fluffingstein down the corridor for the inevitable tearful reunion. Ellie gave instructions to the family for the dog's post-operative care. 'He'll be a little dopey for the next day or two as the anaesthetic wears off.' She handed over a small bag. 'These are his medicines. Some for pain and some to ensure any infection is kept at bay. Keeping the wound area clean is critical for the next few days so no beach time, I'm afraid.'

They all shook their heads soberly. 'We've got a garden in our holiday let so we'll just use that.'

'Excellent. In a few days he should be all right to travel home, and we will make sure to send along all the information to your local vets.'

The mum threw herself at Ellie and pulled her into a huge hug. 'Thank you so much for saving our boy. He's like another son to me and if we'd lost him...' A sob escaped her lips.

'It's all right,' Ellie soothed, returning the hug. 'He's alive and well and will continue to have a happy healthy life as long as he avoids lead weights and the wound stays clean.'

'It'll be the cleanest wound in Britain,' the family's little girl solemnly vowed, holding up her fingers in a Girl Guide salute.

'Well, then,' Lucas said, kneeling down so that he was at eye level with her. 'I shall look forward to receiving pictures of his stitches when they're all healed up. Here...' He pulled out his phone. 'Who wants my email address so they can send me updates?'

The entire family raised their hands and Lord Fluffingstein gave a soft woof.

Ellie laughed, happy and relieved to finally be able to enjoy her time with Lucas. Being on her guard for the past few weeks had been exhausting. It had added a level of fatigue she hadn't needed on top of all the extra work she'd been juggling at the clinic. Despite her best efforts, she yawned.

'Long night?' asked the father.

Lucas smiled. 'I kept her up late.'

Ellie raised her eyebrows until Lucas smoothly finished, 'We were doing some in-depth debriefing after the surgery, you see. We're all about a hands-on approach here. Seeing things through to a happy ending.'

He slipped his arm around her shoulder in what, to the Lab's family, would have looked like an ordinary gesture of happy colleagues, but to Ellie? The gesture and his words meant the world. Maybe Mummy and Daddy could sleep in the same bed on a more regular basis. And not at all like Maverick's cuddly toys.

CHAPTER EIGHT

'FANCY A REAL PINT?' Lucas picked up his empty glass and reached across for Drew's drained soft-drink glass.

'No, mate. Thanks. Painkillers,' he explained.

As if he had to. The poor guy had clearly been through the wringer. Drew lived in a cottage a short walk from the Hungry Pelican, but it had taken him a painstaking twenty minutes to hobble his way down. A walk he'd insisted on when Lucas had shown up in his big old four-by-four that wouldn't even begin to fit in the narrow lanes of the medieval village.

Pins and braces and goodness knew what else were holding Drew together. Grit and determination, most likely.

'Another plate of chips wouldn't go amiss, though!'

'They know how to do them right here at the Pelican, don't they?' Lucas said, swinging his legs out of the booth and heading towards the bar.

After a quick exchange with Ellie's father, whose protective demeanour had become less frosty as the summer wore on, Lucas was back in the booth, enjoying his long-awaited catch-up with Drew.

'And things with Ellie are cool?' Drew asked.

Lucas gave a definitive nod. 'Far better than I could've

dreamt. Maverick's...' His voice grew rough and he gave the table a thump. 'He's one helluva kid.'

'Damn straight he is. He has the best uncle in the whole of England for starters.' Drew said proudly. His mood turned serious as he retained solid eye contact. 'I'm glad things are cool with you and Ellie. I have to admit I was worried when she rang to say you'd offered Henry your job and were coming down to replace him. It felt like—' He stopped himself.

'What?' Lucas had a feeling Drew had just stopped himself from delivering a home truth. Something along the lines of 'It felt like you were taking matters into your own hands again'. He'd never looked at it that way. He'd decided on Ellie's behalf what she would do. The grain of truth was a reminder that just because things were okay now, they might not always be. Life threw spanners into the works. It didn't mean you had to deal with them alone. Ellie hadn't. She had an amazing support system here. She'd been strong enough to admit she'd needed help.

Drew squinted at him then said, 'I don't want to see Ellie hurt again. Or Mav.'

'They won't be,' Lucas said, the words weighted with intent.

Drew gave him a nod. 'You made it extra-tough, staging your comeback when I was in traction.'

'Tough how?'

'It's hard to give someone a black eye from a hospital bed.' The familiar glimmer of fun flared in Drew's eyes as he gave Lucas a shake of his fist.

Lucas snorted. 'I'm on good behaviour alert.'

'But it's water under the bridge now?' Drew couldn't keep the protective note out of his voice. 'If it isn't, or if you hurt her again, you know I'm going to have to run you out of town. Slowly. But I'll do it.'

'I believe you,' Lucas assured him. And he did. Half the village would most likely join him, pitchforks and all. Ellie was one of their own and, famous or not, Lucas was an outsider. An outsider who'd broken the heart of one of the village's favourite daughters. 'I swear to you, mate, my intentions are entirely honourable. And I know I messed up. Things with my family were… They were pretty rough there for a bit.'

'I would ask you if you wanted to talk about it, but…' Drew held his hands out. 'I'm a bloke.'

Lucas laughed. 'Yeah, right. You're probably cuddling up to your cat every night, yapping on about feelings all night with a weepy film on in the background.'

'Sorry, pal.' Drew tugged a hand through his dark hair. 'Books over telly and I don't have any pets.'

'What?' Lucas was genuinely shocked. 'A vet without a pet. That's weird.'

Drew fixed Lucas with a *Shall we look in the mirror?* stare. 'Do you have any?'

Lucas shifted uncomfortably in his seat. Esmerelda was meant to have been his and Ellie's dog. The idea of getting another one…especially with his insane work schedule…even a goldfish would've been neglected. 'Maybe I was choosing the wrong barometer to judge you by.'

Drew waved away the comment. 'I couldn't have a dog now. Not with the way I'm walking.' He feigned some creaky walking frame noises.

'You'll get there. Like everything, it takes time.'

Drew looked away but not before Lucas saw a lance of pain cross his features. Emotional pain this time.

Whether it was the car crash or losing his fiancée a couple of years back, Lucas didn't know, neither did he press. He was going to be around for the foreseeable future, and he knew Drew would talk when he was good and ready. Which reminded him. 'You really think you're going to be ready to come back to work?'

A look of determination pushed Drew to an upright position. 'I've let Ellie down enough these past few weeks. I'll be coming back at the end of September, as promised.'

'You've not let her down in the slightest. She knows you didn't ask your brakes to fail.'

That same shadowed look darkened Drew's blue eyes a second time. 'Yeah, well. It's not fair on her. All the extra work she's taken on.'

'About that…' Lucas began.

'What?' Drew laughed. 'Are you volunteering to stay on?'

Lucas would've preferred to talk to Ellie about it first, but…maybe it was wise to test the waters. 'Yes. If it would help.'

'Always the hero, aren't you?'

The comment slashed through any chumminess they might've had. Drew didn't trust him to stay.

Lucas's gaze sharpened. 'What makes you say that?'

'Sorry, mate. These meds I'm on don't give me much room for charm. I— Oh, hell.' He dropped his head into his hands, gave his skull a brisk rub and then looked Drew straight in the eye. 'Mate, it didn't seem very *you* to dump me and Ellie—mostly Ellie. We'd planned to set the clinic up together. When we saw you swanning around on those red carpets with that woman on your arm—'

'She was my producer!' Lucas said forcefully, too late

to dial his tone back to contrition. 'There was never anything between us. Not on my part anyway. And after that, well…anyone else you saw would've been me trying to convince myself I'd moved on.'

'So, you still love her, then? Ellie?' he added, as if there was anyone else in the world they could be talking about.

Lucas nodded. Of course he did. Always had somewhere beneath that weighted cloak of family responsibility he'd put on six years back.

'Any plans to…you know?' Drew wiggled his ring finger in the air.

Lucas gave his jaw a scrub. 'I don't think we're quite there yet, mate.' Winning Ellie's full trust was of paramount importance and until he had it he was going to play his cards close to his chest. Well…pretty close.

'Fair enough.' Drew gave his hands a decisive clap as if the matter had been discussed, settled and need never more be revisited. He put out his hand for a shake, any friction between them now laid to rest. Lucas took it with gratitude.

Drew and Ellie had been his best friends back in the day. They'd known his father had been unwell. That his brother liked one drink too many. Why hadn't he reached out to them?

Pride.

Fear.

Powerful enemies at a time of crisis.

Drew took a studied sip of his soft drink then said, 'About the clinic. I'm going mad over there in the cottage doing nothing so…talk me through what a man who's hobbling about can do to ease the load.'

'Get better,' Lucas said solidly. And then, 'Actually, do

you remember Ellie telling you about a Bernese mountain dog Henry had scheduled for a prosthetics op? Moose?'

'Moose!' Drew's expression visibly lightened. 'I love that big old bear of a dog.' His brow furrowed. 'Has he not done well? Ellie hasn't told me much about any of the cases.'

Lucas could see why when it came to Moose. The poor dog had been hit by a car careening out of control and had nearly died. She'd done her best with his internal injuries, but his 'rear legs cart' wasn't really up to the job of helping him lead a normal healthy life.

'Henry had planned to give him two prosthetic legs, but I have another idea.'

Drew's face lit up. 'Tell me everything.'

The two friends spent the next hour talking over the case, possible options and then moved on to the actual business of how the clinic was running.

'I think you could do with another full-time vet. One who could come with a cash injection.'

Drew raised his eyebrows. 'Only partners give cash injections.'

'Yup. I know. I've been thinking about ways to show Ellie I'm here for the long run and I thought it might be a good show of faith. Would you be happy if I were to propose—' He stopped himself and changed his choice of words. 'Would you be happy if I were to ask to become a partner?'

'I'm happy if Ellie's happy.'

'Excellent.' He lifted his pint glass and Drew raised his soft drink. 'Cheers to that, mate. To new beginnings.'

Drew pulled his glass back an inch. 'Aren't you getting a bit ahead of yourself?'

'Maybe,' Lucas agreed. 'But you can't blame a man

for wanting to be part of one of the best clinics in the land, can you?'

'Not for a second, mate,' Drew said, letting his glass clink against Lucas's. 'Not for a second.'

'One…two…three…*go!*'

Ellie, Lucas and Maverick started cheering and calling their puppies.

'C'mon, little one! You can do it!'

'Here, Mr Purple! Come to me. No! Not Mummy, me! Mav!'

'Come to Papa, Miss Green!'

Ellie shot Lucas a glance. *Come to Papa?* She snorted as the little golden Lab pranced towards him then veered off to climb up the slide.

When the little chocolate Lab she'd chosen for the race, landed on Ellie's lap first, Lucas pronounced them the winners. She was a gorgeous little thing. Getting big. She was also astonishingly obedient for a young pup. She gave her head a little stroke. Perhaps Drew might like—

'Mum!'

She looked up and realised Lucas and Maverick were both staring at her. 'Sorry. Yes?'

'Can I take Lucas to the petting zoo? I want to introduce him to Barnacle. Maybe we could take him for a swim?'

Lucas raised his eyebrows and gave her an inquisitive look. 'Barnacle?'

'He's our resident buck goat. He should also be a contender for the Olympic swimming team. He loves it.' She nodded at his untucked shirt. 'You'll want to watch that. He eats anything. And by anything I mean anything.'

Maverick nodded intensely. 'She's not lying. The reason we have him is because where he used to live he ate all of their laundry.'

Ellie smiled and ruffled her son's hair. 'Maybe not all of the laundry, but let's say Barnacle's former owners would've been wise not to keep him in the back garden.'

Maverick put his hand in hers. 'Will Lucas be coming to school with us next week?'

'Oh!' She glanced across at Lucas, who suddenly busied himself with getting the puppies back into their pen. 'Well...' Most of the villagers had figured out Lucas and Maverick's relationship as the pair of them looked so similar and her mother refusing to confirm or deny whenever people nipped into the pub to 'casually enquire'.

'Would you like him to come?'

'Yes,' Maverick said. 'And you, too,' he added, his little forehead crinkling as he waited for her answer.

Lucas cleared his throat then turned to them. 'I'd be honoured. As long as you're happy.' The last part was obviously for Ellie.

'Sure,' she said, in a much higher voice than her normal one. 'That'd be great!'

'And can he come to the Christmas play, too? Last year I was a star and this year I want to be a sheep. Or a donkey!'

Lucas laughed, but Ellie could see the questions in his eyes. The same ones she was asking herself. Would he be here in December? Would she want him here?

'C'mon! Let's go get Barnacle,' Maverick tugged on Lucas's hand, the topic clearly not important enough to decide upon now. Thank goodness.

She waved the pair of them off after Lucas promised he'd be back after dropping Mav off with her parents for the afternoon so he could get to the surgery.

As she watched them head off to the small petting zoo, two blond heads, one big hand holding one little hand, Mav skip-running to keep up with his father's long strides, her heart near enough burst. As much as she was loth to admit it, she loved having Lucas here, watching him with Mav. He was brilliant with him—surprise, surprise.

A soft smile hit her lips as she remembered the way he'd run into the ocean with all of his clothes on the other day when Maverick had come off his boogie board and given himself a proper friction burn. Never mind the fact she'd been a nanosecond ahead of him. Knowing Lucas's instincts when it came to Mav were the same as hers made her feel complete in a way she'd never felt before. As if having both parents there to look after her boy had filled an emptiness she hadn't realised needed filling.

But would this be enough for him? It was summer in Cornwall. What wasn't to love? Sun, sand, surf…the odd foray between the sheets with an ex-lover… But what about when the rains came? Lambing season. A cranky little boy refusing to get up on dark mornings for an early start at school. Summertime in Dolphin Cove was 'bed of roses' territory. Not reality. Even the sleeping-together part. That was the pair of them caught up in some absurd lust bubble that would no doubt pop when the clocks went back and Lucas headed off to whatever it was he was going to do next.

And that was the crux of it. Instead of believing he'd be around for ever as Mav was, there was a part of her still wondering when he would pack his bags and go.

She gave the pup a final cuddle then made a solemn vow.

Until Lucas told her what he was going to do after his stint here, she needed to keep her heart firmly under control.

'So this is your big plan?' Ellie looked across at Lucas, who had just finished drawing on the Bernese mountain dog's X-rays. When she saw his big ear-to-ear smile, she couldn't help but grin, too.

'Yup!' Lucas was excited. Kid in a sweet shop excited. 'Drew likes it, too.'

Ellie swotted at his arm. 'You told Drew before you told me?'

'Well...' He slipped an arm along her waist and lowered his voice and his lips until they were brushing against her ear. 'I would've told you last night after I got back from seeing him, but someone was feeling a little bit naughty.'

'It takes two to tango, *mate*,' she said primly, then, unable to resist, gave his bum a quick squeeze as she glanced over her shoulder at the door.

You never knew when one of the surgical nurses would pop in to check up on things. Ever since Lucas had arrived there had been quite a lot of spontaneous 'popping in to check on things'. Something they'd learnt to be hyper-vigilant about once sneaking the odd kiss had appeared on the agenda. She knew it wasn't really the best way to steel her heart against him but...once he left who knew how long it would be until she had sex again?

Because of that, each morning after they untangled themselves from one another she would remind herself. *This doesn't mean anything...nothing definite anyway.*

Either way, for the time being, she felt happy. Warily

happy but… Work. Play. They were all melding into one and it felt lovely after so much stress with getting the business up and running and then poor Drew's accident. When she was being really, properly honest with herself, she knew that the past couple of weeks had been just like…her breath caught in her throat…falling in love.

'Ells…' Lucas's tone had changed. 'I want to talk about something.'

'What? Is everything all right at home?'

'Yes, fine.'

Adrenaline charged through her. 'Has Mav's surf school rung?'

'No, no. Don't worry, he's fine. It's Drew.'

'Drew?' Her hands flew to her heart. 'Has something happened?'

'He's worried about you.'

'What? Why? I'm the one who should be worried about him.' She started hammering Lucas with questions about Drew, his emotional state, his eating habits, his leg. Lucas answered them the best he could, but Ellie persisted. She should've seen him more. Made more of an effort to pull him out of this funk. 'Did you get the impression he was walking as much as he should? Whenever Mav and I have gone over, he's never mentioned it.' An idea struck. 'I was thinking of giving him one of Esmerelda's puppies. The chocolate one.'

'What? Are you sure he could handle a puppy? He's going to be on crutches for weeks yet.'

Ellie waved his concerns away. 'The pups are almost ready to leave their mother now. In fact…' She did a quick tot up on her fingers. 'This is perfect. It gives Drew time to develop a bond with his puppy and will mean he has a chance to get out and about with her before he's threatening to come back at the end of September.' And you're due to leave.

'Desk duty?' Lucas checked.

'Desk duty,' Ellie confirmed, then dared to voice a deepening concern. 'He shouldn't even be coming back then, but I thought I'd better have a plan in place if he showed up. No way am I letting him anywhere near the surgical unit.' They spoke for a while longer about ensuring they visited him more, sending Mav over with a basket of some of his favourite things from the bakery and the pub—he'd always been a sucker for Wyn's fishfinger sandwiches—and, of course, to play board games. Cool Uncle Drew was the only human on earth who had enough patience to play games with Maverick for hours on end.

'Sounds like a plan,' Ellie said, pleased someone else was helping her lure Drew out of his man cave. She glanced over at the wall clock. 'I'd better get back to the main building. There's a list of patients as long as my arm coming in for afternoon clinic.' She stifled a yawn. She'd never admit it, but she couldn't wait for Drew to come back. And maybe a locum. If they could afford it.

'Ellie.' Lucas stopped her. 'Drew and I also talked about the fact that I think you—and by "you" I mean the clinic—need more help. There's too much work for the two of you and definitely too much for one.'

She rolled her eyes. 'More help' had been a recurring theme in her life for the last six years. 'And where exactly are we going to get the money to pay for this much-needed help?'

He gave her one of his cheesy Uber-Vet grins. 'You're looking at it, baby.'

What? Was he offering to stay?

'Oh, Lucas…it's a big commitment.'

'Yes, I know. And along the same lines we need to discuss Maverick.'

She stiffened. 'What about him?'

'I know we haven't discussed visits or anything, but…'

Here it was. The request for joint custody.

'I'd like to move here. Permanently.'

Her hearing began to feel fuzzy. 'Where, here?' Like… into her flat here?

'Dolphin Cove. I'd like to buy into the partnership.'

Her heart didn't know what to do with itself. Squeeze tight. Sink. Pound with joy?

It wasn't a marriage proposal. It was a business proposal. It was Lucas playing it safe.

Just like she'd asked him to.

So why did she feel sad?

Because maybe a little bit she did want him to ask her to marry him?

Would that be enough? Working together? Sharing Mav's care? Raising him together, but…no relationship? Not a romantic one anyway.

She instantly regretted the regular habit of lovemaking they'd fallen into far too easily. If he lived here permanently, she didn't want him as a friend with benefits. It was too intimate if something went wrong. So what did she want him to be? Her husband? Really? After all they'd been through?

She stared at him. Hard.

And then it hit her.

When it came to Lucas Williams she wanted the whole package or nothing at all. But now that he knew about Maverick, Lucas would have to be in her life. One way or another. And it looked as though he wanted it to be on the business end of things. She swore under her breath. Guess that lust bubble had well and truly popped.

'Ells?'

'I don't know, Lucas.' She looked anywhere but at him.

'Don't give me an answer yet.' He ducked down to try and catch her eye. Intimate contact she really wanted to avoid right now. 'It's a lot to think about. Why don't you take the next couple of weeks and if you need more time, I'll hang on as long as you need?'

She didn't need two weeks. Having him here on a daily basis, believing they'd grown closer than ever, it had all been a lie she'd told herself. A stupid dream she'd clung to all these years.

'We don't have the funding for that, Lucas. Once Drew comes back, the insurance—'

'I'll work free. And Caro will as well. For the project on Moose anyway.'

She finally met his gaze, utterly confused. 'Who?'

'Caro Barnes. The inventor who drew up these plans.' He pointed at the roll of sheets they'd just been poring over. 'Remember? My contact from the Uber-Vet days.'

Ellie glanced at them, the complications doubling as she did so.

Of course she wanted him to do the surgery. Moose deserved nothing less than the very best. She also wanted Lucas to stay on at the clinic. Her brain did anyway. It more than made sense, but her gut? It wanted to send Lucas packing right now so she could go back to life the way it had been before Drew's horrid accident.

'I don't know…'

'Oh, c'mon, Ells,' Lucas persisted, clearly oblivious to her emotional turmoil. 'How is this any different from the students you've had down from uni or having Henry here? The Dolphin Cove Veterinary Clinic already has a great reputation for pushing the envelope. You should be pulling in the big guns and, let me tell you, Caro is one of them.'

It's not about her, you idiot. It's about you.

'How do you know her again?'

'She used to work for a really innovative robotics company out in California. They helped us with a couple of tricky cases on the show.'

She tuned in a bit more. Relationship problems aside, Lucas did have some amazing contacts. If he could persuade more of them to come down for special cases like Moose's, the clinic's reputation would grow.

'Did the robotics work?'

'Absolutely. There was some trial and error, but if you want someone who thrives on burning the midnight oil to see an idea through, Caro's your girl. And, double bonus, she's right down the road.'

'In Cornwall? Why's she here?'

Lucas shook his head. 'Not sure. Something about breaking free to work on her own ideas outside the corporate machine, I think. She's not exactly super-chatty. Neither is she asking for a pay cheque.'

Weird. 'Doesn't she need money?'

'Eventually. But for now Caro wants to see if this will work. She's an inventor. Trialling something experimental is a key step in making those giant leaps.'

Ellie nodded. Bringing Caro on board for trial treatments would be a real boon for them. More to the point, having Lucas Williams—aka the Uber-Vet—at the surgery would be about a hundred times more amazing. Famous or not, he was a brilliant vet. Always had been. He'd always been able to put two things together other veterinarians didn't have the guts for. He was a thinker, whereas she was a reactor, which was why emergencies were her forte. So…if she was coming at this whole 'I want to be a partner' thing from Drew's perspective? It'd be stupid to send him packing. At this point anyway. Especially if Moose had a chance at a normal life. Drew would go mad for that type of surgery.

'Okay. I'm happy to give the go-ahead for Caro. Start small, aim high, right?'

Lucas grinned. 'It's how the best dreams come true.' He pulled a few sheaves out of the drawings tube and handed them to her. 'Let's take another look at these, shall we?'

Ah. The clinic.

Despite her muddied emotions, she was drawn into the fascinating proposal.

'They look like architectural drawings.'

'They are in a way.' Lucas helped her spread the large papers out on the surgical table.

'It's all very modern.'

'Robotic legs usually are.'

Ellie shot him a goofy smile. 'I don't mean that, it's just…there aren't that many dogs wandering round the planet with robotic legs.'

'Good point. Although there is a Rottweiler over in the States who's got four.'

'He had four leg amputations?' Caro was shocked. 'What happened to him?'

'Frostbite. His owner kept him outside in sub-zero temperatures and—'

Ellie stopped him. 'Don't. I can't even imagine a dog being treated that way.'

They spent a few minutes poring over the details and

when she finally felt she had her head wrapped around the concept she stretched and grinned. 'I think it'll be brilliant. Do you want to call Moose's owners or shall I?'

'Your clinic…'

'Your patient,' she countered, knowing she would have to make a decision soon as to whether or not she'd like it to be his clinic, too.

Maybe she did need those couple of weeks to think about it after all.

A couple of days later Lucas found himself being dragged to the whelping pen for some puppy time with Maverick. Willingly escorted was a better description, Lucas thought as Maverick pushed through the swinging doors into the puppy unit. He had a million things to do to prep for the robotic leg surgery the following week, but if he'd learnt anything over the past few weeks, it was that time was precious and if his son wanted him to spend ten minutes playing with puppies he'd find that ten minutes come hell or high water.

As for the surgical prep, that's what coffee was for.

'Which one's your favourite?' Maverick asked.

Lucas, who was sitting in the middle of the pen and being used as a climbing frame by the rambunctious pups, gave the puppies a considered scan. 'Depends on what you want the puppy for, I guess. Most of these are going to be trained to be therapy dogs, right?'

Maverick nodded, his face very earnest, as if he took responsibility for the dogs and their futures himself. 'Hearing dogs. Therapy dogs. They do all sorts.'

'Esmerelda's an amazing mummy to have all these lovely puppies, isn't she?'

Maverick nodded happily. 'Esmerelda's the best. She's going to come and live up in the flat again soon.'

'Once the puppies are weaned?'

Maverick gave a solid little-boy nod. 'Mummy is going to get all of the puppy carers to come over then. Then they'll all be gone.' He stroked a little black Lab who jumped up and licked him on the nose. Mav's expression turned gloomy. 'I know they're going to lovely places and that they will be helping people, but…'

'But what?'

Mav choked back a small sob. 'I'd like it better if they could stay.' He looked up at Lucas, threads of anxiety woven across his cute little-boy face. Lucas couldn't bear it. He knew what Maverick was really asking. Would Lucas be leaving, too?

Lucas pulled his son onto his lap along with Mav's favourite puppy, Mr Purple, a golden Lab with a black button nose and a little purple collar to differentiate him from the others. Lucas knew he could spot his boy in a crowd of thousands of blonds. He held him close, so grateful to Ellie for having raised a son who was kind, smart, inquisitive, funny and just about everything a man could ever dream of. He owed her a debt of gratitude he would spend his life repaying.

'I know the puppies have to leave. It's part of growing up, but…' Oh, this was tricky territory. Territory he really should cover with Ellie first. 'How would you feel if I were to stay longer?'

Maverick whirled round in Lucas's lap, the puppy tumbling back into the jumble of happy furballs. 'Are you going to stay?'

'I'd like to. I'd like it very much.'

Maverick whooped with joy and threw his arms round

Lucas's neck. Lucas wasn't a crier, but it was hard to focus with tears swimming in his eyes. This was a moment he would cherish for ever.

A movement caught his eye.

Ellie.

She was standing in the doorway and from the look on her face had been listening to their conversation. Her eyes glistened with tears. Was this it? The sign he'd been waiting for that Ellie had forgiven him?

Maverick scooped up Mr Purple. 'What about Marvin?'

Ellie began to giggle, crossing to join them. 'Marvin? I thought we were going to wait for the puppy carers to give them names.'

Mav looked at her like she was missing half her brain. 'This one's definitely Marvin.' He shot his mother an impish look. 'He's an Uber puppy! And he told me he'd like to stay with us. In the flat. Not next door.' His eyes darted to Lucas then to his mother, his eyes in full *Please, please, Mummy, can we?* mode.

Bash.

Lucas's heart was going to be bruised to a pulp if things continued in this vein. Bruising he could totally get used to.

To her credit, and obvious skill as a mum used to receiving her son's wide-eyed appeals, she laughed and gave Marvin a little scrub on the head. 'All in good time.' She popped her mouth into an O as if an idea had struck. 'Why don't you, me and Lucas all head down to the beach tonight? Have a barbecue before the sunny days start drawing in?'

Mav clapped his hands, a life with Marvin temporarily forgotten. 'Can we have marshmallows?'

Ellie nodded. 'Absolutely. And sausages. And…' Her sparkling green eyes shifted to Lucas. 'What do you like?'

'You,' he said.

Her cheeks flamed hot and bright. 'Well, of course you do. I'm fabulous.' Then she turned on her heel, muttering something about needing to see to a pregnant hamster.

Lucas grinned. She would come round. In time. And time was something he had oodles of.

CHAPTER NINE

THE CLINIC WAS absolutely buzzing with excitement. Today was the day Moose would finally receive his prosthesis. News Ellie was quite certain her mother had spread rather liberally round the village.

Once he had healed and was trialling his robotic legs along the beach and in the countryside, who knew what sort of crowd they'd draw?

To steady her nerves, Ellie took extra care in the scrub room, watching through the glass window as the operating theatre filled with staff, all equally charged up to change the Bernese mountain dog's life.

She and Lucas had had several meetings with Caro over the past week, but she'd opted not to come down to the clinic for the actual surgery, even though Ellie had assured her she was welcome.

She was a quirky one, Caro Barnes. Model-gorgeous, she was all flowing blonde hair and lean athletic body—a proper California girl—but she liked her own space and, from the sound of her working schedule, her own style of timekeeping. She'd mentioned looking out at the shooting stars late at night more than once when asked to explain how she'd come up with this or that idea.

Ellie gave her arms a final scrub then wove her way

through the surgical nurses so that she and Lucas were on opposite sides of the operating table where Moose was still awake, happily receiving the adoration of the chief surgical nurse.

'You ready?' she asked Lucas.

The crinkles by his eyes fanned out above his surgical mask. 'As I'll ever be.'

Ellie grinned. She was absolutely fizzing with excitement. More than ever, the past few days had felt exactly as they had back in the day when they'd poured big mugs of coffee or hot chocolate and hit the books and their laptops, researching everything they could to make sure the complex surgery they were about to do went well.

They'd agreed to put the question of whether or not Lucas should become a partner on hold because what they were about to do warranted their full attention.

'Have you told the *Dolphin Cove Gazette*?' Lucas teased. 'I've never seen the reception area so full.'

'In Dolphin Cove, there's no need. Especially if Mum knows what we're up to.' Ellie laughed. 'You should see the beach!' A warm fuzzy feeling filled her heart. 'It's happened a few times when one of the village's favourite pets was about to have their life changed. The family needs support, and we all just pull together when the going gets tough.'

A few weeks back Lucas would've winced at something like that. This time? Ellie was relieved to see him smile and nod and say, 'As it should be.'

'Right, everyone.' He got the busy surgical room's attention. 'Welcome to Dolphin Cove Clinic's first percutaneous fixation to the skeleton.'

He began to explain the intricacies of the surgery. He would be implanting an internal peg and plate to each of Moose's rear legs onto which the robotic prosthetics would be attached in three or four weeks' time when the soft tissue had healed.

Everyone leant in as he showed the implant. It was a small but incredibly complex piece of technology. 'If you can see the special coatings here…' he held up the endoprosthesis '…this will become an integral part of Moose's skeleton. In other words, the bone will grow onto the metal of the implant. There are further precautions to ensure a robust, bacteria-proof seal.'

One of the nurses raised her hand. 'Will he be able to walk straight away?'

'Not straight away,' Lucas said, his calm authoritative voice drawing them all in the same way millions of television viewers had been captivated when he'd been the Uber-Vet. Ellie felt a swell of pride she hadn't felt before. Her brainiac nerdy boyfriend from vet school was now an assured, intelligent, passionate veterinarian at the top of his game. It felt incredible to feel pride in place of the darker feelings that had once consumed her—loss and insignificance.

One of the nurses asked about Moose's rehabilitation process.

'Good question,' Lucas said. 'A colleague of mine is coming down from London in a couple of days. A physiotherapist who's worked on a few similar cases with me. She'll work with a couple of local canine physios until they're confident with these specific treatment techniques. By week three, we should have a good idea when he can start using his bionic legs and get on with the business of being a healthy, happy dog.'

'And will Moose stay here at the clinic the entire time?' asked another nurse.

'Yes.' Lucas gave the big old dog's head a loving scrub. 'He'll become a member of the family here for up to four weeks. His own family will be welcome, of course, but I'm sure you'll all join Ellie and me in making him feel at home.'

When their eyes met, Ellie could see a solitary question in them. 'Will you let me stay, too?'

She wanted to. Heaven knew, she did, but…how could she know for sure that Lucas wouldn't change his mind again?

Their eye contact broke.

'Right, everyone! Lucas clapped his hands. 'Let's change a pet's life for the better.'

'Uh-oh.' Maverick looked down at his shirt, where a large blob of strawberry jam had just landed.

Ellie laughed. 'Uh-oh, indeed. I'm guessing you don't want to be wearing strawberry jam on your first day back at school?'

Maverick shook his head. 'Not really. Can I change?'

Normally Ellie would've scrubbed it off, just as she did all her son's other mishaps, but today was a special day. The first day back at school.

After he'd lifted his arms to have his shirt tugged off,' Maverick threw an anxious look at the door. 'He's coming, right?'

'Absolutely,' Ellie said, hoping her little boy didn't hear the tiniest sliver of concern in her voice.

After the success of Moose's surgery, the three of them had celebrated down at the Hungry Pelican with fish and chips. It had felt like a proper family night out. Grandma and Grandpa had even joined them. The handful of days following the surgery had been a blur. Ensuring Moose had been healing properly, seeing the scores of other pet patients, earmarking the retriever puppies for their increasingly excited puppy handler families and, of course, getting school clothes for Mav.

She glanced at the clock. She'd heard Lucas leave his flat earlier and presumed he'd gone for a run.

Twenty minutes later Ellie gave in to the urge to ring Lucas. They had to leave. Now.

It went straight to voicemail.

Her blood ran cold.

He wasn't doing this. Not on her little boy's big day. She gave Mav's blond curls a stroke. 'Love, I'm just going to run down to the clinic, all right? I'll be back in two.'

Maverick's expectant little face creased with concern. 'Do you think Lucas has had to do a surgery?'

He did that sometimes. Took the out-of-hours calls when she'd had a long day. It had been a welcome reprieve from those first, long months after Drew's surgery when she'd been on call night and day. But usually he consulted her about the case because she knew most of the animals and their histories.

She grabbed her phone to see if there had been any missed calls or texts. 'That's what I'm checking. He could be showing the new physio around.' Or stuck in a ditch. A flat tyre? Or— No. No, he wouldn't have gone to London, would he?

Not today. Surely not today. And not without telling her. His life was here now. At least he'd said he wanted it to be.

She ran down the stairs to the clinic and rounded the corner, only to run into a thirty-something woman holding a duffel bag in her hands. 'Ellie?'

'Hi! Hi…um…' She looked over the woman's shoulder. No Lucas. Crumbs. 'You must be Rebecca, right?'

The specialist physiotherapist gave a nod, her thick specs falling to the tip of her nose.

Ellie looked round again, listening intently for a car. Still no Lucas.

Weird. This wasn't like him.

Rebecca pushed her glasses up and shifted her bag to the other hand. 'Oof! Sorry. My arms are about to fall out of my sockets.' Rebecca shifted her bag again.

Distractedly, Ellie threw her an apologetic smile. 'Would you like to put your bag upstairs?'

'That'd be great. Taking the overnight train down here wasn't the best of decisions. I don't know what made me think I could sleep sitting up!' She yawned and stretched. 'I know it's not the best of intros to make, but I'd like a short kip if I can, before I see Moose.'

'Of course.' Ellie scanned the area again, her eyes darting from building to building see if she could see any lights being turned on.

Nope. Nothing.

Why wasn't she asking Rebecca about Lucas? Surely there was a simple explanation. Like…he'd picked her up at the station and got caught up doing something in the village.

'Did Lucas drive you in?'

'No, he booked a cab for me. Said he had something to do.'

He had to take his son to his first day back at school was what he had to do.

Had she dithered too long about accepting his offer to be a partner? She should've accepted there and then. Whether or not she wanted to marry Lucas shouldn't have been a factor. She was an adult woman who needed to make adult decisions about her son, and her son wanted his father.

She scanned the car park again.

Nope. Nothing.

She was scared. Scared her instincts were right. That Lucas had done a runner.

'Ellie?' Rebecca shifted her bag again.

Ellie's voice sounded foreign to her as she spoke. 'The clinic's not officially open until nine, but the morning nurses are in with him now, so if you like I can let them know you'll be in around ten or eleven?' And then figure out a way to console her son.

'Sounds great,' Rebecca said through another yawn.

Ellie led her up the stairs to the guest flat, where Lucas had made up the sofa bed.

Mav appeared on the balcony outside the two flats, his eyes wide with hope. 'Did you find him?'

This, she thought grimly. *This was why you didn't say yes when he asked to be a partner.*

'No, love. I...' She turned to Rebecca, humiliation sending streaks of heat up into her cheeks. Rebecca's eyes flicked between Ellie and her son. 'Lucas didn't tell you when he'd meet you, did he?'

'Yeah.' She nodded, stifling another yawn. 'He said he'd meet me in the clinic after he did whatever it was he had to do in the morning.'

Right.

Well, at least she knew which way she was leaning on the partner question.

Not a chance, pal.

Not when you hurt her son.

And just then his car pulled into the car park, Lucas

bounding out of the driver's seat as soon as the car had lurched to a halt. He looked anxious but happy, his eyes instantly going up to the balcony. When he saw Mav he threw him a big wave. 'Ready for the big day, son?'

'Daddy!' screamed Lucas, barrelling down the stairs to throw himself into Lucas's arms, only to miscalculate the steps and take a terrific tumble.

Lucas could see the accident happening in slow motion. He threw himself towards the stairs but not in time to break Maverick's fall.

No!

He raced to his son, a crumpled heap at the bottom of the stairs, barely looking up when Ellie arrived.

'Don't touch him,' Ellie snapped.

'I just want to—'

'I know.' She held her hand up between them. 'You've done enough.'

It took all his willpower to pull back, but he knew she was right. They needed to call emergency services. Get the first-aid kit. Two people fussing over a boy who might have sustained neck injuries was one person too many.

Ellie pressed her fingers to the side of Mav's throat.

'Pulse?' Lucas whispered.

She nodded. 'Thready, but...' She looked up at him, tears in her eyes. 'Why didn't you tell him to slow down?'

He would've. He'd barely waved before Mav had come running and by then it had been too late. Instead of answering, he pulled out his phone and rang for an ambulance.

Rebecca appeared at the bottom of the steps. 'Anything I can do?' she asked in a low voice. Lucas stood up and took her a few steps from where Ellie was gingerly examining a frightening gash on Maverick's forehead. 'Do you mind going into the clinic? If you go to the back door, one of the nurses will get you the first-aid kit. Wait. No. It'll be faster if I do it. Can you go to the end of the lane?' He tossed her his car keys. 'Flag the ambulance down, okay? This place can be tricky to find.'

He raced into the clinic, grabbed everything he could. A first-aid kit, braces, gauze, antiseptic wipes, instant ice packs. With any luck it would just have been a bad tumble and cut that required a butterfly stitch or two.

By the time he got back, Maverick was lying on his back, his eyes fluttering open, tears pouring down into his ears. 'It hurts, Mummy.'

He tried to pull his right arm to him then began to cry in earnest.

'I know, love. You may have broken it, so—' She cut herself off when she saw Lucas. She gestured for him to hand her the first-aid kit. 'Can you clean up the cut on his forehead? I think it's superficial, but it's just on his hairline. I need to pack his arm in ice until the paramedics get here.'

'I'm sorry, Daddy.'

'What? What are you sorry for?'

'Ruining our first big day together.'

'You didn't ruin a single thing, son. It was just an accident.'

An accident he could see Ellie blamed him for. In a few hours she would've calmed down. He huffed out a breath. In a few hours he had been hoping Ellie would be agreeing to be his wife. That plan would have to go on ice. He spread out all the equipment he'd grabbed from the supplies room.

'Here. Just in case.' He handed Ellie an inflatable neck

brace that was meant for canines, but…needs must and all that.

She glanced across at him as he handed her the equipment. 'Thank you.'

There was little warmth in it, but he'd take it. She wasn't telling him to bugger off. Not yet, anyway.

As she saw to Maverick's arm and examined a pair of scraped knees and a bump at the corner of his eye, she issued an odd request. Gauze. Antiseptic wipe. Scissors. She spoke in the same way she would if it were an emergency operation in her clinic, but her voice was utterly bereft of emotion. As if allowing herself to feel anything would pull the seam on whatever it was that was holding her together. A mother's love, no doubt. That, and the core of strength he'd seen in her that very first day they'd met.

He focussed on the cut. The wound, as predicted, was not nearly as bad as it looked. Head wounds always bled a lot and this one was no different. Seeing the streaks of red in his son's hair was unsettling, though. As painful as seeing his father succumb to the cruel effects of Parkinson's. Painful to see and not really be able to do anything. He was cleaning the wound and preparing it for inspection by the paramedics, but really? All he wanted to do was hold Maverick in his arms, pull him in tight and tell him how much he loved him. Apologise again and again, even though he knew it had been an accident. If he just hadn't been so damn excited. Getting the ring had been— It had lit something up in him he had hoped was in there. Strength. Determination. A willingness to be vulnerable. A vulnerability he hadn't expected to have to show so soon.

A car screeched into the car park.

'What the—?' Ellie curled herself protectively over Maverick even though the four-by-four was nowhere near them.

'It's Viola.'

'Why's she here?' Ellie asked, though the answer was pretty obvious. No one drove at high speed into a veterinary clinic before they were open because everything was all right.

Lucas pushed himself up. 'You stay with Mav. I'll go and check.'

Ellie gave him a curt nod. A nod that said, *I wasn't planning on going anywhere, pal.*

He jogged over to Viola's car, reaching her just in time to help her climb out of the enormous vehicle. Her Irish wolfhound, Constanza, was in the passenger seat. Not entirely a health and safety situation to write home about, but it didn't look like Viola was up for a lecture right now.

'Viola? Everything okay?'

She looked more birdlike than ever. And ashen-faced.

'What is it, Viola?'

'It's Wolfgang!'

The mate of Constanza, Wolfgang was Viola's favourite, even though she'd said again and again she knew she shouldn't have one, but she loved Wolfgang to within an inch of her life.

'Where is he?'

'In the back. He's fitting. Last time it was just the once, but this time it won't stop.'

'Last time?' Lucas asked as he ran to the back, trying to get a quick glimpse of Ellie and Mav. She was daubing at his forehead, even though he had been certain he'd stemmed the bleeding.

'Yes.' Viola was following him as he headed to the

back of the large four-by-four. 'It was on the day you were doing that fancy surgery and neither you nor Ellie were available and— Oh! I asked them to get Ellie, but they wouldn't!' A huge sob erupted from her small throat. 'I *knew* he wasn't getting the best treatment. Where's Ellie? Can Ellie come out?'

He didn't have to look to know the answer. 'No. There's been an accident.'

'With Ellie?' Viola's legs wobbled.

'No.' He reached out to steady her. 'With Maverick, but…he'll be all right.' He prayed with every fibre in his being that he was right. 'Are you happy for me to treat Wolfgang?'

'You'll do,' Viola said dismissively, her attention no longer on Lucas now that they'd open the back door of the vehicle. 'I just want my boy not to be in any pain.'

Lucas knew that feeling. In spades. It felt physically painful being away from Maverick right now, but one look at Wolfgang and Lucas flew into action. From everything Viola had described about the recurring episodes, Wolfgang was in status epilepticus, a series of epileptic seizures the poor dog had no recovery time between.

He ran back to Ellie and grabbed a roll of gauze for a temporary muzzle.

'What's going on?'

He quickly explained the situation.

Ellie gasped and handed him a pair of scissors and a couple of extra rolls of gauze. 'For his legs if he's really fitting.'

'Would you like to treat him? You know him best.'

'Are you mad? Of course not! My son's lying here bleeding and in pain because of you! Just go! Do your best because Viola's an incredibly important patient. You can do that, can't you? See to a patient without causing even more damage?'

If she'd slapped him it would've hurt less. She blamed him for Maverick's fall. What was worse, she didn't want him anywhere near Maverick.

He quietly turned to go. 'Don't forget to take blood samples after you get the IV in,' she instructed.

'I know.' For her benefit he ran through the list. Blood glucose, electrolytes, packed cell volume. She was stressed. Emotions were getting the better of her. People lashed out when they were scared, and she was definitely scared. He was too but this wasn't the time to show it. He changed his voice, his hand lightly touching Maverick's hair. 'I'm sorry, Ells. I want to be there with you. At the hospital.'

She nodded her acknowledgement but said nothing.

He gave his son's cheek a soft brush with the backs of his fingers then ran back to Viola.

They needed to get the dog on an anti-epileptic drip and onto some oxygen fast. He quickly wrapped the gauze round Wolfgang's muzzle, calling to one of the nurses who'd just come out to check on Maverick to get a gurney. Wolfgang weighed nearly sixty kilos. Lucas was strong. But carrying sixty kilos of fitting wolfhound would not be a wise decision.

He heard sirens approaching as he finished the wrap and tried to get a blanket under the dog so he and the nurse could do a quick transfer.

He glanced over at Ellie. Her ear was cocked. Good. She knew help was on the way. Help she'd accept, anyway.

The veterinary nurse arrived with a gurney just as the ambulance pulled into the drive.

He felt completely torn in two. One of those rock and hard place moments.

Just like he'd found himself in six years ago.

Ellie's business meant the world to her. She'd never let an animal suffer if it was in her means to care for and protect it. He had to be the one to care for and protect her business while she looked after their son. It caused him actual physical pain to not be there by her side, but he wasn't going to screw this up again.

While he slid the dog onto the gurney, he watched helplessly as the paramedic team slid his son onto one and strapped him in.

As they drove away and he ran into the clinic, he prayed he'd made the right decision. That Ellie would realise everything he'd done, he'd done for her.

'Here you are, love.' Ellie's mum handed her a cup of tea. 'I put some sugar in it. For the shock.'

Ellie blew on the cup. 'Thanks, Mum.' She leant against her mother when she sat down in the hard plastic chair beside her.

'Any word from the A and E staff?'

Ellie shook her head. 'Nothing different from what the paramedics said. Double fracture of his arm. They'll put it on soft bandages tonight, a proper cast in a couple of days.'

They both looked at the empty bed where Maverick had just been. Ellie's voice grew shakier. 'The doctors wanted to do another head scan to make sure there wasn't any damage to his skull. You know, danger of internal bleeding or anything. That's where he is now.'

'And Lucas? Have you heard from him?'

About ninety-seven times. Texts. Calls. To her phone and to the A and E.

Despite herself, she laughed.

Her mother gave her a light nudge. 'Is that a yes or a no?'

'It's a yes.' She flicked a bit of dirt off her knee. 'He's on his way here, actually.'

'Good. I knew you could rely on him.'

'What? Rely on *Lucas*?' Ellie sat up, her tea sloshing over the side of her flimsy plastic cup. 'Ow! God. *Mum!* Do you really think this is the time to wave the Lucas Williams fan club flag?'

Wyn looked at her appraisingly. 'Why? You said it was an accident.'

'It was, but—'

'But what?'

Ellie told her the story. Maverick being so excited. Lucas promising to be there. Lucas not being there. Lucas showing up just when she'd convinced herself he wasn't going to be. Maverick flying down the stairs with no one there to catch him. 'Lucas wasn't there in time. Plain and simple. He never will be. I need to own that now.'

'I thought you said he wasn't here because he was treating Viola's beloved hound?'

'No, Mum!' Ellie whirled on her mother, spilling yet more tea. 'Lucas should've been there for Maverick. Earlier. *Much* earlier than he was. If he'd been there when he'd said he would, Maverick wouldn't have had to run down those bloody stairs and he'd be at school, learning something, and I'd—' She stopped herself. She'd what? Be in Lucas's arms? Be dithering even more about whether or not to say she'd absolutely love him to be a partner in the clinic? Getting on with a thousand other things she'd love to spend the rest of her life doing with Maverick and Lucas by her side.

'It's tough, isn't it?' Wyn said, taking the tea gently from Ellie's hand and placing it on the floor. She handed her a packet of tissues.

'What is?'

'Being so very much in love.'

'Pah! Love? This isn't love. This is pure, unbridled fury. That's what it is.'

'No, it isn't, Eleanor. You know that and you need to stop putting anger in the place of forgiveness. You should've asked that man's forgiveness long ago. Then *none* of you would be in this position.'

'You think I should've asked him to forgive me? For leaving me in the lurch? For swanning off to "help his family"?'

'Eleanor Stone, I did not raise you to be this way. I've tried and tried and tried to get you to see sense through the years but now I'm going to have to be blunt. You were wrong to keep Maverick a secret from him. No matter how angry you were or hurt or heartbroken, you needed to remember that Lucas was in love with you, too. Can you even imagine how painful that must've been? Choosing between you and caring for a family who needed so much help? For a young man like that? It must've been terrifying.'

Ellie pushed her hands between her knees and pressed them tight. It was a good point. One she hadn't fully considered. Definitely not at the time, anyway.

Her mother continued, 'You gave birth to Lucas's son. Anyone who breaks his own heart to look after his own family in their time of need deserves your sympathy. He should be furious with you. If you'd been in his shoes, what would you have done? Sued for custody? I bet you would have.' Her mother was on a roll now. 'So what if he ended up on television? So what if you saw him with some girl on his arm. You didn't wait for facts, did you?'

Ellie bit down on her cheek. No. She hadn't, but he'd broken her heart too and— And what? She'd not considered the fact that he might've had to rip his own heart out to do what he'd done.

She looked at her phone again. Ninety-seven missed calls and messages.

Well.

Ignored calls and messages.

The only reason she knew he was coming was because he'd rung the hospital and got a nurse to tell her he was on his way if she needed to take a break or wanted anything.

Lucas still loved her.

She still loved him.

The only thing that stood between them was fear of something bad happening again, and bad things happened. It didn't mean it would break them up again.

A tear trickled down her cheek. 'I've been a selfish cow, haven't I?'

Her mother wrapped an arm around her and pulled her in for a tight half-hug. 'No, love. You've been a mama bear. Same as I probably would've been.'

'But…' She blinked away her tears. 'I thought you said—'

Her mother cut in. 'Oh, now that I'm old and wise I can see all the mistakes I made and the mistakes you made, too. So you have that to look forward to one day. Being as wise as your old mum.'

'Oh, Mum. I was just so scared.'

'I know, love. Loving a child is terrifying. Trusting

someone else to love them as much as you do is just as frightening. Loving a man is terrifying. You don't think I wasn't scared out of my wits when your father suggested we run the pub? Work with the same man day in day out for the rest of my entire life? Trust him to stand by me when I kept putting the wrong ingredients in everyone's orders?' She laughed. 'I remember sending out a Cornish breakfast with Yorkshire puddings once! Imagine. Yorkshire puddings in a Cornish pub.'

Ellie gave her a strange look. 'When did you do that?'

'When I was pregnant with you.'

A twist of guilt tightened in her chest. She'd had some strange quirks when she'd been pregnant. Drew and her parents knew about them, but there had been others she'd silently told Lucas. Quirks only he would've laughed at or sympathised with. The truth was she'd missed him all along. Had picked up the phone she didn't know how many times to ring him when she'd found out she was pregnant, but it had felt so weak!

'The point being, my darling girl...' her mother planted a kiss on top of her head '...loving someone involves a lot of blind trust. Whether you like it or not.'

'I guess that's my problem.' Ellie hiccough-sobbed as she pressed a fresh wad of tissues to her eyes. 'Of course I love Lucas. I guess in order to preserve what little pride I had after he left, I'd convinced myself that he wasn't the kind, amazing, incredible man I'd met, and that if I told him what had happened, he wouldn't love Mav as much as I did. Or me.'

'Not possible,' said a rich voice that definitely wasn't her mother's. 'I love him every bit as much as I love you.'

CHAPTER TEN

WYN GAVE Lucas a warm smile, and his arm a pat as she rose from her chair. 'I think that's my cue to go and get some fresh cups of tea.'

When she'd left, Lucas sat down next to Ellie, his heart hammering against his ribcage. 'Is he okay?'

Ellie nodded. 'Broken arm and a few scrapes and bumps. They're doing a final head scan, but it's more precautionary than anything. They think his arm took the brunt of the fall.'

'Ells, I am so sorry. If I hadn't gone out—'

'No. No. It was me. I—I thought you'd gone again. That you'd left us.'

'What?' He cursed his decision not to leave a note. Getting stuck behind a tractor on a narrow country lane definitely hadn't been part of the plan. Neither had dropping by her parents' pub for a 'casual little chat,' but life didn't run by a script, did it?

Ellie threw up her hands and sighed. 'I added two and two and got zero. That's why I was so angry. Not because you were late. Well…' a few more tears welled up in her eyes. 'It was also because you were late, but mostly it was me thinking the worst when you were probably out doing something completely boring, like getting milk for the physio.'

He pressed his hand to his jacket pocket. He had been on an errand. But he'd picked up something much longer lasting than a carton of milk.

'How's Wolfgang?' she sniffled.

'All right. I was a bit worried he'd suffered some brain damage.'

'Why?'

'It took Viola a while to get him into the car.'

Ellie's eyes popped wide open. '*Viola* got him into the car?'

Lucas nodded, every bit as astonished. 'She said she knew she had to get him to the clinic as soon as possible and that it would take too long to wait for us, so…' He laughed. 'She called it Herculean love.'

'What?'

'Whatever it was that enabled her to hoist that dog into her vehicle. They must weigh about the same.'

Ellie begged to differ. 'Wolfgang weighs more.'

'How do you know?'

'I was worried about her a few months back, so I had her get on the scales with him.'

Lucas grinned. 'But you already knew what he weighed, right?'

'Right.'

'And you've been doing it ever since?'

The bashful smile told him all he needed to know. 'You're amazing, Ells.'

'Why? For secretly weighing my clients?'

'For looking after the pets and their owners so well. No wonder she thinks the world of you.'

Ellie's cheeks pinked up. 'She probably loves you more now that you've saved Wolfgang.'

'No,' Lucas admitted. 'She made it pretty clear the entire time I was treating him that she trusted you far more than she trusted me.'

'Why doesn't she trust you?'

'She said…and I quote… I was "too pretty to trust."'

Ellie hooted with laughter, giggles taking over where the tears had just abated.

Damn, she was beautiful. Oh, hell. He pulled her into his arms, relief pouring through him when she leant into him and let him take some of the weight. This was as it should've been all those years ago when he'd wanted nothing more than to pull her into his arms when he'd been told his family needed him and he'd had to step away. What an idiot. They'd always been better together. As a team. The fact he'd managed to help his family as well as he had done had been little short of a miracle. One he would've rather shared with Ellie. Nothing had felt entirely right without her. A joke hadn't been as funny. An incredible surgery not as satisfying. The pillow next to his had never been right—not without that fan of flame-gold hair spread across it. It was an emptiness he'd felt as acutely as if he'd lost a limb. And yet he'd thought he'd done the right thing, stoically 'setting her free'. All those years gaslit by his own stupid decision-making.

Hindsight. Hindsight could be a real bitch.

'I was wrong, Ells. To do what I did.'

'What? On the stairs?'

'No, not that.' He checked himself when she stiffened. 'Obviously, that. Of course I wish I'd caught him. The last thing I want is for Maverick to suffer even the slightest pain. He fell so far down the stairs. I just couldn't get there in time. Believe me, Ellie. If it had been within my power, I would've been there.'

Just as he knew in his heart he would've been there for her if he'd known about Maverick all along.

'I know,' she said, crying again. After a few jagged breaths, she pushed herself back from his chest and looked him in the eye. 'I know it was an accident and I owe you an apology for reacting so poorly.'

'No. Ells—'

She cut him off. 'See this?' She pointed to a small chip on one of her teeth.

'Yes.'

'I got that when I was rollerblading towards my mum and she turned around to say something to my father just as I fell flat on my face.'

'Ouch.' He grimaced. 'Remember this?' He pulled up his sleeve and pointed to a scar on the inside of his arm.

She stared at it a moment then smiled sheepishly. '*Crumbs.* Was that the time Drew was supposed to be holding the barbed wire up for you when we were trying to get through a fence to an injured deer?'

'Sure was.'

Ellie clapped her hand to her mouth. 'And I was the one who distracted Drew, who let go of the barbed wire and...'

'Rip!' Lucas said, smiling at the memory. They'd all stared at his wound in horror, then Ellie had done some lightning-fast triage on him whilst barking orders at Drew to help the deer that had got itself properly stuck in someone's chain-link fence. They'd all gone out for drinks together afterwards and laughed and laughed. Not a cross word between them. There never had been. Any problems? They'd talked them out.

'Didn't I buy a nurse's uniform to wear when I changed your wound dressing?' Ellie tipped her head to the side, a tumble of curls shifting onto her forehead.

'Yes, you did.' He nodded, teasing her hair away with a finger. 'I seem to remember you wearing it more than once.'

'That nurse's uniform saw quite a bit of action over the years, didn't it?'

'Yes, it did,' Lucas confirmed with a grin, and then, more seriously, said, 'But not just because we were hurt.'

'No.' Ellie's smile faltered. 'No, it was for other things, too.'

Lucas took one of her hands in his. 'Ells, I know things are crazy complicated between us, but… I love you. And I know it's only been a few weeks, but I love Mav, too. Fell in love with him every bit as fast as I fell in love with you. I know this is hilarious coming from me, but…'

'But what?'

He looked her straight in the eye. 'Don't you think we'd be better off doing this together? As a team? A proper team?'

Ellie felt a lump form in her throat. She was pretty sure Lucas wasn't talking about being a business partner this time.

He dug into his pocket and produced a small red box. 'I know the timing isn't perfect and the setting is about as opposite to romantic as you can get, but… Ellie Stone? Would you do me the honour of being my wife?'

'In sickness and in health?' she asked, even though she knew she didn't need to.

'Better. Worse. Richer. Poorer. Stressed. Chillaxed. But mostly? To love and to cherish.'

She watched as he popped open the box.

It was a new ring. Completely different from the one he'd proposed with all those years ago. It didn't look immaculately smooth like a traditional engagement ring. No shiny solitaire. She'd never liked those really. Had said she'd wanted the perfect veterinarians' ring but wasn't quite sure what that was.

This was it.

'It's sand cast,' Lucas explained. 'I was at the jeweller's this morning, picking it up.'

'Sand cast?'

'Yup. I hadn't heard of it either, but I wanted something Cornish.'

'Why?'

'To prove to you I see my future here, with you and Mav.'

She looked into his eyes and saw nothing but love in them. Genuine commitment. And, most importantly, trust.

She picked up the ring and held it up to the light. Did she share that level of trust? Have the blind faith her mother said she needed to have to pull together as a couple?

'It's an eternity ring,' Lucas said, pointing to the tiny ring of glittering jewels tucked into the delicate white gold band. 'Sapphires for the sea. Diamonds for the stars. And, of course, some sand from Dolphin Cove.'

'It's beautiful.'

'Not as beautiful as you are, Ells.'

She tipped her forehead to his. 'Do you think we can do it this time? Trust one another with our problems? Even when they seem insurmountable?'

He pulled back and tipped her chin up so that their

eyes met. '*Especially* when they seem insurmountable. We did pretty well this morning, didn't we? Miscommunications aside.'

'I think next time—if there is one…' Their eyes met as Ellie began to giggle. Together they said, 'There will be more than one.'

Lucas dropped a kiss on her forehead then, pulling back, his gaze dropped to the ring. 'Is that a yes?'

Her heart skipped a beat when she saw just how hopeful he looked.

'It's a yes,' she said, grinning like a loon as he slipped the ring on her finger.

Mid-kiss they heard a throat being cleared.

'Mum!' Ellie's cheeks flamed red, but she didn't care. Not any more. 'Sorry. We…um—'

'I take it you said yes, then?' her mother asked.

Lucas looked at Wyn in surprise. 'How did you know I'd propose here?'

She tapped the side of her head. 'I'm a wise old thing. Never forget that. Especially now that I'm going to be your mother-in-law.'

Lucas gave her a jaunty sailor's salute. 'Yes, ma'am.'

Wyn gave a curtsy then pulled the curtain open wider. 'I think you both might want to share your news with this young man.'

'Mum!' Maverick ran to his mother, pulling himself short of a hug to protect his arm. When he saw Lucas beside her his smile doubled. 'Daddy! Look! I'm going to have a scar!'

Lucas laughed. 'I have it on good authority women like a man with a scar or two.' He dropped Ellie a wink that unleashed a spray of heat inside her. He was mostly

right. It wasn't the scars she loved. It was the man who'd
weathered the pain and come out the other side smiling.

She held up her hand and wriggled her ring finger.

Maverick went wide-eyed and gave a dramatic, 'Ooh!'
His eyes ping-ponged between the pair of them, absorbing their happy smiles, and then he burst into tears.

Both Ellie and Lucas dropped to their knees and, being
careful of his arm, help him, whispered consoling words
and, thanks to a handkerchief Lucas produced, wiped
away his tears.

'Love, do you not want us to get married?' Ellie asked.

'I do!' Maverick insisted, a smile finally breaking
through the wash of tears. 'I really, really do! This is me
being happy!' His watery blue eyes landed on Lucas.
'Does that mean you're going to stay?'

Lucas gently combed his fingers through his son's
hair. 'That it does, son. That it does. For ever and a day.'

'Yippee!' Maverick cried, then yelped as he'd stretched
out his arm with joy.

After a quick check with the doctor, who confirmed
Maverick's scan was fine and that the only further treatment he'd need was for his arm, they were ready to go
home. As a family.

Ellie's mum doled out kisses and invited everyone to
the pub for supper, but only if they were up to it. They
all agreed they would definitely be up to it, particularly
when Lucas asked Wyn to make sure there was some
chilled champagne ready for their arrival.

After Wyn left, Ellie gave Maverick her hand to hold.
'Shall we get you home, love?'

'Yes, please.' He nodded then threw a hopeful look
up at Lucas. 'By for ever, you mean you'll be coming to
the Christmas play?'

'I'll be coming to all of the Christmas plays, Mav,' Lucas confirmed. 'Wild horses wouldn't keep me away.'

'Good! Because Mummy says the wild horses have to stay out on the moor and that they're actually tame.'

Ellie shot Lucas an embarrassed look. No more pulling the wool over his eyes on that front.

'And this year?' Maverick sent Ellie a mischievous look. 'I've decided what I really want to be in the nativity is Barnacle!'

The laugh the three of them shared meant so much more to Ellie than she could have ever explained. It was a laugh built on happiness, hope and the loving expectation of many more times like this to come. A love that would grow and enrich all their lives. A love she couldn't wait to share.

CHAPTER ELEVEN

'THIS IS BONKERS, RIGHT?' Ellie grinned at Drew as he put the flower crown on her head.

'Yes, but I wouldn't expect anything less from you. Where's my right-hand man?'

'Mav? He's trying to put all the puppies onto leads without them getting tangled up, all with just one arm'

'Ha! That'll be interesting. And Esmerelda?'

'She's with Lucas.'

They both glanced out of the window of her flat towards the beach cove, but Drew pulled the curtain across before Ellie could see the full scene. The sudden movement made him wobble.

Ellie reached out to steady him. 'Are you sure you're up for the walk down the aisle?'

Drew brandished his 'fancy' cane. 'I'll be fine. Are you sure your father doesn't mind I'm going to be sharing the walk with him?'

'What?' Ellie feigned disbelief. 'The man who singlehandedly dragged his little girl out of her funk by helping her create one of the best vet clinics this side of London? He's honoured.' Her smile softened. 'He really is, Drew. Besides...' her grin returned to full wattage '...he thinks eloping on the beach next to Dolphin Cove is akin to eloping in Timbuktu, so…you're helping him in foreign climes.'

A car horn tooted. 'Speaking of foreign climes…' Drew nodded towards the car park '…it looks like the Londoners have arrived.'

Ellie ran to the window, grinning as Lucas jogged out to the car park, pulling his brother into a huge bear hug the second he got out of the car. His mum had come as well. Her body language spoke of a shyer disposition, but even from up at the flat Ellie could see the pride in her face.

Ten minutes later Maverick headed down to the cove with all ten Labrador puppies sort of under control. He made his way down the aisle past friends, family and the staff from the clinic, as if he was the King of Cornwall himself. It was hilarious. Her mum was beaming away at the front, as was Lucas's mother. The vicar, who'd brought his cat in the day after Ellie had agreed to marry Lucas, had barely lifted a brow when they'd asked him to marry them just as soon as humanly possible. Love, he said, waited for nothing and no one and, as they were promising a fish pie and pints at the pub after, why not?

Lucas's eyes lifted from his son's to hers. A smile so proud and happy filled his face she couldn't help but return it. Though her father was on one arm and Drew was on the other, she only had eyes for one man. The gorgeous blond she couldn't wait to call her husband.

When it came time to exchange vows, the vicar took a step back, knowing they had written the vows themselves and needed no prompting to say what was already in their hearts.

Lucas took Ellie's hands in his, his eyes shining with happiness. 'Ellie Stone? I promise here in front of everyone we love to be your best friend.' He threw an apologetic smile to their shared best man. 'Sorry, Drew. I know you're up there, but… I think it's a post that has room for more.'

'You're not wrong there, mate.' Drew nodded his approval. 'You've always been welcome.'

'Thank you,' Lucas said, from his heart. He turned back to Ellie, his eyes connecting with hers with such depth of emotion she could feel it in her soul. 'I promise never to keep anything from you. Even if it causes one or both of us pain. I know now that a burden shared is a burden halved and that together we can turn that pain into something that will heal and help us grow even stronger. Unless, of course, it's Christmas or your birthday and then all bets are off.'

The small crowd laughed and filled the air with a few hoots of appreciation.

Lucas kissed her cheek. 'I promise to love you. To honour you. To respect you, but most of all I promise to cherish you and our family as the most important, precious people in my life. With you…you and Mav… I know we can do anything. Achieve anything.'

Ellie said her own vows with matching intensity. How could she not? She finally felt whole again. Whole after learning so much about herself and life and now, most importantly, love.

After they'd exchanged rings, the vicar pronounced them husband and wife. 'I suppose you'd like to kiss the bride?'

'I thought you'd never ask,' said Lucas, already pulling Ellie into his arms. From the moment their lips touched, Ellie knew they'd made exactly the right choice to wed straight away. Love didn't wait. So when you had it? She knew they had courage on their side as they embarked on their new lives together, as a family.

* * * * *

HEALING THE VET'S HEART

ANNIE CLAYDON

MILLS & BOON

To Stuart
With grateful thanks for simple answers
to complicated questions

CHAPTER ONE

DREW TREVELYAN EASED himself out of his car, pausing for a moment to take a deep breath of sea air. He'd always loved the clarity of early mornings here, the way the sea seemed to stretch out beyond the sheltered curve of the bay in an endless swell of ever-changing colours. When the construction of the new buildings of the Dolphin Cove Veterinary Clinic had been underway, he'd often come here just to sit for half an hour before going on to work in the cramped quarters of the veterinary practice he shared with Ellie Stone...

Drew smiled. A lot had changed in the last few weeks. He'd returned home to Dolphin Cove, after months in hospital and then rehab, to find that his stand-in at the clinic had left. His old friend and Ellie's estranged partner, Lucas Williams, had been Ellie's only option as a replacement and all Drew could do was look on helplessly at the time at the resulting turmoil. Now, another far more joyful turn of events meant that Drew had to remember to refer to Ellie as Ellie Stone-Williams, not Ellie Stone.

The clinic hadn't changed though, and the early mornings here were still as peaceful as they'd been when he and Ellie had first moved in, two years ago. The buildings were starting the long process of becoming one with their surroundings, and moss was beginning to grow on the stone-built technology centre and operating suite on the other side of the ten-acre plot. Here, the wooden frame of the general practice building had begun to mellow, taking on the early autumn colours of the woodlands that lay beyond the drive. The low sun glinted on the high sheets of glass, making them sparkle like the sea.

He was back. Not officially—this visit was a matter of reacquainting himself with a place that he loved, and his diary was as blank as it had been for the last four months. But coming here was one more step that carried him away from the past.

Drew turned, catching up his walking stick and leaning on it heavily as he made his way around to the back of the car, clipping Phoenix's lead onto her collar and lifting the ten-week-old chocolate Labrador down to the ground. She sniffed the air, and then started to tug on the lead, seeming to know that she'd come home too.

Phoenix had been Ellie's idea. A puppy to love and care for, when everyone else around him seemed to think that he should stay down and accept their care. Drew appreciated their concern, but he longed to have a conversation that didn't, at some point, include a solicitous enquiry about his physical and emotional health.

People were kind, there was no doubt about that. They'd been kind when his fiancée had been killed in a diving accident in Puerto Rico two years ago. And when fate had decided that it wasn't done with him yet and the brakes on his car had failed, the village had rallied round again, writing notes and cards and visiting him in hospital. His smashed leg had taken a long time to fully heal, and even now his exercise regime was challenging. But being here gave him a sense of how far he'd come.

'You know where you are, Phoenix?' As he unlocked the main doors to the reception area of the clinic, the puppy started to yelp excitedly, pawing at the glass. 'Not too loud, eh, girl? Ellie and Lucas will hear us.'

There wasn't much chance of Phoenix's barking travelling to the apartment that Ellie and Lucas shared upstairs at the other end of the building. But Drew wanted to be alone here for a moment. He walked into the reception area, past the oak tree that stood in a large tub at its centre. Maybe it was his imagination, but it seemed to have grown a few inches. Nothing else seemed to have changed all that much.

'Everything's fine, Drew. We're managing without you, all you need to do is concentrate on being well again...'

He'd known that was a lie, even if Ellie had told it with the best of intentions. She'd found it hard to keep the practice running without him, and the last few weeks in particular had taken their toll on her. She'd been in turns deliriously happy and deeply despondent, and it had been touch and go as to which would win out.

'Forget it, Drew. Ellie and I will work it out. Stay down for a while...'

Lucas had taken a more direct approach, although the message had been pretty much the same. Lucas and Ellie *had* worked it out, and Drew had been staying down for far too long now. He was more than ready to get back up again.

The deserted reception area smelled of wax polish and hope. The consulting rooms were still the same, one of them filled with a mass of photographs of Ellie's canine patients, and another with a more restrained set of framed photographs that belonged to Lucas. Drew's was…empty. Neat and tidy, without a speck of dust. Drew smiled. It was ready and waiting for him.

'Drew! What the blazes are you doing here?'

Ellie's tone generally became firmer, in proportion to the size and momentum of the animal she was dealing with. This must be the one she reserved for charging rhinos.

Drew did the only thing possible and let go of Phoenix's lead. When he turned, he saw the puppy barrelling along the corridor, the lead trailing behind her, and Ellie fell to her knees, scooping Phoenix up into her arms. Worked every time.

Or… Every time apart from this one.

'Come on. What *are* you doing here?' Ellie stood to face him, trying not to smile as the puppy licked her neck.

'I could ask you the same question. Shouldn't you and Lucas be staring into each other's eyes over your cornflakes? You are technically still on your honeymoon, even if you are at work.'

Ellie flushed slightly, presumably at the mention of Lucas's eyes. 'You do know what you're doing, don't you? Deflecting one question with another. It so happens that I didn't have cornflakes for breakfast, and Lucas isn't here. He's doing the school run this morning.'

'So you're letting him in gently to the joys of parenthood.' Drew grinned. He imagined that the other parents at the school gate were more of a challenge to Lucas than the whole six years he'd spent as TV's favourite vet.

'He said that yesterday was a bit like running a gauntlet of meerkats.' Ellie shrugged. 'He doesn't mind, really.'

'He loves it. You know that.'

Ellie nodded, smiling. She'd been in love with Lucas

ever since the three of them had studied together at veterinary school. Lucas had left to become a celebrity vet, and Ellie had returned to Cornwall, where she and Drew had set up in practice together in Dolphin Cove. When Ellie and Lucas's son, Mav, had been born, he had been so like his father, and a constant reminder that something was missing in all their lives.

But now Lucas was back. Ellie had never loved anyone else, and Drew was happy for them both.

'You *still* haven't answered my question.'

He hadn't counted on springing this on Ellie today, but since she'd asked, he may as well grasp the nettle. 'Why don't we go and sit down in my office.'

'I'm *really* getting worried now. You're trying to butter me up by sitting down, aren't you?'

Drew chuckled. 'Yep. And I don't want Phoenix running around here until she's had her second set of vaccinations.'

He let Ellie tuck his hand into the crook of her elbow, but Drew was careful not to lean on her as they walked. He'd leaned on Ellie far too much already and he appreciated her support, but it had to stop. Leaning on the people around him was beginning to weaken him.

Ellie plumped herself down into a chair, keeping Phoenix on her lap for more cuddles, and Lucas lowered himself into the seat behind his desk. The surface looked as if it had been polished every day while he'd been away.

'I'm coming back to work, Ellie.'

Ellie's eyebrows shot up, but she took a moment to moderate her reaction. 'We weren't expecting you till the end of the month. Are you sure you're well enough? What does your physiotherapist say?'

'She says that if I think I can manage it I should give

it a try, just for a couple of days a week for starters. She told me to take things slowly and stop if anything gets too much.'

Relief showed in Ellie's eyes. 'That…doesn't sound so bad.'

'You know I've been going crazy at home, Ells. I really need this and I'm going to need your support. I know you and Lucas can do with a helping hand here.'

'Yes, we could.' Ellie's gaze softened suddenly. 'Lucas isn't replacing you, Drew. You know that's never going to happen.'

It might. The complex animal surgery Drew excelled at took stamina and strength, and no amount of concentrating on the positive could tell him for sure that he'd ever be able to do that again. But he still had a lot to give, and if anyone *was* going to replace him, he wanted it to be Lucas. And if anyone was going to replace *cool Uncle Drew* in Mav's affections, he wanted that to be Lucas too.

But the late-night fears about being of no more use to anyone were just paranoia. They weren't what Ellie needed to hear from him at the moment.

'You're not the only one who's pleased to see Lucas back, you know. We were all friends, and I've missed him too.'

'You never said…'

Drew rolled his eyes. 'Of course I didn't, not while you were missing him on a completely different level. And being remarkably tight-lipped about it.'

Ellie heaved a sigh. 'Okay. You have my support, just as long as you don't overdo things. If you do, I won't hesitate to escort you off the premises.'

'It's a deal.'

'I suppose…the accounts need signing off.' Ellie shot

him a mischievous look. No doubt it had crossed her mind that checking them through involved sitting down.

'I can do that.' Drew called her bluff. 'Although I haven't forgotten that it's your turn this year. Or maybe we should give them to Lucas, since he's our newest partner in the practice.'

Ellie didn't take the bait. 'We'll *both* owe you one, then. Mrs Cartwright's coming in this morning, with Tabatha...'

'Okay. You take Tabatha, and I'll take Mrs Cartwright.' It was well known that whenever Mrs Cartwright made an appointment for someone to look at her cat, she really wanted to sit in the waiting room and chat for an hour. The vets at the Dolphin Cove Clinic always made sure that she got a cup of tea and that someone was available to listen to her.

'You're a darling.' Ellie frowned. 'I suppose you're not allowed to drink welcome-back champagne...?'

'At eight in the morning, and with painkillers, probably not. We'll do that another time.'

'Welcome-back coffee, then? Your mug's in your top drawer....' Ellie gave Phoenix one last hug and got to her feet.

'You go and get on. I'll make the coffee.' Drew opened the drawer of his desk, finding pens and his coffee mug stacked neatly inside. He was going to have to do something about all this tidiness.

'All right.' Ellie planted her hands on his desk, leaning over to kiss his cheek. 'I'm so glad you're back, Drew.'

'Don't get sloppy on me Ells...' Drew could feel a lump forming in his throat.

'Tough guy, eh?' Ellie shot him a speculative look.

'Not really. I just don't want you to get *me* started.'

'That might not be such a bad idea, Drew. You've always been there for me, and now Lucas and I both want to be there for you.'

'You are. And I appreciate it.' He just didn't want to talk about it. 'White no sugar?'

Ellie rolled her eyes. 'That's right. Glad to see you haven't forgotten.'

When Ellie left, he took a moment to soak in the feeling. He was here, sitting behind his desk, and already had a few things to do with his day. Looking at the accounts, making the coffee and chatting to Mrs Cartwright might not be quite at the cutting edge of veterinary practice, but it was a start.

Mrs Cartwright had been delighted to find that one of the vets was prepared to give her his undivided attention for a whole hour. At any moment now Ellie was going to appear and tell him he'd done enough for the day, and Drew had opened the accountant's yearly report in front of him on his desk. If the enticement of having someone else focus their attention on the figures didn't chase her away, then he'd use the bulky folder as a weapon to defend his position.

'Hey. Ellie sent me…' Lucas popped his head around the door, grinning.

'Tell her *no*. I'm perfectly all right here.'

Lucas chuckled. 'You'll have to tell her that yourself, and she's busy charming a snake at the moment.'

Lucas was carrying a bound booklet, which he set down on the desk. Drew peered at the cover page.

'What's this?'

'Remember I told you about the dog prostheses we fitted while you were away? This is the write-up on the operation. The robotics engineer we were working with has some new ideas for an enhanced prosthetic and she'd like to work with us to develop them.' As soon as Lucas sat down, Phoenix bounded towards him, and he bent down to scratch the puppy's ears.

'Thanks. I'd be interested in having a look.' Drew was grateful for his friend's thoughtfulness in asking for his opinion.

'I was rather hoping you'd take charge of it all. I don't have the time.'

'You're sure about this? I can take some of the weight elsewhere, you must want to see it through yourself.' Drew's hand moved towards the booklet and then he pulled it back. The project sounded fascinating, and he was pretty sure that Lucas wanted to steer it himself.

Lucas grinned at him. 'I'd rather not be working during my evenings and weekends at the moment. You'd be doing me a favour.'

'In that case…thanks. I appreciate it.' Drew picked up the booklet and opened it. The introductory page bore the names of everyone who'd worked with Lucas in fitting the prosthetics, including one that he didn't recognise.

'This Caro Barnes… She's the robotics engineer?'

Lucas nodded. 'Yes, I consulted with her on some of my Uber-Vet projects. She's incredibly talented, and one of the few people I wanted to keep in contact with from my time as a TV vet. We struck up a correspondence, and when everything went south on the robotics programme she was involved with in California, she picked up on an off-the-cuff suggestion I'd made, and decided to investigate animal prosthetics. She came back home to the UK, and was in Oxford for a while, fending off various offers for research fellowships.'

'She must be good.' Research fellowships from Oxford University were usually hotly contested.

'Caro's at the top of her field. She can be a little odd at times...'

Drew could handle odd. In fact, the more challenge involved, the better. 'You said she abandoned the robotics programme. What happened there?'

'I'm not sure. Some kind of spat over patents—apparently she lost the rights to something she'd developed. She clearly didn't want to talk about it, and when Caro's not in the mood to talk about something there isn't much point in asking. But she's not one to abandon anything lightly, if that's what you're thinking. She's committed to this project and she'll see it through.'

'You're frowning...' Drew picked up on a note of uncertainty in Lucas's manner.

'When I say she'll see it through, she'll do it in her own way. I find it easier not to ask about her process.'

'Fair enough.' Drew nodded. 'So what does she need from us?'

'I'm not entirely sure. She says she only wants to discuss it on a need-to-know basis, and apparently I don't need to know just yet. I get the impression that this patent business has made her a little paranoid.' Lucas grinned. 'She's living at Smugglers' Top.'

'What?' If anyone wanted isolation then Smugglers' Top was perfect. 'The house up there is in a terrible state, surely she's not living there?'

Lucas chuckled. 'You're behind the times, mate, it's been renovated as a holiday let. Caro managed to get a reduced rate for the whole of the winter.'

'She's serious about her privacy, then.'

'Yeah, Smugglers' Top really suits her. But she's a

good sort when you get past the whole mad scientist thing she has going on, and the not speaking to you for days because she's thinking. I went to see her at the weekend and took Mav with me. She gave him a miniature drone with a grab mechanism at the bottom. It's a cool thing, we've been flying it around the apartment, picking things up and putting them down again.'

'I'll bet Ellie *loves* that.'

'There were a few abject apologies after we crashed it into her favourite vase...' Lucas grinned, clearly relishing the apology side of the process. 'You'll have to come over for dinner very soon, Mav can't wait to show it to you.'

Drew wondered if the last bit was a pity gesture, and decided it wasn't. If Lucas had thought that Drew was in need of pity, he would have taken him down to the Hungry Pelican and they could have drowned their sorrows there.

'So... I'm taking on a mad scientist who'll only tell me what I need to know, when she's speaking to me at all, that is, and who lives in an isolated spot that's difficult to get to... Anything else?'

Lucas grinned broadly. 'Nope, that's about it. Are you in?'

Drew chuckled. 'I'm in.'

CHAPTER TWO

DREW PARKED AT the mouth of the gully that led down to the beach. The high outcrop of rock that was known locally as Smugglers' Top was inaccessible at high tide, unless you happened to have a boat. At low tide, it was possible to make the climb up to the house from the beach.

In three hours, the tide would be in, and Smugglers' Top would be completely cut off. But that was enough time to get to the top, meet with Caro Barnes, and get back down again. Drew had spent the whole of yesterday resting at home in preparation for the climb today.

'All right, then, Phoenix.' He opened the back of the car, and the puppy immediately raised her head, sensing that they were about to go for a walk. 'This might be a bit of a stretch for both of us, but we'll make it.'

He slung the canvas bag that contained Phoenix's mid-morning snack over his shoulder, and the puppy capered at his feet as he walked slowly across the beach. She had very little appreciation of the adage that slow and steady wins the race, and she'd be exhausted before they got to the top and wanting to hitch a ride.

He was relieved to find that the old steps had new handrails on both sides, fixed firmly into the rock. With the aid of his walking stick, he was able to pull himself up with less effort than he'd anticipated.

All the same, it was a long climb. Ellie had fussed over him, saying that it was impossible he should go all the way up to Smugglers' Top, but he'd cordially ignored her suggestion that he take up Caro's offer of meeting at the veterinary centre in favour of meeting Caro on her own turf. There was no better way of getting the measure of someone.

'We're going to take a rest now…' They were halfway up, and the pup was beginning to tire. Lucas sat down on the stone steps, taking Phoenix onto his lap. After a couple of minutes the pain in his leg began to subside, and the top didn't seem quite so far away.

'Next time it'll be less trouble, eh?' Drew had fallen into the habit of thinking that his own recuperation ran approximately parallel to Phoenix's development. One day soon they'd both be able to walk for a day without having to take a rest.

But right now Phoenix couldn't climb any more. The puppy was curled up in his arms, shielded from the wind, and looked to be snoozing. Protecting her made him feel strong again. Drew opened the canvas bag, pulling out the baby carrier he'd brought with him and fixing the straps under his coat. It was perfect for carrying a tired puppy when you needed both hands to support yourself, and he felt Phoenix snuggle gratefully against his chest.

Another rest seemed in order at the top of the steps, because pride dictated that Caro's first impression of him shouldn't be to find him collapsed on her doorstep. He took the opportunity to extricate Phoenix from the baby wrap, and she began to caper around at his feet. Smugglers' Top was much as he remembered it from playing here as a child. Trees were gnarled and bent in the wind, and hid a dilapidated stone house. But there was a newly laid path from the top of the steps and as he approached the house, he could see that was different too. The old boards that covered the doors and windows were gone now, in favour of a brightly painted door and triple glazing. The thick walls had been cleaned and there was a new slate roof. The place looked positively homely.

Oddly enough, there was a doorbell. Casual callers were unlikely in this isolated spot, and leaving the front door unlocked for an expected visitor seemed the more practical option. But when he lifted the latch and pushed the door with his finger it didn't move, so he rang the bell.

He was starting to wonder whether the bell was actually working and thinking about trying it again when the door flew open. The words *mad scientist* flew at him like a missile.

Caro Barnes was a head shorter than him. Blonde hair, some of which was caught up in a messy plait, with the rest pushed behind her ears. She was wearing a pair of sweatpants that had probably been red once but were now a washed-out dark pink, along with a T-shirt and a large green cardigan that dwarfed her small frame.

'Ah! Sorry! You're…um…' She pressed her lips together, looking up at him.

'Drew Trevelyan. Maybe I'm a little early…?' Drew looked at his watch. He was actually five minutes later than the time they'd arranged.

'Um… No. Probably not. I was working on something and I forgot the time…' She shrugged helplessly, as if that was something that happened a lot. 'Come in.'

She stood back from the doorway, watching uncertainly as Phoenix nosed her way inside. When she went to sniff Caro's fleecy slippers, Caro stepped back suddenly.

'This is nice. A bit different from the way I remember it.' Drew decided that introducing her to Phoenix could wait as Caro obviously wasn't used to being around dogs.

'You know this place?' Caro frowned suddenly. 'I suppose you must do, since you live around here.'

'Yes, I used to play up here when I was a boy. This house was deserted and very ramshackle then.'

'You've always lived here, then?' Caro was looking at him as if he came from another planet. Which wasn't an entirely unpleasant sensation, as her eyes were wide and brown, the colour of dark honey. Knowing and beautiful, all at the same time.

That was entirely irrelevant. Imagining how her hair might shine if she gave it a brush was also irrelevant. He was here to appreciate Caro's intellect.

'Yes, I'm a Cornishman, born and bred.' That was a matter of some pride to Drew. 'I grew up in Dolphin Cove.'

'That sounds nice, growing up somewhere.' Caro frowned, as if the sentence didn't entirely cover all of her intended implications. 'I mean… I grew up, of course. In quite a lot of places.'

'That sounds nice too.' The sudden urge to make her feel at ease gripped Drew. 'Lucas tells me you were working in California before you came here?'

'Yes.' Caro didn't seem to want to elaborate on that. 'I'll get you some coffee and…um…freshen up if you don't mind. I'll only be five minutes.'

It occurred to Drew that Caro had probably been up all night, working on something, and he suppressed the urge to tell her that whatever it was could probably have been done just as well after a good night's sleep. How she chose to organise her life was none of his concern.

'Take your time. I can make the coffee if you show me the way to the kitchen.'

'No. That's all right.' Caro's glance flipped to his walking stick. 'You should probably sit down. I actually really wish you would, it'll make me feel a bit better for bringing you all the way up here and then answering the door in my pyjamas.'

Somehow, the invitation to sit didn't carry with it the tang of frustration and humiliation that it usually did. Standing next to Caro made him feel strong and steady, in a way he hadn't felt for a long time now. And she was charming, in an odd kind of way. Nakedly honest, although he really shouldn't include the word *naked* in any sentence that referred to her. The green cardigan seemed to be inviting him to imagine the figure it so effectively hid.

She waved him towards a pair of sofas that stood next to the hearth, at one side of the open-plan living area. Drew sank down onto the cushions, trying not to heave a sigh of relief and keeping Phoenix on her lead so that she didn't wander off and get under Caro's feet. The pup sprawled out on the hearth rug, her gaze following Caro as she skittered nervously into the kitchen area.

The conversion had been nicely done. The ceiling beams were new, but the oak would mellow with time. The large space was divided into two by a breakfast bar, and the pale colours in the kitchen and on the walls of the sitting area made everything seem spacious and clean. Wooden floors and the pale, natural tones of the furnishing fabrics added a touch of warmth.

And the house looked entirely unlived-in. Nothing was

out of place, not even the cushions on the sofa. It was as if Caro had been parachuted in here to add a little delicious mess to her magazine-cover surroundings.

She was banging the doors of the kitchen cupboards, obviously looking for something while the coffee brewed. Drew watched as she stood on her toes, reaching to the back of one of the units and bringing out a packet of chocolate biscuits.

'Would…um…he like some biscuits?' She pointed towards Phoenix, who returned her gaze steadily.

'She. Her name's Phoenix. She shouldn't have chocolate.'

Caro frowned, tipping half a dozen biscuits onto a plate and then adding a few more for good measure. 'What does she eat, then?'

'She loves cheese, if you have any.' Phoenix's ears began to twitch at the mention of the word, and Drew wondered whether he should have spelled it out.

'Oh! Really? I've got cheese…' Caro fetched two large blocks of cheese from the fridge, and Phoenix jumped to her feet. 'Which does she prefer? Extra mature, or mild and creamy?'

Phoenix wasn't a connoisseur, she just liked cheese. 'Mild and creamy will be fine.' Caro unwrapped the package, hovering her knife somewhere in the middle of the block. 'Not that much. Just a few small squares.'

Caro shrugged, cutting some squares of cheese and putting them onto a saucer. 'What made you call her Phoenix?'

Drew resisted the temptation to say that not everything had a meaning attached to it. In Caro's world, he suspected it did. 'I guess…she's helping me rise from the ashes.'

'Nice thought. Rising from the ashes is always good.'

Drew wasn't entirely sure what she meant by that, but Caro didn't seem to think that the comment required any further explanation. She poured two cups of coffee, taking a quick swig from hers before balancing the biscuits and cheese on top of the mugs to carry them over. As she set everything down on the coffee table, Phoenix decided to stake her claim and came to nuzzle at her hand.

Caro pulled her arm back quickly. If she was going to be studying animals, and her work in making prosthetics made that inevitable, she was going to have to get over her nervousness.

'She won't hurt you.' Drew smiled, picking up one of the squares of cheese. 'Why don't you give it to her?'

Caro shot him a querying look, and he flattened his hand, perching the cheese on top of his fingers to demonstrate. She nodded, sitting down cross-legged on the hearth rug and holding her hand out. Phoenix was keeping her eye fixed on the cube of cheese and her head arced round as he placed it on Caro's fingers.

'Oh!' Phoenix wolfed down the treat, and started to lick Caro's hand, on the off chance she'd left anything behind. 'I thought her tongue would be raspy, like a cat's...'

Drew couldn't remember the first time a dog had licked his hand. And he couldn't imagine a childhood that wasn't surrounded by all kinds of animals.

'You haven't been around dogs much?'

Caro pressed her lips together, as if slightly embarrassed by the question. 'No, not much.'

'But you're spending a fair bit of time and energy making animal prosthetics.'

'Yes. I always wanted a dog when I was little, but I couldn't have one because my parents moved around so much.' She gave a little smile. 'So I made my own. I built my first robot dog when I was ten. It couldn't do much, and one of its legs kept falling off, but I really loved it.'

'But you couldn't feed it treats.' Drew put another square of cheese onto her hand. Almost as soon as he'd done so, Phoenix ate it, and then climbed onto Caro's lap.

'No. I could probably make one now that responds to treats. She smells them, I suppose…' Caro's mind was obviously exploring the possibilities, and she started to examine Phoenix carefully, parting her coat with her fingers. 'She's so soft…'

'She still has her puppy coat. In a couple of months she'll start to shed that, and she'll grow a double layer coat. The top layer is waterproof with a warm underlayer.'

'Hmm. I'd like to see that.' Phoenix had mistaken scientific enquiry for love and was nuzzling at Caro's chin. Perhaps Drew was the one who was mistaken, and love and science weren't so different for Caro.

'You probably wouldn't like vacuuming up all the dog hairs. They get everywhere.'

'Oh, that's all right, I have a tortoise… Tony does my vacuuming for me.'

Drew decided not to ask. Caro's attention was all on Phoenix, and she was stroking her carefully. There was the kind of magic about it that brought a lump to his throat.

'I've…um, I've got to move.' Caro looked up at him questioningly.

'That's all right. Just push her off your lap, she'll get the idea.'

Caro gently pressed her fingers against Phoenix, and the pup ignored her completely. Drew grinned. 'You need to be a bit firmer with her… Phoenix, come here.'

Phoenix took no notice of him, clearly reckoning that Caro was far more interesting. He held out another square of cheese, and Phoenix scrambled off Caro's lap to reach him.

Caro got to her feet. 'I won't be long...' She swiped two of the biscuits from the plate, putting them into the pocket of her green cardigan. Then she picked up another, taking a bite from it as she walked towards a door that led from the open-plan living area to the other side of the house.

Phoenix was eyeing him with that *I-haven't-eaten-in-months* look, and he put the saucer containing the last cube of cheese on the floor. She wolfed it down and started to lick the saucer. Drew took a gulp of coffee, almost choking it was so strong. If this, and her obvious requirement for calories, was anything to go by, Caro definitely *had* been up all night.

Not his business. Not even close to being within his remit as a professional consultant. And however entrancing Caro contrived to be, or rather didn't contrive to be because it was quite obvious that she had no idea just how fascinating she was, *professional* was the word that should cover every aspect of their relationship. He'd made his mind up about that.

He had good reason. Drew had loved Luna with all his heart. He'd only hesitated in proposing to her because his own parents' marriage would give anyone pause for thought. But when Luna's shining optimism, her enthusiasm for the here and now had led her to propose to him, Drew hadn't hesitated to accept.

He'd grieved for her when she'd died. Had gone through all of the stages, starting with disbelief then pain and guilt. He'd blamed himself for not being able to persuade Luna to work a little less and blamed her for diving when she'd been tired from travelling and should have waited a day.

Finally, he'd come to accept it. Luna had been very different from him, she'd travelled the world with a team of conservationists, seeking out catastrophes, while Drew had concentrated his efforts on long-term projects here in Cornwall. They'd both worked hard, but Luna would push herself beyond her limits, never satisfied with what she'd already achieved.

Love wasn't enough. Living together for more than six weeks at a time was the real test, and Luna and Drew had never done that. Their relationship had been a succession of promises to miss each other every night that Luna was away, followed by joyful reunions.

He stretched his limbs, rubbing his face. It was all in the past now, and Drew's relationship with Luna had been more like his parents' than he'd thought. They had been different too and had argued their way through twenty-three years of marriage, until they'd finally come to the conclusion that they liked each other far better now that they were divorced.

Caro was obviously just as blinded by her work as Luna had been. She was enchanting, beautiful and they were like chalk and cheese. He should remember that the next time he felt the impulse to reach out and touch her.

When Caro reappeared, he hung onto that thought as tightly as he'd gripped his walking stick on the way up here. Her cheeks were pink from the shower, and her hair *was* shining, all of it caught back in a newly-braided plait. She wore jeans and a fresh T-shirt under the same green cardigan and was holding two sheets of paper as if they were about to burn her.

'I've…um…got something for you to sign. There are two copies, one for you and one for me. It's just a… I showed it to Lucas and he was happy with it.' She put the paper down on the coffee table and fished a pen from her pocket.

If Lucas was happy with it, that was enough for Drew. He reached for the pen and Caro started, a look of panic on her face. 'You should read it first!'

Fair enough. Drew focussed on the words on the page, reading them through carefully.

'So, according to this, the work we do here is confidential.' That was as he'd expected, but the final clause was surprising. 'And any designs you produce will be available to others under a creative commons licence. I was assuming you'd hold the rights to your own designs.'

'I want them to be of use to as many people as possible. This agreement means that you can't assume any rights that would prevent me from doing that.'

The idea hadn't occurred to Drew, and he suspected it hadn't occurred to Lucas either. But Caro seemed unwilling to trust in that, and her plan to allow anyone to use her work free of charge was more than generous.

'You're sure you want to do that? Holding the patent would mean you'd make some money from your work.'

'I have an income from other patented work I've done. I don't need any more, and this is…a holiday.'

'A holiday?' Drew raised his eyebrows and Caro shrugged.

'It's what I love the most. And there's a beach down there, isn't there?'

Right. Drew would lay odds that Caro hadn't explored the beach or her tiny island home. He reminded himself that it wasn't his business what she chose to do on this so-called holiday, and that if she just wanted to work then that was entirely up to her. He couldn't deny the potential benefits to the veterinary community.

'Okay.' He picked up the pen. 'Can I sign now?'

'Yes. Please do.' She allowed herself a smile. 'Now that you know exactly what your responsibilities are.'

As far as Drew could see, his responsibilities extended to not meddling with Caro's generosity. He had no problem with that. He picked up the pen, signing both pieces of paper, and Caro snatched one up.

'Right, then. I'll show you where I am with everything... Ew!'

Drew followed Caro's gaze and saw that Phoenix had taken advantage of the fact that he wasn't looking and was pretending that the puddle she'd made was nothing to do with her. Luckily she'd chosen the tiles in front of the hearth...

'Oh. I'm sorry, I should have taken her outside. I'll clean up—do you have an old cloth and some disinfectant?' Drew got to his feet as quickly as he could manage.

'That's okay. Tony'll deal with it. Tony!'

Before Drew could ask, the sound of whirring caught his attention. Out of the corner of his eye he saw something shoot across the floor towards him, and he stepped aside to get out of its way. The small, tortoise-shaped machine stopped at Caro's feet, and a little head poked out from under the textured carapace.

'Tony. Liquid spill. Hearth.'

The little creature—because it was hard to see it just as a vacuum cleaner—responded immediately. Zipping over to the hearth, it seemed to be searching for the puddle, and when it sensed it another whirring sound indicated that it was dealing with it.

'That's…impressive.'

'He's just a prototype.' Caro was smiling fondly. 'I think I might make him move a little slower. As he's a tortoise.'

'And it responds to your commands.'

Caro nodded. 'And to my voice. Try calling him.'

It felt a little odd, but Drew called the vacuum cleaner's name. It ignored him completely, its mechanical mind set on sucking up the spill and then buffing the tiles of the hearth.

Phoenix was keeping her distance, crouched on the floor, clearly wondering what this was. But she overcame her mistrust quickly and padded up to Tony, her nose twitching. When she extended her paw, the whirring stopped, and the tortoise head moved back and forth, seeming to try to sense the source of the movement. Phoenix took that as an invitation to be friends and pawed at Tony's shell.

'Tony. Go to the kitchen.' Caro issued another command, and the tortoise pushed slowly past Phoenix. As soon as the puppy was out of range it gathered speed, shooting back towards the kitchen. Phoenix was caught up in the game, racing after it and trying to make friends again. Tony slowed down when Phoenix approached, moving gently from one side to the other as the puppy jumped around.

Drew chuckled. 'Outstanding. Does the vacuuming *and* plays with the dog.'

'Tony doesn't know what a dog is. He's got sensors that make him respond whenever something moves close by, it's a safety thing. Phoenix is just confusing him.' Caro called out another command. 'Tony. Sleep.'

The tortoise stilled, but Phoenix still wouldn't let it

alone. Drew called her, and she ignored him completely. She could take a few lessons in obedience from her new mechanical friend.

Caro seemed suddenly unaware of his existence too, watching Tony and Phoenix thoughtfully. It occurred to Drew that perhaps she was considering extending Tony's range to take in play, but at the moment Phoenix looked as if she was trying to tip the vacuum cleaner over. He walked across to the kitchen, shooing Phoenix away.

'Interesting…' Caro seemed to be making the observation to herself, and then her gaze found Drew. 'I'll think about that later. Come and see what I'm doing.'

She led him towards what seemed to be the back door of the house, but when she opened it, it revealed a bright, warm conservatory overlooking the sea and protected from the wind by triple glazing.

The magazine-cover neatness of the rest of the house suddenly made sense. *This* was Caro's home—the rest was just a collection of things that might come in useful from time to time. The large space had been cleared of furniture and boasted a row of benches, some at sitting height and others standing. The standing ones were piled up with various electrical and mechanical components, in various states of assembly. There were two large computer screens, piles of books and papers, and the small lobby that led out to a path that ran behind the house contained a large 3D printer. The overall impression was of a mad scientist's lair.

At the far end was a sofa, with cushions piled at one end and a throw tumbled at the other. If Caro *had* had any sleep last night, it had probably been right here.

'Sit.' She marched over to the sofa, quickly clearing the throw and spreading the cushions. Drew sat down, and Caro pulled up one of the office chairs. He caught a faint thrill of her scent as she leaned across to put a thick, spiral-bound booklet on the sofa beside him. *Initial Design Specification for Animal Prosthetics.*

'You can take it home to read. As long as you don't show it to anyone…'

'Of course not. I signed an agreement, remember?'

She nodded, obviously pleased that *he* remembered. Caro jumped to her feet, gathering up a selection of components from one of the workbenches and setting them out on the small table in front of him. Then she reached for a laptop, opening it and tapping on the keys.

'Before you start reading, I'd like to show you these…'

At first, it seemed like a jumble of concepts. Models of human and animal limbs, wire-frame computer rendering, and explanations that seemed to defy limitations that Drew had taken for granted. Then, slowly, he began to get it…

'You're saying that you want to make a prosthetic that can respond to the movements of an animal.' Drew hadn't seen anything like this even attempted before. 'It sounds almost impossible.'

'The possible is only something that's already been done.'

There was a light in her honey-brown eyes that made Drew shiver. Walking past the realms of the possible and making the impossible work seemed suddenly as if it was the only thing he wanted to do. And he wanted to do it very much with Caro.

CHAPTER THREE

WHAT WAS IT with vets? Ellie was gorgeous, in a way that Caro had never even hoped to be. Lucas was handsome, good at his job, and it didn't take him as long as most to get his head around extreme possibilities. She'd imagined that Drew would probably be a counterbalance to their dazzling attractiveness, since every extreme implied that another extreme should restore the sum of its parts to the average.

But Drew didn't do anything to confirm that theory. He wasn't merely handsome, or gorgeous, he was amazing. His voice was softened by a Cornish burr, and those blue eyes seemed to take in everything. Dark curls gave him a slightly windblown look even when he was inside, and he had a body to die for, even if it was a little stiff and battered at the moment. Even that was thrillingly attractive, and Caro wondered how he'd feel about playing the patient while she played the nurse.

That would lead to consequences. Inevitable ones that Caro wasn't prepared to face. Leaving America, and what had become the only home she'd ever really had, and coming back here had been her way of saying an irrevocable goodbye to matters of the heart. Her work was the only thing that mattered.

He was turning the prosthetic that Lucas had used at the clinic over in his hands, examining it carefully. He seemed to get it. The work that had gone into it, and where it could be improved. His obvious approval sent a throb of desire through her whole body.

'So…where do we start?' He looked up at her.

With the eyes. She could start by staring into his eyes. Or with his hands. So gentle in such a strong man…

'Work's already been done on how dogs and other animals move. I want to take those findings and add to them to give me an idea of how the natural movement of a dog might control a prosthetic.'

He nodded, frowning. Obviously applying his mind to the problem. Caro wondered if his mind was as beautiful as the rest of him.

'So the joint will have the ability to flex, in response to the animal's movements, rather than being rigid like this one.'

He got it. A warm swell of gratification filled Caro's chest, before she'd had a chance to remind herself that someone who appeared to *get it* had still been capable of betraying her.

'Yes, that's right.' Her voice sounded a little squeaky and she cleared her throat.

'And the first thing you need to do is capture the movements of real dogs and quantify that, using the software you showed me.' He nodded towards her laptop, and the camera that lay beside it on the table.

He *definitely* got it. Maybe Caro was hallucinating, and she'd find something wrong with this guy when she'd had a good night's sleep and something more to eat than just three chocolate biscuits.

'Yes. I'm hoping to film real dogs and then use the software to quantify their movements.'

Drew nodded. 'How do your robot dogs move? Can you show me?'

Oh, yes. She could show him.

'Clarice!' She called her robot, who she preferred to think of as a *proper* puppy, despite the presence of the wriggling reality at Drew's feet. Clarice was in sleep mode in the corner of the room and raised her head in response. 'Come here.'

Clarice trotted across the room. A lot of work had gone into that gait, but it wasn't quite the same as Phoenix's unpredictable movements. Caro stroked Clarice's head, and when she nuzzled against her legs Caro saw Drew's eyebrows shoot up.

'It responds to you?'

'*She* responds…'

'Sorry. Do that again, will you?'

Caro stroked Clarice's head again and this time she pawed at her legs. 'Her programming mimics real life. She learns, and she has a range of different reactions to any one action.'

'She learns?' Drew shook his head. 'How does she do that?'

'The same way we do. If she responds the way I want her to I reinforce it with my approval.' Caro bent down, stroking Clarice's head again. 'Clarice, well done.'

Maybe she'd gone too far. Moving around so much as a child had meant that Caro's only permanent companions had been her robots. She knew they weren't human, or even proper animals, but sometimes they felt a great deal more dependable. She expected that Drew would think the way most people did and consider that giving her love to a mess of circuitry and plastic was a character flaw. His derision would be harder to bear than usual and betraying her feelings for Clarice would be a mistake.

'It's fascinating. Challenging…' He held his hand out to Clarice and her head swivelled towards him. 'She's very cute.'

'She's *programmed* to be that way. I could equally easily programme her to snap and growl at you.'

He laughed. 'Then you programmed her well. Maybe that scrap of humanity I see in her is really yours.'

Was he for real? How did he understand that Caro felt that she'd put a little of her own personality into Clarice? She felt herself blush.

Perhaps working with someone who knew nothing about robotics wasn't going to be like wading through mud after all. Drew seemed to understand the bare bones of what she was trying to do.

'So our first challenge is to find dogs to film. I imagine that'll be where *I* come in.'

Caro had been thinking that it was more a matter of what challenges *she* would face. In the singular. The vets at the veterinary centre were just there to provide her with the things she needed. But she couldn't resist those eyes. Suddenly it didn't seem so bad to share some of the challenges with Drew.

A loud beep sounded, and he pulled his phone from his pocket.

'That's my alarm call. The tide's coming in.'

Oh. Up till now, the tide coming in had seemed like a good thing. Something that naturally cut a visit short and allowed Caro to get on with her work in peace.

'That's a shame. We were just getting to the interesting part…' She turned the corners of her mouth down.

The interesting part was actually Drew at the moment, and he had to go.

He looked at his phone speculatively, not meeting her gaze. 'It'll be going back out again this afternoon.'

That sounded like an opportunity that was there for the grabbing. 'Would you like to stay? I'm…um…getting a bit hungry…'

He grinned. 'When did you last eat? Something other than chocolate biscuits.'

Caro thought back. 'Yesterday.' Sometime yesterday, at least. Perhaps he'd jump to the conclusion that she'd had a hearty home-cooked meal yesterday evening.

'Okay.' Drew didn't seem to be jumping to any conclusions. 'I can go out and get us something before the tide comes in, and let you get on with what you're doing.'

'I have plenty of food in the fridge…' Lack of supplies wasn't the issue. Tearing herself away from her workshop to go and prepare a meal was sometimes tricky. 'Would you like some cheese on toast?'

'Sounds good, thank you. Why don't you let me do that? I could do with stretching my legs.'

He never mentioned being in pain, or finding it difficult to walk, but Caro had caught him wincing a few times when he'd thought she wasn't looking. If her little secret was the last time she'd eaten a proper meal, then his might be that he'd be pulling painkillers out of his pocket as soon as he was alone.

'If you don't mind. That would be really nice, thank you.'

'My pleasure.' Phoenix raised her head as he got to his feet, and he bent stiffly to stroke her head. 'Maybe you can persuade Phoenix to let you film her…'

Maybe. Caro picked up the camera, but as Drew

walked out of the room, it wasn't Phoenix that she started to film. It was him.

Cheese on toast apparently took a little longer than two minutes to half-melt the cheese under the grill, and when Drew called her out of her workshop, the cutlery laid out on the breakfast bar was an unequivocal hint that she wouldn't be eating at her desk. But it was actually worth it. The bread was crispy and there was ham underneath a golden layer of toasted cheese. And there was coffee as well, even if the way Drew made it didn't take much of the edge off her tiredness.

'She's not having cheese for lunch?' Phoenix had scampered through from the workshop with her at the sound of Drew's voice, and was currently demolishing the contents of a feeding bowl on the floor.

'No, cheese is a treat. She has a properly balanced formula, four times a day.'

'Right.' Caro eyed the fruit bowl that Drew had placed next to them. Apparently, he was aiming for a properly balanced formula for her as well. She'd be willing to bet that if given the chance he'd be an *eat-your-vegetables* freak.

Although the results of vegetable freakery bore thinking about. With the obvious exclusion of his leg, he looked outrageously outdoorsy, well rested and healthy. His strength might well be the kind to impress a girl indoors too.

'Have some more.' Drew was still on his first slice of ham and cheese, presumably chewing each mouthful the prescribed number of times. Caro hadn't been able to stop herself from wolfing her two slices down and wishing that there was more. Drew tipped his second slice onto her plate.

'No…um…that's okay. Aren't you hungry?'

'I had breakfast.' Somehow he managed to avoid making that sound like an accusation.

'In that case…' She picked up the slice. 'This is really good. I'm a bit tired, and I get hungry when I'm tired.'

He nodded. 'Yeah. Your body's looking for a quick uptick in energy. High-calorie foods will fool it into thinking it has that for a while.'

Okay. He was beginning to sound like her mother. Caro could ignore that for the time being, since he didn't look anything like anyone's mother. She wondered whether pheromones were fooling her body into thinking she wasn't tired as well.

'I get an idea and I run with it. That's the way it works.'

He nodded, picking up an orange from the fruit bowl. 'Want some?'

Peel me an orange. Not quite so obviously seductive as *Peel me a grape*, but it still allowed her to appreciate the delicate precision of his strong hands.

'Yes. Thanks.'

He deftly stripped the peel from the orange segments, putting more than half on her plate. Was there *anything* that Drew Trevelyan did that didn't bear a closer look?

'You broke your femur. Along with your patella?' She could see through all the things he didn't say, just as clearly as he seemed to see through her.

Drew stared at her, suddenly tense. 'What?'

'I caught you on film. I was going to try filming Phoenix's movements while you made lunch.' Suddenly this felt like an intrusion rather than a reply to his fixation with her diet and how much she slept. Maybe she should have asked first.

'And you got that just from my gait? That software's pretty good, then.'

'It doesn't catch everything. But, yeah, it's pretty good at picking up deviations from the norm.' She shouldn't have done this. 'Sorry. Sometimes I forget that everything isn't an exercise in logistics.'

'Yeah. This is a lot more personal.' He shot her a warning look.

'Like wanting to know when I last slept?'

For a moment she thought he was going to take offence. Then suddenly he laughed. It was a nice laugh that emphasised a *with* instead of an *at*, and Caro couldn't help smiling.

'Touché. It's just like that. And I *am* impressed with the logistics, I think they could be very useful.' He reached for the jug of coffee and refreshed both of their mugs. 'I was in a car accident.'

'Lucas told me. He didn't say that you had trouble walking, I would have come down to the veterinary centre for this meeting.'

Drew shook his head. 'Then I would have missed the delights of your workshop.'

It sounded like a compliment, and Caro decided to take it as one. 'Thanks. I like it too. A bit too much sometimes...'

He nodded, as if he'd already come to that conclusion himself. Caro wanted very badly to know what had happened to him but didn't dare ask.

'The brakes on my car failed. I was on a coast road, and I managed to avoid plunging off a cliff and ended up in a headlong collision with a tree.'

Caro took a gulp of her coffee. She was too tired to filter her reactions through the fine mesh of what was appropriate, but maybe that wasn't such a bad thing. 'It sounds horrible.'

'Yes, it was.' His hand shook a little, and he glared at it as if it had betrayed him. 'I broke my femur, and my patella's been partially replaced.'

'It must hurt you still.'

'Yes, it does. You're very direct.' Drew smiled suddenly, as if that wasn't a problem.

'Sorry. I don't mean to pry.'

He shrugged. 'That's okay. I sometimes wish that everyone would be a bit less tactful.'

So she didn't have any tact? If that was true, she'd have already made many more personal enquiries about his body, somewhere along the lines of whether it was actually as beautiful as it seemed.

'If we're going to be having business meetings, then it would be easier if you told me what you can and can't manage. Then I wouldn't have to guess.'

He seemed to like that approach. Drew reached across to the canvas bag he'd brought with him and took a blister pack from one of the small pockets at the front.

'I have prescription painkillers, but I'm scaling them down. I only take them when I need them.'

'Like now?' The blister pack had two tablets missing.

'Yeah. I'm still struggling a little with climbing steps.'

'You might have said. We could have made other arrangements…' Caro wrapped her thick cardigan around her, as if the warmth might be of some comfort to the guilty feeling of letting Drew come all the way up here.

'I'm a little tired of being the one that everyone else has to make their arrangements around.' There was a trace of annoyance in his voice.

'Okay, so if I promise not to mention sitting down or

taking things easy, will you promise to mention if things really are getting too much for you?'

Drew smiled suddenly. 'That sounds like an excellent work arrangement.'

Did he think that was all it was? Caro suspected that Drew was made for play as well as work, but she'd already experimented with mixing work and pleasure, and the results had been conclusive. Big, bad mistake.

But she was really too tired to think about it. Her back and legs were aching from fatigue and she wanted to sit down on the sofa. Walking across the room seemed like a gargantuan effort, but it would be worth it just to sink into the cushions for a few minutes...

Someone was calling her name. Caro was wide awake before she even realised she'd been asleep, sitting up before she'd known that she was lying down on the sofa. Maybe he hadn't noticed that she'd dropped off. Caro hoped she hadn't given the game away by snoring.

Only... The throw from her workshop was spread over her legs. Her slippers were lined up neatly on the floor. And she was sure that she felt a pillow crease on her cheek. She decided to brazen it out.

'So...what do you think?' That was always a good holding question. People were always happy to expound for ages on what they thought and it was a good opportunity to catch up if her mind had wandered.

Drew grinned. 'I think your ideas are great. I've just been reading about them.' He indicated her design specification, which lay open on the coffee table. He either read at the speed of lightning, or her eyes had been closed for more than five minutes.

Caro puffed out a breath, bowing to the inevitable.

'I've been asleep, haven't I?' She craned around so that she could see the kitchen clock, focussing blearily on it. *Three o'clock?*

He nodded, getting to his feet. Clearly he'd been resting too, because his movements were more fluid than they had been.

'I'm so sorry…'

Drew shrugged, as if it was just one of those things. 'You were very tired. I would have let you sleep longer, but the tide's on its way out again, and I should be making a move soon.'

'Okay. Give me two minutes, and I'll walk down with you.' Maybe she could carry his bag or something. Anything to make the journey back a little easier for Drew than the one here had been.

'I can manage. And I can't believe I'm the one saying this but stay down for the rest of the day.' There was a look of quiet humour in his eyes, and Drew was clearly appreciating the irony.

'People tell you to stay down quite a lot, do they?'

'All the time. I thought I'd try it out on you to see if you like it any better than I do.'

'Actually… I don't mind it.' Being looked after like this was a novel experience.

'I'll give you the full treatment, then.' His lips curved into a delicious smile. If she'd been greeted by that when she's woken up, goodness only knew what might have happened, and Caro thanked her lucky stars that he'd saved it until now.

Phoenix had wandered over, it obviously having occurred to her that something might be happening without her. Caro swung her legs off the sofa, and Drew arranged the throw across them carefully, lifting the puppy up and putting her onto Caro's lap.

'Uh…what am I supposed to do now?' Caro was beginning to wonder exactly what *the full treatment* would entail.

'Same as you do with Clarice…' He shot the words over his shoulder as he walked towards the kitchen.

Presumably that didn't mean tinkering with Phoenix's programming. Caro stroked the little dog, and she started to lick her hand. 'She's not going to bite me, is she?'

'She might give it a go, but it'll only be in play. Don't bite her back.' He grinned, opening the fridge door.

That was all very unpredictable. As was the way that Phoenix snuggled into her lap, looking up at Caro as if she was at the very centre of her world. But it was nice to have someone there who could make her feel that nothing was so urgent that it couldn't wait a little while.

She stroked Phoenix while Drew clattered around in the kitchen, looking up when he walked towards her, carrying two mugs. 'What's this?'

'It's the next stage. Random drinks.' He put the mugs down on the coffee table.

'Hot soup. That's nice.' Caro had rather been hoping for coffee, strong enough to jolt her out of this feeling of delicious laziness.

'Yeah. Nourishing and unlikely to keep you awake.' He lowered himself onto the sofa next to her. 'Now. Afternoon TV. I'm quite an aficionado.'

He reached for the remote, turning on the television that was mounted on the wall in the corner of the room. 'What do you fancy? Home improvements?'

Caro shook her head. You needed to *have* a home in

order to improve it. He flipped through the channels, listing the options.

'Or you can have a whodunit... Sherlock Holmes?'

'I don't mind that.'

Drew grinned. 'Perfect. You don't want anything that you like too much in case it encourages you to think.'

'You're enjoying this a bit too much, Drew.'

He chuckled, leaning back against the cushions. 'You have to admit that I'm very good at it, though.'

Yeah. Something told Caro that Drew was good at everything he did. Even the process of letting an afternoon slip by, without having done anything constructive. He'd probably had a little too much of that recently.

She leaned forward to pick up her mug, and Phoenix escaped her lap in favour of Drew's. 'Okay. So when we've done with the hot drinks and the afternoon TV...?'

'I'll go home. You can watch some more TV and then get some sleep.'

'That sounds thrilling. And what about the project?'

'I've got a proposition for you.'

'Sounds exciting.' Damn! That had just slipped out. The proposition was almost certainly work related...

'Wait till you hear it.' Drew took a moment to reach for his own mug and take a sip from it, and Caro wondered if he was trying for a Master of Suspense effect, or if the soup and the TV were having an effect on him also.

'Write a couple of introductory paragraphs about your project. You can be as vague as you like, there's no need to give away anything you don't want anyone to know. I'll append that to an email asking some of our dog owners if they'd like to participate in the initial study.'

'Okay, thanks. I'll do that...' Caro pulled the throw away from her legs. She could apply her mind to that simple task while Sherlock Holmes tackled the more difficult question of tracking down a criminal mastermind.

She felt Drew's hand on her shoulder, and Phoenix scrambled out of the way as he leaned across to arrange the throw across her legs again. 'Tomorrow's soon enough. Are you going to stay put?'

Who in their right mind would want to move now? When he was so close and the bulk of his body, along with the tenderness of his hands, were so very apparent.

'If you insist.'

He smiled. Before Caro could wonder whether his lips were as soft as they looked, he'd moved away.

'Of course I insist. Are you doing anything tomorrow? If you want, we can meet up at the clinic and send out the email. Maybe you could set up your testing equipment and show me what's involved.'

'You're going to help me, then?' Caro hadn't wanted to take his participation for granted.

'Yeah, of course I am. It's an exciting project. I want to see where it goes.'

'Thanks. What time shall I come?'

'Any time after eight?'

'Okay. Eight's fine. I'll be there.'

'Great.' He drained his own mug and picked up hers. It was probably better not to tell him she'd deal with the mugs, and she watched the TV while Drew added them to the rest of the things in the dishwasher and set it running.

'I'll see you tomorrow, then.' He seemed positively breezy now. Moving more easily, even taking a few short steps without his stick. Obviously an afternoon spent sitting down and reading, while she'd slept, had satisfied both his restless mind and his need for physical rest.

'Yeah, okay. You're sure you'll be all right down the steps?'

'Positive.' He called Phoenix and she leapt off the sofa and went careening towards him. He clipped her lead onto her collar and put his coat on, shouldering his canvas bag. 'Watch the TV. And don't sleep in your clothes tonight…'

Caro shot him a look, calculated to imply that sleeping in her clothes was the last thing she'd ever consider doing. Drew chuckled, opening the front door and waiting for Phoenix to follow him through it. Then he was gone.

Now she could stop this game and get on with something. Caro couldn't quite think for the moment exactly what. Maybe she'd just watch through to the end of the film…

Beneath all the playfulness, Drew was obviously frustrated and bored. He still needed some downtime to recuperate from his injuries, but his restless mind also needed stimulation, and quite by accident she'd managed to contrive both today.

Allowing him to look after her had just been a joke, but… It had obviously fed a deeper need for Drew. Maybe a deeper need for her too. No one had ever looked after her like this.

Not even Blake Harmer. He had been the handsome lecturer and she the budding inventor. Ten years older than her, and touched by the California sun, she'd felt pale and unworldly next to him, but somehow he'd chosen her. She'd fallen in love harder and faster than she'd realised was possible, and when he'd asked her to move in with him Caro had finally found the home that her parents' itinerant lifestyle had never given her.

She'd ignored the voices that had whispered behind their backs, saying she was the more talented of the two. They hadn't understood.

But then it had become obvious that it was Caro who didn't understand. The water feature in their garden had been leaking, and she'd fixed it by making a self-cleaning valve. By the time she'd realised the potential for its use in developing countries, Blake had patented it as his own.

She'd hoped it was all a mistake, but had then found out that the companies Blake had been negotiating with wouldn't waive their exclusive rights to the new valve for charitable and non-profit agencies. They'd argued, and she'd seen the glint of avarice in his eyes.

'Suck it up, Caro. You can play with your robots and your wild dreams all you like, someone has to deal with the money side of things. Since you don't seem capable of doing that, you should leave it to me...'

When the news had got out that Blake had lucrative offers for the rights to the valve, and was leaving his teaching post, the whispers had begun again. What had he seen in Caro anyway? Had it only been the chance to make money from her inventions? This time Caro believed them. Blake hadn't ever wanted her for herself, just what she could do for him.

She'd run. Put her legal claim against Blake into the hands of an attorney and fled back to England. *This* time her designs would be used for the purpose that she intended. *This* time her heart wouldn't break.

Now she saw things more clearly. Someone like Drew could never find her attractive. He might want to work with her. He might even like her a little. He'd even attempted to address the cost of making her wild dreams work, in effort and time, which was something that Blake had never done. But she shouldn't get carried away and think that there was anything more to it than just an attempt to be nice.

Caro shifted on the sofa, curling up under the throw. She was warm and comfortable, and felt more relaxed than she had in a long time. She could accept that one small favour from Drew, even if she could take nothing else.

CHAPTER FOUR

DREW HADN'T BEEN able to stop thinking about Caro. She was obstinate, entrancing, and he'd never met anyone like her before. Maybe that was it. He'd just never met anyone like her, and she fascinated him.

Fascination wasn't the way to go. Interest would be sufficient. An evening spent thinking about Caro had only confirmed his first impressions. She was talented and beautiful, any man's dream. But she was also a workaholic, and that meant that she couldn't be *his* dream.

But his eagerness to see Caro again had peeled him out of bed early and taken him to the veterinary clinic almost before he'd had a chance to think about how his leg was feeling today. He sat in his office, drafting the email that invited the clinic's dog owners to participate in Caro's study.

His phone rang, and Tegan's voice sounded on the other end of the line. *'Drew...!'*

'Yep...' He wasn't sure who else Tegan might think it was, but since he'd been back, their receptionist had been enunciating his name with an excited emphasis every time he completed the simple task of answering his phone.

'You have a visitor. Ms Barnes is here to see you.'

Tegan made that sound fabulous and exciting too, and Drew resisted the temptation to agree with her.

'Great, thanks, Tegan. I'll be right out.' He hung up before Tegan could volunteer to bring Caro through to his office.

He was halfway along the corridor that led to the reception area when he saw Caro burst through the swing doors at the far end, wheeling an equipment case. Drew was so surprised that he forgot to keep walking...

Her hair shone in the overhead lights, caught back in a complicated plait that seemed to owe something to nature and something else to design. She wore a pair of slim, dark trousers with a red jacket, and the material of her cream blouse looked as if it might be silky to the touch. Caro was immaculate. And...it was so blatantly obvious that he couldn't ignore it...beautiful.

'Good morning.' She stopped in front of him, and he realised that her honey-brown eyes were yet another thing he should have noticed. All part of her softness.

'You made it...' Drew felt suddenly tongue-tied.

'Looks like it.' She gave him a bewitching smile, leaning confidingly towards him, and Drew felt the back of his neck tingle in response to her scent. 'It was the evil stepfather.'

'What...?' Maybe this was one of those confusing non sequiturs that dreams threw up from time to time.

'Sherlock Holmes deduced the answer, though.'

'Oh! That. I was wondering if you'd go straight back to work after I left.'

'No, I stayed on the sofa all afternoon. Did Phoenix make it home all right?'

The mischief in her eyes told him that she was really

asking about him. Her concern didn't feel diminishing, though, as if he couldn't manage on his own.

'Yeah. We both rested up yesterday evening.'

He turned, the sound of Caro's dry laughter echoing in his ears. He could get used to that. Making her laugh a little more and work a little less...

Although today was all about work. Obviously. Why else would they be spending time together?

He led the way to his office, and she parked her case in the corner and sat down. Drew printed out his email and handed it to her, and she read it through, nodding her approval.

'Here's mine.' She pulled a memory stick from her handbag, and Drew plugged it into his laptop.

'It's too long.'

'You haven't even read it yet!' Caro frowned at him, folding her arms in a clear signal that he'd better do so, and that she'd wait while he did. Under her delicious scrutiny, Drew focussed his eyes on the screen.

'This is all interesting.' And his original comment still stood. 'But it's too long. People don't need to wade through all of the reasons that the project's interesting, they just need to know what we're asking of them and the positive good that their participation will do.'

She rolled her eyes. 'You're not one of these people that likes to oversimplify everything, are you?'

Drew pursed his lips. Caro's idea of simple wasn't the same as most other people's. 'I don't fully understand the second paragraph, and I've read your initial specification.'

She frowned, walking around his desk to peer over his shoulder at the screen. As she leaned across, seemingly unaware that her arm was touching his shoulder, he felt the hairs on his forearm raise in response.

'Okay, delete para two. And the third para rather relies on the concepts explained in the second, so you'd better get rid of that as well...'

It didn't take long to distil the description down, but by the time she returned to her seat, Drew's head was spinning. So much for keeping things professional. Maybe if he concentrated on looking and sounding professional, then his instincts would get the idea and follow suit.

'I'll send this through to Tegan, then? She has the mailing list and she'll send the emails out.'

'That's great, thank you.' There was a hint of excitement in Caro's tone. It was the beginning of a new challenge, and suddenly it all seemed new and exciting to Drew, too.

He led her through to his consulting room, showing her where she could set up her camera and the force plates that would measure the animal's gait and the force generated by each foot strike. Caro looked around the room thoughtfully.

'I want to quantify climbing movements as well...'

'We have a set of steps that will help with that. Lucas is going to bring them from the storeroom when he's finished his morning surgery.' Drew's phone rang and he answered it.

He knew that Caspian Smythe-Bingham always kept his phone handy to respond to emails and social media, but he hadn't expected him to be this quick. Or this positive. Drew smiled, asking him to hold on for a moment.

'We have our first participant. Caspian can bring his Pekingese in any time this week. When are you free?'

'Tomorrow!' Caro's enthusiasm sent a tingle racing

down Drew's spine. 'Or any time this week. Whenever suits you.'

Drew smiled, speaking into the phone. 'How would tomorrow at ten suit you, Caspian?'

The date was set, and Caro was finding it difficult to conceal her excitement.

'So we're ready to start. I'll have to calibrate my equipment, I don't suppose you have a dog with nothing to do right now, do you?' She made it sound like a wonderful adventure that was just waiting for them to plunge in.

'I'll ask Ellie if we can borrow her Labrador for a few hours.' He laughed at Caro's sudden expression of dismay. 'Esmerelda is Phoenix's mother. And she's very placid, she won't eat you.'

'I'll take your word for it.' Caro was obviously willing to negotiate any danger to push her project forward. She unbuttoned the sleeves of her blouse, rolling them up. The perfect, pristine version of Caro was beginning to give way to the mussed-up work version, and Drew wondered which he liked the most.

Both. He liked them both.

Caro had always been of the opinion that you didn't actually have to *like* anyone or anything in order to invent something. Sure, you had to know a bit, so that the work was appropriate and solved a problem. But treating every dog that came into the surgery as if it were a long-lost uncle or auntie wasn't necessary.

She supposed it was necessary for Drew. He must like animals, otherwise he wouldn't have become a vet. They had ten people on the list to be seen today, and Drew's manner with each of the dogs calmed them so that it was easier to put them through the various exercises that

Caro had devised. There was a different side of Drew to see each time. Man and dog. Handsome man and puppy. Smiling, disastrously attractive man, taming a trouble-some Pekingese. And so it went…

'Peter…' He smiled broadly at the young lad who entered the consulting room with his mother and a brown and white puppy. 'Thank you for bringing Rolf along…'

'How are you, Drew?' Peter's mother asked the inevitable question. Everyone seemed to know Drew, and they were all concerned about him.

'I'm good, thanks, Laura.' Drew's smile didn't betray the fact that this had already been asked and answered more times than Caro cared to count this morning. 'Very happy to be back at work. How's Brian? I haven't seen him in a while.'

'Oh, fine. Pretty busy at work. Everyone's car seems to have something wrong with it at the moment…' Laura's hand flew to her mouth. 'Sorry…'

Drew grinned, shrugging off the gaffe, and bent down towards Rolf. The pup nuzzled at his outstretched hand, seeing only a new friend.

'This is Caro. You've seen the information about her research? Do you have any questions?' Drew introduced her in much the same way he'd done before, and Caro smiled at Laura.

'We'll leave the details to you, Drew. We're happy just to participate.' Laura smiled back, eying the camera and the force plates. It had already occurred to Caro that most of the people they'd seen this morning were here because they liked and trusted Drew.

'Do you want to film us?' Peter looked up enquiringly at Caro, and she was about to show him how the tread-mill worked when Drew broke in.

'Yes, that would be great. Perhaps we could just walk Rolf up and down over there for starters.' Drew pointed to a space to one side of the area that had been set aside for filming.

Caro flashed him a questioning look and Drew gave a small nod. If that was the way he wanted things...

They'd said that they would be filming, and Caro supposed she'd better do so, even if this wasn't one of the exercises that all of the other dogs had done. She disengaged the camera from the treadmill, switching it on as Peter walked Rolf up and down. Drew was concentrating hard on the puppy, and Caro thought she saw concern on his face.

There was something he wasn't saying. Peter had obviously already given his heart to his puppy, and the thought that there might be something wrong with him tore at Caro. Drew seemed intent on watching the way that the puppy moved, and she asked Peter to walk him up and down a few times more.

'Okay, that's good.' Drew shot her a smile. Please... *please*...let that be a good sign. Maybe he'd decided he was mistaken in whatever he thought he'd seen. But when he gently lifted the puppy up onto the examination table, Caro saw an extra tenderness in the way Drew gently stroked him and knew that everything *wasn't* all right.

'I think we should take an X-ray, Laura.' Drew spoke quietly, and Laura nodded. She'd seen the way that Drew had carefully examined the puppy's back, legs and hips.

But Peter hadn't and Caro could practically see the questions forming in the boy's eyes. If she couldn't help with the puppy, this was something she could help with.

'Hey, Peter, I'd like to give you a little thank-you for helping with my research.' She reached into her bag and the boy's head turned, his attention drawn away from what Drew was doing.

She'd used the 3D printer to make a few small carapaces, equipped them with sensors and circuitry, and put them into her bag. As she drew the model of the tiny tortoise out of her bag, Peter's eyes widened, in just the way she'd hoped.

'What is it?'

'There's a little switch underneath, just push that...' When Peter pressed his fingers on the spot she'd indicated, the tortoise's legs started to work. 'Now put him down onto the floor.'

Peter started to cackle with glee as the tiny tortoise began to scurry across the floor. When Caro put her foot in its path, he caught his breath as the tortoise swerved out of the way, avoiding the obstacle and making its way towards Drew.

He reached for his stick, planting the end in front of the tortoise until it had turned full circle to make its way back towards Peter. The boy caught it up, turning it over in his hands.

'Can it see me?' Peter was staring intently at the tiny head.

Caro was about to explain that the tortoise couldn't actually *see* anything, and that the sensors simply registered any obstacle that was placed in its path. But Drew had a different answer.

'I think he's taking a look at you right now.'

That satisfied Peter. He put the tortoise back down onto the floor, running to place his foot in its path, and beaming when it swerved out of the way.

There was something in Drew's eyes. He knew that she was trying to divert Peter's attention. 'Why don't you and Caro go and show it to Tegan, while your mum and I finish off the research with Rolf?'

'That's a wonderful idea.' Laura beamed suddenly. 'Thank you so much, Caro.'

'We'll bring one along for Tegan, shall we?' Caro reached into her bag, taking out two more of the tortoises. Putting them on a tabletop, and watching them avoid the edges of the table and each other would keep Peter occupied while Drew did whatever it was he needed to do for Rolf.

The plan worked. Peter followed Caro out into the reception area, and Tegan let out a little scream of excitement when he showed her the tortoise. When Caro handed her one, she planted a red lipstick kiss on its carapace, and walked over to the coffee table, clearing it of magazines.

'Tortoise wars, eh, Peter?' Tegan knelt down on the floor at one end of the table and motioned for Peter to sit at the other end. The phone rang, and Tegan ignored it completely in favour of watching the two tortoises swerve to avoid each other, so Caro leaned over the reception desk to answer it.

'Oh… Um… Hang on a moment, please…' She saw Lucas, looking around for his next patient, and beckoned him over. 'Someone would like an appointment…'

'Okay, thanks.' Lucas took the phone, tapping on Tegan's computer to make the appointment, and then bidding the caller a cheery goodbye. Then he turned to Caro, frowning, as Tegan shrieked with laughter.

'What's going on?'

'Don't disturb them. Drew's taken Peter's puppy to be X-rayed and… I think there's something wrong with it.' Caro shrugged miserably. 'I don't know what, but he seemed pretty keen on keeping Peter occupied with something else.'

Understanding dawned in Lucas's eyes. 'I see. I'll stay and answer the phone, then. My next patient isn't here yet.'

'That's okay, I can do that. I'll take messages and Tegan can phone everyone back.' Caro slipped behind the reception desk, sitting down and taking the last tortoise from her pocket. Wordlessly she handed it to Lucas.

He found the switch and grinned when the little legs began to move. 'That's very cool.'

It seemed that tortoises had the ability to take everyone's mind off the one thing that was consuming her thoughts. What if Drew found something seriously wrong with the puppy? How would Peter react then?

'I hope…' She was desperate for the reassurance that she knew Lucas wasn't in a position to give. Lucas looked up at her suddenly.

'Drew's the best at what he does.' His quiet words slowed the thump of Caro's heart.

'Not you?' She managed a smile.

'I'm the best when he's not around. You're sure you'll be okay here for a minute?'

'I'll be fine. Go…' Lucas would be able to reassure Peter better than she could if he decided to question what was going on with his puppy.

'All right. Call me if you need me. And thank you, Caro.'

'My pleasure.'

Caro watched as Lucas walked over to the coffee table, motioning to Tegan to sit back down again when she saw him and jumped to her feet. Peter chuckled with glee as the three tiny tortoises wove around each other on the tabletop. Now all she had to do was sit and wait and hope that Rolf was going to be all right.

Drew had explained everything to Laura, and when he made his way back to the reception desk he found Caro answering the phone, while everyone else was crowded around the coffee table. She seemed very alone, and the agonised look she gave him after he'd dragged Peter away and sent him on his way with his mother tore at his heart.

'They are such fun!' Tegan bounced back to the reception desk, handing her tortoise back to Caro with a hint of reluctance. Caro found a smile from somewhere.

'Keep it, if you like.'

'Can I? Thank you! I can paint its shell…' Tegan displayed her purple sparkly nails, in an indication of how her tortoise might look like when she'd finished with it. 'I'll put it on the table and the kids will love playing with it.'

'Perhaps we can commission some from you, Caro?' Drew wasn't sure whether Caro knew just how much she'd helped by keeping Peter entertained.

'Great idea. How much are they?' Lucas asked.

Caro shrugged. 'They don't cost anything much to print, and the micro-electrics are pretty standard. I'd be happy to make some more for you.'

Lucas looked as if he was about to protest, and Drew silenced him with a shake of his head. They could sort all that out later, and he'd make sure that Caro was recompensed for her work, even if they just bought new supplies for her 3D printer. Caro obviously had something more important on her mind, and that meant that Drew did too. He hurried her away and back to the consulting room.

'What's the matter with Rolf?' The question came almost as soon as he'd closed the door behind them.

'First things first. He's going to be all right.'

'Oh! Thank goodness.' Caro flopped down into a chair. 'I should have known, really. Lucas said you were the best at what you do...'

Warmth flowed through Drew's veins. Not just because Lucas had said it but because Caro had heard it. 'I'm the best when he's not around.'

'He said the same about you.' Caro smiled suddenly. 'What about Ellie?'

Drew chuckled. 'Ellie's in a league all of her own. Neither Lucas nor I presume to compete with that.'

She nodded. 'Wise move. So what did you see, Drew? Something to do with Rolf's gait?'

She was perceptive, noticing everything. That was probably one of the things that made Caro so good at what she did. Along with a liberal helping of hard work, which Drew preferred not to think about at the moment, because it always prompted a flutter of concern for her in his heart.

'Yes, I noticed that he's got a slightly swaying gait, which is one of the signs of canine hip dysplasia.'

Caro's eyes widened in alarm. 'I don't know what that is...'

Drew sat down opposite her. 'It's quite a common genetic condition, where the hip develops laxity early in a puppy's development. If left unchecked, it can cause a great deal of pain and stiffness, but we've caught it early so there's lots we can do to prevent it from developing. I think that Rolf will be able to live a perfectly happy and pain-free life.'

She nodded, clasping her hands together. 'That's…
good. What are you going to do?'

Caro needed all the information she could get so that
she could fit all the pieces of the puzzle together. Drew
smiled. He was beginning to like the way that her mind
worked.

He got to his feet, fetching the model of a canine hip
from the glass-doored cabinet, and when he turned he
found her standing at his elbow. 'Okay, here's how it
works. In the first few weeks of a puppy's life the liga-
ments that stabilise the joint can become loose, eroding
the cartilage so that the bone doesn't develop properly.
When the puppy moves, the joint is displaced, like this…'

Caro winced as he demonstrated. 'That looks…hor-
rible.'

'If it's allowed to develop it can be. But I've given
Laura an exercise and feeding programme for Rolf that
will help stabilise these joints, and I'll be checking on
him regularly. That'll mean he doesn't develop all of the
secondary wear and tear that will start to cause him pain.'

'He's not in pain now?'

'No, he isn't.'

A tear suddenly rolled down Caro's cheek. For all her
insistence on the science, she had a soft heart that was
just as beautiful as her mind. Drew wanted to hug her
but didn't dare, telling himself that this wasn't the right
place. In truth, nowhere was ever going to be the right
place, because he knew that hugging Caro would reach
parts of his own heart that were forbidden.

Instead, he handed her the model of the joint. She nodded, trying the movements for herself, and then seemed
to notice the tear, which was now travelling across her
chin, and brushed it away impatiently. If hugging her was

a step too far, then Drew supposed that kissing the tear away was a giant leap across the boundaries that he'd imposed on himself.

'Thank you for looking after Peter. It was a great help, and he didn't need to know that I was concerned. Laura will explain everything to him when they get home, and she'll be able to tell him the same as I've told you, that Rolf will be all right.'

'It was…nothing.' Caro shrugged. 'I couldn't bear to think that he might be worried about his puppy.'

'It was everything…' A lump blocked Drew's throat. He took the model from Caro's hands, putting it back into the cabinet, and turned away. Whatever he did next, he had to keep his distance to avoid anything that had even the slightest chance of turning physical.

'Would a wire-frame model help to isolate the differences in movement?' Her mind was obviously starting to work, embracing all the possibilities. 'I expect that's already been done…'

'There are a lot of studies on canine hip dysplasia, and since early diagnosis is so important many of them concentrate on how to diagnose accurately. I can get some of the literature for you if you're interested.' He lowered himself into a chair.

'Yes, I'm interested. I probably wouldn't be able to contribute anything, but you never know…'

Drew knew. Caro had a way of stripping a problem down and seeing it in many different ways, and if she set her mind to it he'd be surprised if she couldn't add a little something to the sum total of knowledge on any subject.

'You're not going to get diverted from the prosthetics project, are you?'

She grinned suddenly, rubbing one hand in a circle

over her stomach and using the other to tap her head in an impressive show of co-ordination. 'I can do more than one thing at a time.'

'Right, then.' Drew ignored the hard spike of desire that shot through him. Finding out how many things Caro could do at one time, and then concentrating her mind on just one, over-arching sensation was an entirely inappropriate thought, and there wasn't a situation that was going to change that. He seriously needed to get a grip.

'So... Are you ready for our next visitor?'

'I need to take a break.'

The words were surprisingly easy to say, even if they did prompt a grimace of disappointment from Caro. In the three hours since they'd started work, her manner had changed a little, her quiet wariness of their canine test subjects beginning to dissolve. She'd even stroked a particularly docile spaniel without glancing at Drew first for reassurance, and Drew had fought to hide a smile.

But now he was tired. His leg was beginning to ache, and he knew that he'd reach a point soon where he would *have* to sit down.

'Lucas is still doing his morning surgery, and if you wanted to join him, I'm sure he wouldn't mind. Perhaps he could send some of his patients your way for the study.'

She raised her eyebrows, as if he'd suggested something that was beyond outrageous. A little stir of gratification nudged at Drew's heart.

'No, that's okay. I think I have what I need for this morning. Anyway, I've trained *you* up now.'

Drew chuckled. He was finding it more and more difficult to resist Caro's forthright manner and the way that she reddened slightly when she realised that she'd said what was on her mind without applying the usual filters.

'Glad to hear it. I'll try and remember the drill for the next time.'

'Good. Shall I go and get us some lunch from the cafeteria?'

He'd really like to stroll over there with her and get his own lunch. But something about Caro always made him feel stronger and more useful than he usually did these days, and it didn't seem quite so galling to let go of the reins from time to time.

'A ham and cheese toastie, if they have one, and some coffee. Put it all on my account.'

'Okay. Lunch is on you, then, thank you.' Caro made it sound as if he'd just asked her to dine at an exclusive restaurant. But in truth nothing was more luxurious than the chance to just watch her as she crossed the room, the overhead lights teasing the shine from her hair.

CHAPTER FIVE

CARO COULD GET used to ham and cheese toasties. These weren't as tasty as the ones that Drew had made, but she was a great deal more awake to appreciate them. They'd gone to his office to eat, and the ashen tiredness in his face had begun to lift a little. He'd stayed put while she'd taken her laptop from her bag, opening it on his desk and scanning through the data from the force plates.

'You have what you need? Or are you still at the stage where vets shouldn't interfere with your process?' There was a sudden tension in his voice that told Caro he was expecting an answer that he didn't want to hear. A week ago, he probably would have got it, but now... She'd seen Drew work, and he was truly dedicated to the welfare of the animals under his care. Caro didn't feel the same need to keep him at arm's length.

'No. Vets are very welcome to interfere with my process at the moment.' *One* vet. Carol liked Lucas and Ellie, and she was sure that they were both completely trustworthy. But Drew was the vet she was beginning to actually trust.

'That's reassuring. I wouldn't want to meddle.'

She supposed she'd asked for that one, making him sign the non-disclosure agreement. But since she had, perhaps it was okay to share a little. However risky her heart told her it was.

'I don't suppose you'd mind taking a look through these results, would you? I can analyse the data from a mechanics point of view, but it would be good to get another perspective.'

He looked pleased. A little surprised as well. 'Yeah, sure, I'd be happy to. I'll come to you and we can review them together?'

'Yes. Thanks.'

Nice. It felt nice to have someone to share her ideas with. The taste of danger in the thought only seemed to add a bit of extra spice. Maybe that was what had been missing from her work in the last few months. The sense of reaching out into the unknown that drove her forward.

'I know that the people who came today did so because *you* asked them. I really appreciate that. They're all very kind…'

Perhaps *too* kind. Everyone seemed to be so careful around him, and it clearly made Drew uneasy. But Caro shouldn't say it, Blake had told her more than once that voicing whatever was on her mind wasn't her most attractive trait.

He was looking at her questioningly. 'Don't let me down now, Caro. I was starting to appreciate your habit of saying exactly what you mean.'

'I just… I was wondering if this "*poor Drew*" thing that everyone seems to have is helping. It's not my business…'

He let out a short, barking laugh. 'One of the things about living in a village is that everyone knows your business. I don't see why you should be any different.'

Caro took a deep breath. '*Is* it helping, then?'

'Everyone's been really supportive, and I appreciate it more than I can say. And, no, it's not helping. I feel as if no one has any expectations of me any more.' He smiled suddenly. 'Apart from you, of course.'

'Is there anything else I should know? That might make me rethink my expectations?' If he wanted honesty then Caro was up for that. It saved a lot of time and beating around the bush.

'You don't need to rethink anything.' He narrowed his eyes, searching her face, and it occurred to Caro that she wasn't the only one who had reason to be cautious. 'Two years ago I lost my fiancée in a diving accident.'

'I'm sorry. You've had a lot of hurt to bear in a very short time.' Caro's own troubles seemed insignificant in the face of this.

'It doesn't define me.' There was a trace of defiance in his tone.

She didn't know what to say to him. And then it occurred to Caro that this was Drew's problem. Everyone knew what had happened and no one talked about it.

'Were you there? When your fiancée died?'

Something ignited in his eyes. An understanding between them that it was okay to ask, because Drew wanted to answer.

'No. Luna and I had a shared interest in marine conservation, that's how we met. She was a member of a team that travelled a lot and I was busy here, building up the practice with Ellie.'

'So you didn't get to see her as much as you wanted?'

Drew puffed out a sigh. 'Luna was very determined, and I always knew she'd stop at nothing for the things she believed in. It was one of the things I loved about her. She'd driven for two days to get to the team's encampment, and she was exhausted, but she went diving anyway.'

A prickle of embarrassment travelled down Caro's spine. She was no stranger to working for two days straight and fighting exhaustion to do just that bit more. Drew's insistence on food and afternoon TV the other day hadn't been a whim.

'And you think that if you'd been there, you might have stopped her?' Caro shook her head. It was a natural enough reaction, but it could only lead to more grief.

He shrugged. 'I can't say that the thought didn't occur to me. But I couldn't have stopped her from taking risks. That was in her nature and you can't change the people you love.'

'You reckon not?' Blake should have taken note of that. He'd spent an appreciable amount of time suggesting clothes that would suit her and pointing out what she shouldn't say or do. It had all been a terrible waste, though, because he hadn't really wanted her because she was beautiful or charming. She had just been someone who had ideas that could be turned into hard cash.

'I'm not sure I could ever change who I am. Could you?'

Caro swallowed hard. 'No. I don't think so.' It seemed like an admission of failure. Drew made her wish that she *was* beautiful and charming.

'I guess we'll just have to be what we are...' He quirked his lips downwards as if he didn't really want to think about that. 'Would you like to come for a walk? We have a beach, and some woodlands...'

Suddenly she didn't want to be near Drew any more. He'd never once criticised her, but she couldn't stop the things that Blake had said from echoing in her mind.

'No, thanks, but… I should be getting back. The tide…'

'Yes, of course. I'm running late too, I'll have to hurry home if I'm going to catch the last of this afternoon's TV.'

Caro breathed a sigh of relief. She'd be home soon, in her workshop, where she didn't have to think about any of this. 'I'm told it does you a lot of good.'

'Whoever told you that?' Drew smirked at her, getting to his feet.

What? What had that all been about? Drew let himself into his cottage on the outskirts of the tiny village of Dolphin Cove, scarcely having time for the thought before Phoenix came hurtling towards him.

'Hey, there, girl.' He bent down to stroke the puppy, lifting her up into his arms. 'You missed me, then?'

The answer was unequivocal. Phoenix started to lick his neck, and Drew couldn't help smiling. She was the most uncomplicated part of his life at the moment.

Caro, on the other hand…

He'd known her for two days. And found himself spilling things he'd kept from people he'd known his whole life. It was puzzling, and a little outrageous, and maybe just the result of her blunt honesty. But he couldn't shake the feeling that Caro somehow got him in a way that most other people didn't.

It was almost as if she knew him, right down to his bones, the way that Ellie did. But Ellie's knowing was the result of them having grown up with each other. Brother and sister. Caro's knowing was warm and wild and confronting, and he couldn't seem to get enough of it. It had followed him home, digging into his heart, like a sharp longing for what he couldn't have.

And he *couldn't* have it. He couldn't change Caro,

any more than he could have changed Luna. His parents had argued their way through his teens, both trying to change each other. The divorce had been a long time coming, postponed until he and his brothers had all left home, and it had probably been the best thing that had ever happened to his parents. Finally, they'd learned how to be friends, and they got on together much better than when they'd been married.

Man's best friend was still making an excited fuss of him. He scratched behind Phoenix's ears, and the puppy wriggled with pleasure.

'Sorry to leave you for so long. When you've had your final round of shots, you can come to the clinic while I'm working.'

Phoenix didn't seem to care about anything other than this moment, she was just happy that he was home now. And maybe looking just a few moments ahead, in anticipation of some dog treats. He set her down, and she trotted ahead of him as he made his way into the kitchen.

Caro had been staring at her computer screen for two hours, ever since Drew had replied to her text, confirming that he'd be coming to see her later on today. He'd clearly forgotten all about the tide, because he'd said he'd be there at noon, and he'd replied to Caro's reminder with a thumbs-up emoji. Whatever that meant. Thumbs up for the tide? Or for not arriving until later in the afternoon?

In the meantime, though, she was safe from visitors. That was the whole point of living up here, but at the moment it seemed an annoyance. She stared out of the window of her workshop at the sea, following the movement of a small rowing boat that was making its way around the peninsula.

Whoever that was must be mad. Wherever they needed to get to it couldn't be more than five minutes' drive, and pitching yourself out into the water just for the sake of it seemed perverse. Maybe she should go outside, just to make sure that the small craft didn't capsize while it was traversing her small slice of the horizon.

She may as well. She wasn't getting anything done here, and perhaps the breeze that continually danced across her small island would clear her head a little. Caro pulled on the sweater that was draped over the back of her chair and squeezed past the printer, unlocking the door.

Whoever it was was pulling strongly on the oars. Caro narrowed her eyes at the splash of red at the prow of the boat. Was it two people…?

She let out a little yelp of surprise. It was a small dog, wearing a bright red lifejacket. And the man pulling at the oars was Drew.

That put a different complexion on the whole thing. Now the raw power in his shoulders made her heart beat a little faster. And the desperate foolhardiness of the venture became a little more personal. Caro ran to the edge of the cliff that dropped down towards the sea and shouted.

'Drew… Drew!'

He didn't hear her the first time, but when she screamed at the top of her voice, he stopped rowing, grinning up at her. That wasn't what she'd meant him to do. He should be heading for the beach, where he'd be safe.

'What are you doing? Be careful!'

He seemed to be allowing the tide to bring him closer to the foot of the cliff.

Drew swung one of the oars into the boat and waved at her. He was just twenty feet below her now, the boat bobbing up and down on the water, and he seemed to be looking for something. Then he reached forward, pulling the boat right up against the rocks.

'I said I'd be here at twelve.' He looked up at her, his face all innocence. He could cut that out right now.

'I didn't expect you to row here. What are you going to do now?' The cliff face that separated them was a sheer expanse of rock. No one could get up it, and certainly not a man with an injured leg and a puppy to contend with.

'Have you been down into your basement?'

'Only once.' The agent had insisted on showing her the whole of the house, but the dark, empty space hadn't much appealed to Caro.

'I'll meet you there.'

'What?'

Too late. The boat had disappeared into a crevice and taken Drew and Phoenix with it. She could hear the puppy's excited barking, but short of throwing herself into the sea there was no way of seeing what Drew was up to now. Caro wrapped her arms around her, tramping back to the house.

The door into the basement was locked, and she twisted the key, switching on the light and walking down the stone steps. What was she supposed to do now? Caro looked around and caught sight of a new-looking door at the far end of the space.

That too was locked, but the key was in the lock and the mechanism turned smoothly when she tried it. The door swung open, and she saw Drew, walking towards her with a torch in one hand and Phoenix's lead in the other. The puppy seemed to be having a fine old time, still wearing her lifejacket and yelping excitedly.

Drew grinned at her. His shoulders seemed somehow broader now that she'd seen them powering the fragile craft through the waves towards her, and he looked deliciously windswept. That was something she could think about later, when she'd questioned the advisability of arriving this way.

'What do you think you're doing, Drew? Couldn't you just wait for the tide?'

He shrugged. 'Rowing's a lot easier than climbing steps.'

'And it's a lot more dangerous as well. Goodness only knows what might have happened to you. And Phoenix.' If he had little heed for his own safety, then she knew that he'd baulk over having put Phoenix at risk.

'It's an easy row, around from Dolphin Cove. If it was dangerous I wouldn't have come this way, but it's a nice day and these waters are sheltered enough. I've been rowing back and forth in them since I was a kid.'

'You're a *vet,* Drew. Not a crusty old fisherman.'

He chuckled. 'True. But my grandfather's a crusty old fisherman, and he was the one who taught me how to row and showed me every inch of this coastline.'

Caro puffed out a breath. 'All right, then. I still don't like it.'

'What on earth did you do when you were in California? I hear there's a great deal of sea there.'

'They call it ocean. And, yes, there is, but...' She shrugged awkwardly.

'You were a bit busy with other things?'

'Yes, as it happens, I was.' Caro peered past him into the darkness. 'What is this, some kind of secret passage?'

'It's an open secret, most people around here know about it.' He turned, beckoning her into the gloomy space.

When her eyes adjusted to the darkness, Caro could

see that it was more of a cavern than a passage. She could hear the sound of the sea and see light at the other end.

'So this is a landing? For any visitors who can't be bothered to climb the steps?' The small wooden rowing boat was pulled up out of the water, inside the mouth of the opening onto the sea.

'You really don't know? What's this place called?'

Ah. Smugglers' Top. 'This is an old smuggling route?'

'That's the story. I don't know whether it's true or not, but why else would anyone go to the trouble of opening up this cavern? It's big enough to land any amount of contraband, and it would be pretty difficult for the excise to lie in wait and capture you here.'

'What do you do with it once you've got it here, though?' Caro looked around the cavern, half expecting to find a long-abandoned crate of brandy in one of the corners.

'I suppose you could bring it down onto the beach when you know it's safe. Or take it along the coast by sea.' Drew shrugged. 'It's just an old story.'

'And how did you know that the passage hadn't been filled in, when they renovated the house?'

'I gave Stella a call, at the letting agents. She told me that it was still okay to land here, and that they'd just put a lock on the cellar door so that no one could get through into the house.' He grinned. 'I think she must have mentioned it when she showed you around.'

The perils of a small village. And not listening to everything that the letting agent had had to say. Caro had switched off when Stella had launched into yet another story about the history around here.

'And so you decided to do it the traditional way. In a

wooden boat.' Phoenix clearly approved of the craft as she was pawing at the side of it, wanting to get back in.

'What's wrong with that?' Drew raised his eyebrows.

'Nothing, I suppose. Only a motor would have been easier. Along with something to help you steer.'

'You steer with your oar strokes. And in a small boat like this, an outboard motor doesn't let you feel way the tide's running.'

Of course. How come she didn't know that?

It was because they were so different. Caro worked with absolutes, data and programming, robots that would react according to a set range of values. Drew relied on his senses to deal with the unpredictable behaviour of the world around him. How two people with such different approaches could understand each other so well was one of those imponderable questions that had a habit of keeping Caro awake at night.

'*You* can feel it. I'd be over the side as soon as a wave hit me.' She grinned up at him.

'Nah. You'd invent something and fly over the tops of the waves.'

'Probably. You want to come upstairs for some rum and hard tack?'

He chuckled. 'You got me hard tack? How did you know that was my favourite?'

CHAPTER SIX

THEY'D WORKED FOR a full five hours, trading ideas over a steady stream of snacks from the kitchen. Drew had enjoyed himself, and when the time came for him to row the boat back to Dolphin Cove, he felt his body thrumming with strength. His leg still hurt a little, but he was nine tenths alive now, instead of feeling half-dead.

Phoenix tugged at her lead when she saw the boat, eager to resume her position at the prow. Most dogs liked the water but, much to his grandfather's delight, Phoenix was turning into a real sailor.

'Will you be all right?' Caro stared out at the sea, as if it really did conceal monsters.

'Yeah, we'll be fine.' She didn't seem particularly reassured, and Drew tried again. 'Think of it this way. I've been messing around in boats all my life, and so far it's proved less injurious to my health than driving.'

Drew smiled. He could practically see the cogs turning in her head, weighing up probabilities and risk. Then Caro shook her head, as if the equation was too complex for her.

'I wouldn't know about that. I've never messed about in boats, so I don't have the data.'

An idea sprang into Drew's head. Probably not a good

one, but it was enticing, like a siren's call, and he couldn't
resist it.

'Would you like to come out for a trip on my dad's
boat? We could go one weekend.'

She was turning the idea over in her head. Work or a
boat trip. Drew knew how strongly work pulled at her,
but Caro was interested in everything, and a new experience was difficult for her to resist as well.

'Can you swim?'

'Yes, I'm a good swimmer…when I'm in the swimming pool, that is. Why, were you thinking of pushing
me overboard?'

'Only if you disobey the captain's orders.' Drew
chuckled as Caro shot him an exasperated look. 'We can
borrow a wetsuit from the diving centre, and if the weather's good I'll show you how to snorkel. There are lots of
things going on down there that you've never imagined…'

He was deliberately pushing all of Caro's buttons. The
idea of things going on that she couldn't imagine was ir-
resistible to her. Drew had done plenty of swimming and
water exercises as part of his rehab, but he hadn't been
in the sea since his accident. It was about time he reacquainted himself with the capricious mistress that he'd
loved ever since he could walk.

'I'd like that. Can we go down deep?'

He should have known that Caro didn't do anything
by halves. 'Not unless you can hold your breath for half
an hour. You want to scuba dive?'

She shifted awkwardly from one foot to the other. 'I
don't know…'

Drew wasn't quite sure about that either. Since Luna
had died, he'd judiciously avoided being responsible for
anyone while diving, and had given up his teaching ses-

sions at the diving centre. Maybe it was about time he reacquainted himself with that part of his life, too.

'I'll tell you what. We'll pop down to the centre tomorrow and sign you up for some lessons. They do short courses that last a week and just teach you the basics. If you like it, then you can come out with us the Saturday after next.'

Caro thought for a moment. 'Okay. Thanks. I'll see what's involved tomorrow, and I might just do that.'

Drew nodded. He'd tempted Caro into this, but now that it was a reality his throat seemed a little dry. Maybe he'd prefer it after all if she stayed safely on the boat, but now that Caro had the idea in her head there wasn't going to be any stopping her.

'All right. One thing, though…'

'Yes?' She tipped her head up towards him, and in the shade of the cavern, her eyes seemed to glisten, full of unknown possibilities.

'If you've been up all night, working, you don't get to dive. Ever. Safety's always the number one consideration.'

He heard the sudden blunt assertiveness in his own tone and saw Caro's face soften. Maybe she understood… Drew fought back the temptation to smile. She *needed* to understand this.

'Okay, I hear you. No going into the water unless I've had a solid night's sleep. I promise.'

'Thanks.' Drew could smile now. And that brought with it a new temptation, to kiss her goodbye. It seemed that there was no getting away from wanting just that little bit more with Caro. 'I'll see you tomorrow?'

'Yes.' She bent down, giving Phoenix a hug and a kiss. 'Safe journey back, sweetie. Perhaps you can persuade the old grouch to send me a text when you get home.'

'I'll remind her to remind me.' Drew pushed the small craft down into the water and then stepped into it. Now that his legs didn't need to hold him up, he felt strong again. And if he needed to be a grouch to keep Caro safe, he'd had plenty of practice over the last few months.

She stood watching them as he manoeuvred the boat around and started to row. Ten yards. Twenty… Her figure was becoming smaller, standing in the mouth of the cavern like a sweet, golden-haired lover, standing at the water's edge to watch the boats go out. His grandfather had told him that his grandmother had done that every time when he put to sea, and Drew had never really understood the impact of the statement.

Then she waved. Drew raised his hand in reply, and then started to row again, pulling hard on the oars. *He* was the one who needed a good night's sleep, to regain some much-needed perspective.

Caro had decided not to mention diving to Drew. She'd been carried away by the thought of exploring new worlds with him, and she'd probably gone too far. His attitude had become suddenly authoritative, and Caro had been reminded that Drew had conflicting feelings about the sea, and diving in particular. He clearly loved both, but they'd taken his fiancée from him.

This morning it was as if he'd pushed their conversation of last night to the back of his mind and was pretending that it had never happened. That was fair enough. Caro was disappointed, she'd gone to sleep last night thinking about drifting mermaid-like under the sea, finding new and unimagined wonders. But she'd do it with someone else, in another place. There would always be new places, and Drew's peace of mind was far more important.

'So.' They'd eaten their lunch and he leaned back in his seat. 'Are you still up for the diving centre this afternoon?'

'Yes!' She couldn't help replying too quickly and maybe a little too enthusiastically. 'If you are, that is.'

He gave her that gorgeous lazy grin of his. The one that said he'd finished work now, and he was going with the flow. He had a built-in off switch that he seemed to be able to flip at will, and Caro wondered what that might be like.

'Yes, I'm up for it. I'm looking forward to getting back to diving.'

That was that, then. There was no resisting him now, no telling herself that Drew probably wasn't ready for this. He wanted to do it and holding him back was the one thing that Drew really didn't need at the moment.

'Okay. Where's the diving centre?'

'Down there.' He jerked his thumb towards the window, and Caro saw a low, stone building, nestling in the sheltered curve of the beach next to a small jetty.

'There's a diving centre here? Is there anything that you *don't* have?'

Drew grinned. 'Ellie and I developed this place as a resource for the community and a learning centre for all aspects of the natural world.'

'How do you manage it all?' She peered at Drew. 'You don't have an old treasure chest under your bed, do you? Or a rich uncle…?'

'No, nothing like that. We were given the land by a local benefactor, and we've had grants to help develop some of the community and learning aspects of the centre. Ellie and I have been in practice together ever since veterinary school, and when we got the opportunity to expand we grabbed it.'

'So you do diving…and conservation…?'

'Hasn't Lucas shown you around?'

Caro shrugged. 'He gave it a go. I was concentrating on my stuff, and he had stuff with Ellie to think about. Between us, there wasn't a great deal of time for anything other than what was strictly necessary.'

Drew chuckled. 'You think you can tear your head away from your work for a few hours?'

Yes, actually she could. Drew's ability to tear her head away from almost anything was a little frightening, and if Caro wasn't careful, she'd lose focus. But she could worry about that tomorrow, when the sun wasn't shining and his smile wasn't so close at hand.

'I've got a small window of opportunity.'

'I won't let it go to waste, then. I'll give you the guided tour, and then we'll go and see Jake at the diving centre. He's probably having lunch at the moment.'

She followed Drew through the reception area, giving Tegan a wave as they passed. He made for the trees, walking along a woodland path until they were out of earshot of the clinic car park. Leaves were beginning to carpet the ground, and there seemed to be all kinds of rustling going on but Caro couldn't see where it was coming from. Drew sat down on a bench.

'What's here?'

He smiled. 'Wait and see…'

She sat next to him, suppressing the urge to tap her foot. Drew stretched his legs out in front of him, seeming wholly at peace.

Silence. Nothing was happening, and Caro wondered

how long they would have to wait before Drew either gave up or they saw something. And then, suddenly, the empty woods began to come to life.

A small pinkish brown bird, with a black beak and bright blue flashes on its wings, seemed to be foraging amongst the undergrowth. Drew leaned over, whispering.

'It's a jay. Looking for acorns to bury for the winter.'

Caro watched the bird as it made its way amongst the fallen leaves, moving them to one side with its beak. Sliding towards him on the bench seemed very natural. They *were* whispering after all…

'Do they remember where they've put them?'

'Often enough, I guess. When they don't, you'll get an oak tree.'

Caro was suddenly very aware of his arm, slung across the back of the bench behind her. If keeping quiet and still meant they wouldn't disturb the wildlife, then it also meant that she could keep this feeling of being close to Drew for a moment.

A chaffinch flew down onto the path, almost in front of them. A rustle amongst the leaves turned out to be a fox, treading warily and stopping every now and then to sniff the air.

'I never thought that if you stayed still for a moment, you'd see all this.'

Drew smiled. 'We manage these woodlands very carefully to encourage all kinds of different wildlife. We have hedgehog boxes in a more secluded spot over there and if you come down here at night, you can hear them all snuffling around in the undergrowth. There are a few badgers too, and we're thinking about having a beaver enclosure.'

'Beavers? I didn't think you had them in this part of the country.'

'We don't, but they've been reintroduced in enclosures in various parts of England. When they build their homes, a natural wetland forms so you get an increase in those plants and animals too. We're also looking at building a red squirrel enclosure.'

'Don't they catch something from the grey squirrels?' Caro racked her brains for the name of the disease that had decimated red squirrels and came up with nothing.

'Yes, SQPV. Squirrel pox virus. The greys carry the virus, but it doesn't affect them.'

'And that's why you'd have to keep the reds in an enclosure?'

'Yes, there's been some research into administering a vaccine to wild squirrels, but until that's been perfected, it's not possible to establish colonies in England.' He smiled. 'But maybe Mav will take *his* children into these woodlands and find red squirrels roaming free.'

'You're in this for the long haul, then.'

Drew nodded. 'An oak tree can support up to a thousand different species of wildlife. I won't live to see the ones I planted last year grow to their full size.'

'Good thing someone thought to plant a few for us, then.'

'Yes. We're just trying to pay that forward, so that future generations will still have the species that are becoming endangered now. Not just the ones that hit the headlines but the lesser known ones. You know who runs the planet?'

Caro thought for a moment. 'I'm guessing the answer isn't going to be us.'

'Well, in some ways we do. But the wart-biter bush-cricket, the shrill carder bee and the bog sun jumper spider are all endangered species in Britain, and they're part of a vast number of different insects that keep our eco-system going.'

'Great names. Someone should definitely save them. So saying that I'd rather watch hedgehogs than have a wart-biter cricket crawling across my foot isn't the way to look at it?'

'That's a reasonable enough reaction. But there are a lot of entomologists working very hard to encourage various species of insect, some of which are very important to our natural habitats.' Drew smirked at her. 'It's an endlessly complicated interaction. I thought you might like that.'

It was definitely growing on her. 'I prefer to confine myself to robotics. It's a lot more predictable.'

He nodded, looking up as the sound of voices floated towards them. When Caro saw a young woman, leading a group of children, she automatically moved away from Drew a little, feeling the sweet pressure of his arm around her lift.

'Ah. One of our school trips. They'll be here to see the reindeer.'

'You have reindeer!' Caro couldn't conceal her excitement. '*Real* reindeer?'

'No, they're plastic ones with red noses…' he joked, and Caro frowned at him. 'You want to tag along?'

'Yes. Please. I've never seen a real reindeer before.'

He got to his feet, greeting the woman at the head of the group, and introducing Caro to Angie, a teacher at one of the nearby schools. Drew fell into step with the group, talking to the children and telling them about the wildlife that lived here in the woods.

He was so at ease here. Caro could imagine him tramping these woods, strong and alert to everything that was going on around him. Never alone, because he understood the complex language of the countryside, which Caro had always just hurried past without giving it a second thought. What cacophony did he hear in the rolling waters around her home? Suddenly, she wanted very much to dive with him and find out.

CHAPTER SEVEN

CARO SEEMED AS excited as the children were when they approached the cluster of low barns that housed the petting zoo. Eddie, the manager here, had brought the most docile of the reindeer in from the pasture, and was waiting for them in the barnyard.

A chatter of excitement ran around the group, and Eddie introduced Dasher the reindeer to the children. He saw Caro clutch her hands together, almost jumping up and down with excitement, and Drew decided to hang back a little, sitting down on a bale of hay. The afternoon sun caught the golden highlights in her hair, and he smiled.

Under Eddie's close supervision, each of the children was allowed to approach Dasher, with a little hay to feed him with. Angie took her turn, but Caro was hanging back, talking to a little boy who didn't look inclined to go anywhere near Dasher. They seemed to be coming to some decision, and Caro put her hand up, along with the other kids who wanted to feed Dasher.

She approached Dasher gingerly, turning to look back at the little boy she'd been talking to. Clearly both of them were a little nervous of getting too close to the reindeer. Eddie handed her some straw, and she held it out, seeming ready to snatch her hand away if Dasher made any sudden moves.

Dasher amiably took some of the straw from her hand, and Caro gasped with delight. Carefully, she reached out and stroked Dasher's neck. This was what the petting zoo was for. Kids of all ages.

Meanwhile the little boy was edging closer, emboldened by Caro's bravery. Both Eddie and Caro let him take his time, but finally he reached out, taking some straw to feed to Dasher. Caro turned, and the look of delight on her face made Drew want to laugh out loud with happiness.

'Hey, Drew, I wasn't expecting to see you here this afternoon.' Kirsty, one of the animal care assistants, walked towards him.

'I just dropped in. How's everything going?'

'Fine. Um…are you back at work yet?' Kirsty eyed the walking stick propped up against the bale of hay.

'Yes, I'm back. Anything I can help with?

'Well, I was going to call Ellie but since you're here… I noticed this morning that Missy's very slightly lame in one of her back legs. I've kept her inside, and I think it's just a stone bruise, but it would be great if you could take a look.'

'Yes, of course. You're going to go and help with the children?'

Kirsty nodded. 'Yes, just while Eddie takes Dasher back to the pasture. I'll be as quick as I can.'

'That's okay. I'll wait.'

Drew wondered whether Caro would be going in to see the rabbits with the rest of the group, but when Kirsty ushered them towards the long, low building where the smaller animals were kept, she turned, walking towards him.

'You're not going to see the rest of the animals?'

'No, I've seen a reindeer. That's enough excitement for the day.' Her face was shining, and she plumped herself down on the hay bale next to him. 'The little boy I was with was scared, and I said that I'd go and stroke him for both of us. But he ended up coming to stroke him too, did you see?'

'Yeah, I saw.' The magic of the moment hadn't been lost on Drew. It was so easy to relive the wonder of touching an animal for the first time through her.

'Are we going back to the diving centre? Or do you want to take a rest first?'

'Neither. I've got to take a look at one of the Shetland ponies.' Kirsty had disappeared with the children, and Eddie was leading Dasher back to the pasture, and a thought occurred to Drew. 'I don't suppose you'd come and keep her still for me, would you?'

'I can try. I don't know how to keep a Shetland pony still, though.'

That was one of the things he liked about Caro. She didn't back off from things she knew nothing about, she tried them anyway.

'You just hang onto her bridle. Missy's getting on a bit, and she's not going to give you any trouble.'

He led her into the stable block, found Missy's stall, and showed Caro how and where to hold the bridle. She wrapped her arm around Missy's neck, whispering to her, and Missy quietened. Caro might not have much experience with animals, but she was a natural.

'What's the matter with her?'

'Kirsty thinks she may have trodden on something and bruised the sole of her foot.'

'Ouch! Poor thing. I hate it when that happens.' Caro twisted round, watching as he bent down and lifted Missy's leg a little. 'What are you doing now?'

'Just scraping away the dirt so I can see. It doesn't hurt her.' Drew carefully cleaned the sole with a knife and examined it. There was a red area that looked like a bruise.

'Is she all right?' Caro interrupted his train of thought.

'Hold on. Let me examine her properly.'

Caro gave a little huff of impatience and started whispering to Missy again, who seemed a lot more unconcerned about the procedure than she was. Drew went back to feeling the pulse on Missy's leg and checking the temperature of the sole. He could see no evidence of a cyst or laminitis, which would have been far more serious.

'It looks as if it's just a bruise. She'll need to be rested up a bit, but she'll be fine.'

'Good. D'you hear that, Missy?' Caro was stroking the pony's mane. 'Can I give her something to eat?'

'No, she's fine.' Caro looked so downcast that Drew relented. 'You can give her a little hay from that bale over there.'

Caro scooted out of the stall, pulling at the bale to get a good handful. When Missy took the hay, then nuzzled against Caro's arm, her face lit up again.

It had been so long since he'd really felt the magic he saw in Caro's face. Since he'd felt the wonder she saw in things around her, and in every new experience. Drew could spend a lot of time just watching her and still feel that it wasn't enough.

Kirsty's arrival broke his reverie, and he quickly relayed his findings and went through everything she should do for Missy. Caro gave Missy one last stroke, and then followed him out of the stable.

'Are we going to the diving centre now?' She grinned up at him.

'Wait. Hold on a minute.' Drew shot her a mock-serious look. 'You're taking the afternoon off, even though you haven't worked yourself to a standstill. And you're actually enjoying it?'

Caro's laugh seemed rather more carefree than before. Joyous even. 'Yes, I was wondering about that myself. Seems I am.'

Kirsty had dropped them off at the diving centre, and Drew found Jake in the office at the back, shuffling through the papers on his desk.

'Drew!' Jake got to his feet and their handshake turned into a hug. 'So you've found us at last.'

'Yeah. I've brought someone to see you.' He turned to Caro, who was hovering in the doorway. 'Caro's interested in scuba diving.'

'Oh, thank goodness for that!' Jake grinned at Caro. 'This paperwork's been driving me crazy.'

Drew chuckled. 'Jake always gets a bit itchy around this time of year. Not so many people want to go diving in the autumn.'

'You can say that again. And I've been missing my diving buddy.' Jake slapped Drew on the back. 'When do you want to go, then?'

'I have to learn first.' Caro gave Jake an apologetic smile.

'Ah. Great. Well, there's an introductory manual I need you to read through...' Jake caught up one of the wire-bound manuals from a large box in the corner of the room, handing it to Caro.

'All of it?' Caro opened the first page, scanning the contents list.

'You can skip chapters six, seven and eleven, they're for the more advanced course.'

'Read all of it.' Drew knew that Jake didn't cut corners, but he wanted Caro to be more than prepared before he took her into the water. Jake shot him a querying look and then shrugged, obviously reckoning that the extra chapters couldn't do her any harm.

'Okay. That's my weekend sorted. Then what?' Caro tucked the manual under her arm.

'Then we do three two-hour sessions in the pool. Now, that'll just give you the basics, and I'd normally suggest you go on a dive with the class after that, but if you're with Drew it'll be fine. He's a qualified instructor.' Jake picked up his diary and flipped through the pages. 'I'm doing lessons next week on Monday, Wednesday and Friday mornings.'

Caro hesitated. Drew knew exactly what she was thinking.

'We could continue with the study on Tuesday and Thursday. I'll be at the clinic on Wednesday, so maybe I could take some of the measurements you need then as well.'

Caro looked at him as if he'd just asked her to cut off her own arm. 'Perhaps it would be better to do the lessons the following week.'

'Then you'll miss out on a few days that week. You can run through everything with me on Tuesday if you like.' Drew already knew exactly what to do, he'd watched

Caro do it enough times. But if it made her feel better, she could go through it one more time.

The cogs in her head were working overtime at the moment. Maybe she just didn't trust Drew. Then she turned and smiled at Jake. 'Monday, Wednesday and Friday sounds great, thank you. I'll need to hire a wetsuit as well.'

'Okay, so you have a choice. A thicker wetsuit will probably be all right at this time of year, but a drysuit, like the one that Drew has, will be better.'

'We'll take a drysuit.' Drew interrupted.

'That's going to mean an extra session in the pool, to show you how to deal with the buoyancy and so on. We can do that on Monday afternoon.'

Caro looked a little downcast. Yet more time away from her work. Then she nodded. 'Okay, in for a penny, in for a pound. I'll hire a drysuit, like Drew says.'

Jake nodded. 'As you're working with Drew, I'll throw the drysuit hire in. We don't have much call for them outside the tourist season.'

'Thank you, but… I don't want to take advantage…' Caro was clearly determined to pay her way.

'Why don't you give Jake a couple of those miniature tortoises? His little boy is two and he'd love them,' Drew interjected.

'Oh, yeah. I heard about those. That's definitely a deal.' Jake grinned. The diving centre was nominally a part of the outreach side of the veterinary clinic, but in practice Ellie and Drew left the management to Jake.

'Four's best. They go crazy, trying to avoid each other, if you put them on a tabletop.' Caro didn't have much concept of bargaining anyone down, but then neither did

Jake. The arrangement seemed to suit them both, and Drew decided not to interfere.

'You're coming along to help out, Drew?' Jake was scribbling Caro's name down in his diary.

'Um…no. I said I'd do some work at home on Monday. Friday I'll probably rest up a bit.'

Drew had been so sure that he wanted to show Caro the hidden world that lay beneath the waves, and so sure that she'd be fascinated by it. But now it was turning into a reality, his own fears were kicking in. If he left Caro's training to Jake alone, then there would be no possibility of Drew becoming distracted by her smile or his own fears about taking her into the water and forgetting something vital.

'Okay.' Jake gave him a searching look. He knew that since Luna had died, Drew had given up the responsibility of teaching, and had only gone into the water with experienced divers. But he said nothing.

'Is that all agreed, then?' Drew pushed his fears to the back of his mind. He really needed to get back into the water, and this was a great opportunity. Jake was the best instructor he knew, patient and knowledgeable, and very thorough. Nothing bad was going to happen to Caro. This was an opportunity that no one should miss.

'Yep.' Jake grinned at Caro. 'Monday at nine, then? If you want to come here, I'll give you a lift up to the pool.'

Caro nodded, smiling suddenly. 'Thanks. I'm really looking forward to it.'

Drew had made his mind up not to phone Jake. But Jake knew him too well and phoned him instead, launching exactly into what Drew wanted to hear.

'Has your lady got a photographic memory or something? I got the distinct impression this morning that she had the whole of the manual off by heart.'

'She's not *my* anything. We just work together.' Expressing his relief that Caro had actually read the manual, and absorbed all of the information, might suggest that Drew had entertained the thought that Caro did anything by halves.

Jake chuckled. 'She's a bit too good for you, mate.'

Shorthand for 'Caro would be perfect for you'. Drew had told Jake the very same thing when he'd first set eyes on his wife, and Jake had upped his game significantly in response. Drew had no game left.

'Caro's only interest is her work.' Jake knew what that meant. He'd known Luna.

'Well, she swims like a fish, and she pays attention to every detail. Just thought you might like to know. She's solid, Drew, and she doesn't compromise on safety.'

'Yeah. Thanks.' Drew considered mentioning to Jake that he might like to throw in something unexpected to gauge Caro's reaction but he was an experienced instructor, and he knew how to test his students.

'I'll catch you later, then...' Drew heard the sound of Jake's son in the background and knew he had to go.

'Soon. We'll go down to the Hungry Pelican for a pint.'

'Definitely. Tell Caro that Ollie loves the tortoises. Gotta go...'

The call ended abruptly, and Drew smiled, dropping his phone on the sofa. Caro would be ready—Jake would see to that. And his own doubts about going diving again were receding in the face of wanting to show Caro a part of the world that he loved. For the first time in a long time he was beginning to shake off his fears and look forward.

'Want to go for a walk, Phoenix?'

Phoenix twitched her nose. An early evening walk probably didn't sound so fabulously exciting when you were already curled up in front of the grate. Drew got to his feet, automatically reaching for his stick and then changing his mind.

'We'll just go a little way. I'll try leaving the stick at home this time…'

CHAPTER EIGHT

CARO HAD BEEN through her training, and she was ready. Jake had told her she'd be fine. All the same, a little quiver of excited uncertainty had been making her heart pump faster ever since she'd woken up this morning.

She'd carried all her diving equipment down the stone steps and across the beach to her car. Living here *did* have its disadvantages, even if the tides did provide her with the solitude she needed to work. But Drew and Jake didn't see water as any obstacle, and while that was reassuring in someone who was teaching you how to dive, it was rather more challenging when it applied to Drew. More than once she'd woken in the night and wondered what it might be like to look out of her window and see a glimmer of light out to sea as a rowing boat carried him towards her.

Night thoughts. It was the morning now, and Drew was just a friend. If trusting him enough to continue her study alone on Wednesday had been a challenge, then trusting him to take her diving was a piece of cake. There was no need to wonder about the inconsistencies of that, because life could be complicated and inconsistent at times. That was why she liked robots.

She arrived early at the small jetty that was attached to

the diving centre and saw Drew walking towards her car to meet her. He was windblown and cheerful, wearing a drysuit with a pair of deck shoes and a windcheater. The stick seemed incongruous next to the spring in his step.

'Hi. Ready to go?'

'As ready as I'll ever be.'

'Got your papers from Jake?'

Jake had bet her another one of the tortoises that Drew would want to see them, and Caro had already paid up. She pulled the list of topics covered and Jake's scores out of her pocket and gave them to him.

Drew scanned them, nodding. 'A hundred percent. Very impressive. Did you bribe Jake?'

He knew full well that she hadn't. 'No, bribery's a contravention of Jake's and my safety standards. Do we change here?'

'Yes, it's easier than trying to do it on the boat.' He led her across to the diving centre and unlocked the main doors. 'The changing rooms are over on the left.'

Locked in the white-painted cubicle, Caro took a deep breath. She was really doing this. She carefully unrolled the drysuit. All she had to do was to apply what she'd learned now. That started with getting into the suit.

First there were layers of clothes to keep her warm, two thermal vests and two pairs of thermal leggings. It took a bit of wriggling and cursing to get into the suit, and she was glad of the zip hook that hung next to the mirror, but she made it. Jake had said that thick socks and trainers would be fine for the boat, and she pulled them on, along with a warm jacket. Bundling her clothes into her bag, she found Drew sitting on the jetty, watching a small blue and white painted fishing boat make its way towards them.

'That's your dad's boat?' It looked a very small craft in which to brave the sea.

'Yep. It looks as if my grandfather's at the helm.'

When the craft neared the jetty, Caro saw a white-haired man standing alone in the small, white-painted cabin that provided the only shelter from the wind that the boat afforded. He cut the engine and threw a mooring rope to Drew, who caught it expertly and then turned his attention to Caro.

'Welcome aboard, young lady.' He held out his hand in a gesture of old-fashioned courtesy. Caro climbed down the steps from the jetty and found that she was guided onto the deck by a firm, steady grip.

'Thank you, Mr Trevelyan.' The boat wasn't wobbling as much as she thought it might, but it she still had to concentrate on keeping her balance.

'Call me Gramps. No one but the excise man calls me Mr Trevelyan.' Gramps's dark eyes twinkled.

'Leave it out, Gramps.' Drew was handing their diving equipment down to his grandfather and shot Caro a smile. 'He loves to sit in the harbour during the summer and tell all the tourists his smuggling stories. He's never smuggled anything in his life.'

'That's what you know, boy.'

Gramps gave Caro a confiding look, tapping the side of his nose. When he turned his back, Drew rolled his eyes, mouthing his words silently. *'He hasn't.'*

'Where's Dad?' Drew swung down into the boat.

'He's gone off somewhere with your mother.' Gramps shook his head. 'I'll never understand those two if I live to be a hundred.'

Drew shrugged as if he didn't understand either, and Gramps nodded.

'Sit down, lass, we'll be ready to go.' He motioned her towards a bench that ran around the side of the boat and Caro stumbled towards it, sitting down heavily next to the diving gear. Drew sat next to her as the engine of the boat started up again and they began to move across the bay.

'I hope we haven't put your grandfather out. Coming out this morning…' She grimaced awkwardly. Fish out of water was an entirely appropriate cliché as all of this seemed so new and different.

'Nah. The only way you can put Gramps out is to leave him behind on dry land. My parents have a habit of disappearing off together on day trips from time to time.'

'That's nice.' Caro was searching for something to say, and that seemed to be the least contentious, but Drew chuckled.

'My parents are both very different people, and they argued their way through twenty-three years of marriage. Now that they're divorced they get on like a house on fire.'

That seemed very personal information. But in the context of a village, where everyone knew everyone else's business, Caro supposed not.

'I guess…whatever suits them.'

'Yeah. That's my view. They were never going to change each other, although they both tried. Living apart gave them the opportunity to make their peace, and they found that they really liked each other.'

He seemed so at ease out here. As if the wind and the waves were absorbing all the woes that the land held for him. Drew even seemed better on his feet on the rolling deck than he was on land, using handholds on the boat to steady himself instead of his stick. Caro watched the land recede, wondering whether she was going to be sick.

A wave of nausea suddenly hit her, and then disappeared as quickly as it had struck.

'You want to take a turn at the helm, lass?' Gramps called back to her, and Drew gave her a nod that indicated this was something of a privilege that wasn't afforded to everyone.

Be brave…

'Yes. Thank you.' Caro eyed the distance between her seat and the helm, wondering how she was going to get there without falling overboard.

'On land you always keep one foot on the ground, yes?' Drew murmured to her, and Caro nodded. 'On a boat, it's one foot on deck, and one hand to hang on with.'

'Right.' Caro got to her feet, grabbing onto the side of the boat. This was easier than it sounded.

Gramps positioned her hands on the helm, pointing to a spot on the horizon. 'Keep your eye right there. That's where we're going.'

Caro nodded. This was easy enough, like steering a car. But the boat seemed determined to go left when she wanted to go right. She turned the wheel a quarter turn, but still couldn't manage to correct their course.

Suddenly she felt a strong body behind her and Drew's hands on hers. 'You need to turn the helm more than you do a steering wheel on a car.' The wheel spun under her fingers, and the boat began to move out of the cove and into the open sea.

'Got it?'

Yes, she had it. But his body felt so warm against her back. So strong. She could so easily just sink into that warmth.

'A bit to the left.' His breath caressed her cheek, and Caro turned the wheel. 'Bit more…'

'You want to go to Trethaven Point? There might be dolphins there.' Gramps's voice reminded her that it wasn't just her and Drew, alone in the universe.

'Dolphins?' She heard the excitement in her own voice and Drew's deep chuckle reverberated through his chest. 'But what about Dolphin Cove?'

'Dolphin Cove got its name from the shape of the headland, which looks like a dolphin's head. If you want to see dolphins, then Trethaven Point's the place to go.'

'Can we go there, then?'

'We'll go wherever you want, lass,' Gramps replied. 'Bear to port.'

'Turn left.' Drew's voice guided her, his hands helping her turn the helm so that the boat described a gentle arc in the water.

It took half an hour to get to Trethaven Point, which was on one side of a huge, sheltered bay. Caro was windblown and very excited, but Drew insisted on checking her drysuit and all her equipment, turning her round to make sure that everything was just so.

'Now you.' She grinned up at him. 'Jake told us that we must check each other's equipment. He showed us how.'

Drew gave her a lopsided smile. 'Okay. Since Jake told you…'

Caro repeated the acronym that Jake had taught them under her breath, going through the procedure. The boat was bobbing gently at anchor on a calm sea and Gramps was leaning against the helm, his arms folded and with a broad smile on his face as Drew submitted to being turned and turned again as she ran through the checks.

'Happy?' Caro nodded. 'Right, then. Jake's taught you how to sit on the edge of the pool and turn into the water?'

'Yes, he said that was the easiest way for beginners.'

'Okay. I'll go in first and Gramps will help you. Give me the signal when you're ready. You know the hand signal to make if you're in trouble?'

He'd read her papers closely enough, and Jake had given her ten out of ten for hand signals. Caro decided to humour him.

'*Not sure* is this.' She flattened her hand, palm down, rocking it back and forth. 'And *Help* is this.' She raised her arms above her head.

'Great. Now I want you to stay within reach of me all the time, but if we do get separated, what do you do?'

Caro closed her eyes, visualising the page in the manual and reeled off the bullet points. When she opened them again Gramps was chuckling.

'I think she's good to go, son.'

'All right.' Drew shot Gramps a glare. 'Just making sure…'

Of course he was. Caro had submitted to all of Drew's questions because she knew that he needed to ask rather more that she needed to answer. But she was ready now, and she couldn't wait any longer.

Drew put the regulator into his mouth, holding it in place and executing an impressively smooth back roll into the water. Gramps held out his hand to steady her as Caro swung her legs over the edge of the boat.

'All right, lass?' Gramps smirked. 'Better give him the signal, he'll only make a fuss if you don't.'

Caro signalled an *okay* to Drew and he signalled back. Then a sliding turn brought her into the water with a splash. Now, at last, she could put what she'd learned into practice.

They sank together into a deepening blue, the light

dancing on the waves above their heads. The awkwardness of breathing through the regulator and managing the buoyancy of the drysuit were suddenly secondary irritations, compared to the shimmering beauty around her.

Drew was taking this first dive slowly and gently. Keeping within reaching distance and not letting Caro swim as strongly as she knew that she could. But there was enough to fascinate her as they travelled downwards through shoals of small fish to the sea bed. He pointed out crabs and strangely shaped creatures, their large eyes swivelling to take in as much light as possible. Jake had told her about *maerl*, the rock-hard, red skeleton seaweed, and there was some here in the well-lit shallow waters. So many new forms of life that were equipped to deal with their environment. Suddenly tortoise robots seemed just the tip of an ever-expanding iceberg.

It seemed that they'd only been down there for a moment when Drew signalled it was time to surface again. Caro's heart sank, but she knew she must follow his instructions. She'd seen the tension in his face when they'd prepared themselves for the dive.

They surfaced next to the boat, and Caro saw Gramps sitting on the deck, a pair of glasses perched on his nose and reading the newspaper.

'Okay, Gramps?' Drew removed his regulator, shouting up to him.

'Back already?' Gramps raised his eyebrows. 'I haven't got to the sports pages yet.'

Drew grinned. 'You want to go down again, Caro?'

'Yes, please. We haven't seen any dolphins yet.'

He was less solicitous the second time, allowing Caro to dictate the pace a little more. Drew was beginning to enjoy this too, and he even allowed himself to unclip his camera from his belt and take a few photographs. Caro took her time, inspecting the sea floor carefully, and Drew let her to swim a little further.

Finally he tapped his watch, signalling that they should surface again. Caro took one more look at this underwater kingdom, silently bidding it goodbye until the next time. Then she felt Drew's hand on her arm.

He was pointing, towards a flash of movement to their left. It was impossible to see what it was, but then the shapes wheeled around, coming into view. Caro's heart beat a little faster, bubbles spinning upwards from her breathing gear. Dolphins.

She wanted to swim towards them, but Drew had told her she mustn't. She felt his hand curl around hers and she squeezed it tight, watching the creatures whirling playfully in the water. Then they were gone.

He kept hold of her hand. As they drifted back upwards, she wanted to hug him, but was afraid of dislodging some of the breathing gear. When they surfaced, Gramps had abandoned the sports pages and was standing at the side of the boat.

'You saw them, Gramps?' Drew called up to him, and Gramps nodded.

'I managed to catch them on video.' Gramps brandished an up-to-the-minute smartphone, which he presumably kept well hidden when he was playing the old seadog for the tourists.

Caro could have spent all day here, but Drew swam over to the boat, beckoning to her to follow. They climbed aboard, stowing their gear carefully, and then Drew sat down, his face wreathed in a delicious smile.

'You enjoyed yourself?'

'Yes, I did. Thank you so much, Drew. Can we go again?'

He chuckled. 'I think I'm going to insist on it. I've had six months cold turkey, and now I'm well and truly bitten by the diving bug again.'

'Your leg's all right?' Caro had noticed that Drew's movements underwater had been far more effortless than they were on land.

'Yes, no problem. Call it water therapy.'

It had been water therapy in more ways than one. He was smiling and relaxed now. Whether that was because the dive was over, or because he'd finally broken through another barrier in the long climb back to full fitness, Caro wasn't sure. But she was sure that this had been an achievement for Drew and being part of it was special.

He unzipped the pouch at his waist, taking out a smooth flat stone and dropping it into her hand. 'Here. A souvenir of your first dive.'

The stone had a round hole, right through the centre of it. It was the most beautiful thing that Caro had ever seen.

'It's called a *milpreve* in Cornwall. It'll ward off snakes.' Drew glanced at Gramps, who nodded sagely.

'Thank you...' Caro closed her fingers around the stone, holding it to her heart. This morning had been a succession of wonderful things and words weren't enough. And the strangest and most wonderful thing had been that, quite unexpectedly, she'd found herself trusting Drew.

Drew was intoxicated by her eyes. Warm honey brown and reflecting every last bit of the magic of the morning. Caro *was* the magic. The way her forehead had puckered slightly in concentration as she'd quoted the diving manual, which he'd helped Jake to write, straight back at him. The way she'd leaned back a little, almost in his arms, as they'd steered the boat together. The way she'd squeezed his hand under the water.

He watched her as the boat moved steadily back to the diving centre, with Gramps at the helm. Her hair blown dry by the wind and stiff with salt, her fingers a little red from the cold and curled around the cup of hot soup from the flask he'd brought. Her nose was a little red, too, and it was enchanting.

She thanked Gramps, waving to him from the jetty as the boat drew away. Drew opened the diving centre, carrying their tanks inside and leaving them with the others that needed to be refilled. Caro made for the changing rooms, stopping to ask Drew if he'd undo the zip that ran across the back of her shoulders for her. He'd done that a thousand times before for his fellow divers, but it had never seemed so intimate. He decided to wait for her out on the jetty.

She joined him, her face shining. 'Thank you so much, Drew. That was one of the best things I've ever done.'

'Right up there with robotics?' If that was the case, it was praise indeed.

'Definitely. It's given me some ideas as well.' She shot him an impish smile.

'Don't…' Drew held his hands up in an expression of surrender. 'If I find that your tortoise has been banished to a cupboard in favour of a cleaner fish, I'll feel very guilty.'

'That's not going to happen. Tony will always have a place in my heart.'

He should get into his car and go home now. But Caro didn't move, and he couldn't leave. Drew reached out, skimming his fingertips across the arm of her jacket.

'It's been good to get back to diving. Thanks for giving me a good reason.'

She nodded. Caro had a habit of thinking about every aspect of a given situation, and no doubt she'd thought of that, too.

'It must have been hard. After everything that's happened, you must have wondered if it would still be the same.'

'It'll never be the same. But this was as good as the best of what I had before. Better, because...' He shrugged, unable to put his feelings into words.

'Because you knew you'd come close to losing it?'

No. Better because Caro had been there. Something suddenly fell into place and for a moment it seemed as if the void inside him could be filled.

Trapped in her gaze, he reached for Caro's hand, bringing it to his lips. She moved closer, stretching towards him as if she were about to kiss his lips. Then suddenly a tear rolled from her eye and she backed away, her hand over her mouth.

'I'm sorry...' Drew didn't know what he'd done wrong.

'No... It was nice of you. I'm just not that girl...'

She seemed upset. Drew couldn't let this go. 'Not that girl?'

'You know. Pretty girls who say the right thing and don't speak their minds.' Caro wrinkled her nose. Perhaps she thought *that* was speaking her mind a little too plainly.

'You're definitely not that girl, then. You're a beautiful woman who says the things that should be said.' The words came easily because they were true. And suddenly it seemed that Caro needed to hear them.

She blushed suddenly, shaking her head. She really

didn't know how beautiful she was, and words weren't enough to convince her. Drew reached for her.

'Caro, I would like very much to kiss you.'

'Would you? Really?' She looked genuinely surprised. 'I'd like to kiss you too.'

He brushed his lips against hers and felt her melt against him. Then he kissed her again, this time a little more insistently. She gasped, smiling up at him, and he kissed her again.

All thought was gone. All he wanted to do was carry her away and make love to her. And then Caro flung her arms around his neck, pulling him down for another kiss that was sweeter and wilder than the rest.

She drew back a little, her eyes still warm with desire. Her hair blowing in the breeze. One last thread of sanity tugged at Drew. They had to stop this.

'This morning… I had the best time. Thank you.' Caro seemed to know that they had to stop, too.

'Yeah. Me, too.' He pressed his lips to her cheek in quite a different kind of kiss. One that allowed the possibility of a parting.

'I think I need to go now.'

'You have work to do?' The thought seemed more bitter to Drew than usual. Caro would always put her work before anything else.

She reached into her pocket, bringing out the stone he'd given her. 'First of all, I have to find somewhere nice to put my *milpreve*. I want to be able to look at it.'

That didn't seem so bad. Caro's rented house didn't contain anything that seemed personal to her, and it was warming to think that this one thing was important enough to her to break that rule.

'I'll let you get on, then.'

If she kissed him again, he wouldn't let her go. Drew stepped back, and all the wild possibilities that had been swirling in his head began to fade.

She nodded, and then turned, shouldering her heavy diving bag, and made for her car. If she looked back…

Caro didn't look back. She already had her eyes set on what was ahead of her, and she'd probably be working late tonight in her workshop to make up for the time she'd lost this week. He watched as she got in and drove away.

That was the first time he'd kissed a woman since Luna had died. Apart from his mother, of course, and Ellie, but that wasn't the same. It was the first time that his body had thrilled to a woman's touch.

And strangely it was all right. Gramps had said that guilt and loss wouldn't always paralyse him, and that one day he'd wake up and find he was moving on. And Luna would have wanted that, her zest for life wouldn't have tolerated him remembering her any other way.

He picked up his stick and began to walk to his car. The one thing that he couldn't move on from was the present. Caro's work was all-important to her, all-encompassing. That was her choice to make, but Drew had choices too. He couldn't deal with it, and this mustn't happen again.

Why? *Why?* Caro hauled her heavy bag up the stone steps of Smugglers' Top. The morning had been a whole kaleidoscope of delights in all shapes and sizes, the greatest of which had been the Drew-shaped one.

She'd kissed him. It had been wonderful, and Caro was in no doubt that Drew had liked it too. He'd said that she was beautiful, and Drew didn't lie. She'd known he wasn't lying; no one could fake that kind of passion.

And then she'd cut and run, like a scared rabbit.

It was the only thing possible. If she let Drew into her life, then what happened next? The light out at sea? The rowing boat, braving the swell of the tide in the darkness? The knock on her door at midnight by a handsome adventurer? She'd trusted once before, and then she'd lost one of her most important projects *and* her home.

She balanced the equation carefully in her head. On one side, Drew. On the other side, everything else. If he seemed to outweigh everything else, then that was just faulty calculation.

She dumped her bags in the hall and walked into the bathroom, staring at herself in the mirror. Her fingers grazed her lips, and she could almost feel his kiss, still there.

Beautiful. The word made her smile.

'Nonsense,' she reproved her reflection. Drew had reclaimed a part of his life this morning, and it was natural that he would feel a sense of euphoria. He'd got carried away.

She took the *milpreve* from her pocket, turning it over in her hand. It *had* been a wonderful morning, and the glistening stone, worn smooth by the sea, would always remind her of his kiss. But now she had work to do.

CHAPTER NINE

CARO WAS BRIGHT and early on Monday morning, and looking as smart as she always did when she visited the clinic. The briskness of her manner told Drew that she'd made the same resolution as he had. Their kiss had been wonderful, and if it had settled the question about whether Caro was beautiful or not, he would be completely happy. But it was something that shouldn't be repeated.

'I made something. It's a thank-you gift for the clinic.' She dumped the box she was carrying in front of him on his desk.

'That's nice. May I open it?'

'If you don't, it's not going to be a great deal of use, is it.'

Okay. Logic trounced pretty much everything else in Caro's book. Drew flipped open the lid of the box and saw a small robot dog crouched at the bottom.

'Oh. That's great. Thank you.' Drew wasn't quite sure what they were going to do with it, they had enough *real* dogs around here, but it was a nice thought.

'You haven't seen what it does yet.'

He lifted the dog out of the box and tried to stand it on its legs on his desk. The legs weren't stiff enough to hold the body and the dog collapsed into a sitting position. Maybe there was something wrong with it.

'It's supposed to be lying down. This is a very specific, sole-purpose dog.'

Sole-purpose dogs were a new one on Drew, but he went with the flow. No doubt Caro was about to dazzle him with something clever. 'What's its sole purpose?'

She rolled her eyes as if that should be obvious to him. 'I noticed last week that there was a pup in an incubator. It seemed a bit lonely.'

The pup had been very sick, although it was improving now. It had had blankets and a favourite toy but hadn't taken much notice of either. Drew found the on switch for the robot, hidden behind its ear, and pressed it. The robot's small frame began to expand and contract in a regular rhythm.

'It's breathing!'

Caro gave him a reproving look, but obviously decided that she didn't need to tell him that it wasn't *actually* breathing, just that its chest was moving up and down.

'I've heard about breathing pet comforters, and it seemed like a good idea. If the pup's mother were with it, she'd be breathing.' Caro frowned. 'She'd be furry, too.'

'Well…yes.' There was that to it, but breathing was a good start. 'I guess we could make it a coat.' He wondered how Caro might feel about the clinic making alterations to her designs.

Finally, she smiled. 'Yes, that's what I was hoping you might do. You know best the kind of thing that would be most comforting and what's hypo-allergenic and so on. I'd like you to complete the design.'

Drew was conscious of the honour that was being accorded them. Caro never hesitated in asking for the information she needed. But she didn't just turn her half-finished designs over to someone else for the finishing touches.

'Thank you. This is really amazing. Perhaps we can get Tegan to sew it a furry coat while she's sitting at the reception desk.' Perhaps not. On second thoughts, Tegan probably didn't do a lot of sewing but Drew didn't rule out the possibility that she might have hidden talents in that direction. He decided that the question of who would actually do the sewing could be shelved for the moment.

'So you like it?'

'It's a brilliant idea Caro, thank you. You did this at the weekend?' Drew wondered whether she'd had any sleep at all.

'It didn't take long. I've got templates for all kinds of dogs that do all kinds of things. The thing that took longest was printing out the body, and I just set the printer going and went to bed.'

That was a relief. 'I'm going to show Ellie and Lucas.' He picked up the dog, switched it off again, and made for the door. 'Are you coming?'

It seemed that the appeal of the dog had ended now that he'd confirmed that it was fit for purpose, and the problem at hand had been solved. 'You go. I'll go and calibrate the equipment in your surgery, if that's okay.'

'Sure. Go ahead. And thanks again, Caro, this is an innovative solution.'

That made her smile. Caro was all about solutions. Drew tucked the dog under his arm, surreptitiously switching it back on again as he walked along the corridor. Caro had got the movement just right, and it really did feel as if it were breathing. Unless he was very much mistaken, Ellie would love this.

* * *

Back to normal. It was a relief, even if it was a disappointment as well. Drew hadn't mentioned the kiss once. Caro had thought that was an excellent idea and neither had she.

Ellie had made a great fuss over the breathing dog, although its movements and reactions were so simple as to be verging on the mundane. Drew seemed to want everyone to like the robot, and Caro was secretly pleased at the pride with which he showed it around.

Caro had agreed to make another two of the dogs, and Ellie had insisted that the clinic should pay for them. When Caro had refused any payment, Drew had stepped in and settled the matter by ordering a box of printer filaments in return for the dogs.

He'd promised to help put the dogs together, and Caro had left the larger plastic pieces to print overnight. But almost as soon as he arrived at Smugglers' Top the following morning, his phone rang. He listened carefully to the voice at the other end of the line, his face darkening.

'I'm sorry. I have to go.'

'You've only just got here.' It wasn't like Drew to allow anything to interrupt what he was doing, and this must be important. 'What's the matter?'

'That was Ellie. There's been an oil spill out at sea...' He shook his head, running his fingers through his hair.

'Is it bad?'

'We don't know the scope of it. Just that an oil tanker's run into trouble, and the crew have been airlifted off. Apparently it's still afloat, and it's being towed, but there is an oil slick forming.'

He looked worried. Ashen.

'What are you going to do?'

'Ellie says that there's help on the way from the environmental agencies, but they won't arrive until later in the day. We're here now.' He'd already pulled his jacket on and was halfway to the door. Phoenix seemed to sense the urgency in his movements and was trotting quietly behind him.

'Wait. Drew, I'll come with you.'

He turned, his hand on the door latch. 'It's not your battle, Caro.'

'What, because I'm not from Cornwall? We've only got one sea, and it's as much mine as it is yours. Don't you dare tell me it's not my battle.'

'It's going to be hard work. Distressing at times, too.'

'Well, if you're up to it, I'm sure I am.'

Drew smiled suddenly. 'Okay. Bring a warm sweater and your drysuit. We can lend you an oilskin jacket.'

Luckily, the drysuit that she'd been lent was packed neatly away in her diving bag, along with the warm underclothes that she wore with it. Caro pulled on a thick sweater, following him down the stone steps and onto the beach. They bundled into his car, and Drew stopped off outside a stone cottage in the village, going inside for a moment and then reappearing with his own diving gear. When they reached the harbour, it seemed full of people who knew exactly where they were going and what they were doing, loading boats and setting out to sea.

She saw Lucas and Ellie exchanging a kiss before they split up to board separate boats. Jake wound his way through the crowd, catching up with them.

'Can I hitch a lift?'

Drew nodded. 'Of course. I need to speak to Lucas before we go. I'll catch up with you at the boat.'

Caro could see Drew's father's boat further along

the quay. A woman, with shoulder-length blonde curls, dressed in a woollen coat that incorporated all of the colours of the rainbow, was hurrying towards it, carrying two large bags. The man on board, who looked too much like Drew not to be his father, stopped to greet her.

Jake nudged her. 'That's Diana, Drew's mother. She never lets Peter go to sea without sandwiches and a flask.'

The bag that Diana handed to Peter looked as if it contained a lot of sandwiches and more than one flask. Caro watched as Drew's parents hugged, Diana's long scarf fluttering in the breeze.

Diana bade Peter goodbye and then turned away, catching sight of Caro.

'Ah! You must be Caro.' She thrust the second bag into Caro's arms. 'Drew texted me and asked me to bring my oilskin jacket for you. Here.'

'Thank you. I'll look after it and make sure I get it back to you.' Caro put the bag at her feet, holding out her hand to Diana, who shook it vigorously.

'I've been telling Peter that he must make sure that Drew doesn't hurt his leg again.' Diana leaned confidingly towards Caro and Jake. 'Of course he's a Trevelyan, so he doesn't listen. They all think that they have everything under control and no one needs to worry about them. They'll never change.'

'I'll keep an eye on him,' Jake volunteered.

'Would you, darling? Thank you.' Diana turned to Caro. 'I've been hearing all about you. You're up at Smugglers' Top, inventing marvellous things…' Diana gave a wave of her hand to cover the full range of marvellous things.

'I'm doing my best.' Caro smiled, warming immediately to Diana.

'Fabulous. Creativity's such an important thing. And Jake's been giving you diving lessons…?'

'Try not to make it sound as you've been stalking her, Mum.' Drew's voice sounded behind her. 'Caro's not used to village gossip, she's still under the impression that not everything she does is common knowledge within ten minutes.'

Diana waved her son away. 'Don't listen to him. I'd be fascinated to hear more about your inventions, we must have tea together. There's a little place overlooking the harbour that does a very passable afternoon tea.'

'Thank you. I'd like that.'

'Wonderful.' Diana smiled at her, and then turned to her son. 'Drew, darling, you *will* be careful, won't you? I know that there's no point in asking you to stay behind, but I just couldn't bear it if you were hurt again…'

Drew wrapped his arm around his mother's shoulders, taking her to one side and speaking to her quietly. They must have been words of reassurance because Diana was nodding, and when Drew let her go, she seemed reconciled to his leaving.

Gramps came hurrying along the quay and got into the boat. Drew and Jake followed him, and Drew turned to help Caro. Peter gave Diana a cheery wave, and she waved back, her bright scarf fluttering in the sunshine as they drew away from the dock.

Drew and Jake were talking to Peter, who was at the helm. Gramps patted the wooden bench beside him in an invitation to join him.

'All right, lass?'

'I think so. This is all very sudden, and everyone seems so concerned.'

Gramps nodded. 'Oil spills have done a lot of damage

along this coastline. Drew doesn't remember the worst of them, but he's seen the effect it had on marine life. It strikes a cold feeling in the heart.'

'Maybe it's not so bad. Drew said they don't know yet.'

'That's right, lass. We all need to hope for the best.'

The boat lurched, and Caro felt suddenly sick. She clapped her hand over her mouth.

'Bit queasy?' Gramps leaned towards her.

'When I came out last time, I felt a bit sick for a while. Then it passed off again.'

'Come and stand by the helm. You'll feel better there.'

Whatever worked. A cold sweat was beginning to form on the back of her neck and Caro was glad of Diana's thick oilskin jacket.

'Out of the way, lads.' Gramps selected the spot where Caro should stand and pointed to it.

Drew turned to her. 'Feeling sick? Take a few deep breaths. And don't look down at the deck, look at the other boats. If your brain can gauge the movement, then your stomach will feel better.'

'Or you could just give her a ginger biscuit.' Peter glanced around at her. 'I dare say Diana's packed a few, she usually does.'

'Yeah. That's a good one too.' Drew reached over to the bag that Diana had packed, unzipping it and bringing out a box of home-made biscuits. 'There you go. Mum never forgets.'

Caro nibbled at the biscuit, chewing on the small chunks of ginger. It was difficult to say which of the remedies had worked but she was feeling better now and ready to take on the task in hand. Up ahead, there was an oleaginous sheen across the water, and as they came closer, Caro could see that the white specks that dotted the surface were sea birds.

Drew's face became grim again. Caro moved out of the way as Gramps took the helm and Peter started to talk on the radio. He turned to Drew.

'Ellie says it's a smallish patch of oil, they've just been all the way around the edge of it. Most of the birds are in this quadrant.'

Drew nodded. 'So we'll start here?'

'Yes. Her boat will be joining us shortly, and Lucas is staying over the other side.'

The boat was going slower now and Caro could see a bird in the sea alongside it, smeared with oil and struggling vainly to fly.

'Drew…!' She tugged at his sleeve and his gaze followed the line of her pointing finger. 'Can we get it?'

'That's what we're here for.' Drew opened the storage compartment, under the bench at the back of the boat, taking out two long-handled nets and a bundle of flat-packed cardboard boxes. Pulling a box into shape, he set it down on the deck then picked up one of the nets, trailing it in the water next to the bird. It flapped and squawked, but it was too weak to put up much resistance, and Drew netted it and swung it back onto the deck.

'Are we going to take the oil off now?' Caro couldn't bear to see the poor creature in such distress.

'No, we can't. Cleaning oil off a bird is a traumatic process, and they're already exhausted. We'll keep them at the clinic for at least a day, feed them and keep them warm until they regain their strength.' Drew carefully extricated the bird from the net, laying it down in the box.

'Okay. So we're just collecting them.'

'Yes, both live birds and dead ones. We need to remove as many of the carcasses from the sea as we can to prevent secondary poisoning of predators.'

'What do you want me to do?'

Drew handed her the net. 'Take this and net as many as you can reach. Bring them back to me and I'll put them into the boxes. If you can't reach, don't lean over the side. The most important thing is that you don't fall overboard.'

'Gotcha. Most importantly, don't fall in.'

Suddenly the task ahead of her seemed impossible. Trying to rescue half-dead birds from a polluted sea. It already made her want to cry, and she looked down at the deck, embarrassed at her own faint-heartedness.

'Hey.' She felt his finger curl under her chin, and when she raised her gaze his face was tender. 'I'm really glad you're here, Caro. I would have left you back at home, but you wanted to do something, and you came with me. That means a lot.'

He wanted her here. Maybe even needed her, just a little. Bravery flooded back into her heart. Clutching the net, Caro walked over to the side of the boat.

It was hard work, both physically and emotionally. For as many birds that she leaned over and pulled alive from the sea, there were many more that were dead. Drew examined each bird that she and Jake netted, putting the dead ones into a large box with as much care as he took with the live ones. He fed the weakest birds with a gastric tube, keeping them warm by wrapping them in old towels. He was tireless, and every time Caro wanted to give up, she knew that she only had to look at Drew to receive a smile.

Gramps was manoeuvring the boat slowly and skilfully through the water, while Drew's father was using binoculars to spot the birds. After three hours of back-breaking work, Drew decided that they should take the birds they'd rescued back to the clinic.

Suddenly Caro was very hungry. Very tired. She stripped off her gloves, sitting down next to Drew at the stern of the boat, and he reached into Diana's bag, taking out one of the flasks and pouring some hot chocolate for her. As the boat swung round, he reached out to steady her, keeping his arm firmly around her shoulders as Gramps piloted the boat away from the oil.

CHAPTER TEN

THE BOATS CARRYING Ellie and Lucas were also making their way across the bay, and there were people waiting to receive the boxes of birds. Ellie jumped onto the dock, supervising their transfer up to the clinic, and Lucas was carefully unloading the boxes from the boats. Even Tegan was there, wearing a pair of pink wellingtons and a spotted pink mac, with heavy gloves to protect her nails.

They waited until the other boats had left the dock to make space for them, and then Gramps manoeuvred alongside it. Tegan was coaxing him off the boat with the promise of a cup of tea, and Ellie took his arm, leading him up to the clinic. He was obviously tired, and it seemed he wasn't going to be allowed back out on the boats this afternoon.

Dry land seemed a little strange now, and when Caro got back onto the boat, the movement of the deck seemed far more normal. Ellie was staying behind to supervise the care of the birds, and she stood on the beach, waving at the boat carrying Lucas away from her.

'Goodbye, my lover…' Her accent had taken on a broad Cornish twang. *My lover* was an endearment used for practically anyone, but it was clear that Ellie only had one lover and that it was Lucas.

'Looking at them together now, it's hard to believe that they spent six years apart,' Drew reflected.

Now they were happy, calling out for everyone to hear. And Drew said that people could never change.

'They've changed…' She ventured the hypothesis.

He turned suddenly, raising one eyebrow. 'Nah. Lucas and Ellie were always made for each other. Nothing ever changed, things are just back the way they were always meant to be.'

Jake beckoned to him and Caro was left alone, staring out to sea. A movement over to their left caught her eye. Drew was talking to Jake, and Peter had his eyes on the waves in front of them, so no one else had noticed. Caro hurried to fetch the binoculars, training them as best she could on a moving target.

A sick feeling rose in her stomach as the deck lurched unexpectedly beneath her feet. But she'd seen all she needed to see.

'Drew! There's some wreckage over there. And something's moving.'

Drew hurried across to her, taking the binoculars and training them on the horizon. He turned to Peter. 'Dad, there's something there. Maybe a small dolphin or a seal. The water's clear around it, but it's caught in some wreckage.'

Peter nodded, swinging the helm, and they changed course. As they got closer, Caro could see that it *was* a dolphin, and that the sea around it contained a larger shape, which was circling the creature.

'It's a baby…and the mother's there.' Drew pulled the radio speaker from its clip, speaking into it, and Caro saw Lucas's boat turn towards them.

'What are we going to do? Can we get it on board?'

Drew shook his head. 'If the baby's not badly injured, superficial cuts will heal in the sea. We don't want to take the baby away from its mother if we can help it, not least because there's the risk that the mother might attack us.'

'But...dolphins are friendly, aren't they?'

'They're wild animals. And her instinct is to protect her young.' Drew's face was set in concentration. 'Are you up for coming in with us?'

'Yes, of course.' Drew wouldn't have asked if they hadn't needed her help.

'Great.' He nodded at Jake, who disappeared down the tiny hatch that led below deck. 'You take the cabin; we'll need our drysuits.'

Jake reappeared, hauling the men's diving bags with him. Peter helped her down the steps, and Caro found herself in a tiny cabin, two bunk beds on one side and a row of cupboards on the other. There was about two feet of clear space between the two and everything was rolling from side to side, the movement making Caro feel a little queasy again.

At least there wasn't far to fall. And she'd been given the luxury of a cabin to change in while Drew and Jake changed on deck.

Caro took off her sweater and jeans, putting on the thick vests and leggings that went under the drysuit. Then she crawled into the bunk, unpacking her drysuit. She could just about manage to roll it down and get her feet into it...

A tap sounded at the door. 'Are you decent?'

More or less. The sound of Drew's voice made her feel virtually naked. And the thought of him squeezing with her into this tiny space brought a hot flush to her cheeks. But she wasn't used to this, and she was going to need some help.

She leaned over, opening the cabin door. When Drew entered, the available space seemed to dwindle to nothing. He was wearing just a thermal singlet and thick sweatpants, and his shoulders looked very broad.

'These things are a bit tricky until you get used to them.' His voice sounded much the same as it did when he was talking to one of the dog owners at the clinic. Very professional.

She could do this. Caro fixed her thoughts on the baby dolphin, which needed their help. Drew set about helping her to get her feet into the drysuit and pulling it up over her legs.

'Okay, stand.'

Standing involved allowing him to wrap his arms around her to lever her out of the bunk. They were squeezed face to face now and Caro focussed her eyes on his chest, wishing that she could manage to think about something other than the warmth of his skin.

'Put your arms in.' Some wriggling and tugging ensued, and then Drew pulled the headpiece over her head, leaning round to do up the zip that ran across the back of her shoulders.

'Comfortable?'

The drysuit was fine. She was about to explode…

'Yes, I'm good. Thanks.' She made the mistake of looking up at him. The quickly hidden mischief in his eyes told her that she wasn't the only one who had been considering the possibilities of their being squished together in a restricted space.

'My pleasure.' He backed away, leaving her to take a shaky breath and follow him back up on deck.

Jake was already in the water, along with Lucas and one of the men from his boat. Drew was stepping into his drysuit with the ease that years of practice afforded.

'Here's what we'll do.' Drew was using his *listen carefully* tone and Caro focussed her gaze on his face, trying not to think about the strong, capable hands that had eased her into her suit.

'Jake, Lucas and Terry will be taking the mother and holding her in the water next to her baby, which should calm them both. It looks as if the baby's tangled in some plastic mesh, and if you help me hold it, I should be able to cut it free. You must try to keep its blow hole above the surface or it'll drown.'

'I can do that.'

He nodded, giving her a smile. Pride began to warm Caro's heart. Drew was relying on her and she wouldn't let him down.

'There are a few spots of oil in the water around the wreckage. Try not to swallow any or get it on your skin. Wear your goggles, they'll protect you.' She felt Drew's fingers curl around hers, and he gave her hand a squeeze. Then he was all business again, pulling the headpiece of his suit into place.

Peter handed him a diving bag, while Caro pulled on her flippers. Their exchanged *okay* signal seemed to carry with it more warmth than just a normal safety procedure, and she eased herself into the water, swimming with Drew towards the wreckage.

Lucas, Jake and Terry had managed to manoeuvre the mother dolphin alongside her baby, which was emitting high-pitched whistles, trying to get free from the plastic mesh in which it was caught and only getting more en-

tangled. Treading water, Drew tried to soothe the frightened creature, and it reacted to his presence.

When Caro wrapped her arms around the baby dolphin it was warm to the touch. She stroked its head and
it seemed to calm a little. She glanced at Drew and he
smiled.

'That's right. You're doing fine.'

The other three men were having a bit more trouble.
The mother was large and strong, and they struggled to
keep hold of her, but she was calmer now that she was
with her baby. Drew was between the two of them, tend-
ing to the baby, but they could see and hear each other,
and seemed to be communicating, making sharp trill-
ing noises.

Drew cut the mesh with a knife, looking carefully for
any signs of injury as he went. The mother lashed her
tail, bumping against his back a few times, but Jake and
Lucas were holding her steady, keeping her quiet. Caro
wondered if she knew that they were there to help.

Everyone was cool and calm, watching the dolphins
carefully while he worked. It took half an hour to cut the
little dolphin free, and then Drew wiped the specks of
oil from around its blow hole. Caro's arms were aching
and she was beginning to tire, but it only took one look
at Drew to shore up her resolve.

He signalled to her to get her attention. 'Keep hold of
the baby. I need to clear some of this wreckage away before we release them.'

Caro held the little dolphin as tightly as she dared
while Drew pushed the wreckage out from under it. Finally, Drew seemed satisfied that the dolphin was un-
hurt, and they could release it. He ducked under the

baby, surfacing next to Caro and helping her to hold the small creature.

'We'll release them on my count…' He looked around, receiving the okay signal from the others. 'Three… Two… One.'

Everyone let go. The baby shot forward, its wake pulling her forward in the water. As the mother followed, Caro felt a heavy blow on her chest that drove the air from her lungs and spun her backwards. Instinctively she closed her eyes and held her breath as she felt herself hit the water and her head went under.

She was drifting. Dazed. Before she could wrap her head around what had happened, she felt someone next to her and when she opened her eyes, she saw that it was Drew. His arm snaked around her waist and then their heads broke the surface together.

She heaved in a breath, choking and clinging to him. Okay. She was okay. Shakily she gave the sign, still gasping for air, and feeling her shoulder twinge as she raised her arm.

There was no need to do anything more. Drew supported her back to the boat and together he and Jake boosted her up onto the deck.

'I'm all right…' Jake sat her down and took her goggles off. Then Drew elbowed him away. Apparently this was *his* job.

He leaned her forward, making sure that she could breathe properly. 'Did you swallow any water?'

'No… I don't think so.'

'Okay. Where were you hit?'

'On the side of my chest. My shoulder hurts a bit. What happened?'

'The mother caught you with her tail as she swam away. She lifted you right out of the water.'

'Uh…' Caro put her hand to her shoulder, flexing it. It didn't feel too bad… 'Are they okay?'

'Yeah, they're fine.' Jake had been watching the progress of the pair, and he indicated their curved wake. They seemed to be circling the boats, keeping their distance in case anyone decided to try to capture them again.

'Good. That's good.'

Drew had stripped his drysuit down to his waist, and she felt the brush of his skin against her cheek as he reached around to undo the zip that ran across the back of her shoulders. Actually, she *was* feeling a little shaky. She could do with a hug right now, but she didn't dare ask.

Drew carefully eased the headpiece over her head, rolling the drysuit down. As he did so, Peter wrapped a blanket around her shoulders.

'I'm okay.'

'So you said. Take a deep breath for me.' Drew's voice was gentle, and she felt his fingers on her ribs, feeling for any injury. Her ribs felt fine. His hands…a lot better.

She let him gently test her arms and shoulders, feeling warmth flow through her. It was probably about time she called a halt to this; she was enjoying it far too much.

'Any headache or stiffness in your neck? Do you feel sick?'

'I've no symptoms of a concussion. It's just my shoulder, Drew. And I can move it okay, I think it's just bruised.'

He nodded, wrapping the blanket around her. His eyes were gentle but his mouth formed a tense line.

'I'm so sorry, Caro…' He turned to Peter. 'Dad, we should go back.'

'No! I don't want to go back.' Caro frowned at him. 'And it's not your fault, she could have hit any one of us. I *told* you that I wanted to come and help.'

'The lady has a point.' Jake was leaning against the side of the helm, his arms folded. He held up his hand in a gesture of surrender when Drew turned and glared at him.

Peter stepped in to settle the matter. 'Let's get you down into the cabin, Caro, and out of that suit. Drew, you can bring some hot chocolate. Jake, take the helm for me.'

'Aye-aye, Cap'n.' Jake grinned. Drew hesitated and then nodded, helping Caro to her feet and allowing his father to guide her down into the cabin.

Drew stripped off his drysuit, putting on jeans and deck shoes, and then grabbed the flask of hot chocolate. His father appeared from the cabin, bringing Caro's dripping drysuit with him and signalling to him that he could go down to see her now.

He should get a grip. Caro was all right, but she'd had a shock and she needed him to be calm. She was sitting on the bunk, the blanket wrapped around her shoulders and legs, a small puddle still on the floor where his father had helped her out of the drysuit.

'I won't fuss.' He poured the hot chocolate and handed it to her.

'That's okay. You can fuss a bit.' She gave him an intoxicating smile. 'And I reckon you've still got your training wheels on.'

As usual, she'd managed to divine exactly what he was thinking. Luna's death and his own injuries had made him acutely aware of the senseless accidents that could happen and their consequences. He'd do anything…any-thing…to stop Caro from being hurt.

'I guess I have. Thanks for putting up with me.'

'No problem.' She took a sip from her cup. 'Take a look, will you?'

She let the blanket fall from her shoulders, handing him the cup. Caro eased herself carefully out of her long-sleeved thermal top, and he saw she had a sleeveless vest on underneath. He was both grateful and disappointed that she'd taken Jake's usual advice about layers of cloth-ing, but on reflection he should probably go with grateful.

He was becoming aware that his leg was aching, so he sat down on the bunk next to her. Drew inspected her shoulder carefully, flexing her arm again, and her face showed no pain. A red mark showed where a bruise was beginning to form and she tried to squint down at it.

'How does it look?'

'Not so bad. You'll have a bruise.'

'I'm glad you were there, Drew. Thank you.'

'It's what diving buddies are for.' Caro was a lot more than just a diving buddy to him, but he couldn't go the whole hog in emulating her habit of saying exactly what was on her mind.

'And I could do with a hug.'

'So could I.' Drew curled his arms around her. She nestled against his chest and he felt the last of his own shakiness subside.

Haltingly, she began to whisper. The shock of the blow. Feeling afraid but knowing she was safe when he'd caught hold of her. All of the things that Drew had never talked about when he'd had his accident, and which he proba-bly should have. She voiced her fears and then put them aside, snuggling against him as if he was her comfort.

Maybe a little closer. Maybe a little longer, although Peter and Jake might start wondering what they were doing. He dared to plant a kiss on the top of her head, and then he let her go.

'You'll give the nets a rest for a while?' This time his question didn't involve any of the push and pull between concern and wanting to be strong.

'Yes, I think I will.' She gave him an impish look. 'I suppose that means we're staying out here for a bit longer?'

Drew sighed. 'Yes. We're staying.'

Caro grinned at him as he walked out of the cabin, and Drew took the stairs with renewed energy, using the rails to boost himself upwards. They had work to do.

CHAPTER ELEVEN

THEY DIDN'T MANAGE to collect as many seabirds as they had this morning, but that was largely because there were fewer stuck in the oil. Most of the ones they did find alive were in bad shape, and there were a few other marine creatures as well, a dead starfish and an octopus. They heard over the radio that the boat Lucas was working from had rescued a sea otter and was heading back to the clinic.

They were all tired, and the sun was sinking low on the horizon. Peter turned the boat and they made for home. Drew looked over his shoulder more than once, obviously thinking the same as Caro. The job was only half-finished, and there was still more to do, but they'd done all they could today.

Ellie and Lucas were at the dock and helped to unload the boxes of birds. Caro saw Jake stride across to a woman who was carrying a drowsy two-year-old, hugging them both and kissing his son before they walked to their car together. Drew asked Lucas if there was anything he could do at the clinic and was told no.

'The tide will be in soon.' Drew walked to his car with Caro in the gathering dusk.

'Yeah, I'd better be getting back.'

'Or you could come to the Hungry Pelican and we'll get something to eat. You can stay at mine tonight, and we'll be ready to go back out again in the morning.'

No question about whether she was going or not. He knew that he couldn't keep her away.

'I've heard the food's really good there, Ellie's mum and dad run it?'

Drew chuckled. 'That's right. You must be getting used to village life if you're hearing gossip. Although as it goes, that isn't all that juicy.'

'I might have to try and do something with my hair first...'

'Your hair's fine. No one dresses up for the Hungry Pelican.'

The quayside pub was already busy, and Caro excused herself to go to the rest room while Drew made his way to the bar. She combed her hair, wincing as her shoulder protested and the comb snagged in a knot. At least the day at sea had brought a bit of a glow to her cheeks, and that, along with fixing her hair back in a slightly lopsided plait, was about as good as it was going to get.

Drew was talking to a man behind the bar, who had a shock of white hair. He introduced him as Gordo Stone, and the man leaned over to shake her hand.

'I'm Ellie's dad. I heard you've been out with Drew today.'

'Yes, we just got back.'

'Ellie says it's not as bad as we'd feared.'

Drew shook his head. 'It's a small spill. Hopefully it won't be coming onto the shore.'

Gordo nodded. 'What are you having?'

'I'll have a sparkling water.' Drew turned to her. 'Do you want to try the local brew?'

Gordo was already moving towards the pump and there seemed to be no escaping it. 'I'll have a half, thank you.'

Drew reached for his wallet and Gordo shook his head. 'First round's on me for everyone who's been out today. Something to eat, Caro? We do a mean fish and chips, even if I do say so myself.'

'Fish and chips sounds great. A large portion, please.'

Drew chuckled. 'Gordo doesn't know how to do small portions. Same for me too, please.'

'Right you are.' Gordo turned, shouting to someone who was working in the kitchen behind the bar, and then got their drinks for them.

Both Gordo and Drew were looking at her, and it appeared that she was expected to taste hers now. She took a sip.

'Mmm. This is *very* good.'

Gordo nodded in approbation and turned to his next customer, while Drew guided Caro over to a table by the fire. When their food arrived, the chips were good as well. And the fish was delicious. They were both hungry.

'Oh.' Caro leaned back in her seat, surveying her empty plate. 'That was lovely.'

Drew was looking pleasantly relaxed now too. He seemed to know everyone here, exchanging a few words with whoever happened to walk past their table.

'You want another drink?'

'What I'd really like is a hot shower and a bed.' Caro wondered whether she should emphasise that both would be alone as she saw that flash of mischief in his eyes again. No, alone went without saying.

'Me too.' He got to his feet, making his way over to the bar, and Caro grabbed her coat and followed him.

'You can put that away.' Gordo had seen Drew's wallet in his hand.

'What's the matter, Gordo? Won the lottery?' Drew raised his eyebrows.

'I'll take your money next time you're in here.' Gordo propped his elbow on the beer pumps. 'But no one would have expected you to go out today, Drew. Not so soon after the accident.'

'You'll take something from me?' Caro had been feeling for her purse at the bottom of her bag and finally found it.

Gordo laughed. 'My Ellie doesn't know when she's beaten either. Off with you both, before I throw you out.'

Drew chuckled, leaning over the bar to shake Gordo's hand. Then he ushered Caro through the door and into his car.

'That was nice of him.' Ellie settled into her seat as Drew drove through the narrow lanes to his cottage.

'He and Wyn are great. I used to hang out with Ellie at their place quite a bit when we were kids and my mum and dad were arguing.'

'You and Ellie...you never thought about getting together?'

Drew let out an explosive laugh. 'What? No. Ellie and I practically grew up together, she's the sister I never had. I think there were about ten minutes, when we were sixteen, when I realised that she might be pretty.'

Caro raised her eyebrows. 'What? Ellie's gorgeous.'

He shrugged. 'She's my friend. I tend not to notice things like that about her.'

But he'd said that he found Caro beautiful. It was better not to think about that, particularly if she was spending the night at Drew's place.

'It must be nice. To have a friend like that.'

'Yeah, it is.' He stopped the car outside his cottage. 'You don't?'

'No. Like I said, my parents moved around a lot, they still do. It's tough enough to keep up with them, let alone anyone else.'

'Apart from the robots.'

Suddenly that didn't seem enough. If she'd had somewhere like this to call home… Caro could see why Drew never wanted to leave.

'I noticed something at the pub tonight.' It was time for a change of subject.

'Yeah?'

'All of the people who stopped to talk to you… Not one asked you how you were.'

He thought for a moment. 'No, I don't believe they did. Perhaps telling everyone exactly the same thing is starting to work.'

'Or perhaps it's just that you seem so much better. You're hardly using your stick now and you move much more confidently.'

'My leg still hurts from time to time, but I don't feel as if it's going to give way under me.' He shrugged. 'My physio told me that I'd get to the point where suddenly I started to forget all about it.'

He broke off suddenly, gazing at her. Nothing that was ever said or done between them made Caro shiver quite so deliciously as the silences. And this silence told her that she'd helped him forget that he was a recovering invalid and remember who he really was.

Drew had done that all by himself. She might have been there when he finally made that transition, but Caro couldn't take any of the credit for it. All the same, the warmth of his gaze was compelling, and for a moment she couldn't break free.

Finally, Drew moved. 'Let's get inside.'

His cottage was…just Drew all over. She could imagine him on winter evenings in the book-lined sitting room, sprawled on the comfortable sofa. Surrounded by the things he loved, stones and shells on the mantelpiece and in front of the rows of books memories dredged up from the sea. Photographs on the wall, of boats, divers and underwater scenes, and one of Drew with his arm around a dark-haired beauty on the beach. The large kitchen diner at the back would be full of light in the daytime, and now it was cosy and inviting. A place where serious cooking and a lot of informal entertaining might take place. At the back, the kitchen lights illuminated a small garden, which was a riot of different shrubs, probably all planted with an eye to giving shelter and nourishment to different species of birds and insects.

He dumped her diving gear in the hall, and Caro followed him upstairs with the smaller bag that contained a change of clothes. The spare room doubled up as an office, with more books and a desk, and a pull-out sofa bed.

'I'll leave you to take a shower.' He jerked his thumb towards a door that led out to the top half of the kitchen extension downstairs and must be the bathroom.

'Thanks.' Caro couldn't suppress a yawn. She was rather hoping that Drew wouldn't want to talk too much now, because all she wanted to do was sleep.

'I'll make the bed up for you now. Would you like a hot drink before you turn in?'

'Um… Thank you. That would be lovely.' She couldn't stop herself from yawning again. A shower, a hot drink and then a comfortable bed sounded wonderful. Second only to curling up with Drew and falling asleep to the soft sound of his breathing, and neither of them were going to let that happen.

'Go, before you fall asleep in the shower.' He smiled, shooing her out of the room.

The warm water on her shoulder made it throb, and when Caro inspected it in the mirror there was a red mark that looked as if it was going to form into a bruise. The dolphin hadn't meant to attack her, she had just got in the way, and the damage was well worth the glimpse of the two dolphins circling the boats.

When she returned to the bedroom, the overhead light was off and a lamp burned by the bedside, throwing soft shadows across the room. The sofa bed was made up, with a warm blanket the colour of a stormy sea draped over the duvet. There was a folded T-shirt with the logo of the diving centre on the back, and Caro smiled, reckoning that this was Drew's way of telling her she'd earned her stripes as a diver. She towelled herself dry and slipped it over her head.

There was a mug with a saucer perched on top of it by the bed, and on further inspection it contained hot chocolate. Drew clearly wasn't expecting her to go back downstairs, and she slipped gratefully under the duvet. She'd only drunk half of the hot chocolate when drowsiness overtook her, and she snuggled down in the fresh-smelling sheets and closed her eyes.

It had been a while since Drew had cooked breakfast for more than one person. Sometimes it had just been him and Luna, and sometimes a whole gang of divers, who'd camped out in the spare bedroom and on the floor in the living room.

He'd woken early and rather than lie in his bed, staring at the ceiling and wishing that Caro was curled up next to him, he'd got up and gone downstairs. When he heard the quiet sounds of her moving around, and the noise of the shower, he started to make breakfast.

Twenty minutes later she appeared in the kitchen, her hair still damp and cascading down her back. Her eyes were bright, and she still had the last traces of a pillow crease in her cheek. Drew wondered if it was possible to kiss a pillow crease away and decided to view it only as evidence that she'd slept well.

Breakfast in company was different from the way he remembered it. Not the bandying of jokes and the hurried gulping down of coffee and bacon sandwiches, but Caro's warm eyes and a succession of questions and ideas, some of them completely crazy and a few that…if you just let go of your preconceptions they made every kind of sense. He forgot all about the insistent push to get out of the house and wanted to spend all day just talking to Caro, bathing in her unique and creative view of the world.

'Why not?' She shot him a laughing smile. *Why not* was the thing that marked Caro out from everyone else he'd ever known. She had a completely different set of boundaries from most people.

'Because… I don't know. I can't imagine sea life sending distress signals to us when something bad happens.'

'But what if they could? What if the dolphins are out there calling us right now? What if we just can't hear them? Or we *can* hear and we simply don't understand.' She took a bite from the slice of toast she'd been waving in the air to illustrate her point.

'What if that toast just shouted, *Don't eat me!*' He grinned at her.

She held the slice to her ear. 'Too late. I didn't hear it. But seriously, warning systems, Drew, triggered by the very organisms at risk. I'm sure that there are loads of surveillance systems in place for endangered species, but what if we could make them better?'

That was always Caro's refrain as well. Refusing to accept that some things were too hard or couldn't be made any better. She extended those principles to him, and her belief that he *would* heal had made him believe it too.

'I'm just a working vet...' Who didn't have the vision or the ability to turn far-fetched ideas into reality.

'Rubbish! You're the one who *gave* me the ideas in the first place.'

The thought that something he'd done had nudged Caro's creative process into gear and focussed her capricious mind was endlessly gratifying. Drew was still trying to get his head around it when his phone beeped, and he opened the text his father had sent.

'Dad says he's getting ready to go now. Is forty minutes too soon to meet him down at the harbour?'

Caro shook her head. 'I'm fine with that, if you are. Or sooner...'

There was still a lot more left to do. And Caro's drive and energy added a new facet to the task ahead of them. He nodded, texting his father that they'd be there as soon as they'd finished their coffee.

More birds. Not as many as yesterday, but a greater proportion of them were dead or dying. But every time they pulled a living bird from the water, and Drew laid it carefully in a makeshift nest in one of the boxes, he saw Caro give a little nod of pleasure.

There were more boats, too. As the day wore on, resources from various environmental agencies arrived, and Drew made his decision.

'I think we should go back in now. Tomorrow's going to be a busy day at the clinic, we'll be starting to clean the birds that are strong enough. There's not a lot more we can add here.'

They made their way back to the veterinary centre to drop off the boxes of birds, and then returned to the harbour at Dolphin Cove. He and Jake shook hands, wordlessly acknowledging the efforts of the last two days, and Gramps came aboard, shooing Drew away when he offered to help tidy up on the boat.

'I'll take you home, then.' Drew loaded his and Caro's gear into the back of his car. She was beginning to look like a proper seafarer, clad in a thick sweater and oilskins and climbing off the boat without waiting for a helping hand. Gramps clearly considered this was all *his* doing and had exchanged a couple of jokes with her before he took up his usual stance, leaning against the helm and watching her go.

'Thank you. I guess I should go now while the tide's out.' She quirked her lips down, and it occurred to Drew that she didn't want to leave him, any more than he did her.

They had plenty of time, and he drove as slowly as he could to Smugglers' Top, without collecting a queue of other impatient drivers behind him. He parked on the rough ground that led down to the beach and opened the boot of the car.

'I'll give you a hand with your gear.'

'That's okay, I can manage. Although…' She hesitated. Drew could wait. 'Would you like to come up and have some lunch? You can catch the low tide again this afternoon.'

'Thanks, that would be great. Mum's reckoning on keeping Phoenix for a few days, so I don't have to get back for her.' Drew tried to sound casual about his reply.

'Right, then.' Caro gave him a delicious smile, picking up the larger and more cumbersome of the two bags and leaving the one that Drew could sling easily over his shoulder. 'You take that one.'

CHAPTER TWELVE

THE MORE THAT Drew did, the better he seemed. Caro
had been reluctant to let him carry anything up the stone
steps to Smugglers' Top, but she knew that Drew was
just beginning to grasp at the reality of being able to do
the things he wanted to. It would hurt him more to take
nothing than it would to take the lighter bag.

All the same, he was limping a little when they got
to the top. Caro unlaced her shoes, leaving them in the
hallway, and made tea. Then she plumped herself firmly
down on one of the sofas in the living area, propping
her legs up on the cushions. Drew took the hint and did
the same.

Once he was there, she could insist that he stay put
while she cooked. Or…pulled something from the freezer
to heat. The smell of part-baked bread, browning in the
oven, made thick, chunky soup seem like more of a meal.
When he stood again, to follow her back to the kitchen
with his empty bowl, he walked without a limp, leaving
his stick behind by the sofa.

'So what are you up to this afternoon? Working up
some ideas?'

Maybe. If Drew left, she'd have nothing but her ideas
to keep her company. She wondered if he knew how much

he was a part of these latest ones. The way he listened and understood. The way he injected a note of practicality, without rejecting the blue-sky thinking.

'I'm just going to let them simmer for a while. Maybe I'll take a break.' Caro wondered if Drew could be persuaded to take a break with her.

'I'll leave you to it, then. I'd better make a move, the tide will be turning soon.'

Crunch time. Time to make sense of the last two days, when she'd felt closer to Drew than anyone else in her life. Time to wonder whether it was possible to create a compartment, away from her work and everything else, where there would be a bit of space for each other.

She watched as he fetched his shoes and sat down to lace them up. Then he picked up his stick... Maybe she should just let him go, but it seemed that he was taking all the air in the room with him. She was already feeling light-headed, and unable to think properly.

'Wait!' He'd pulled on his coat, and there was no time left to think. Just to act.

'What is it?'

Those blue eyes. The dark, slightly wayward curls that gave him an outdoors look even when he was indoors. The thought that someone like Drew couldn't really want her, and then the memory of his kiss, which led her to the inescapable conclusion that he did.

'I'm not very good at this.' She walked towards him.

'Don't sell yourself short. You're good at a lot of things.'

Yeah. Seduction wasn't one of them. Caro was a lot more comfortable when she said exactly what she meant, and meaningful glances weren't really her forte.

Although strangely she always seemed to know exactly what Drew's meaningful glances meant.

'I want you to stay.'

His face softened. 'Because...?'

Drew wouldn't let her down. Not with this anyway. If he left, then he left, but he'd find a reason for doing so that wouldn't disappoint her. Something that probably wouldn't even hurt all that much.

'So that we can keep each other company tonight.' Caro congratulated herself on finding the words that made her meaning clear, without having to tell him exactly what she'd been imagining them doing together.

His eyes darkened suddenly. Pools of velvety black, with iridescent blue borders. So, so beautiful.

'It would be my privilege to keep you company tonight, Caro.'

Nice. That made her feel so good, and she wished she'd thought of saying something like that.

'But...' He twisted his mouth in an expression of regret.

Okay. There was a *but*. Maybe it was time to tell him that everything was okay and let him leave. His gaze fell to the stick in his hand, and his knuckles whitened against the curved top.

'My leg isn't... They say that with time it'll look a little better.'

He thought *that* was a problem? Caro had never really considered that Drew couldn't know how beautiful he was. With or without scars. She tapped the base of the walking stick with her foot, and it moved without any resistance. He wasn't actually leaning on it, and when she kicked it, it clattered to the floor.

'You're the kind of girl who would kick a guy's stick out from under him?' Drew's smile reflected her own hunger.

'Yes. You don't need it, Drew. And I couldn't care less what your leg looks like.'

Suddenly he reached for her, curling his arm around her waist and pulling her against him. When he kissed her, it was mind-blowing. Knee-shaking.

'Do you trust me?'

So he wanted trust. Any man would. Caro took a moment to think about her answer.

'I don't *not* trust you.'

He shook his head. 'That's not the same.'

'I trust you enough to go diving with you. And to want you to stay tonight.'

'And what *don't* you trust about me?' He tipped her chin with one finger, kissing her lips lightly.

'My work's always…something separate. I have to go wherever it leads me.'

He nodded, dropping kisses onto her neck. 'I understand that. We're very different people and I'm not sure that we'll ever be able to reconcile our lifestyles.'

That was a nice way of saying that she was a workaholic. Right now, none of their differences seemed to matter. Caro kissed him, and his response told her that it didn't matter to him either.

'I want to make love to you, Caro. For the rest of the afternoon and…then again this evening. And tonight…'

'That's enough, isn't it?' It would always have to be enough. Caro didn't know how to trust that a lover might truly become a part of her life any more.

'Right now, it feels more than enough.'

When he kissed her again, the ache for him went into overdrive, blinding Caro to everything else. He was slowly picking her apart, owning everything. It was so much more than just blinding physical pleasure this time because she knew that they understood each other.

'Can we go to the bedroom now?' She wanted the luxury of stretching out on the large bed, knowing that Drew wouldn't be struggling to balance.

He nodded. 'Then you can tell me exactly what's on your mind. And I'll tell you what's on mine.'

Drew couldn't believe this was happening. He'd wanted Caro from the first time he'd seen her. Had told himself that he couldn't have her. Known for sure that he couldn't have her, and then… She'd told him that she wanted him. And then they'd found a way to be together that didn't compromise either of them.

Her bedroom was all creams and neutral colours. The kind of room that took its only life from the people who were in it, and the colour of the sea and sky outside the large windows. The only piece of her was the stone he'd given her from the seabed, displayed proudly on the bedside table.

She didn't rush him. He was still a little uncomfortable about the scars on his leg, and she didn't make a thing about him showing them before he was ready. She stripped off his coat and sweater, hurling them at a large wicker chair that stood in the corner. Then her own sweater, which missed the chair and landed on the floor. Caro took a little more time over his shirt, undoing one button at a time. They lay on the bed together, exploring all the subtly different ways that a woman could kiss a man and a man could kiss her back.

'Would you like to take a shower?' She ran her finger across his chest, and he felt a wake of sensation follow its path.

'And wash off the sea…?'

'No. I love the taste of salt on your skin. And your scent.' She trailed her tongue along the path that her finger had just taken, and Drew felt his whole body begin to stiffen. 'I'm giving a gentle hint that I want to see a little more of you. Maybe you want to see a little more of me?'

'I want to do more than just *see* a little more of you.'

She laughed, wriggling away from him off the bed, and disappearing into the en suite bathroom. The sound of running water, and then she appeared in the doorway again. Naked.

'Come here…' He choked the words out.

'No. You come here.'

He was on his feet, pulling off his jeans and undershorts before he'd even thought about it. Her gaze dropped, but she clearly wasn't interested in his leg. That was okay, he wasn't embarrassed at showing her just how much he wanted her.

She let him watch as she soaped her body. It felt as if he should be on his knees before her, but it was Caro who bent to wash his legs, her fingers skimming over the scars as if they were of no consequence to her. He towelled her dry, kissing her at every opportunity, before he followed her back into the bedroom.

His knee twisted and he stumbled. Almost fell, before he grabbed at the footboard of the bed to steady himself. Suddenly he felt weak again, as if it had just been a fantasy that he could take back everything he'd once had.

Caro didn't make a move to help him. In fact, she moved back, swinging her legs up onto the bed and shifting to lean against the pillows.

'Hurry up, Drew...'

She didn't see him as weak or in need of any pity. Forgetting all about his leg, Drew slid onto the bed, pulling her towards him.

'You are so beautiful.'

'You don't need to say that.' She smiled, saying the words as if they didn't matter. She really didn't know... The thought that no one had ever made her feel any different cut him to the heart.

'I can't help it. Maybe you'll trust me enough to believe me before we're done.'

Her eyes widened in surprise. Soft and golden, and as gentle as a warm sea breeze. He kissed her, easing himself over her, his hand exploring the silk of her skin.

She didn't reply, but her gasp when his fingers found her nipple told him that he had her full attention. He wondered how long she could hold out against him and hoped it would be for just a little while.

He told her all of the ways that she was beautiful, all of the things he loved about her. Teased her until she was drunk with the same heady passion that intoxicated him.

'Drew. Please...'

He didn't want her to beg. He wanted her to receive him into her arms, knowing how much he adored her. Slowly he slid inside her, feeling the warm tension of her body.

Something stirred, deep in her eyes. He wrapped his hand around her leg, pulling it up and around his hips. His next thrust was a little faster, a little harder and she groaned.

Strength pulsed through him, unleashing a hurricane. There was no going back now. She was driving him beyond anything he'd ever experienced.

In the sudden calm, before the storm reached its height, he stared down into her eyes, and saw acceptance and trust. It was then that he knew that this was more than just passion. Caro was giving a part of herself to him, and he was giving whatever was left of himself to her.

Who had the stamina to work their way through half a box of condoms in sixteen hours? And who on earth could make things perfect and then manage to improve on that? Warmer and wilder, heart-thumpingly passionate and mind-blowingly intense.

And *then* make breakfast.

She watched him as he carried the tray over to the bed, setting it down. Just jeans, slung low on his hips. The way he used those hips was just so satisfying.

'There *has* to be something wrong with you, Drew.'

He raised his eyebrows. 'Why's that?'

'Because you're too good to be true. You're the most beautiful man I've ever seen.' There was no denying that, she'd already told him. 'And you're gentle and very sweet, and I love it when you forget about both of those things…' She'd told him that too. In rather plainer terms than she could use this morning without blushing.

'Ah. You mean when you agreed with me that you were beautiful?' He sat down on the bed, and the plates and cups slid gently to one side of the tray.

'I think I said that was how *you* made me feel.' Caro was a little hazy on the exact details. Just that he'd coaxed something out of her that she hadn't know was there last night.

'I'd like to make you feel that again. If you'll let me.'

They hadn't talked about that. But it was impossible to deny that they both wanted it.

'I'd like that too.' She leaned forward to kiss him, and the contents of the tray tipped back the other way.

'My place? This evening? I'll go and pick Phoenix up from Mum's after work today.'

Caro had wondered whether his cottage might contain too many memories for Drew to make love with her there. It was also far less likely that an overnight visitor would escape notice in the village than it was here at Smugglers' Top.

'Don't you mind? If you feel better about coming here, I'm accessible via land or sea.'

He thought for a moment. 'No. I'd like it if you came to my place.'

Drew was moving on. She was glad for him, but something deep in Caro's heart sounded a note of warning. She'd moved out, and then moved away, but moving on was a little more difficult. But Drew had shown her how to do so many things, and maybe he could show her how to move on too.

'Okay. Your place tonight. I can come to the centre this afternoon to help out with the birds if you need me.'

'We're going to need all the help we can get. Thank you.'

'I'll see you around twelve, then. That'll give me the morning to work out what I need to do this week on the prosthetics project.'

He nodded, picking up the mugs from the tray and handing one to Caro, then taking a swig of coffee from the other. 'Okay, I'll leave you with the washing-up, then. I'd better get going.'

She ate her toast while he found his clothes and put them on. Then he kissed her, and Caro heard the front door close behind him.

Getting out of bed, she walked across to the bathroom, peering at her reflection in the mirror. All the things that Drew had said last night… She'd never really thought much about her looks, and Blake's betrayal had made her feel worthless and ugly. But she valued Drew's opinions much more than Blake's.

Her hair glinted in the overhead lights. Her eyes were marvels of evolutionary genius, but then so were everyone else's. There was nothing extraordinary about her features or her figure, but if you liked fair skin she supposed both were passable. And, last night, Drew had given her new respect for all her body was capable of. Perhaps, after all, she might accept that he *did* find her beautiful…

CHAPTER THIRTEEN

'YOU'RE LOOKING VERY pleased with yourself.' Ellie put the last of the birds that had been washed this morning in the drying pens. Drew had already perched himself on a stool, unable to stand any longer.

'Am I?'

'There you go again. Answering a question with a question never works, Drew.'

'You asked a question?'

Ellie puffed out an exasperated breath. 'All right, then. Dad said he was driving along the coast road early this morning, and he saw your car parked off the road by Smugglers' Top. He was concerned about you so he stopped to take a look, and he saw you walking across the beach.'

'Right. Does he have photographic evidence, or is this just word of mouth?'

'He said you were looking a bit furtive.'

'I was *not* looking furtive.'

'Ha! So you *were* there!' Ellie clapped her hands together. 'Can't I be a bit pleased for you, Drew? It's time you started dating again. And Caro's really nice, even if she can be slightly kooky at times.'

'Mostly that's just because she's thinking about something that's way over our heads.' Drew leapt to Caro's defence and Ellie shot him a knowing look.

'That's true. I really like her a lot, Drew. And she was an absolute star, coming out with us to help with the birds.'

'Yes, well, she'll be coming in this afternoon to help with cleaning them up. So don't start with her, Ellie. She isn't used to everyone knowing her every move, she has a normal person's expectation of privacy.'

'Of course I wouldn't say anything to make her feel uncomfortable.' Ellie wrinkled her nose at him. 'And it's good of her to come. You could do with a hand, the standing's a little too much for you.'

That and a couple of very gratifying positions last night. Ellie really didn't need to know that.

'Yeah, you're right. I could use some help. But don't start getting carried away, Caro and I are very different. Like my mum and dad were, and you know as well as I do what happened there. Caro has her work...'

'And that doesn't play out so well with you.' Ellie gave him a knowing look.

Drew sighed. 'It's not going to get that far, Ells. We're not really dating, we just have...a thing.'

Ellie nodded, suddenly leaning forward and planting a kiss on his cheek. 'Well, I hope your *thing* makes you happy. You deserve it, Drew.'

'Thank you. And if you want to get sloppy, go do it with your husband. Lucas signed up for it when he married you.'

Ellie chuckled, poking her tongue out at him, the way she used to when they were kids and flouncing out of the room. Drew shook his head, Ellie wouldn't like the term *flouncing* very much.

Caro *did* make him happy. And she'd told him that he made her happy. They just had to be careful and remember that any commitment that they were tempted to make wouldn't work.

And maybe he should try to look a little less happy when he was at the clinic. Although with the prospect of Caro arriving in half an hour's time, that wasn't going to be easy.

It had been a long day. Actually, it hadn't been all that long, but it felt like it. Drew's leg was aching badly, and for the first time in a couple of weeks he'd taken the full dose of painkillers.

He'd wondered whether that would keep Caro away tonight. Maybe she didn't want to run around after him this evening while he sank down onto the sofa to rest. But when he'd hinted that maybe he should rest tonight, and she might like to go home, she'd given him a smile.

'Good. If you're resting, then I can cook for you.'

'What are you going to cook?' He'd never seen Caro cook anything. She was good at taking stuff out of the freezer and heating it up, and she was quite capable of working her way through a mountain of fruit and a stack of sandwiches at her desk, but cooking required leaving her workshop for more than ten minutes at a time.

'Anything you like.' She shot him a frown. 'That's what cookery books are for, Drew.'

'How about spaghetti Bolognese?' *Everyone* knew how to make that.

'Done.' She pulled her phone from her pocket. 'I'll find a recipe, and we can get the ingredients on the way home.'

'That's okay. I have the ingredients…'

When they got back to his cottage he spent a worrying forty-five minutes on the sofa, trying to tell himself that there was a limit to the amount of damage that one robotics engineer and a Labrador puppy could do in someone's kitchen. Caro appeared in the doorway, crooking her finger at him, and he levered himself onto his feet and followed her.

Phoenix ignored him completely in favour of the bowl of food that was laid out for her in the corner. The pans were all cleared away and in the sink. The blinds were drawn and the light over the dining table switched on. There were two plates of spaghetti Bolognese, a dish of grated Parmesan cheese, and a bottle of sparkling water on the table, along with a candle. The smell made his mouth water.

'Sit down.'

Drew regretted his doubts and did as he was told. Caro lit the candle and sat down, pouring the water into a couple of wine glasses while he sprinkled Parmesan cheese onto his food. She picked up her fork and he followed suit, aware that she was watching him.

The spaghetti was perfect. The sauce was wonderful. Drew rolled his eyes as he ate the first mouthful, prompting a smile from Caro.

'This is great. Really nice. Where did you get the recipe again?'

'I found four different ones. So I worked out what each element was supposed to achieve and chose the parts I liked the best.'

In other words, she'd applied the techniques she used in sorting and refining her own ideas. And it had all worked with the same apparent ease as her robotics projects.

'Well, you have to write it down. This is much better than my recipe.'

She gave him a luminous smile. 'You didn't think I could do it, did you?'

He should come clean and admit it. 'You don't cook all that much. I can see why, you get interested in something...'

'Yes, I know. I'm not working now, though.'

Maybe she could be persuaded to work a little less in the future. Drew dismissed the thought. She was who she was, and just because that wasn't compatible with his way of life, it didn't give him the right to try and change her.

'You're as perfect when you're not working as when you are.' He decided on a compliment that covered both of their points of view.

'Thank you.' She waved her fork at him, grinning like a Cheshire cat. 'Eat. Before it gets cold.'

They spent the evening in the sitting room, Caro with her laptop balanced on her knees and Drew sprawled on the sofa with Phoenix. Drifting back and forth between talk and silence, ideas and thought. When Drew started to doze, she left him to sleep while she finished what she was doing and then closed her laptop, walking over to the sofa to shake him gently.

'Come upstairs if you want to sleep.'

'Uh. Yeah... Sorry.'

'Don't be. It's been a busy few days. You're not working tomorrow, are you?'

He thought for a moment. 'I may go in late.'

'That's a good idea. You have two jobs at the moment, and one of them is to heal.'

Drew sat up, and Phoenix jumped down off the sofa.

Stretching, he got to his feet. 'Anything I can get for you? Before I tear off your clothes…?'

Tearing off her clothes sounded just fine to Caro. Now sounded even better. 'Where do you find the energy?'

'I have plenty of energy.' Drew looked wide awake now. 'My leg just gets in the way a bit sometimes.'

Drew had been an active and resourceful lover last night, but now he was hurting. He'd been forced to rest for so long now that all he wanted to do was shake off those constraints, but he was in danger of overdoing things.

'I have a solution. If you'd care to try it?'

'I'm *always* interested in your solutions…'

She followed him upstairs, and he caught her hand, leading her into the bedroom. Drew pulled her close, kissing her, and Caro backed him towards the bed, pushing him down onto it.

'I want you in full working order tomorrow, Drew. You've been overdoing things.'

'Whatever you say…'

'Seriously?'

He gave her a melting look. 'Seriously. I'm entirely in your hands.'

She'd hold him to that. She pulled off his sweater and shirt, started to undress him. Drew meanwhile had found something to do with his own hands, and they were skimming her body.

She wriggled free of him, backing away. Drew leaned back onto the bed, watching her as she undressed.

'I'm liking this *in your hands* business very much.'

'I can see…' Caro pulled back the bedspread, piling two pillows on top of each other. When she climbed onto the bed, flipping her finger towards them, he got the gist of what was expected of him and pulled himself backwards to lean against them.

'Is this where you tell me I won't feel a thing?' He grinned teasingly.

'I have reason to believe that you'll feel everything.' She grabbed a pillow from her side of the bed, propping it carefully under his knee. 'Comfortable?'

'Very. Thank you.'

His gaze followed her every move as she crawled slowly across the bed towards him. He reached up, caressing her cheek, and she felt him shiver as she climbed astride him.

'Caro, this is the best way of resting…'

She smiled, and saw his eyes darken suddenly. They both knew what came next, and the air itself seemed to be trembling with passion.

She bent down to whisper in his ear.

'Just lie back, sweetheart.'

Last night had been something else. Truly something else that owed nothing to the simple mechanics of great sex. Caro had taken him as he was and had turned caring into blinding, nerve-shattering passion.

He felt different. And, however much Drew told himself that this wasn't good, that he'd promised not to get so involved, he couldn't help it. Caro had captured his heart, and everything she did and said only made her hold on it more secure.

Ellie had called him early, not enquiring where he was or who he was with but telling him that he wasn't needed at the clinic today. Volunteers from local charities would be helping out with the birds, and the efforts of the environmental agencies in breaking down the oil slick were coming to fruition.

Drew knew that Ellie's assertion that there was *nothing for him to do* wasn't entirely true. He was sure he could find something, but it was clear that she and Lucas were managing. And in a perfectly co-ordinated pincer movement, Caro told him that she needed his help with the prosthetics project.

He spent the morning in her workshop, his leg propped up in front of him on the sofa. When Phoenix started to fret, jumping up onto the windowsill and pawing at the window, Caro told him to stay put, and that she'd take the puppy out for a couple of circuits of the small island.

Drew picked up the pieces of the prototype that Caro had been printing on the 3D printer, and which lay on her desk. He couldn't see how they fitted together, but there were notes and diagrams. He sat down, placing the pieces in order, and began to fathom how it would all work. He started to clip them together, and suddenly saw the concept clearly. It was simple but ingenious.

'What are you doing?' He hadn't heard Caro come in and he looked up to see her standing in the doorway of the workshop. Her face was like thunder, and he wondered what could have happened to make her so cross.

'I'm just taking a look at this. It's amazing…'

His words seemed to make her even crosser. 'Well, don't. You signed an agreement, remember?'

Okay. He remembered. But he still couldn't see why Caro was so angry. He put the pieces of the prototype back down on her desk.

'You do remember, don't you?' She wasn't going to let this go. 'Because I have a copy…'

'I remember. I'm sorry if I overstepped any boundaries.' Drew got to his feet. Annoyance was beginning to tug at him, but he didn't want to argue with her. Arguing never did any good.

'*Any* boundaries? You know just what the boundaries are, Drew. I told you that my work was separate from everything else and you said that was okay.' She seemed close to tears. 'You *don't* look at my work. It's mine, and I'll let you have the finished product when it's ready.'

'I'm trying to help, Caro. You asked for my help, remember?' He couldn't let this go.

'Yes, I asked you to *help*. I didn't ask you to go behind my back.'

Phoenix was sitting between them, looking back and forth, as if she knew that something bad was happening. Drew knew that something bad was happening, but he just couldn't work out what it was. Caro seemed to have changed so suddenly.

'All right. I'm not going to engage with this, Caro. We're both tired, and we probably need some space.' Drew wasn't sure that space was going to make any difference. But at least it ruled out any more conflict.

'I don't need any space, Drew. I just need you to understand.'

'Okay. Well, I'll go away and think about it. Maybe *you* should think about whether this reaction of yours isn't just a little bit paranoid.'

He turned, wondering if she might protest. All he heard was silence. He knew all about those silences, too. His parents had kept them up for days…

Drew grabbed his stick and called Phoenix, who bounded up to him as if she too wanted to get away from this. Clipping her lead onto her collar, he put on his jacket and walked out of the house without looking back.

This had been his mistake. He'd fallen for Caro, knowing that she was different from him. Knowing how committed she was to her work and knowing he couldn't change her. He should also have known that it was only a matter of time before the differences started to chafe, and the inevitable niggles turned into arguments.

Phoenix started to whine, pulling at the lead and pawing at the front door. 'No, Phoenix. We're not going back.'

The puppy gazed up at him. Phoenix didn't know about the bitterness of being let down, she was all trust.

The thing that had been niggling at the back of his mind suddenly became clear. He didn't understand, and he'd given Caro no chance to explain.

'Did it look as if she was about to explain, Phoenix?' He bent down stroking the puppy's head and she nuzzled against his hand. It was probably asking a bit much of a puppy to mediate between two grown people.

He could do better than this, though. He didn't need to walk away, maintaining the silence the way his parents had. If Caro was angry then she must have a reason, and he wanted to know what that was. Understand a little maybe.

He lifted the latch, pushing the front door with his finger. Caro clearly hadn't locked it behind him, and when the door drifted open a little he could hear the muffled sounds of her crying. That left him no choice. He had to go back and make things right. Even if he had to battle with Caro to do so.

CHAPTER FOURTEEN

It had been a surprise to see Drew sitting at her desk, handling her inventions. She'd reacted when she should have stopped and thought. But Drew was the one person that she'd thought would never betray her, and it had felt as if the bottom of her world had just fallen out.

It was too late now. Maybe he *had* intended to read through her notes behind her back for some reason. That wasn't the most likely evaluation of the situation. They'd shared so much already, and she'd never explained why sharing her work was such a touchy subject for her.

She'd messed up. If he had any sense, he wouldn't be coming back now.

'Caro...'

She almost jumped out of her skin. So much for Drew having any sense.

'I'm really sorry, Drew. You were right to go, and you should...just keep walking.'

'I'm not going to do that. I *want* to do it; I think you know why I can't deal with arguments. But that's my problem, not yours. So you can just throw whatever you want at me, and we'll take it from there.'

'I don't want to throw anything at you, Drew.' She couldn't look at him.

'That's fine too. I think I need to know why you re-acted that way, though. I obviously hurt you, and I didn't mean to.'

'It's not your fault.'

'Maybe not. It'll be my fault if I walk away without finding out what's going on with you. So, if you don't mind, I'm just going to wait here until you think you can tell me.'

Phoenix bounded up to her, nudging and pawing at her legs, as if she hadn't seen Caro for months. Caro scrubbed at her eyes with her sleeve, remembering too late that it probably wasn't a great look.

She felt the sofa move as Drew sat down next to her, handing her a piece of kitchen roll from the kitchen. She tore it in half, blowing her nose with one piece and rubbing at her eyes with the other. He reached forward, smoothing down a lock of hair that was obviously stick-ing up and she turned the corners of her mouth down. She must look an absolute fright...

'You look beautiful.'

'What are you, a mind reader?'

'Sorry. Won't happen again.'

She reached for him, and his arms closed around her shoulders. The warmth of having him close only made her burst into tears again.

'I messed up, Drew.'

'Yeah. Me too.'

'I'm sorry.'

'So am I. Now tell me something I don't know.'

Caro heaved in a breath. It was time to face up to him and tell him the truth. He deserved that at least. She couldn't do this while she was still in his arms, so she sat up straight, looking into his eyes.

'It's not your fault, Drew, it's mine. It's...' Suddenly it hit her. Drew wouldn't have treated her the way that Blake had. 'It's *not* my fault. I don't think it is anyway.'

'So tell me whose fault it is.'

'Blake. He taught at one of the universities I was associated with in California.'

'He was *your* teacher?' A note of concern sounded in Drew's voice.

Caro shook her head. 'If I'm honest, there wasn't a great deal that he could teach me.' This was new, too. She could see Blake from a different perspective now, and it didn't do him any favours.

'Okay. More a colleague, then. To be honest, that doesn't sound quite so inappropriate on his part.'

He knew. He'd put two and two together and realised that no one could hurt you as much as someone you loved. That was why Caro had been so afraid when she'd seen Drew looking at her work.

'I thought he loved me. I loved him, and I thought I'd found my home with him. I shared all my ideas and...' Caro shook her head miserably.

'He took them from you?'

'Worse. When the water feature in our garden kept getting gunked up I developed a self-cleaning valve. He patented it, and I lost the rights to it, which meant I couldn't develop it any further and make it available free in developing countries. He didn't steal it from me, he stole it from all the people who might have benefited from it.'

'What did he do with the patent?'

'He tried to sell it. There was a lot of interest and he was set to make a life-changing amount of money from it. He told me that I was stupid, and that someone had to look after my business affairs for me.'

'Wait. No, Caro. Anyone who ever tells you that you're stupid…well, that reflects on them and not you.'

'Trusting him wasn't my finest hour…'

'Someone deceived you. That doesn't make you stupid.' Drew shook his head. 'Is there anything you can do to claim the patent back?'

'I was so embarrassed. I left him and put the whole thing in the hands of an attorney in the States. She's trying to get the patent transferred to a charity that will do the right thing with it, and it looks as if she'll succeed. I just… I can't get any closure from that, Drew. I just wanted to crawl away and hide. Forget about it all.'

'But you can't, can you?'

Caro sighed. 'I think that's pretty self-evident, don't you?'

'Okay. I'm going to take this as a compliment.'

She stared at him. 'How do you work that one out?'

'You were afraid that it was all happening again. That someone you cared about would betray you. To jump to that conclusion, and react so strongly, means that you must care about me.'

'That's…one way of looking at it. I *do* care about you.'

'And I imagine it's not so easy to trust me after what happened.'

'I'm working on it.'

He pulled her close, kissing the top of her head. 'Yeah, I'm working on a few things too. Neither of us is perfect.'

'What are we doing together, then?' The obvious question didn't make her feel any better.

He chuckled. 'Well, for my part, you're probably the most interesting person I've ever met. You're very clever, and you're beautiful and a good person. And the sex is amazing.'

'I thought it was just me who thought the sex was amazing.' She grinned at him.

'Then you haven't been listening to me. What do you like about me?'

'All of the above. And you have a really cute puppy.'

Drew nodded. 'Yeah. The cute puppy does it every time. Why do you think I have her?'

There was something she had to do, even if it did still frighten her a little. Caro slid away from him, getting to her feet. 'I want to show you, Drew. All of my designs and sketches. The way the prosthetic's going to work.'

He caught her hand, holding on tight. 'No. I don't want to see it. Not until you've finished and it's under licence.'

'But… I want to show you that I trust you.'

'I know, and I appreciate that. Let's just take what we have for the time being, Caro. Know that there are things we can't reconcile yet, and that maybe that will change.'

'Hang on in there until it does, you mean.'

'Yeah. I'm definitely hanging onto you.' He pulled her down onto his lap.

It wasn't everything, but it was something. Something to hope for when Caro had lost hope completely.

'So, while we're hanging on… I don't suppose there's any hope of some more of that amazing sex, is there?'

'Not a chance.' He rolled her over on her back, kissing her. Just as she was starting to melt into what promised to be the greatest make-up sex ever, a shape moved on the periphery of her vision.

'Drew. Drew! We have to go to the bedroom, Phoenix is *watching*…'

* * *

'Can you feel it?' Drew's voice sounded behind Caro.

'No. I can't feel anything. Apart from deep mistrust.'

'Just relax. Let your shoulders do the work.'

Caro pulled on the oars. This wasn't as easy as Drew made it look. The boat seemed to be going backwards, not forwards.

'You've got stronger shoulders than me.' Her tone sounded unpleasantly whiny. This rowing business was bringing out the worst in her.

She felt him slide forward, planting his feet on either side of her and his hands next to hers on the oars. *That* was better. She could feel the raw power of his body against hers, and when he pulled on the oars the boat started to make some headway.

'*Now* can you feel it?'

'Yes. Wonderful.' She relaxed against his chest.

'I meant the tide.'

'Oh. No, I think I'll have to practise a bit more. Maybe when I'm a bit less tired.'

His lips brushed against her neck as he planted a kiss. *That* she'd definitely felt. 'Why don't you go and sit with Phoenix?'

Phoenix was sitting in the stern, wearing her red life-jacket, her nose aloft in the evening breeze. Caro slid forward, careful to keep to the centre of the small craft as she turned around.

'That's much better. I can watch you row.'

He grinned at her. 'I get it. You like watching me work.'

'Yes, I do actually. You make an excellent reindeer wrangler.'

Drew pulled on the oars. 'I wasn't wrangling. I was attempting to hold them still while I did their health checks. And you didn't do so badly yourself.'

Caro chuckled. 'Apart from when I fell flat on my face in the mud.'

'You're particularly delightful when you're covered with mud.'

It had been a good day. Drew had suggested that Caro might like to come with him to see the reindeer, and he'd let her help hold the animals while he gave them a thorough examination. They'd gone to the Hungry Pelican for supper and ended up missing the tide. Caro had a video conference booked with a robotics researcher in Australia first thing in the morning, so Drew was rowing her home.

'I can see why you like it. The sea. It makes you feel that the little things don't matter so very much.'

He nodded. 'Yeah. It's been here so much longer than we have. And it's so much bigger than us.'

'You must have missed it. When you were in hospital.' Drew loved the open skies, whether they were on land or sea. Being cooped up in bed for so long must have been hard on him.

'It was the worst thing…' His face darkened. 'Almost the worst anyway.'

Maybe she shouldn't ask. But talking about the bad things with Drew had helped her to begin to come to terms with them.

'What was the worst?'

He shook his head. 'You don't want to hear that, do you?'

'Yes. I do, actually. Whatever it was, it doesn't frighten me.'

The water slopped against the side of the boat as he

pulled silently on the oars. There were a lot of things that he hadn't said about the accident, and sometimes his flat assurances to everyone that he was okay and doing well seemed more for their benefit than for his.

'When I ran the car off the road, I was alone.' He spoke suddenly. 'I was dazed at first, and my leg didn't hurt all that much. The pain came later.'

'You were in shock.' Caro nodded him on. Drew needed to say this and injecting her own sense of horror into the mix wasn't going to help him.

'Yeah. It was very quiet, and I could hear a dripping sound. I could feel blood seeping through my clothes, and...' He stopped rowing suddenly, leaning on the oars as the boat bobbed up and down. 'I knew that if someone didn't come soon, I'd die.'

'So you held on.'

'I'm not entirely sure that it made any difference. But, yes, I willed myself to live. And I willed whoever happened to drive past to see my car and stop.' He shrugged. 'I've never told anyone that. Everyone assumes that I was unconscious, and I don't remember.'

'I've heard that a lot of people don't remember.'

He nodded, started to row again. 'Yes, I've heard that too. It didn't work that way for me.'

She hugged Phoenix as the boat moved forward in the water. Caro waited for him to say more, but it seemed that Drew had said everything that was on his mind.

'Thank you for telling me.'

'Thank you for listening.' He smiled suddenly. 'I appreciate you not handling me with kid gloves. Probably a great deal more than you know.'

Blake hadn't appreciated it at all. He had always been telling her that she shouldn't be so literal, or so outspoken. But then Blake, and all his put-downs, were right where they ought to be. A long, long way away.

'I could do kid gloves. If I put my mind to it.' Caro covered Phoenix's ears with her hands, and Drew chuckled. He knew what that meant. 'Tonight...'

'Sex with kid gloves. How does that work?'

'I touch you very slowly. *Very* gently.' Caro smiled at him.

'I'm up for that. And leave Phoenix's ears alone, she doesn't know what we're talking about.'

'She knows some things.' Caro spelled out the word *cheese.*

'Okay. Well, if you don't associate the word *sex* with treats from the fridge, then it's not likely to have much significance for her...' He manoeuvred the boat carefully into mouth of the cave beneath her house. Together they pulled it out of the water, then Drew wrapped his arms around her and kissed her.

'You, on the other hand, react very admirably to the word...' she whispered in his ear, feeling his body harden against hers.

Drew chuckled. 'Just goes to show how well you're training me up.' His fingers brushed the side of her face, so lightly that it made Caro shiver. She took his hand, leading him through the cavern and into the house.

Drew struggled to think of a time when he'd been so happy. There had been odd instances, but he'd never before been so perfectly content for twenty-one consecutive days.

It was odd. Nothing was settled between him and Caro. They were still different, and their relationship still wasn't going anywhere. But happiness didn't listen to logic, it just burst in on his heart anyway.

They tramped every inch of the ten acres around the Dolphin Cove Veterinary Clinic. They went beachcombing and diving in the bay. Drew showed her the woods, and the badger setts, and they listened in the silence for birdcalls. Phoenix seemed to be growing in front of his eyes and was developing an even bigger appetite and a gentle but mischievous nature. And he was getting stronger. His leg still hurt from time to time, and would do for a while, but he was beginning to feel powerful and able to tackle anything again.

They shared their nights, and when Drew wasn't working at the clinic he spent his days with Caro. She still maintained a fearsome work schedule, but Drew could make sure that she ate something by cooking for her while she worked. And coaxing her to bed was never that difficult.

He was falling in love. And love brought with it the terror of loss. Drew tried hard not to think about it, because he knew in his heart that he couldn't overcome his fears, and they had the power to tear them apart.

Yesterday she'd finished the first prototype of her animal prosthetic, and they'd packed it into a box and taken it to the clinic. Lucas and a selected group of consultants would be putting it through a whole barrage of tests, and assessing its viability, and he and Caro could take the weekend off. Drew had made cupcakes with candles to celebrate.

It wasn't unusual for him to wake up alone. Caro often got up early, and he'd find her pottering around in her workshop, still wearing her pyjamas. But when he went to find her, calling that he was about to make coffee, she didn't reply. And when he looked out of the window he saw something that almost made his heart stop.

Throwing on his clothes, he rushed down the steps onto the beach.

'Caro! Get out of the water!'

She was wearing her drysuit and had waded into the sea until it was up to her waist. The brisk autumn breeze and a strong tide was buffeting her back and forth, so that she could hardly keep her footing, and a snorkel hung from her hand. Much good that would do her in this rough sea—she was just as likely to get a lungful of water as she was air.

'In a minute.'

'Now, Caro!'

She turned, pulling a face at him. And then the unthinkable happened, and a wave crashed into her back, knocking her off balance. Sudden panic gripped Drew's heart and he waded into the water.

'All right…' She was thrashing around, trying to regain her footing. 'I can manage.'

She couldn't. She splashed around a bit more, buffeted by the tide and weighed down by the heavy suit, and finally she stopped fighting him and accepted his help. Drew marched her out of the water, trying to quell his anger.

'I was just getting what I wanted, Drew.' She brandished the underwater camera that Jake had lent her from the diving centre, and for a moment Drew cursed Jake for being so accommodating.

'What was so important that you had to go into the water anyway?'

'Those little crabs that we saw the other day. I was

thinking about the way they scatter and react, and I wanted to see if I could work out a pattern.'

'And you couldn't wait one second longer and ask me to go with you? You know how strong the tide is on this beach, and there's a riptide further along here…' The mere thought made him feel sick.

'Yes, you told me about that last week. It's fine here, the tide was a little stronger than I'd thought, but I was managing.'

'Managing isn't good enough. You know that.'

He needed to calm down. If he could just get off the beach, then maybe the feeling of nauseous panic at the risk that Caro had taken might subside a bit, and he could reason with her. Drew turned, walking back up the steps to the house, and he heard the swish of the drysuit as she followed him.

Caro marched into the bathroom, leaving a trail of water behind her and slamming the door. Drew's overnight bag was in the bedroom and he grabbed a set of dry clothes from it, bundling the wet ones into a ball and shoving them back into the bag.

Yes, he was overreacting. And, no, he wasn't going to apologise for it. He of all people should know the dangers. And Caro knew why he couldn't compromise on safety and had always accepted that.

She was in the bathroom for a long time. Drew suspected that she was spending most of it cursing him. It would probably be best to wait and talk about this when they were both a bit calmer.

A bit calmer wasn't going to happen any time soon. Drew told himself that this was just a matter of her safety. That was of primary importance, but he knew that it was more than that. Their increasing intimacy was as challenging to Caro as it was to him. And they were both re-acting in the only ways they knew how.

She made coffee in silence. They sat in silence to drink it and finally she got to her feet, making for the door that led to her workshop.

'Don't, Caro…' If she disappeared in there, she'd be lost to him until this evening at least. He'd be cooling his heels, rehearsing all of the things he needed to say to her, and that wasn't going to make things any better.

'What, then? Drew, you're not in charge of what I do.'

'No, but I'm asking you to come back here and sit down.'

She did it, but not without a sulky quirk of her lips. Drew ignored it and tried to organise his thoughts a little. Maybe see things her way.

'Caro, I know that your work is important to you. It's been your home and your companion when you didn't have anyone. But I can't watch you put yourself at risk like this.'

She thought for a moment. 'Going out on my own was a stupid thing to do, I'll admit that. But I didn't *mean* to take risks. I just…got an idea and…you know how it is, Drew. I don't think about anything else.'

'What I see is that you don't trust me. I get too close, and suddenly you're hiding behind your work. It's all-consuming, Caro, and I can't just stand aside and watch you working every hour of the day and night just to pro-tect yourself from me.'

Drew shook his head. He'd thought that if they talked about this rationally, they'd find some solution. But all he'd done was convince himself that it would never work between them.

'I'm not sure I know how to do things differently.'

Her eyes softened suddenly. 'I'm not very good at trusting people.'

'I know that, and I understand. But you have to understand how I feel.'

'Yes. I do.'

And that wasn't going to make any difference. He could never change Caro, and he didn't want to. He didn't know how to change himself either.

They stared at each other for a long time. When a tear ran down her cheek it almost broke him.

'I'm going to go.' Perhaps she'd say something that would allow him to stay. Give in just a little. But he knew she couldn't.

'You must do whatever you need to do, Drew. I won't ask you to stay.'

She *couldn't* ask him to stay. Caro knew all about moving on, and next to nothing about staying.

There were still a few more moments to turn this around. He called Phoenix and clipped her lead onto her collar. Put his jacket on, taking his time to zip it up. But there was nothing he could possibly say to stop the tide that was carrying them irrevocably away from each other.

Goodbye would hurt too much. *I'll see you* would be a lie. Drew didn't even dare take a last look at her, because he knew she'd be crying, and he doubted he'd be able to stem his own tears. He closed the front door behind him, and this time he wasn't going back.

CHAPTER FIFTEEN

CARO WAS EXPECTING LUCAS. She'd also expected to be up and dressed by the time he arrived, but last night she'd been up late, working. She hadn't made any progress, but it had been better than lying awake, missing Drew, the way she had every night for the last two weeks. Somehow work didn't seem to ease the pain the way it always had before.

The doorbell rang, and she grabbed her oversized cardigan, pulling it on before she went to answer it. Ellie was looking fresh faced and fabulous on the doorstep, a cardboard box tucked under one arm. That was the last thing she needed.

'Ellie... Sorry. Bit of a late night last night.'

Ellie nodded. 'Yeah, I was in my pyjamas until about half an hour ago.'

She was being nice. Extra nice, in fact, because Drew was Ellie's friend, and Caro was on the outside now. She stood back from the doorway, and Ellie grabbed Mav's hand, leading him inside.

'Where *did* you get those?' Ellie gestured towards her blue and green pyjama bottoms. 'I love them, I have to have a pair.'

'Uh...in America. I'll look up the web link, maybe

they have an online shop.' And then what was she going to do? Write to Ellie as if she was her friend, with a shopping link? Ellie was hiding it well, probably for Mav's sake, but she'd be justified in wanting to scratch Caro's eyes out.

'I brought your prototype back. Lucas and the review committee's response is in here as well.' Ellie handed Caro the box.

'Thanks.' Ellie perched the box on top of the packing cases in the hall.

'I'm afraid they've suggested a few changes.' Ellie grimaced apologetically.

'That's fine. It's exactly what I wanted them to do. This is the first step in a long process, and it'll be a while before I get it exactly right.'

Mav was looking up at her expectantly, and Caro remembered the promise she'd made to Lucas. She bent down, plastering a smile onto her face. 'Would you like to see what I've got for you?'

'Yes!'

'Please.' Ellie provided the missing word. Caro hurried into her workshop, bringing out the box she'd saved for him.

The little tortoises were now little crabs. And there were some programming modifications, which meant that their movements weren't controlled just by proximity to anything else in their path. These had an additional interaction with each other.

'Here you go.' She put the box down on the floor next to the coffee table. Mav reached in, taking out a crab and finding the *on* switch without being told. That was one of the reasons why Caro had offered the crabs to Lucas for

Mav to play with. Kids weren't fazed by the complexities of technology, they just tried things out.

'If you're busy, Caro…' Ellie watched as Mav took the crabs out of the box, one by one, switching them on and setting them onto the table.

'That's okay.' Caro shrugged. 'Actually, it would be very interesting to see how Mav interacts with them. I've introduced social and group behaviours into their programming.'

Ellie looked at her blankly and then grinned, walking over to Mav and pulling his coat off, while her son ignored her completely, already fascinated by the movement of the crabs. 'I don't entirely understand what you just said. But thanks.'

'Would you like some coffee?'

'Love some. You see to Mav, I'll make it.' Ellie slung her coat onto the back of a chair and marched into the kitchen, disregarding the plates in the sink and the breadcrumbs on the worktop, and switching the coffee machine on.

She could almost see Mav's mind working, the way he was trying things out with the crabs and learning their behaviour. It was a project in itself, and Caro wondered if she might borrow him for a couple of hours, just to observe. Probably not. Ellie wouldn't want her around him too much, and if Mav knew that she'd hurt his beloved Uncle Drew he'd be throwing the crabs at her instead of playing with them.

'Milk and sugar?' Ellie's voice interrupted her reverie.

'Um… Just a little milk, please.' Caro walked over to the breakfast bar as Ellie sploshed the milk into the cups.

She had to say *something*. 'Ellie, I appreciate your coming.'

Ellie looked up at her, a trace of knowingness in her

eyes. 'What do you mean? We really appreciate you allowing Mav to play with your little robots.'

'I suppose… I meant I appreciate you coming and not trying to beat me over the head with a frying pan. I'm assuming you're not saving that for later…' Caro climbed on one of the high stools and pulled her coffee towards her.

Ellie pursed her lips. 'Look, Drew's my friend. More than my friend, you know he's like a brother to me. I know that he wouldn't want me to take sides, and I have no interest in that either. The one thing I've learned with Lucas is that there are always two sides to everything.'

'That's…good of you.' Caro shifted awkwardly in her seat. 'How is Drew?'

'Oh, like a bear with a sore head. I offered him my services as a vet, I've never treated a bear before, but I could give it a go. He turned me down, though.' Ellie shrugged. 'He knows that Lucas and I are both there for him.'

'Good. That's good.' Caro wondered if she should thank Ellie for looking after Drew, but she'd given up the right to do that. Ellie and Lucas were his friends, of course they looked after him.

'How are you?'

'Um. Keeping busy.'

Ellie plonked herself down on one of the stools on the other side of the breakfast bar. Clearly Caro's answer wasn't the one she was looking for, but Caro hadn't been doing much else other than missing Drew and keeping busy. She took a sip of her coffee, hoping that Ellie might drop the subject.

No such luck. 'Those crates in the hallway…?'

Caro heaved a sigh. 'I was thinking of going back to

Oxford. I can continue with my work on the prosthesis there.'

'I imagine it would be good to be near the university.' Ellie was gazing at her thoughtfully.

'Yes. It would.'

That wasn't the reason. Caro was cutting and running. As a child, she'd learned that looking back never worked, and she'd applied the same principles with Blake when he'd broken her heart, putting as much space between them as she could. Now she was doing it again with Drew because it was the only thing she knew how to do.

'Look, Caro, it's none of my business...'

'That's okay.' Cruel hope flashed into Caro's heart. Maybe Ellie had seen something that neither she nor Drew were able to.

'Drew's miserable. And from what I can see, so are you.' Ellie held up her hands in a gesture of appeasement. 'And if you don't want to be with him, that's your business and you should tell me to take my nose out of it. But he's a good man.'

'Yeah, I know. He's the best.'

Ellie nodded. 'I don't know what he's thinking, he hasn't talked to me. But I'll take a guess that he wouldn't want you to leave because of him.'

What did *that* mean? Caro shot Ellie a questioning look and she shrugged. Ellie obviously didn't know either, she was just making an observation.

But the seed was sewn, and Caro's heart was fertile ground for it. Her parting with Drew had been final, they'd both wanted it that way. But she still loved him. She had no choice but to trust him and stay a little longer. She had to wait for him.

'I… I do like it here. There's something about Dolphin Cove.'

'I think so too.' Ellie smiled. 'Why don't you at least come down to the Hungry Pelican one evening with me and Lucas? I can get Drew to babysit, so you won't be bumping into him unexpectedly.'

It was kind of Ellie to ask. Caro had no intention of taking her up on the offer, however much she wanted to.

'Thanks. Maybe…when things have blown over a bit?'

'Whenever you want.' Ellie nodded, grinning. 'Look, if you're not doing anything this morning, why don't you go and get dressed, and give Mav a hand with those little monsters over there? I'll do the washing-up.'

'No!' Caro looked over at the plates in the sink and felt her ears redden. 'You're not doing my washing-up.'

Ellie laughed. 'Nonsense. You should see how much washing-up Lucas and Mav generate, this is child's play. Go and get dressed and maybe we'll go down to the beach and see how they work on sand.'

Drew had finally come to a conclusion. He'd raged over the fact that he couldn't change, and Caro couldn't either, for three weeks now. He'd been tight-lipped and grumpy with everyone at the clinic, even telling Tegan off for painting her nails in the reception area. When he'd gone back to apologise to her for his show of temper, Tegan had smiled sweetly at him and done her best to console him with the latest action pictures of her horse. Drew appreciated it but it was better to just keep his distance from everyone, Lucas and Ellie included.

He'd shut himself away from everyone when he hadn't been working and had stewed on his own in a slow bubble of anger flavoured increasingly with despair. And then he'd made his decision.

If Caro wanted him, even half as much as he wanted her, then they could work something out. He didn't know how, but maybe he could convince her to at least talk about it.

He took a couple of hours off work and drove into Penzance, without thinking about why he was making the trip. He wandered past shop windows, without properly knowing what he was looking for. But when he saw the ring in the jeweller's window, he knew that this was exactly why he was here.

It was a platinum eternity ring, with blue-green emeralds inlaid all the way around it. When he went inside and asked to see it, the colours flashed and changed like the sea. Like the ever-moving, ever-fascinating workings of Caro's mind.

'What size would you like, sir?'

That was a problem. Drew brushed it away. 'I'm not sure. Her hands are about the same size as yours, does it fit you?'

The assistant flashed him an uncertain look, but she tried the ring on anyway. Drew tried to imagine it on Caro's hand, and the comparison didn't really work for him. This was Caro's ring, and she was the only one who should wear it.

'I'll take it.'

'It would be better if you could find out the size. This is a lovely ring, but it isn't easy to resize something of this design. It's a lot of expense to go to if you're not sure.'

That was the least of Drew's worries. He wasn't sure whether Caro would even accept the ring. Or which finger she'd wear it on if she did. For the moment, all he could think was that he'd keep it in his pocket as a reminder. An expression of intent.

'That's okay.'

The assistant hesitated. He wondered if he should ask to speak to the manager and complain that that an assistant who wouldn't sell him what he wanted wasn't doing her job properly. Actually, she was doing her job very well, and this was madness.

'Please. This is the ring I want.'

'All right. If you bring it back undamaged within the next fourteen days, we'll give you a credit note.'

The assistant put the ring into the box and started to wrap it. Drew found himself smiling at her and realised he'd been under-using those muscles recently.

He drove back to the clinic and spent the rest of the morning and the better part of the afternoon in his consulting room. Somehow the stream of patients didn't seem quite so daunting when he knew that the ring was in his pocket. Drew didn't think about what he was going to do with it, or whether he was going to get a chance to do anything with it. For the moment it was enough that it was there.

When he walked out of the clinic that evening, the air seemed fresh and clean. He wandered down towards the beach, slipping his hand into his pocket and tracing the shape of the ring with his fingers. As the waves lapped against the sand, he stared out towards the horizon. The view here was ever changing and yet still always the same.

Suddenly he knew. It had been staring him in the face, and he hadn't seen it. Now that he did, Drew realised that the answer had been obvious all along. He turned, making for his car. He had to hurry; he had a tide to catch…

* * *

Caro was no particular stranger to crazy ideas, but this had to be the craziest yet. Sitting on the bench that overlooked the open sea, as the sun fell in the sky. She told herself that she was appreciating the view and getting a breath of fresh air, but when she closed her eyes all she could see was a light, fixed in the prow of a small rowing boat. Drew, pulling strongly on the oars, coming for her.

The longing to see him became sharper each day. Sometime soon it would be stronger than the fear of rejection, the dread of what he might say. Until then, she'd wait for him.

This evening, he seemed so real. She could almost hear his voice, calling her name…

'Caro…!'

She almost jumped out of her skin. That actually *was* Drew's voice. Or maybe she was just going completely mad. Caro sprang to her feet, whirling around, and saw a dark shape walking slowly towards her.

'Drew?' A shiver down her spine accompanied the thought that he couldn't really be here at all. 'How did you get here? The tide's coming in…'

He was closer now. Clearer in the failing light. 'I had to wade out to the steps.'

Caro's gaze fell to the watermarks on his trousers, just above his knees. He *had* come. Not the way she'd imagined, but he'd come and that was all that mattered.

She swallowed hard, trying not to allow false hope to take root. 'Why are you here, Drew?'

That smile. The one he always gave when she got straight to the point. It was just one of the things she'd been dreaming about…

'Caro, I've walked out on you twice. If you can find

it in your heart to take me back, I promise you that I'll never do it again.'

A tear rolled down her cheek and she brushed it away impatiently. 'I was waiting for you, Drew.'

He stepped forward, and Caro saw that he was trembling, as if he was afraid to touch her. But when she flung herself into his arms he was there, so solid and unmistakeably real, and hugging her tight.

'I kept you waiting for too long…'

'It doesn't matter. You're here now.' She snuggled into his arms. 'You told me that I was hiding behind my work and you were right. But I've changed. I trust you, and I want to be with you.'

'I've changed too, Caro. I was wrong when I said that it wasn't possible, because loving you has changed me. I want to be with you, and I'll do whatever it takes to make you happy. Go wherever you go—'

'I don't want to go anywhere, Drew. I like it here.'

'Really? You're not just saying that, are you?'

'When did I ever *just say* things? I love it here, Dolphin Cove and the Hungry Pelican, the reindeer…' She hugged him tight. 'And you. I love you most of all.'

'Then you give me no choice.' He sank to one knee, flashing her a delicious smile.

'I love you, Caro, completely and wholeheartedly. Please marry me.'

For a moment she thought she was going to collapse under the sheer weight of joy. Tears sprang to her eyes, and Caro could only manage one word. But it was the word that mattered.

'Yes…'

He caught his breath, pulling her close. If he'd only

stand up now she could kiss him properly. But Drew was feeling in his pocket, his other hand finding hers.

'Yes, Drew... Yes.' She wanted to say it again.

'I heard.' He grinned, holding out a ring that sparkled in the half-light. Caro couldn't see it properly through her tears, but it didn't actually matter. If he'd chosen to tie a piece of string around her finger, she'd treasure it.

They both gasped as he slid the ring onto her trembling finger. Caro pulled him to his feet, kissing him. Everything...*everything* was all right now. They'd made it right.

Drew took her hand, looking at it as if to check that he hadn't been dreaming and that the ring was still there. It *was* gorgeous.

'It's beautiful, Drew. And it fits me. How did you know what size to get?'

'I didn't. The shop assistant tried to talk me out of buying it.'

Caro wrapped her arms around his neck. 'And they say *I'm* crazy.'

'This is the sanest thing I've ever done.'

'Mmm. Me too. Got any ideas about our next sane and logical step?' She was sure he would.

He wrapped his arms around her shoulders. 'Since we're engaged to be married now, I think the least you could do is ask me in for a coffee.'

Caro chuckled. 'I think I should get you out of those wet clothes. *Then* make you coffee.'

'Let's forget all about the coffee, shall we?'

She clung to his hand, pulling him towards the house. The front door slammed shut behind them and they abandoned their coats and shoes in the hallway. There was no time for anything else but kisses.

'Oh!' Caro gasped as he lifted her off her feet, walking purposefully towards the bedroom. 'Be careful…'

'It's all right.' He was limping a little but his leg held firm. They'd already made the greatest journey, and now it was just a matter of a few steps.

EPILOGUE

Eight months later

ELLIE SEEMED VERY CALM. Annoyingly so. She also looked immaculate, in the way that only Ellie could with the breeze tugging insistently at her riot of curls.

'You're sure you don't want a sea sickness tablet? I've got some in my bag.' Ellie brandished the small, embroidered drawstring bag that she had looped around her wrist.

'No, I'll be fine. I always feel sick on boats for the first five minutes, and then it wears off.'

'You're sure about that?'

No. Caro wasn't sure about anything at the moment. Whether Drew would really want to get married on a boat. Whether being pregnant would tip the balance and mean that she was going to be sick all over her wedding dress...

She looked out to sea, taking deep breaths. Thinking of Drew's smile calmed her, because she knew that Drew would be waiting for her, and that he wanted today as much as she did. He wanted the rest of their lives as much as she did.

Gramps climbed aboard, looking dapper in his suit,

and planted a kiss on Caro's cheek. 'You look beautiful, lass. Are you ready?'

'I'm ready, Gramps.'

'Then we'd better get going before the lad decides he's not going to wait any longer.'

'Gramps!' Ellie protested. 'Don't say that!'

'We'll find out soon enough.' Gramps waited for Peter and Diana to board, then started the engine, manoeuvring the boat away from the dock.

Drew would wait for her however long it took, Caro knew that without question. The sea was glittering in the sunshine, and the day was going to be perfect. As the boat sailed out of the tiny port of Dolphin Cove, she felt the queasiness in her stomach subside.

Drew had stayed the night with Ellie and Lucas in their apartment above the veterinary centre. Ellie had left at the crack of dawn to help Caro with her dress and the final arrangements for the wedding, both of which Caro had managed to keep secret from him.

He was already happier than he'd ever thought he could be. When they'd found out that Caro was pregnant, they'd decided to bring their wedding day closer, and Caro had told him that she wanted to surprise him and organise everything. She'd been making furtive phone calls for the last three weeks, and Ellie and Lucas's flat had become a no-go area for him, their spare bedroom having been given over to mysterious *things for the wedding.*

At eleven o'clock Lucas had announced that it was time to go, and chivvied him and Mav down to the deserted beach.

'Okay. So we're here. Now what?'

'Wait and see.' Lucas was looking annoyingly smug.

'Mav…?'

Mav shrugged. 'I don't know. No one told me.'

That was probably just as well. Mav wouldn't have been able to keep the secret, so he and Drew had both been kept in the dark.

'You've got the rings, though. Tell me you have the rings, Lucas.'

'Yes, I've got the rings. Simmer down, mate.'

That was one thing sorted at least. Lucas would be giving Caro away, and Ellie had agreed to be Drew's best man, on condition that *this* best man was going to be wearing a dress. Mav had been given the responsibility of carrying the rings, but not until they arrived at the unspecified venue, in case he lost them on the way.

Drew turned towards the sea, taking a deep breath. Caro would be coming for him. Carrying the small spark of life with her that would grow into their child. It was everything that he wanted, and he'd marry her anywhere that took her fancy.

Then he saw the boat. Bedecked with flowers, rounding the corner of the bay. And Caro. Standing at the prow, waving. Behind it was a small flotilla of boats, which were sounding their horns on the off chance that no one had noticed their presence. Drew started to run towards the dock, hearing Mav shouting with excitement behind him.

He couldn't take his eyes off her. Her blonde hair shimmering in the breeze. Her white dress moulding the curve of her hips and floating out behind her. The bouquet of summer flowers, bright in her hand, as she waved it above her head. It was Caro through and through, different and delightful, and he couldn't wait to be standing next to her.

Gramps steered the boat up to the dock and he jumped aboard before anyone had a chance to secure the mooring rope. Caro stepped carefully down from her perch, straight into his arms.

'Do you like it?' She looked up at him, her eyes dancing.

'I love it. I love *you*, Caro.' He found her hand, raising it to his lips.

'Shall we get married, then? We brought the registrar with us.' Caro gestured towards the local registrar, who was wearing a suit with a lifejacket and beaming at them from the deck.

'Yes. Let's get married.'

Phoenix, Lucas and Mav tumbled into the boat and they cast off, Gramps navigating the craft to the centre of the bay and then dropping the anchor. The other boats clustered around, forming a small floating cathedral bedecked with flowers under the wide arch of the summer sky. When it was time to say their vows, they faced each other, Caro clinging tightly to his hands as he steadied her against the roll of the sea. And when they were pronounced man and wife, a deafening chorus of horns sounded from the other boats.

Drew lifted his new wife out of the boat and onto the dock. The beach was beginning to fill up, with people who'd come overland from the village and family and friends from the boats. But all he could see was Caro. When she looked up at him, her eyes brimming with love, he knew for sure that he was the happiest man alive.

Their wedding day had been perfect. The food truck, which had raised a few eyebrows when it had arrived on the beach, had won everyone over with gourmet pancakes and delicious finger food, while another truck had dispensed drinks. The cake had been big enough to feed the whole village, and when darkness had begun to fall she and Drew had kicked off their shoes and danced together in the sand.

And now they were going home. They'd decided to spend the first few days of their marriage here, and then two nights in Florida, visiting Caro's parents for a second celebration. Then, ten days in the Caribbean, with nothing to do but relax and be together.

'What was your favourite thing?' Caro asked the question as Drew drove back towards the village.

'Hmm. Not sure. Mav almost dropping the rings overboard? Phoenix trying to snack on your bouquet?'

'What! All the things that went wrong, you mean.' Caro smiled. They'd been two of her favourite things too.

'What could possibly have gone wrong? You married me, didn't you?'

'I did. And you married me straight back.'

'Yes, I did.' Drew stopped the car outside their house, leaning over to kiss her. 'How could I do anything different when you came sailing across the sea to find me?'

He got out of the car, opening the tailgate to let Phoenix out and then folding her in his arms. 'Our home. Our family.'

'My lover...' Caro intimated his soft Cornish burr, and Drew laughed.

'Yes. Always.'

The house, up in the hills above Dolphin Cove, had come onto the market just a few months ago. It was perfect, big enough for the family that they both wanted, along with a book-lined study for Drew and even an old conservatory at the back, which could be renovated as a workshop for Caro. Drew had pulled out all the stops to make sure that the sale would go through in time for him to carry her over the threshold after their wedding. He lifted her up gently into his arms and Caro clung to him.

'You don't have to carry me all the way up the front path. That's just showing off, Drew.'

'I've been thinking about this for a long time now. I'm not doing it by halves.'

His leg was fully healed now, and Drew could do everything he'd done before the accident. He strode up the path, stopping at the front door.

'Keys. In my pocket.'

Caro felt in his pocket to find the door keys and unlocked the front door. Drew kicked it open and Phoenix bounded past him. Then he carried her over the threshold.

'*This* is my favourite part of the day.' She snuggled in his arms, kissing him.

'Yeah. Mine too.'

* * * * *

COMING SOON!

We really hope you enjoyed reading this book.
If you're looking for more romance, be sure to
head to the shops when new books are
available on

Thursday 17th September

To see which titles are coming soon, please visit

millsandboon.co.uk/nextmonth

MILLS & BOON

MILLS & BOON

Coming next month

SECOND CHANCE WITH HIS ARMY DOC
Charlotte Hawkes

'Kane?'

Kane stopped, paused, then swivelled around to stare back down the corridor to where Mattie was standing immobile, as though rooted to the spot, and ignored as something kickstarted deep in his chest.

'It is you,' she muttered, and even from a distance he could see the stunned expression playing over her striking features.

Suddenly, his hands itched to smooth them away and he had to clench them into fists and punch them down, deep into his pockets in a very non-military way.

Thank god he wasn't in uniform.

'Hello Matz.' The name that only he had ever used for her. He couldn't help himself. 'It's been a while.'

'Fourteen years,' the words were clipped, sharper.

As though it still mattered.

Kane hated that his heart twisted in some perverse hope. Of course she didn't care, she was just surprised, even shocked, and he was just reading into it what he wanted to see. He had no idea how he managed it when so many emotions were charging through him right at this second, but he folded his arms across his chest and affected a lighter air.

'What are you doing here, Kane?'

'Just visiting…someone,' he didn't think she detected the momentary hesitation where he'd stalled. Wanting, for a split second, to tell her more.

Suddenly needing to unburden to someone – he refused to admit it was only because it was her – that he was here visiting a former army buddy. The only other survivor of a mission gone wrong a few years back, and who was only in this hospital now because he'd let the guilt of it eat into him.

Kane slammed the shutters in his mind in an instant. He had no intention of following his old buddy down that dark path. And baring his soul to Mattie wasn't going to help anyone.

'Which ward?'

She bit her lip, her brows furrowing together in a hint of irritation which was so painfully familiar that it caused a sharp band to tighten around his chest. Still, he was fairly certain her question had slipped out before she could check herself and it felt as though there was some comfort to be drawn from that.

Still, saying anything to her about his visit was bound to have her demanding to know how he – army-hating as he had been as a kid – had even come to sign-up. And then he'd have to tell her where he'd disappeared to all those years ago. And why.

Continue reading
SECOND CHANCE WITH HIS ARMY DOC
Charlotte Hawkes

Available next month
www.millsandboon.co.uk

WE'RE LOOKING FOR NEW AUTHORS FOR THE MILLS & BOON MEDICAL SERIES!

Whether you're a published author or an aspiring one, our editors would love to read your story.

You can submit the synopsis and first three chapters of your novel online, and find out more about the series, at **harlequin.submittable.com/submit**

We read all submissions and you do not need to have an agent to submit.

IF YOU'RE INTERESTED, WHY NOT HAVE A GO?

Submit your story at:
harlequin.submittable.com/submit

MILLS & BOON